THE HEALINGS

Oana

ALL THINGS
THAT MATTER
PRESS

ISBN: 978-0-9846154-8-3

Library of Congress Control Number: 2010911658

Cover design by All Things That Matter Press

Published in 2010 by All Things That Matter Press

To Central Phoenix Writing Workshop people,
who have inspired me in ways known and unknown to me.

Special thanks to Jacob Shaver, my kindred soul and editor;
Kenneth Weene, my guardian angel in publishing; Dr. Melissa Price
for her unconditional support and encouragement; Preston Bigler,
Mark Miller, Philip MacGregor, and Patricia Perek for their amazing
insights; and Geoff Cross for being the driving force of the group.

Oh, and to Becky for being the driving force of Geoff ☺

THE HEALINGS

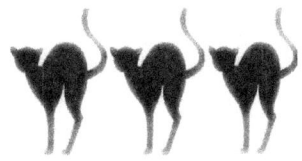

There is nothing more rewarding than watching your favorite football game. This is the essence of masculinity. I open myself a beer, burp vigorously, and get ready for some passive action. My cat jumps into my lap and looks me in the eyes while hitting the remote control with her right paw. She wants tuna crackers. I assure my furry significant other that we will get them first thing in the morning. This is not a good answer. She rephrases. She wants tuna crackers now. *I get up and grab some money in hatred and resentment. She is like a wife, and we enjoy the dynamics of a heterosexual couple. I am single, yet married to a cat.*

The Healing Session with
Evgeni Heavy Feather

I have been spending the past few days – or maybe years? – in the dark solitude of my bedroom, arranging gummi bears on the bed. I place them in random situations and positions. I make them interact socially: gummis at the office; gummis reading books together; and gummis having hot, sweaty sex.

Some of them break the rules by having sex at the office. I am a man of strong principles. I do not like my settings to overlap. I remove them forcefully and place them in solitary confinement for breaking the rules – bad, bad gummi.

One mature male gummi doesn't need to be placed in confinement. He has isolated himself and doesn't want to interact with anybody. He's sad and hasn't showered or eaten in a very long time. However, he refuses to change his setting. He will not move an inch. He's stunned. What's wrong, boy gummi bear?

While I try to hold a conversation with the little bear, an angry paw pushes all of them aside. The principles vanish. The gummi social structure is a mess.

It's my cat that interrupts my adorable depressing game. She shows me an older picture, in which she was overweight and happy. Then she points at her protruding ribs. The message is simple: she's hungry.

I need to get food for her, so I crawl to the grocery store in pajamas and barefoot.

When I get back from the store I pass one of the mirrors hanging in the hallway, accidentally looking in that direction. A pale reflection of what used to be me stares back at me. What? I have covered all the mirrors in the house myself! I don't want to see my face! I refuse to see my face! I hate to see my face! I summon the cat and force her to take a look at us. She screams her throat raw and closes her eyes. She might have uncovered the mirror with her tail by mistake. She promises not to do that again if I feed her. Okay, I will feed her.

The doorbell rings but we don't move. Maybe they will leave us alone.

I spot a shadow standing right in the middle of my bedroom. It's

Shlomo, who stopped by to bring us Matzo ball soup. We inhale the fragrance of the soup. I wonder if someone could make little bottles of Matzo soup perfume. I instantly picture my cat advertising exotic fragrances by even more exotic designers, "Matzo" by Ball, "Moussaka" by Dill. We used to love to eat.

Inspired by our original setting – covered mirrors – Shlomo starts saying the Prayer for the Dead.

We politely inform him that we are not dead. Not yet. The soup is good, though. We haven't had a decent meal in a very long time.

Shlomo is happy to hear that we are not dead. We try to show our stiff, ridiculous liveliness to Shlomo by walking from the window to the bed and back, asking him about the weather and about my dear Aunt Lyla's apricot trees. An hour later, a concerned Shlomo leaves us, but not before handing me a letter.

The anonymous letter informs me in a stern tone that I have been accepted for a healing session with the well-known and rarely seen Shaman Evgeni Heavy Feather. I should probably go see him.

It is no secret for me that my condition has worsened. In the past, I used to lead the same boring existence as everyone else, consisting of repetitive actions that took me *nowhere*: laundry, grocery shopping, clean up and maintenance of my own body. The problem is that even when I enjoyed, temporarily, a nicer activity – coffee with a hot woman – I usually ended up in the same place, which is *nowhere*.

I've asked myself many times why is my life so miserable? No answer. Now, I no longer ask this question. I don't care. My new question is will it be miserable forever? And while a temporary pointless life is acceptable, the perspective of a long term *nowhere* makes me shiver.

I start packing slowly. I'm due to meet the Shaman tomorrow at dawn. Needless to say I cannot sleep. I wake up many times and check the letter, reading and reading it over and over again. I'm about to have my twenty-fourth coffee and my fifty-ninth cookie when I decide to stop reading the letter. My cat thinks I'm obsessive and compulsive. Who, me? I crawl to bed, however, and try to catch a few hours of sleep, seasoned with nightmares.

***

I arrive at the isolated hut of the Shaman just before dawn. The hut is small and oddly shaped. It resembles a cloud sketched by a playful child more than a man-made structure. It is real and surreal at the same time. There is also an intense heaviness to it, making it so weighty that I can barely continue to look at it. Naturally, I do what we all do when we want to avoid unpleasant situations. I close my eyes.

As I sit on the doorstep I am silent and in awe. What an odd fellow, this shaman. I suddenly realize that my hair is not combed and must resemble a mop on my head. It strikes me that my eccentric hairstyle can be perceived as a poor maintenance of the physical body. And, unlike the mind or the soul, the body is visible to the human eye.

At that same moment Shaman Heavy Feather opens the door, or what might be a door, and I'm forced to leave behind the worldly and shallow thoughts about hairstyle. I'm carried away by admiration and fear of the Shaman. I feel like a miserable cockroach. Maybe I'll grow antennas and crawl on the ground, yearning to be smashed by his heavy foot of wisdom and infinite Knowledge.

The Shaman – imposing masculine presence, no facial features, penetrating gaze – intimidates me. I don't like this! Where is his face? Where is his face? Oh, he has an owl face. No, he doesn't. There is an owl involved, but she's perched up on his right shoulder. The Great Shaman is faceless, but I can feel in him something powerful and meaningful. So I follow him, without saying a word.

Once inside the hut, I realize that the place is entirely built on and made of…feathers. Huge, medium, and extremely small and delicate feathers each play their own important part of this amazing structure. Words are too poor to render the beauty of the feathers, and I wonder if they have ever known the miracle of flight. Maybe they are just magical creations of the Shaman, crafted in his dreams.

Each object reflects light in a strange way that moves over my pale body as I pass by.

Yet I am a son of an architect – true, an unaccomplished architect. The desire to understand things runs in our family. I don't leave anything unchecked. I'm curious to see how one can build such a structure.

I'm not only curious. I am clumsy as well – grandson of an unaccomplished pizza dough juggler. I tear a feather from the wall. As I try to stick it back, the Shaman's heavy presence passes beside me but seems not to pay attention to my exposed clumsiness. I realize the feather must weigh at least ten pounds, and I stand there staring at it, overwhelmed by a deep fear. I dare not to question the heaviness of the feather. I'm afraid this will upset the Master. Finally, I manage to stick it back, but I have a nasty surprise. The incredible heaviness of the feather has somehow stayed with me.

Puzzled and ten pounds heavier, I try to catch up with the Shaman. I'm carried away, deep into what I thought was a small room.

The moment has come.

I'm genuinely embarrassed because, although I haven't said anything yet, I feel my words will be shallow, empty of substance, weightless and meaningless, floating in the air like balloons. I feel that all my life my expressions have been as *nothing*. Yet, I've been saying *nothing* with such dedication and so passionately that I ended up thinking that *nothing* was actually *something*.

I start by sharing my sufferings, my ordeal of struggling with my base instincts. I use simple words. "Great Shaman Heavy Feather, I don't know who I am or where I am going. I feel I am drowning. My life is limited by my own desires. I have become a slave to my body, desperately seeking carnal pleasures. I wonder what the purpose of education is, since I am nothing but an animal that went to school. I see myself in every hungry, horny and impulsive animal that's out there."

His voice interrupts me and I can distinguish sarcasm, yes, sarcasm in his tone. "Yeah, so do we."

"But, Great Shaman, I've also been drinking like a pig."

The Voice resumed with an amused tone, "So have we."

Who is "we"?

"But, Shaman, you don't understand. I've been surrounded by shallow, empty people whose names I cannot even remember."

This time the Voice sounds serious. "Have you walked all this way to tell me you cannot control your instincts? Take a look around you and tell me who can? The question is not what and how you do it, but WHY? And who else can answer this question but you?

"The feather you picked up earlier seemed heavy, is that right? Yet to another being that same feather might seem weightless. If what you're doing now makes you heavier and clumsier, stop doing it, then see how you feel. You may also discover that, in time, some of those feathers will seem lighter and lighter and very easy to live with. Only time will tell. Right now, I see you're asking for more, so I am giving you … more. Now, go home!" commanded the Great Shaman.

His voice is profound, vibrating, and shattering my being. His words are also very different from what I think of as words. For the first time since I mumbled "ma-ma," words seem to have shape and weight and substance.

As I sit there being struck by the Shaman's words, I try to pick a few, but they all appear to be extremely heavy, raw and unpolished.

I stand up, disoriented and frustrated. I'm still ten pounds heavier, and the weight I am coping with is not physical. I almost feel hatred for Shaman Heavy Feather, for he added more to my ordeal. Why did he do that? I had expected his feathers to be light, delicate and resistant, yet these treacherous Shaman's feathers are like lead. I notice, on my way to the door, that the feathers seem to crumble easily, so I touch as many as I can on my way out. Now, fix your feathers, Great Shaman!

***

I wake up at home, lying face down on the floor. My cat insists that I had a seizure. There's so much pressure inside and outside my head that I can barely breathe. I'm not even sure that I'm alive except that I observe two ants and one multi-legged insect I cannot name. One of them is climbing the newspaper that my neighbor slides under the door every morning, *knowing* that we will not read it. He is always there for us, ready to offer help no one asked for. Maybe that's why he's been crowned "best neighbor" for seven years in a row.

For the first time in years, I open the newspaper randomly. It smells nice. I didn't know that our neighbor wears "Omelette." I notice an article about a famous homeopath. I don't know much about homeopathy, but from what I'm reading, I understand that illness can be cured by illness, kind of like vomiting can be stopped by being made to vomit, to get rid of what is making you sick. I don't know if this applies to my condition. *Can depression be stopped by being forced into even more depression?* This "homeopathic" concept reminds me of the cruel Shaman Heavy Feather, who does nothing but add more heaviness to already unbearable heaviness.

Suddenly I feel tired and lost. Maybe Shlomo is right, and I should be around people. Yet, as of now, their presence has become extremely heavy to me. My own voice has even become heavy and so, too, have my thoughts. I'm heavy inside out, and people appear like two dimensional paintings with no depth, only unbearable heaviness.

In the morning, I pick up the lonely gummi. He will not surrender. He will soon leave the house. He will look for answers. Where? Everywhere.

The Healing Session with Dream Master Dust Devil

I decided to take it slowly with the help seeking. Enough with the unpleasant, seedless and fruitless experiences like the one I had with Heavy Feather. What a poisonous feathered snake!

However, yesterday, while I was watching my cat pulling weeds, it hit me that all my life I've yearned to be a Dream Master, sending beautifully crafted dreams to everyone, including myself. Having beautiful dreams would change people's lives forever. Isn't this life miserable enough? Do we really have to continue our traumatizing existence even when we rest?

I do not expect to get a degree in dream mastering. I just crave to learn more about dreaming and maybe, just maybe, alleviate my pain…

Even my cat agrees. She can no longer tolerate the screaming I deliver at midnight and 7:00 a.m. with the precision of a Swiss clock.

Can she go with me? I deliver three no's with my mouth full of crackers.

On my way to the pharmacy I have this short unprecedented conversation with two of my neighbors. They are going on and on about awesome positive dreams in which they fly over the mountains and they can turn into either haystacks or needles, depending on the circumstances. Really?

I used to like these people but my feelings shift steadily as I listen to their stories. Why can such insipid individuals enjoy sweet dreams while I cannot?

I don't feel like sharing my nightmares with them. If they only knew! My signature nightmare is the one with the demons who stand in front of me stating simply, "Loser." No, my demons are not sophisticated. They don't throw daggers at me or chase me. They don't drink blood. They drink martinis, smile a lot, and always win.

I tell the stupid neighbors that I don't have such amazing dreams, and I do not crave them. I prefer to stay connected to the real world.

I LIED. The truth is I would very much like to eliminate the demons, be in a continuous state of dream, and never come back and face reality.

I do not believe in coincidences. The conversation about dreams was not an accident. The thought stayed with me through lunch while walking the cat, and continued even to dinner. The persistent feeling told me I had to do something about it. After calling several times, being put on hold and listening to the latest hit "Keep Dreaming" for at least three hours, I manage to get a verified appointment with the Dream Master Dust Devil, who lives in the secluded Cerulean Blue Mountains.

My cat suggests that I should verify the Dream Master's credentials. I have no intention to involve her in my personal quest, but what if the animal is right? What if the so-called master is a fake? I'm not small prey. Or am I?

A thousand phone calls later I am *almost* convinced that Dust Devil is an expert in teaching lucid dreaming and helping his scholars with programming the most beautiful dreams around.

YOU got my attention, Dust Devil!

Armed with the directions I got over the phone, I walk and hike for a day and a half. Why does Dust Devil have to live in such a secluded, tough-to-get-to place? Where does his name come from? There's no dust in the Cerulean Mountains.

As the trip is longer than I thought, I make plenty of pit stops and fall asleep a few times on the side of the road, carried away by the thirst for dreaming. I do dream a short dream. It's about a hungry cat, meowing desperately from behind locked doors. I'm not sure that this is a dream. At this point I can't remember if I fed the cat before I left the house.

I finally reach a meadow. Is this place on Earth? In awe and horror I realize that Dust Devil's residence is just a small hut situated in the middle of a circle shaped area. Not good. Reminds me of another hut I visited recently. Ewww....

Everything inside the circle is yellow and dead, and the only décor is a tumbleweed in full motion, rolling to and from the edges of the circle. For some reason, the tumbleweed never seems to leave the circle no matter how close it gets to the edges. Maybe it fears the green waiting outside the lifeless circumference.

As I enter the dusty space I, too, start rolling a couple of times to and from the edges, full of enthusiasm. I'm in!

In front of the hut a woman sits by the fire. I perform my post-seizure signature roll, landing gracefully at her feet.

The woman – nice voice, cold chipmunk face, baggy clothes – greets me warmly, but there is no time for small talk. I'm not here for her. I'm eager to see Him. She tells me that the Master is still dreaming, but he will meet me soon.

I can't help asking how they can cope with the ugliness and dryness of their dusty residence. She smiles. "What dryness?" She doesn't see it. Instead she sees lush endless green. I wish I could dream like these guys do.

While waiting for the Dust Devil, I get my small "Dream Toolkit" consisting of a dream catcher, a little candle, and a knife – I learn that the knife is meant to cut off the connections with the demons.

Wait! I wasn't told demons were involved. I'm here to achieve a sweet, continuous state of joyous dreaming, not to battle demons again.

I'm instructed by the woman at the "Front Desk" how to start my initiation journey. There are three steps. She is the one who will reveal them to me. Dust Devil will only help me to polish my abilities, remotely assisting me from his office.

She gives me a brochure. Simple instructions for a simple creature like me:

Light the candle. Keep the dream catcher close in case dream demons try to send you nightmares. Keep the knife under your pillow to cut the unwanted connections. Then follow the steps:

Relax completely and repeat "I know I am dreaming." Visualize yourself in a situation where you know you are dreaming – e.g. you are rich, you get laid every day, et cetera. Carry out a particular action – e.g. fly, walk on the ceiling, et cetera.

Walking on the ceiling would be nice. The neighbors downstairs complain all the time about me and my cat passionately exercising our Flamenco steps.

Puzzled and disappointed, I ask the Master's assistant if this is all I have to do. She says yes.

As I stand there staring at the dream toolkit in total denial, Dust Devil – gray complexion, long hair, bored demeanor – shows up unexpectedly and delivers a short, full-of-substance message: DREAMING IS SIMPLE.

I hate them both, but I smile just like my dream demons do. I do want to dream and I will.

The mysterious dream team delivers an equally friendly grin and then dissipates into the hut.

At this point I really don't know what to say. So much effort to meet an ugly woman and a moody Dream Master who sends me home with a dream toolkit and some instructions.

But who am I to undermine Dust Devil's authority? So I'd better do what he says.

Days have passed by. I don't even remember when and even if I ever met the Dream Master in person. At home, my cat does not believe that my meeting actually took place. She thinks that I landed in one of those cheap taverns, got drunk and had another nightmare.

Who cares? I lost grip on time a long time ago anyway.

As I try harder and harder to follow the instructions and dream my favorite dream – which is making love to Agatha, my long-lost lover from twenty years ago – a nasty dream about me getting a blowjob from a cheap Korean prostitute keeps coming back, over and over again. The Asian fellatio must be good though, as I wake up refreshed and happy.

I call Dust Devil and ask him politely to remove the ugly Korean woman from my dreams. Not only does he seem oblivious to my pain and unfulfillment, but I start having this dream about my beautifully shaped Agatha being caressed and touched everywhere, and I mean *everywhere*, by a stranger with no face. At the end of this nightmare, which I don't ever remember to have asked for, I manage to get closer to them and…surprise! It is Dust Devil! His greedy hands are touching her passionately and relentlessly. Get out of my dreams, treacherous filthy old man!

My old demons moved up. Literally. They no longer stand or sit in front of me, sipping their drinks and calling me names. Now I keep waking up – am I awake, really? – with them resting on my chest and giggling.

I no longer sleep with the knife under my pillow. Eyes half-opened, I hold it firmly with both hands. It doesn't seem to help. What really pisses me off is that the only thing my dream catcher managed to catch is a small fly.

I am not alone. Apparently, Dust Devil's demons are haunting my feline friend as well. She complains about repeatedly dreaming that she steals a juicy sausage, but when she starts eating it, the sausage turns into a fresh carrot.

Dust Devil rarely answers my calls, and when he does, he politely listens to my drama then he tells me to work on polishing the dreams and giving them depth. I think he's had enough of my complaints, for he visited me in my dreams recently telling me to "fuck off."

So I did, but with no results.

My dreams are filled with characters I have avoided with tenacity all my life. People I do not want to see, like Aunt Lyla's cousin, Uncle Safari. Although I've never been close to him, Uncle Safari now stops by my house to tell me his boring stories about fly fishing and bread baking.

I also dream I have to account for all my hunting trophies – including the bear with ugly lips I shot ten years ago in Alaska. My trophies are alive and they want to know if taking their lives has enhanced mine.

Not only have these creatures and situations taken up precious time from my real life, now they are invading my dreams as well.

I can no longer tell reality from dream. I meet people and I connect with them only to discover later that they're actually people I've met in my dreams. I don't know who is real and who is a dream anymore.

The postman brings me a letter. I know he is a real postman, the man I have known for years. I open the letter only to discover that the sender is actually a woman I've met in one of my tormented surreal journeys.

Although I do dream, it is definitely not what I asked for. I have less control of what I see or do in my dreams than before.

Reality, no matter how repulsive, might be an attractive option.

The Healing Session with Chamomile, the Storyteller

I sit on the bench in front of the house. My cat congratulates me for having the strength to get out of the house again after the scary encounter with Dust Devil. I couldn't agree more. It wasn't easy. I had to take no less than thirteen steps, skillfully putting one foot in front of the other.

But I made it and now I watch two happy teenagers making out to the background of a joyous chirping. It's springtime. Again? Where is my gun? Where is my gun?

While the cat is in the house, looking for the gun, my neighbor's mother-in-law stops to say hello. She asks me where I've been. I reply respectfully that I just got back from a trip in Hell. She informs me about Chamomile, the storyteller, who supposedly helped the daughter of a neighbor of her father-in-law get over a painful divorce and her brother overcome his gambling addiction.

Hmmm. Interesting. I learn that Chamomile has the unique gift of "mirroring" and is capable of developing amazing plots and characters. He makes the listener a central winning character in his stories. He makes the listener feel accepted and understood. His tales, I am told, reflect Beauty, Harmony, and Completeness, all coming from inside out and going from outside in.

While I can't understand this "inside out and vice versa" thing – familiar words in an unfamiliar setting – I do understand one thing: Chamomile's listeners leave soothed and happy, just like little children who stop crying after drinking their herbal tea.

My cat is skeptical. Why can't we seek therapy in our ancestors' fairy tales? I look at her, surprised. She doesn't get it. The fairy tales are not about *me*. They are about beautiful, intelligent, supernatural beings. How can I relate to that? Why can't I have my own story?

The animal is clingy. She wants to go, too. I explain to her that Chamomile has a dog, and, from what I have heard, a mean one. She feels insulted. The cat is the best friend for someone who questions everything. A dog is basically the typical follower, the approves-of-all friend. I end our dispute telling her that I do not want my meeting with Chamomile to end at the Animal Hospital.

I slam the door in her face and leave the house somewhat disoriented.

I get there at dusk and learn quickly that in the small rural settlement, Chamomile is a very popular presence. I am directed to the butcher's shop. I reach the butcher's shop only to have the pleasure of catching some fragments of one of his famous stories. The village crowd stands there mesmerized, tasting fresh sausages and pondering the fate of Chamomile's characters. I find the story of a little girl abused by an evil grandfather captivating and yet way too primitive, lacking the fantastic elements that tormented souls would expect. The little girl cannot fly, cannot change shape, and cannot escape her fate, since the mean cruel grandfather always wins. She can't even turn into a haystack or a needle, like my stupid neighbors do! I start wondering what the therapeutic role of such stories is, other than inducing even more depression. A villager distracts me by offering fresh oven-baked bread and sausage. I give up questioning Chamomile's therapeutic powers.

Mmmmm…what a good sausage.

As I sit on a stump in front of the butcher's shop, indulging in my sausage, someone taps me firmly on my left shoulder. Oh, my God! It's Chamomile himself! I stand up, sausage flying in the air, landing on the ground and from there into Chamomile's dog's greedy mouth.

Chamomile is short, hefty yet imposing, with big brown piercing eyes and hair that resembles one of my late mother's wigs – curly, dusty, a few patches missing.

I tell him in a soft, shattered voice that I am in desperate, oh, so desperate need for a story to heal my soul. He smiles.

I also tell him I need guidance. He smiles again.

I add that I have been searching for a while and meeting other healers as well.

I expect him to smile again. He doesn't…hmmm…which makes me wonder if he is friends with the treacherous Shaman Heavy Feather or Dream Master Dust Devil, whom I had the "pleasure" to meet recently. I admit I've become very suspicious and see enemies everywhere.

He tells me to meet him in an hour at a place called "The Crossroads." It's an actual crossroad between the main village road and a trail that goes into the woods. Cool, no problem, see you there, famous storyteller!

I get there early – I think I might be desperate – and I find the crossroads to be a very cozy setting. The main road is dusty and lifeless, yet the trail that intersects it is vibrating with green life. An antithesis of worlds and a place of meditation, "The Crossroads" could be inviting or less inviting, depending on where you're coming from. If one approaches it coming from the village, the green trail appears to hold salvation and relief. If one comes from the deep woods and hits the dusty road, depression settles in, no questions asked!

I lay down in the dust, motionless. The only thing I can think of right now is that I am an idiot. A humble idiot. An idiot who is trying to figure himself out.

I fail to sense Chamomile's presence. But his dog's sticky tongue brings me back to reality.

"Once upon a time," starts Chamomile, "there was a lonely man. His loneliness was so deep and so broad he himself could not see its limits. It was like a city spread in the desert, or maybe worse, like a desert spreading from one ocean to another. Some people's loneliness is greater than others'. This man's was definitely one of those greater ones. He tried repeatedly to connect with people, yet people didn't seem to understand his language and what he wanted to tell them. He would tell them about real problems and real concerns. He would try to reach some depth. But they would always deliver stupid lines like 'I missed the mattress sale again!' He would ask them questions and they would smile, oblivious to their own existence, immersed in their trance-like state."

I can't help thinking, "Oh, my God, that's me!" And for the first time in years I feel warmth around me.

I look at the Master Storyteller. Chamomile's gaze is piercing my Being. Maybe he is a mind reader as well? He continues in a soft voice, "And this man, looking for answers, is lucky enough to meet amazing, gifted people, who guide him through his journey…"

I start liking this little man from the Camomilesque story… I just know him. I like everything about him.

No, I take that back. I indulge, *in-dulge*, in this story.

What I do not like, though, is Chamomile's ugly dog chewing on my shoelaces; it appears to me that this is his favorite pastime. I try to physically remove Chamomile's canine follower. He comes back. I squeeze his nose. He growls and then goes back to my shoelaces. I pull his tail. He pees on my shoes.

Caught in the fight over shoelaces, I lose track of time. I manage to temporarily get control of my left shoe. Okay, now let's go back to the story. "What story?" Chamomile smiles. He just finished it.

I missed the climax of Chamomile's story. I was too busy defending my shoelaces. The dog seems to get it, though, for he stops chewing for a while and nods his head slowly, with deep respect for his Master's craft. Then he resumes what appears to be his favorite pastime and here gains control of my left shoe.

Honest and open as I am, I let Chamomile know right away about two things. First, I found his dog's habit extremely annoying; and second, a dog chewing on your laces is one thing, but an ugly one is highly unacceptable.

Chamomile's reaction to my statement is shocking, to say the least. The great storyteller and healer stands up, revealing his imposing figure, pointing at me in such an aggressive manner that even the dog freezes with a piece of my shoelace hanging out of his mouth.

I learn that what I call "ugly dog" happens to be a carefully crafted and designed mix between Schnauzer, Poodle, Bichon, and Pomeranian, also known as Schnoo-bich-pom. I fall on my knees, humiliated by my own ignorance. I feel an urge to offer Chamomile's dog my shoelaces, or what's left of them, anyways. Maybe this offering will help?

Yet Chamomile gives me the stink eye. He's not even trying to hide his disgust, for God's sake! I don't remember to have seen so much disgust in one single facial expression. What have I done?

What have I done? Chamomile starts laughing and his laughter makes me even more desperate and disoriented. He tells me that I missed the point.

Will he be kind, repeat the most important part of his story, and forgive my distraction?

Chamomile says no. Kindness is not what he is here for. He is here to deliver a teaching and I missed it. I ask him why is he so merciless? He explains, "In life we have many opportunities; each of them is unique, and once it is missed it cannot be brought back."

The ugly curly-haired dog is laughing at me. Yes, I swear, the dog is laughing, while Chamomile takes me through his mean teaching to the bottom of the ocean of human depression.

I cannot believe Chamomile is so mean. Maybe I should've listened to my cat and checked his references. I wouldn't be surprised to learn he is the brother of the other two charlatans…and his real name is Nettle…the only person who finds his company soothing is his mother…

Oh, I cannot take it anymore! I need earplugs. The more I hear the more suicidal I become and, although tempted, I have always been afraid to commit suicide. I don't want to hear a true story! I want a nice story!

I don't remember many details from my return trip.

I reach home with tears in my eyes, dragging one foot – no shoelaces – and thinking that the only thing that made this trip worthwhile was the sausage I brought back home for my cat.

The Healing Session with
Medje, the Gypsy Tarot Reader

For some reason, I ended up reading the local newspaper every day. Since I started doing so, the neighbor stopped sliding the paper under our door and now I have to get out of the house, walk ten yards, and get it myself.

In the paper I look for a cure for my pain. A disease of the soul might be tough to heal using scientific methods, so I can't help searching mostly under "Magicians, Witches, and Others."

What does "Others" mean? That I don't know.

My cat comes across a purple ad: "Magnificent traditional Gypsy Tarot reading that makes your jaw drop." My jaw drops not from Tarot readings, but from the stroke I had last winter. I wonder what other harm those readings could do to me.

I call the Gypsy woman named Medje and she informs me in an erotic voice – mmmmmm – that she also offers hypnosis, high-quality hypnosis. Hypnosis that will take me back in time to the beginning of the universe.

An hour later I am face-to-face with dark-haired Medje. Now I see why her hypnosis can take me and, generally speaking, any man on this planet, back to the beginning of the universe. She is probably in her late twenties, has a pretty face, long legs – from what I can guess under those Gypsy rags – and the biggest breasts I have ever seen. Every part of her body is carefully groomed. The hair, the makeup…I bet she wears nice lingerie, too. Medje is glamorous in every detail.

Her smile is lovely, and her nails, well manicured and polished, pull the cards with great grace and skill. She shows me the Tarot deck, explaining some of the cards to me. Yet I am an animal, thinking of her big breasts along with my best friend's sexual fantasy about lactation. Back then I could not get it, but now I think I'm eager to delve deeper into this one. Lactation, that is.

Aunt Lyla told me once that any true Gypsy Tarot professional has a black cat.

When Medje excuses herself to the restroom, I seize the opportunity. I look discreetly for the black cat. I cannot see it. I'm about to give up when I see what appears to be a black tail coming out from under the table. I pull the tail. Nothing. I pull the tail again. I hear a very familiar hiss. This encourages me to try to get the cat out. I manage to do so only to be unpleasantly surprised. It's my cat who has followed me, curious to see where I was going. I kick her out through the window. We will have to address this situation later when I get back home.

The beautiful Medje is back. She asks me to focus on "my problem." No problem, I think of it all the time. How could I possibly forget about it?

Then she asks me to deeply envision a person or fact that might be of help. I can't envision anything really, but I play along, pretending to be caught in "envisioning." After all, what is she going to tell me? That I won't get laid for another year?

You'd better tell me something I don't know, Big Tits.

Medje starts chanting some weird songs in an even weirder language, and she invites me to pick a few cards. She puts them aside, and then she shuffles the remaining cards so fast that I barely find time to blink. Wow, she must be good I'm thinking, full of hope.

Medje smiles at me and turns the cards upside down. She keeps smiling until she sees the last one. Her smile freezes. The air in the room is suddenly cold and damp.

"What happened?" I ask in desperation, but Medje shushes me and keeps shuffling the rest of the deck.

When she finally starts talking I see awe in her eyes, and even her voice has changed tones, from warm and soft to coarse and cold. "From what I can see, you are trapped in a no-way-out situation. Someone insignificant, maybe someone from your past, might or might not come to the rescue. Think of someone or something you do not find relevant, something really insignificant. This person might set you free. That is all I can see now," Medje says, lighting up a white candle and making what I call funny faces while trying to send imaginary waves of blessing towards me.

What? I want answers! I want details! Wha- wha- what is that creature with big ugly eyes on the card she is holding? I want to know how this reading thingy works. Do you ask the cards? Is there any spirit behind this? Is Medje a witch? Is she a true professional or is this just a part-time job?

I wake up in the street. Literally. I don't even remember finding my way out from Medje's small apartment. As I walk down the narrow filthy streets I keep thinking of her reading, trying to find mysterious signs in the everyday life. A tiny girl passes me by, chanting "Fresh plums, fresh plums." I stop her to get a fresh plum. I already see a mysterious significant message in the way she holds the bag with plums.

I keep walking, nibbling the plum. I don't know anyone around here so this is definitely not the best place to look for answers. But I can't help it. I just cannot help it!

I reach an intersection and stop. There's a sign right there, and what does it say? It says "One way." Is this a "sign," or just a sign?

A man walking his dog stops me to ask for directions. I don't care about him, but his dog has curious eyes, and I remember what Grandma taught me in childhood about curious eyes. "They are evil," she told me, "and whenever you see a critter with curious eyes you must walk in a circle around them three times and repeat 'Curious eyes will never get me.'" I am more than curious myself to see if this works, but this is a big Rottweiler and he's showing his teeth to me. Grandma never taught me how to do the circles around those without getting bitten. I naturally pass.

However, I repeat the "curious eyes will never get me" thing as I keep walking. I realize that I don't even remember the face of the man who stopped me, yet I can describe in detail the dog's face. One would think this is not important at all, but what if the police stop me and ask, "Sir, do you happen to remember this dog?" It is always a good idea to be an alert and active citizen.

Pit stop at a Chinese restaurant.

I swallow a few hot dumplings, burning the tip of my tongue. I also get a fortune cookie. Aha! My hands are literally shaking as I unfold the tiny piece of paper. I read: "He who asks is a fool for five minutes but he who does not ask remains a fool forever." Wow, these Chinese cooks are so sophisticated nowadays. I can't help thinking that I do not want to be a forever fool. No, it's not funny. I get a second fortune cookie. I'm curious to see what other messages of wisdom Chinese thinkers pass on to us along with their delicious food. This one reads: "This is *not* your fortune cookie."

I think I shouldn't have swallowed the second fortune cookie. It made me sick. Maybe it was indeed not meant to be mine. I enter the restroom at a small coffee shop just to freshen up. I get stuck inside. The door won't open. Two hours later, people who free me are surprised to see that I'm rather a quiet thinker than a panicky person. I think of Medje's reading. But I doubt that getting locked in a restroom might have some significance, unless it involves extremely hot women.

On my way back home I stop at a furniture store. I need a couch for my den. I'm told they just received the new collection of the well-known Asian designer, Master Architect Pok-Pok. I also learn that while furniture designers strive to bring together beauty and practicality, Master Pok-Pok is original, for he brings together ugliness and impracticality. This is a must see!

An enthusiastic salesperson guides me through the world of impracticality. The showrooms are incredibly small, which gives the poor space management more perspective.

The most successful project is the room named "No way out." This showroom has a docent, not a salesperson, assigned to it. He is a highly trained athlete, who can show the customers that living in space designed by Master Pok-Pok can be harmful, not only to the mind and soul, but to the body as well. The bruises on his knees, arms, and legs are there to prove it.

Anyone would question the necessity of a hostile design. Not me. I am way beyond kindergarten questions.

The "No way out" room lives up to its name. It is a tiny twelve-by-twelve-square-foot living room. Right in the middle of the room – two round tables. One small, the other one big. What is the purpose of having two tables? I learn that not only do they take up space and raise the blood pressure of the tenant, but they also offer the opportunity to show profound hospitality to our guests, by seating them at the bigger table.

Three corners host items that would be naturally placed in the proximity of the table: a TV set, a computer, a chair.

Access to the fourth corner, however, is blocked by the door. The door opens inward, blocking access to the corner and brushing off one of the tables. One has to be indeed very skilled to get into the room. Or out. Mostly out, I'm thinking.

I'm carried away by antagonistic emotions. I must be hooked, though. I picture fake, ugly flowers in between the two tables.

My antagonistic emotions are brutally severed. A little man – humpback, short legs, black sunglasses – passes me, followed by a consistent flock of worshippers. This must be the Master Architect Pok-Pok himself.

Time to move in. I literally push aside the gray mass of inspiration-free people. I demand to interact with the master right away.

Oddly enough, Master Pok Pok encourages me by pushing away a few of them as well. He delivers his words of wisdom without introducing himself – have we met before? The secret of his work relies on maximization of the apparently insignificant element. "Let's take the door in the No Way Out project," he says. "Everything in the room seems to be in the way. However, the only element really in the way is the door. You see, nobody notices the door. And the door cannot be moved. Hahahaha. The key is to use the insignificant element to create significance."

The master architect waves at me with grace, ready to move on.

I'm once again, puzzled. My mind is flooded with insignificant thoughts, overcast by the significant ones.

I look him in the sunglasses, boldly, unfettered by minor emotions. "Why? Why?"

I can distinguish pride in his voice. "Why? Because I hope my new design will finally force people into thinking. People take everything for granted. They assume they deserve to relax. They assume they have the right to enjoy a welcoming environment. They assume they are entitled to comfort. Guess what? They're not! You have to work hard to find your most comfortable spot! You have to find your way out on your own. And my design is here to prove it!"

I take a deep bow, kissing the ground before the Asian thinker. As I struggle to get out of the crowded store, I pass three young people. Fragments of their conversation, bullshit of nothing, reach my ears. I know that fifteen years from now, their conversations will be exactly the same.

I think again of Medje's reading. Are we truly forced to live our lives in a "No way out" environment?

I leave the store in silence, respect, and meditation.

The Healing Session at the Psychiatric Ward

It's been a month since I joined – as an employee, of course – our lovely local psychiatric ward. I left behind the world of mysticism and twilights. This time I will settle for the scientific approach. Adieu Shaman Heavy Feather, Dream Masters and Tarot readers. Hello Mother Science! You got my attention!

I know, I know, I have some minor issues, but who doesn't? Therefore, I decided to put some time into careful observation of various medical conditions and see if they were similar to mine or not.

If they are, they are. If they're not, oh well, then, they're not.

I love my workplace. It's quiet and peaceful, except when the residents start roaring and screaming. But I used to rent an apartment in Brooklyn, and, honestly, this is much better. This is actually music to my ears.

I also like my co-workers – silent, happy and optimistic human beings, big smiles 24/7, no ups and downs – who give me faith that my quest is worthwhile. We literally love each other, vigorously shaking hands at the beginning of our shift, gracefully returning farewells at the end of the day.

Since I am basically a rookie I was assigned to Dr. Schnauzer's team. An honor I didn't deserve, a right I didn't earn. I feel blessed, yes! Blessed. For Dr. Schnauzer is a well-known physician who even studied in Vienna – at least this is what our cleaning lady claims. And there is no secret that all the good shrinks either come from there or had Wiener Schnitzel at least a couple of times in their lives.

My task is to shadow Dr. Schnauzer and assist him when giving medications. I love medications! Sure, I don't quite understand what they are made of, but no one seems to know, really. Besides, they are smooth and glossy and they have such funny shapes…some pills are even square, something I wasn't aware of until I joined Dr. Schnauzer's team. *This* is knowledge, my friends.

I feel aroused when the amazing Dr. Schnauzer barks at me to bring him thirty-five mg of "Nitopitopholosphorine" pointing with his steely fingers at the shelves with medications. "I'm coming!" Here I am, holding "the cure," offering it to my boss and mentor with respect, admiration, and submissiveness.

I also hold the patients down for him while he pokes them. Believe it or not, some even bite! Not that Dr. Schnauzer is some whining chick. He bites as well, especially when his wife calls and bothers him with useless information about upcoming opera events.

Since he cannot bite her over the phone, he redirects his aggression, occasionally biting us.

I personally believe a bite from such a scientific genius is a gift, so I don't mind.

Days are passing by and I feel better than ever. When I'm tired I go to our beautiful Garden of Nonsense, a small retreat amidst tall trees and neatly trimmed bushes.

I sit down and play with my gummis. If anyone expresses their desire to join me, I swallow the gummis impulsively and smile, relaxed. I really, really don't need company right now.

This place is lovely, lo-ve-ly! I feel like singing and dancing, and sometimes I even do it. After all, aren't we all a big, happy family?

To be quite honest, I don't even feel like going home anymore. This is better than home. I haven't discovered many residents with issues like mine. Most of them suffer from sophisticated conditions like multiple personality disorder, or schizophrenia. Mine is just a heavy cloud of ongoing depression that seems to follow me everywhere. But the journey has just begun! My cloud and I are eager to discover more and more about the unknown conditions of the mind and soul.

I work in the East Wing of the Ward, where Dr. Schnauzer gives his treatments, holds his conferences and occasionally teaches his students. I also have the amazing opportunity to listen to and learn from those well-schooled people. I usually sit under one of the conference room's windows, eating pasta and allowing the knowledge to flow in. Flow, knowledge, flow!

For example, yesterday Dr. Schnauzer held a short lecture on the importance of being original while still blending in the scientific research flow.

I was wolfing down donuts, receiving the divine message, when a short statement caught my attention. It was Dr. Schnauzer's powerful bark.

"...not being able to connect with the scientific community is, pardon my French, intellectual masturbation, where the young researcher, selfish and unwilling to share the pleasure of discovering new worlds, keeps it all for himself; neither giving, nor receiving. A dangerous path to follow, since both the researcher and scientific community must understand that this is a two-way street! And no matter how difficult scientific togetherness can be, the pleasure both sides will derive is immense."

Wow, I almost choked. "Intellectual masturbation," "Scientific togetherness"... how come some people can take two words, stick them together and get such funny new meanings? I cannot. Maybe that's why I am a humble servant of Dr. Schnauzer's. For he can. And I cannot.

Although blissful and content, a naughty thought started dancing in my head some time ago.

I know the hopeless cases are lodged in the West Wing. I have never been there. What if I stop by, just like that, to quench my thirst of knowledge, huh?

Maybe now is the moment, yes? After seeing the Ward inside and out I think I am strong enough to step into the world of those who will never come back.

Careful not to be seen I put on Dr. Schnauzer's scrub top and grab the stethoscope, sneaking out of the East Wing like a true health care Ninja. Getting to the West Wing is a piece of cake for me, as I know the Ward well enough. I open the big back door and get into the main hall, smiling with fondness at my playful shadow.

My immaterial shadow slides on the walls, trying to follow me while simultaneously being faithful to Dr. Schnauzer, whom I have been shadowing for some time now. Speaking of which...Dr Schnauzer's voice...can't be! What's he doing here at this late hour of the night?

But then I hear another voice...shh...oh, no! I know this thunder-like voice. I try to open the door but it is way too heavy for me. I grab a little chair and try to reach the small window in the wall, built for discrete observation of the extremely aggressive patients. I watch and I am shaking...yes! It is him, the Shaman Heavy Feather himself. Hahaha, knock knock! Look who's here! The "healer"! I try to get some of their conversation. I cannot believe my own ears. "Great Shaman Heavy Feather, I cannot sleep. My one and only relief, the inflatable doll with qualities no woman possesses – silent, graceful, orgasmic smile 24/7 – somehow got a hole in her head and she is losing air! I patched it, yet I'm afraid our love is doomed."

I shake as Heavy Feather delivers his mean wisdom. "Do not despair, Dr. Schnauzer. Can't you see most women have holes in their heads, constantly losing air, and, unlike yours, they cannot ever be fixed?"

I witness Heavy Feather advising Dr. Schnauzer how to handle his most complicated cases. A patient suffering from "parental support syndrome,"a forty-five-year-old living with and off his parents, is, according to the Shaman, a "parasite." Shame on you, Heavy Feather! You think you have an answer for everything. You laugh at human suffering. Someone must stop you before you make other victims!

But Dr. Schnauzer doesn't seem to be outraged. He thanks Heavy Feather for his insight.

What? What is this? I demand an explanation! Dr. Schnauzer is seeking help? I want to scream, "Run, Dr. Schnauzer. Run! The shaman is a fake!" But my voice is sore and so is my mind. I step down, thunder-stricken, and look for the exit, but on my way out I'm passing another room. I can't help but peek inside. I see Dr. Schnauzer's favorite nurse, Maya, enjoying a worry-free sleep in one of the tiny beds and dreaming. Wait a minute! Who is by her bed, gently caressing her hair? Isn't that the deceiving and treacherous Dream Master Dust Devil? I don't understand anything anymore. Can anyone tell me, please, what is going on here? Who is who?

I'm way too overwhelmed by the latest revelations to pay attention to my surroundings. Instead of taking the exit door, I find myself in a room where Medje gives Tarot readings to a few patients while confessing about her manic depressive episodes.

I leave right away, but in the hallway I find myself following, again, my great mentor. He's not alone. A stocky gentleman walks with him, telling him a story about a physician who could cure all the people but himself. Who are you? Dr. Schnauzer is a scientific genius, and science is not storytelling. How dare you! I keep calling him names until he turns around and I see his face. It is Chamomile, the devilish storyteller. Wow, what a night! I'm stunned, yet Dr. Schnauzer gives Chamomile a hug along with a prescription for his hysteria episodes.

I'm shocked and numb, unable to move my body. I wake up only to see concerned faces – where have all the happy personnel gone? Why are their scrubs spotless? Why spotless? Why? I want spots, I want imperfection, and the spotlessness makes me feel shaky and insecure.

Why does nobody talk to me anymore?

Where is the friendliness, the vigorous handshake and the warm farewell? I want to know!

I am indeed very frustrated. Here I am, again on my own.

Who is this familiar character bending over me and putting her dirty paw on my forehead? It's my cat who came to take me home. I overhear the conversation the cat is having with Dr. Schnauzer. According to them I should be fine.

And how are things back home? Good, the cat cleaned the house, paid the bills and cooked soup. I can't wait to get home.

While I get my stuff, the cat follows me asking me the same simple question over and over again. Are we alone? Are there any other people with problems like ours? I look at her, puzzled. I don't know. Why don't we find out? We need to get out of here. We need to check out the real, palpable world.

The rest is…intellectual masturbation.

The Healing Session with
Astrakhan, the Animal Spirit

A letter with an ugly baby crow on its header informs me that I'm offered a tour at one of the most prestigious wildlife rehabilitation centers in the country. The tour itself does not appeal to me as much as does the fact that it will be given by Astrakhan, also known as the Animal Spirit. Astrakhan is famous for connecting with animals at a deeper level, delivering wisdom from the animal world to us. After all, where seek wisdom if not there? People don't seem to be too wise these days.

And human rehabilitation does not sound convincing to me. Bring the animals on!

I make the mistake of sharing my plans with my cat. She looks at me with contempt. She says that in every being there is a dormant idiot and mine just awoke. Don't I have enough bad, unpleasant experiences? Do I really need more of these?

I close the door behind me with great relief, yet without really understanding what she's trying to convey to me. Who listens to a cat, anyway?

I get there early in the morning, anxious to interact with the depressed and/or wounded wild fellows.

Astrakhan – reddish hair, ridiculously small ears, strong orange teeth – seems happy to show me around. I clap hands and bounce in joy.

My first impression is that I have been lied to. This is not the cute and worry-free animal kingdom I've seen on TV, sprinkled randomly with dog food commercials.

Where is the hot, clean-shaven animal control officer who works together with the wildlife fellows to save our endangered species from extinction?

I didn't know that wildlife rehabilitation involves dirty people handling aggressive animals. I pass them slowly, looking at them intensely. Who are you?

However, while touring the center I notice that the animals in the enclosures have much more interesting expressions than most people I have met in my life. I pass a sad fox that is peeing in the fresh water bowl – defiance, says Astrakhan – a joyful wolf chasing a little bird – teenager – and a pissed juvenile bald eagle. Astrakhan says he is just a maniac.

We also pass an enclosure where an opossum enjoys his afternoon nap. I can't understand why Astrakhan storms into the enclosure, shakes the poor opossum a few times and then smiles, relaxed. The opossum wakes up and gives him a "fuck you" look. Astrakhan explains to me that, some time ago, one of these lazy critters slept for three days in a row. The animal caregivers kept supplying him with fresh food and water, envying him for he did not have to be up every day at 6:00 a.m. Some of them even held one-way conversations with the animal, "Sleep, little angel, what do you care?"

When Astrakhan, the Animal Spirit, tried to "connect" with the little fellow, he noticed that the small critter had been dead for more than a week.

So what? I remember we had a similar case at the psychiatric ward when I was working with Dr. Schnauzer. At least the opossum didn't have a greedy family to sue them, ha!

I'm also shown the log where the workers carefully follow the health status of the patients. I'm told that animals are rescued, checked in, treated, and then released or euthanized, depending on their condition. I think human hospitals should offer the same options. Just a thought.

For some reason Astrakhan's words bring back old images from the past. I think of Uncle Yolkie. He endured miserable years of excruciating pain in his hospital bed, connected to multiple devices meant to keep him alive. But was he alive? Judging by the empty eyes resembling two huge egg yolks, he had the awareness and the clarity of thought of a medium-sized eggplant. However, according to his wife and the rest of the family, Uncle Yolkie was *there*, alive and connecting with them on a daily basis – "He moved his fingers again!" Why were they so cruel? Because they loved him and they did not want to let go of him. His suffering didn't matter. I think love is selfish. Just another thought.

I'm back with Astrakhan and his stories.

He tells me that the wildlife workers are instructed to minimize interaction with the wild guys. Wild animals should stay wild, in order to increase their chances of surviving out there. I totally agree.

I, too, am a wild one, and I plan not to interact with humans more than I have to, in order to increase my chances of surviving.

I observe everything in silence and am truly immersed in Astrakhan's words. I learn that most animals with a major physical defect – a bird with a broken wing, for example – can no longer function in the wild. I am so proud to be human, for our society first turns a healthy individual into an impaired one and then encourages him to survive.

Astrakhan doesn't approve of my thinking. We move towards a cage where a Mexican gray wolf howls non-stop. He explains, "Not long ago the wolf lost his mate and now he is calling her." Astrakhan tried to move other females in, but it didn't work.

I totally understand the wolf. When I lost Agatha, I, too, tried other females, and it didn't work. Then I tried alcohol, and it worked for a while.

Animal Spirit shows me a bunch of baby turkey vultures snoozing. They're cute in their ugliness. I want to take a closer look at these creatures but Astrakhan explains that when they are stressed, they vomit. Hmmm. Thank God humans don't manifest like this under stress; we would be vomiting continuously.

Astrakhan shares other wildlife stories with me. I listen with extreme interest to these amazing encounters where the Animal Spirit mediates conflicts between bears and antelopes, gives marital advice to a Red-tailed Hawk, and helps a beaver build an extension to his old house.

I'm deeply moved by these stories. I tell Astrakhan I have always liked to communicate with animals more than with humans. He agrees.

I tell him about my cat who meows every time I open the refrigerator. She is so smart! Astrakhan looks at me with pity. Really? I look at him amused. Show me what you got, Animal Spirit.

I tell my guide that I want to see the big, powerful animals, the ones that I used to impersonate when I was a kid at school parties. Mom and Dad were always proud when I was playing the lion and very pissed when the teacher had me play the bunny or the bee.

As a matter of fact, I remember parents getting involved in school activities well before Christmas. They were doing it not because they cared, but because they wanted their kids to be bears, wolves, and big cats. The principal had tried once to explain to the parents that in the animal kingdom size doesn't matter. Naturally, most dads protested. They asked a simple question: Who would want to be eaten? A few moms blushed.

I share my childhood memories with Astrakhan. He approves of the principal. However, on our way to the big cats' enclosure, he offers me a feather as a sign of friendship. It is a feather from a bald eagle, not from a house sparrow.

Animal Spirit shows me a bored lion. He tells me that the lion does nothing but flash his mane, eat, and get laid.

The lion is not fun to be around; he is boring, infatuated with himself, and horny. He is the ultimate male.

I don't find "being the ultimate male" interesting at all. The only thing I might have in common with this lion is the fact that now and then, I allow my instincts to take over and become an animal.

However, although I occasionally follow women, horny and misunderstood, they never seem to respond to my joyous mating signals. The only way I can get closer to women is to buy them a drink or two, while I inhale the air around them deeply.

One more question for Animal Spirit. I know my cat would say it's a very stupid question, but I'm going to ask it anyway. How come wild animals bite us occasionally, in spite of what appears to be a long-lasting friendship?

Astrakhan smiles and explains to me the mystery of human-animal interaction. "When we raise baby raccoons, for example, we teach them that they are humans like us. We cannot teach them raccoon habits because we are not raccoons. So they grow up *thinking* or at least *trying* to be like us. But one day they take a closer look at themselves in the mirror and say, 'Wait a minute! I am a raccoon!' Then they turn to us, 'You lied to me.' Then they bite us. Yeah, it's that simple." Astrakhan finishes his lesson licking his right paw.

Animal Spirit's wisdom is astonishing. He is so right! I think of myself. All this time I've been a baby raccoon, adopted by a very religious family. I just didn't know it.

Pit stop at the neighborhood pub. I enter the place I have known for years and go straight to the bar. It's not until I get my favorite drink that I notice that the customers' behavior doesn't differ much from the animals'. I turn around and take a second look at the citizens enjoying quality, worry-free time.

I suddenly picture them all locked up in enclosures, just like the animals Astrakhan showed me. Once in a while an animal caregiver – bartender – supplies them with food and fluids. The cases that cannot be locally handled – overdoses, intoxications – are sent to the animal hospital. Only a few are released; a few keep coming back – fear of coping with freedom. Some never leave their cages, even if the doors are wide open – fear of trying out freedom.

I call the waitress. One more drink and I'm out of here.

I feel an overwhelming urge to leave. I want to go and hide in the cage I built myself for my own rehabilitation program.

I want to go home.

The Healing Session at the Detention Center

I admit I have been very concerned lately. What if I missed something? What if the "essence" was right there in front of me, and I was unable to spot it? I have freedom of choice, yet I always make bad choices. Maybe freedom is in my way. Maybe if I limit my freedom I'll make the right choices.

After all, why do we have soooo many options? Just to make our lives unbearable, if you're asking me.

I know you're not asking. But I do. I like to ask.

I walk around the house with a concerned face. It's not a mask. Who said that what is inside is also outside? I think it was my last girlfriend, the one with the bulldog eyes.

My preoccupied brisk walk is abruptly interrupted by three policemen busting a guy right across the street. I walk up to them, grateful for this unexpected opportunity. Isn't this one of the most exciting professions? Sometimes police officers go undercover, real undercover, with makeup and role-play. They also help old ladies to cross the street.

I am not only concerned about inner freedom and such. I'm also interested in individual, social freedom. Let me take a closer look. A bored police officer gives me all the details I need – why bored, when you have such an exciting profession? Nothing out of the ordinary; just the average burglar sneaking into people's houses.

As I watch them handcuffing him and pushing him into the car, naughty thoughts start to flow in again.

I need to talk to people who have hands-on experience with limited or no freedom.

I need it badly. I need it NOW.

I am indeed a man of action, so after I write tens of letters and memos, I'm finally allowed to take a short tour of the detention facility they just built outside the city.

As I get closer to the D-Day, a phone call from the detention center disrupts the harmony, the excitement, the anticipation ... the tour has been canceled. Oh, no!

Have you ever seen a two-year-old who is refused his favorite toy? That's me right now.

The question is, will I let the depression take over? Heck, no! A warrior like me cannot surrender to minor enemies such as cancellations.

I hear movement in front of the house. It's the milkman. The milkman brings me milk, yogurt, and occasionally exciting news from the gray communities of gray people populating this planet.

As I taste the yogurt, inspiration strikes. I ask the milkman if they're hiring at all at the detention center.

Actually, they are! Well, they need someone to sweep the hallways in between meals. The milkman gives me in-depth explanations.

Apparently some of the personnel steal from the meals while serving it to the inmates – smart, smart. They stick it in their pockets, mostly muffins, and they leave a mess of crumbs on the floors.

I, too, want to steal something. I want to steal a few crumbs of Knowledge, if possible.

I have to hurry. I gracefully blow a kiss to the milkman and I rush into the house. I grab my resumé, highlight the recent and most outstanding moments in my career – apprenticeship with Dr. Schnauzer, delete the insignificant ones – Ph.D. in Social Sciences, the short-lived yet intense career within the intelligence community, and … I am on my way!

The job interview is condensed and to the point.

The detention officer in front of me is eating a muffin, *accidentally* dropping a few crumbs on the floor.

I rush to pick them up with intense submissiveness. A relaxed smile on his face tells me that I'm hired. Yes! It pays off to have a Ph.D. in Social Sciences. Or, to have worked a few months at a psychiatric ward.

I show up early, anxious to steal the crumbs of Knowledge. The hallway that separates the cell rows is narrow and indeed very sticky. My co-worker, who is in charge of serving the breakfast, tells me how stuff works. He serves the meals; I follow him with the clean up.

I make my first step in the hallway observing the décor in the cells. Nice comfy beds, excellent bed spreads, overall a refreshing design. The first guy who gets his breakfast is a linguist – gorilla eyes, tiny mustache, caterpillar-like eyebrows. A short conversation brings us together. I ask him if he likes muffins. He says yes. Me, too. He looks at me with contempt. Then he delivers in a few sentences the fundamentals of words, messages, and intimate experiences.

I learn that the statement, "I like muffins," refers to a very personal experience. It involves my being, the muffin, and my perception of the muffin. Okay, I did not know that, although I kind of sensed it at some point in my life when I realized that my depression is not yours.

Yet I just cannot leave the impression that I'm some sort of rookie in languages and communication. I, too, can teach this fellow something. I expose my original theory about minimizing the amount of words in a phrase, cutting out the unnecessary, keeping *the essence*. I know, I know, it takes years and practice to become a master. For example, why bother to phrase such difficult concepts as, "The aroma and the taste of this coffee are outstanding," when you can deliver a much more powerful message by reducing the sentence to, "Outstanding coffee!" All you have to do is take it gradually, small steps, cutting out the insignificant words, one by one. Going from, "The aroma and the taste of the coffee are outstanding," to "Aroma and taste – outstanding" and finally to, "Outstanding coffee," requires years of practice. There is also "Mmmmmmmmmmmmm," but this is reserved for the chosen few, the ones who reach true enlightenment in the spheres of human interactions.

Human beings always have a sick tendency to give out more information than they should.

The linguist seems to embrace my theory. Moreover, he is skilled enough to be able to apply it right away with amazing results. He points at me with disgust, "You – stupid."

I keep sweeping with an indifferent, yet stern gaze. One might think I'm focused on sweeping. Not at all. Far from it. I observe, check out, make mental notes.

I pass a guy who got punched in his face so bad that his eyes resemble my niece's stuffed Panda Bear.

Panda Bear, what are you doing here? I learn he is getting his Master's in Time Management.

Spending so much time with so much time on his hands inspired him. He decided to help people make Time fly by faster. What is the purpose of that? I don't know. Everyone seems to crave to stop Time or at least turn it back. Yet Panda Bear insists that only people who know what they want should attempt this. The rest of them, he says, don't know what they want. So they have to get to the final destination faster and suffer less.

Panda Bear doesn't sound convincing to me. I move on, pushing my cleaning gear. I think I made it very clear that I only stop to connect with those who appear to have a teaching or two for me.

I keep picking up muffin crumbs while searching for a potential source of wisdom.

Next! Oh, my God! The next cell hosts a fine, polished gentleman wearing a top with playful chic dots. The pants feature dots as well, just with a slightly different pattern. A little bit too eclectic for early morning. Nonetheless, a feast for the eye hungry for harmony.

I learn that he just got moved here. Reason? Depression. The counselor who occasionally services the inmates is truly a revolutionary mind. He doesn't treat depression with medications. Nor with dreams or asking animal spirits like those I've met before. When depression moves in, he just moves the inmates out.

He seems convinced that the change in environment is "it." In plain English, "Hey, Depression, want to move in? 'Cause I am moving out."

The subject wakes up in a cell that is exactly the same as the previous one, just different.

I really want to meet this counselor. But now, back to the guy in front of me.

He smiles and he doesn't seem depressed at all. He skips the intro – my favorite – and tells me he is a former fashion designer who hoped for a change, an escape from the dull, organized fashion trends of the outside. Interesting approach. Looking for answers in places where they're less likely to be found.

He points at the shoes of the guy who serves the meals. "See," he says, "you can tell who you're dealing with just by looking at them. New shoe, vigorously scratched, soaked and polished in order to have that 'old' look. A true believer, a person dedicated to introspection, interpretation, and mystification of fashion."

It hits me why I used to be so welcomed in certain high spheres when I was wearing my grandfather's old, worn out shoes. They looked really antique. So that's why everyone praised my good taste. The truth is that back then I had no money to buy better ones. Had I known my poverty was so trendy I wouldn't have tossed them out when I got my first paycheck at the grocery store. Life is indeed a learning process.

It is true what they say, enlightenment presents itself in various shapes and forms. Thank you, sophisticated fashion designer.

I am indeed overwhelmed by what I have seen so far. My thoughts are burning inside my head. Someone, either my grandfather or my handler at the ski resort, I cannot remember who, taught me once, "When your thoughts burn you, burn them as well." I feel an urge to go home, put everything on paper and then burn it…kneel in front of the fire, humbled and free. Burn, thoughts, burn! I visualize some of them burning nicely, some of them slowly, and some, resisting death, making huge flames, leaving behind the perfume of the thought yearning for completeness.

On my way out, surprise! I bump into the counselor. Yay! This one I do want to meet.

The counselor – stern gaze, small squirrel eyes, five big moles on top of the nose – is reserved, but eager to share some of his wisdom.

He informs me, on an optimistic note, that he accidentally overheard my short conversations with some of the inmates. He reserves the right to reject my theory about rendering the essence with the help of just a few words. He backs up his thirst for elaborated wording by giving me the example of Panda Bear, the inmate I just met. Panda Bear was actually having dinner with this hot woman. Instead of letting the avalanche of words flow in the air – *You are so special, your hair is soft like the most precious silk, my eyes are glued to your gazelle-like silhouette* – he rendered his intense emotions in three simple words: "I want pussy." Sadly, the hot sexy woman was an undercover police officer who was investigating sexual harassment cases. So, before she arrested him, she took great pleasure in punching his face as hard as she could.

It's okay, counselor. I will survive. I will make changes to my theory. For example, we can keep working on short, essence-filled messages only in men-to-men interactions and keep those long, blurry sentences for special circumstances, like when we need to convince women they *must* have sex with us. As you see, I'm pretty flexible.

While looking for the exit sign, I meet a man who starts talking to me. For some reason I can't hear him at all. I'm shocked to discover I am actually wearing my earplugs. This means I totally missed the words of wisdom the Counselor *might have had* for me. But then, how come I can recall the entire conversation?

Maybe the conversation did not take place at all. Maybe it's just a creation of mine.

I look with disgust at the few crumbs I'm holding in my hand. I exercise my freedom of choice by tossing them into the first garbage bin available. This is definitely Knowledge I do not want to keep.

The Healing Session at the Kindergarten

I have been on-off with society lately. After all, society has always seemed to me a job, a place where I go and perform certain activities, only to rush back into my world.

Besides, every time I go there, I feel like I have to appear in court. It's a mean court, and I am always sentenced for crimes I'm not even aware of. I will not burn the bridges, though. I practice self-discipline. I don't need someone to punish me. I punish myself well enough on my own.

Yesterday, for example, I spent three hours on my knees, facing one of the corners in my living room. It hurt. But it was worthwhile.

The truth is, I need guidance, I need pressure, and I need a higher authority, even if I don't understand the deeper meanings of the restrictions imposed on me. Who am I to fight society?

Does a puppy understand *why* he gets punished every time he poops in the house? Heck, no! All he knows is that he is not allowed to do it. He has no concept of cleanliness. Nor does he know about house, city, country, and world. I, too, have no concept of "world." I can only see myself and the Society I belong to. All I know is that the Society wants to keep it clean, which means that I'm not allowed to poop in the house. I have to play by their rules and keep my original opinions to myself.

I'm headed to an exciting session with an old African witch when the phone rings. I am not pissed. I am overly pissed. I roll my eyes, pull both my hair and the cat's tail, spill coffee. What is it this time?

It's my niece who wants to ask me a huge favor. She wants me to pick her daughter up at Aunt Lyla's, then drop her off at the kindergarten, and then pick her up again and take her home. I look at my busy schedule and, yes, I can help.

I will take care of the kiddo in between my African witch, karate lesson, and the clowns' meet-up.

I'll have to hurry, though; I'm on a tight schedule here. I hate to be late, especially since I am dealing with witches, martial arts experts, and clowns. They all can be vengeful, and they can harm you, each in his own way. Witches target the soul, martial arts experts can target the body, and clowns, oh well, those can make you cry instead of laugh, targeting your mental sanity.

Aunt Lyla welcomes me warmly. I don't like to see kids at her place, though. There are certain things hard to explain to a three-year-old. Like, why do we have to sit on old, shaky chairs, when a beautiful, inviting and covered-with-plastic couch is right there in front of us?

I know Aunt Lyla is right. How are we going to keep the couch new and shiny if we actually use it? I'm used to "preserving" things and passing them on to the fifth generation.

My little niece might not be. Not yet.

Aunt Lyla wants to know if I still have the egg holder she gave me twenty-eight years ago. But, of course. Have I ever used it? I'm a little bit insulted by her question. Never!

I am suddenly carried back in time, thirty years ago. I'm in the same room. My father is there, too, drinking fine French wine from what used to be a mustard jar.

I look at the beautiful mahogany cabinet filled with precious porcelains. Oh, I *so* want to touch them. My father tells me in a grave, official tone that one day they will be mine. But how can they become mine tomorrow if I break them today? Back then it didn't make sense to me. Now it does.

I'm three-years-old and I eat my breakfast from what used to be a doggy bowl. I like it. It even has cute poodles on the sides.

Back with Aunt Lyla and my niece. My niece has a little makeup kit and she asks Aunt Lyla to help her "be pretty." Aunt Lyla gives her a lecture about the girls who put too much makeup on their faces. "They do that because they're feeling insecure," Aunt Lyla says. Aunt Lyla is right. I will bring this up at the clowns' meet-up.

In between helping the little girl with her makeup, Aunt Lyla gives me the latest news. Yesterday she ran out of salt. She went in the neighborhood to borrow some. Oddly enough, all the neighbors pretended not to have it.

One would think everybody put on their tables salt-less, tasteless food. Aunt Lyla was very, very upset.

I agree. I picture all the humanity, silent and selfish, hiding in their houses, firmly holding big salt jars. Liars!

Indeed, the smallness of human race cannot surprise me anymore.

I assure Aunt Lyla of my deepest respect for her suffering. I leave her surrounded by expensive porcelains, furniture, and jewelry no one has nor ever will use.

The kindergarten is small but very, very welcoming, a gray dome decorated with amazing paintings meant to distract the young generation from the real world. The paintings are so cute. I see purple squirrels, blue monkeys, and even pink lions. I admit that they're cool; however, I do not understand what the purpose is of teaching the kids that bears are orange. Aren't they going to be disappointed when they'll finally realize that real animal coats are pretty... dull?

Let's take a closer look at the curriculum designed for the little people. Today's classes are listed by the main entrance. I read with passion and curiosity. The curriculum hasn't changed too much in the past thirty years. Music lessons – "Me me me mu mu mu." Grammar and spelling – "I have a cow. You are a cow." Dance lessons for the little girls – "Graceful ballerinas." Trip to the shooting range for the little boys – "Shaping aggression." I like that. We didn't have that back then, just some plastic knives and homemade slings. And of course, extracurricular activities, like "Little cook" – same boring fatty meals, no change here.

As I stand there immersed in the educational highlights of the day a bored four-year-old passes me, dragging his feet. He looks *through* me, conspicuous, with hatred. Is it me, or does the little fellow seem depressed? That's cool. I think it is a good idea to familiarize them with depression at this early stage in life. It is indeed a beautiful morning.

I take my little niece to her classroom. My greedy eyes take a quick peek inside.

Here they are, little creatures...waiting to grow up and become lawyers, salespeople, police officers, CEO's, bored housewives, and pimps...right here in front of my eyes, enjoying their childhood. Isn't that awesome?

A tiny redhead, hiding in the back sucking his fingers, catches my attention. He is the nonconformist of this small social group.

This becomes obvious as the teacher shows up and starts the music lesson. All the kids sing along *Me me me mu mu mu* except for this fellow, who delivers short, bored *boo boo's*, with his mouth full of peanuts.

I need to bring this insubordination to the teacher's attention. I wait outside until the bell rings.

The teacher – short hair, freckles, Nazi uniform – informs me that she has already mentioned this to her superiors. The nonconformist kid will soon be enrolled in the revolutionary educational program, *Regression for the Smartest*. Wow! It's good to know that the society who constantly punishes me has something for the younger ones as well. I don't feel alone anymore.

I am all ears, anxious to quench my thirst for knowledge. *Regression for the Smartest* is a complex, unique program meant to level off the creativity and originality. All kids with extraordinary abilities are subjected to a very rigorous regression program, until their perception of reality matches the one everyone else has.

This way, I'm told, we have a happy, united society. This program is indeed mind-blowing!

Competition is totally eliminated. Everybody is a winner. Why should they compete when everything they need is delivered? There's food, boring cartoons, boring lessons, and boring quizzes with all the answers written at the bottom of the page. Most important of all, they are kept *busy*, so they do not have time to *think*.

I'm hooked. One question, though. How can we spot those enemies early enough to take action? I learn there is a special counselor whose task is to carry on informal, relaxed conversations with those gremlins and weed them out before the originality spreads. Originality is worse than a disease. True, very true.

But what if, knock on wood, the regression program doesn't work?

The Obersturmbannfuhrer smiles. She shows me their album with *before* and *after* shots. I see a picture of a five-year-old little boy with sparkling, penetrating black eyes. His *before* abilities are listed under the photo. Musical genius, bilingual, writes poetry. The *after* picture needs no comment. The boy's eyes are empty. I read with tremendous joy that they emptied his head as well. Now his vocabulary has returned to normal, in only one language. He's no longer interested in Chopin, and the only poems he reads are those from the "Thank you" cards his mom sends to the other housewives following a baby shower.

Impressive. Impressive healing programs. Had they had this amazing tool when I was young, today I would have been healed and happy. I'd have fit in. But, for me, life has been nothing but a series of missed targets.

I think I am done here. Before I go, I take the opportunity to ask about my niece. Is she, God forbid, a future hostile element? Far from it. She is a true follower. Good. That's my girl. Can't wait to deliver the great news to her mom.

I need to go now; otherwise, I'll be late for my healing session with the African witch. I shake hands with the teacher, ready to part ways. I notice that my cat has a tendency to stick with her. The teacher must be very smart. One can't guide people, even children, through intellectual regression if they're stupid.

I can't say I am surprised by my cat's behavior.

She's done this before with Dr. Schnauzer and, generally speaking, with all the smart people I've met in my life.

I've had many conversations with her; she is like a moody wife who is never ready on time. I have to wait for her, beg her to stay with me and not with others. It's ridiculous. I constantly have to check around me to see if she's there. Lately, I panic when my cat is not with me.

I drive like a maniac to the African witch's tent, counting seconds. I get there, jump out of the car, and crawl under the protected, magic shelter. I express my joy for not being late, but the African witch looks at me with sadness, "You might be on time, but your cat is not. She's still at the kindergarten."

I stare around in disbelief. The witch is right. My cat is not there. I can picture the clowns at the meet-up making fun of me. I can't take that much humiliation. Time to find that bitch!

We will have to reschedule. I kiss the African bearer of wisdom on both her cheeks, humbly receive a pickled snake from her – talisman – and rush back to the kindergarten. I storm into the classroom only to create havoc, since Snake falls out of my pocket and kids have never seen a pickled snake in a classroom. Neither had I.

My cat is not there. I call Aunt Lyla. She puts me on hold while looking for her. I hear strange words coming from the phone. "Fuck off, okay?" And, "Leave me alone!"

This cannot be Aunt Lyla. This must be my cat. Aunt Lyla is back on the phone.

Aunt Lyla managed to find her. She was hiding in one of her cabinets, behind the Chinese collection. I knew it!

Apparently, my cat likes to be around things that I can't get close to.

And, unlike me, she can't be trapped. Or punished.

The Healing Session in Painting

The idea to sign up for painting lessons came when I picked up my niece from kindergarten. My thinking is simple: if other people can grab a brush and paint, why can't we? My cat agrees. Aunt Lyla says that art can help people to understand themselves better.

And then there is my friend, Xavier the writer. No matter how diverse, Xavier's works have one thing in common: no one would bother to read them. Even members of his close family would learn the synopsis by heart, reciting it later, and avoiding Xavier's questions about the characters.

Reading his works became a challenge for us. After torturing myself and the cat with a few pages, I came across a chapter entitled *The Image, the Self, and the Identity.* Obviously, I didn't read the chapter, but the words stuck with me.

I wake up and fix myself a coffee. The cat has a concerned face. I know, I know. I, too, am profoundly disturbed by the conflicts in the Middle East. Yet she is so sensitive. I'm worried this might have a negative impact on her appetite. I turn off the TV so she can't watch the news and sob at the sight of so much injustice around the world.

I pick the Mad Master Painter to be my guide in the world of colors and shapes. I'm lucky; he's just starting a new class. Detail-oriented as I am, I perform a thorough background check in the neighborhood. I ask the butcher's wife, "Why Mad?" I learn that he is mad at mankind because no one seems to understand the clarity of his thoughts. I feel the same, just the other way around. My thoughts are blurry, not clear.

"There is a small problem, though," says the butcher's wife. "The openings are limited, as the Mad Master insists on having a multicultural, diverse class. There is only one opening left and only a Dutch fisherman will be considered."

I kiss her hands and rush to do my homework.

I manage to get all the gear in one afternoon, including a smoked fish I will hold in my right hand, just like that, to emphasize the deep connection with my Dutch ancestors. My cat looks at me intensely. Yes, I know. We can be whomever we want. *We just can't be ourselves.* But that's what we're trying to understand.

I am an avid, motivated learner. I quickly absorb basics like "Wie bent U?" – *Who are you?* and "Goedemorgen" – *Good morning.* I also pray no one ever asks me in detail about Pieterburen, the small Dutch village where I was born, wink, wink.

Why am I doing this? Because I'm a humble satellite, trying to launch myself on an orbit around great minds. I like this Mad Painter guy. I feel we can connect. The sooner I see him the better!

Like all the special people I have met so far, the Master Painter – big smile, conic teeth, sheep-like face – is actually very excited to share his knowledge with a Dutch fisherman.

He shows me with great pride his masterpiece, *Self Portrait of the Soul*. As he unveils the work, I look at it with great curiosity. It's a … it's a … it's a … bunny. Yes, the great master's true nature is that of a shy, cute bunny. He tells me that he'd enough with traditional painting that limits creativity by imposing painters to render overrated egos. Everybody likes to think they are lions, bears and eagles. Nobody wants to be the mouse, the bee, or the Portuguese-man-of-war. Time for a change. I agree.

I sign up for classes on the spot. I'll start the following morning.

Here I am, a humble, aspiring artist. I enter the "classroom," which is the Master Painter's shed. I tune out the discussions on the latest news – chicken fever outbreak in Congo, car crash in downtown Paris, hold up at a remote inn in Peru – as I broadcast a polite smile.

I notice that most students are painting, or at least aspire to, still life: potatoes, cauliflowers, and cabbages. This is very intriguing, especially since the students are of various ethnicities and nationalities. I wonder if we could all work on a common project and paint a vegetable. I have always dreamt of a bunch of children of all colors and religions, working together on a…on a…universal, international cauliflower, for example.

My presence does not go unnoticed. I hope it's not the smoked herring I'm holding. The others demand to know right away what I expect from my brushes and colors. Everybody stares at me and a thick silence falls. Even though a beginner, a Dutch fisherman is not easy to intimidate. I pull out my fishing knife and skillfully carve a fish-shaped hole in the Silence. Then I deliver my wisdom of nothing.

I tell the sophisticated, enchanting students of high standards that I humbly envision a future when I will be able to paint thoughts: suicidal thoughts, treacherous thoughts, and last, but not least, peaceful thoughts.

My plans also include, but are not limited to, depressed caged souls, as well as boring bored people drinking tea or listening to their inner voice of boredom. Or both.

I share only a few of my artistic expressions-to-be. I don't intend to shock and scare. So far they seem to respond well to my creative impulses. They say "Oh" and "Eee."

An older woman sitting next to me catches my attention. She's trying to recreate the image of her grandson eating pasta with tomato sauce. I look at the unfinished work. She put too much red in his lips and he looks like he is spitting blood. She tries to fix it, with no success. I advise her in an encouraging tone to just change the title to *Tuberculosis*. She shows teeth. Some artists just lack imagination and playfulness, I guess. I didn't picture her in our international cauliflower team of talents anyway.

The painting lessons are intense and vivid. It's their simplicity that makes them so appealing. The rules are as follows: the Mad Master hovers from one student to another, giving directions. We follow them or not. Yeah, it's that easy.

"More white," he says, or, "less blue." Then he leaves, only to hover back to us at the end of the lesson, and add, "More purple."

The Master stops by me. I like to shadow, so I followed on his steps. I decided to work on a self portrait. I'll call it *Cancer of the Mind.*

My mentor is excited and shows enthusiasm. We get the message: It's our turn. We have to look at each other's paintings and evaluate, give advice, show enthusiasm.

As I start displaying enthusiasm, it hits me that deep inside I believe that artists should never evaluate artists since their "targets" are not other artists, but simple people.

Yes, simple people, simple minds, the man from the street. However, this can be relative. My cat and I once decided to test the average audience for our short philosophical poem *Disaster*. We walked out of the house and we randomly picked out what appeared to be the average citizen – average height, average weight, average hair length. We showed him the poem. He gave us a harsh critique. We smiled proudly and we asked him in a contemptuous tone if he was some connoisseur. He said, "Yes." We then learned in awe and disgust that the randomly selected average citizen was teaching Liberal Arts at the University.

I will not fall for this again!

I ask the Master why can't I paint something amazing, just like that? He explains, "All the great works emerged as a direct result of immense suffering in the artists' lives. Most artists endured poverty, depression, rejection, insurmountable pain." He's right. I rub my full belly – had twelve donuts for breakfast. There's no pain right now, just a blissful smile.

I run back home overwhelmed and ready for action. Usually, I'm very independent. I don't like to involve my cat, but this time I will have to ask her for help. She approves of my new lifestyle. She'll be there for me.

We turn off the heat and sleep in cold and darkness. A few candles provide us with the light we need, in case inspiration strikes and we need to paint. Our meals consist mostly of plain bread and water. We also ask Aunt Lyla to avoid and mistreat us, and put us down on every occasion. This way we can feel rejected, misunderstood, and special.

After experiencing the harsh fate of a genius for more than a week, we decide that it's time for feedback from the audience. I take my *Cancer* and drag it – it is really heavy – to the flea market. I show it to a peasant, who is proudly standing by his tomatoes and peppers. I ask him, "Hey, what do you think of this?"

The peasant – bald head, soiled shirt, one missing tooth – doesn't hesitate. "I don't know what the fuck this is, but I can tell you that whoever painted it must have a rotten brain indeed. Want to try a fresh baby tomato?"

This positive feedback gives me hope. For my audience is peasants, small manufacturers and … fishermen.

Yeah, those categories are always left behind. I offer the *Cancer of the Mind* to a family of farmers in exchange for fruits and vegetables.

Deep inside though, I started losing interest. This artistic ordeal is taking me nowhere. My paintings are dull and lifeless.

I stand in front of the easel inspiration-free. A meow in the background awakens me; my cat must be hungry.

This reminds me that I, too, am hungry as hell. I open the refrigerator only to see an empty cold box. I hate being a poor artist. Screw those masterpieces, *I want a burger*!

Sleep-deprived and grumpy, I crawl to the grocery store. A woman stops me in front of the produce aisle. Honestly, I don't remember her ugly face or name. From what she's telling me, we're deeply in love with each other. Oh, when did this happen? I know! I know! This must be the one night stand from two weeks ago. Why didn't I call her? Hmmm, I can't tell her that I deeply regret our short encounter which triggered my 52nd attempt to quit drinking. I tell her that I've been out at sea, fishing. I hug the anonymous woman with passion, and I move on to the cat treats aisle.

I get fish crackers, my cat's favorite snack, and I'm on my way!

The cancer must have totaled my brain already. I don't remember where I live anymore. Naturally, I look for my driver's license staring at it in disbelief. According to this piece of plastic my name is Elwin Van Roessel and my address is somewhere in Pieterburen, Holland.

I take a deep breath. I don't know who I am yet, but I think I know who I am not.

The Healing Session with
Master of the Words Whiteout

A short, casual conversation with my cat, followed by a terrible misunderstanding made me think that maybe, just maybe, the words I use do not render the thoughts and expressions crafted in my mind.

I crave to talk immediately with someone who has mastered the art of expressing themselves, able to tell exactly what they want, without hesitations or fears.

As I start desperately looking up writers in various newspapers and magazines, the neighborhood midwife and babysitter knocks at my door. She needs help with moving a table from one room to another. While pushing the table I ask her about writers. Does she happen to know a good one?

But, of course! Actually, she happens to know a famous one, Master Whiteout. She herself delivered a nephew of a cousin of his wife into this world. She tells me that this writer's words express exactly the emotions or judgments involved; there is no *more or less.* Needless to say, I want to experience this Master Whiteout right away!

If I could catch at least a few tricks and add them to my daily vocabulary, I would consider myself very blessed.

I run home happy with the Master of the Words' phone number in my right hand. My hands are shaking, so I have to dial five times until I hear the Voice. I try to introduce myself but I only manage to mumble some hilarious sounds, empty of meaning. The Master tells me in a very polite tone that he knows who I am. The sister of the cousin of the midwife informed the milkman, who in return delivered the information along with the 5:00 p.m. batch of fresh mozzarella.

I have never done drugs, but right now I feel high. If this is how it feels when you're under the influence, then yes! I too want to be under the influence. Under the influence of the Master of the Words, that is.

Master Whiteout not only agrees to share his wisdom with a worm like myself; he proposes early morning coffee in his beautiful garden. I feel, again, blessed and spend the rest of the day trying on all my better outfits. Long sleeves or short sleeves? White pants – purity of intentions, or dark pants – official tone? Red, white and blue scarf – French and chic, or green scarf – blending in Nature? I settle for a beige neutral tone with a warm orange scarf – strong feelings of respect.

Humble and shy as I am, I dare not to knock at the Master's door. I freeze with my hand in the air, in a timid attempt to touch the door.

I must've spent some time standing there and *trying,* when Master Whiteout opens the door to let the dog out and notices my presence.

The Master of the Words – bald head, left eye half-closed, rabbit teeth – does not waste time with useless introductions. He greets me and asks me to follow him to the kitchen, where he will prepare the delicious Turkish coffee. I follow him in silence, and watch the ritual of the Turkish coffee making.

The Master pours the coffee in two precious little porcelain cups and places them on two cute little plates. But then the misfortune strikes. The Master notices he only has one napkin left. I sense the embarrassment of my amazing host, and I express my deep desire to enjoy the coffee *without using a napkin.* The Master insists. I, too, insist. The Master insists again. I use my diplomatic skills and excuse myself to the restroom. I masterfully tear a piece of toilet paper and fold it twice. Then I go back to the Master and announce to him with tremendous joy that I will replace the napkin with toilet paper. The Master wants to use the toilet paper himself, since my intentions cast shadows over his hospitality. We both end up using toilet paper.

The Master starts sharing his thoughts with me. Yes, it is true what they say, he can make use of any word that exists. And, when he cannot decide which one to use, he invents a new word.

However, he doesn't want me to think that he's some sort of sorcerer or magician.

His powers are limited. He is paid *by the word* and publishers hate to see too much ballast – lumber – in the literary works. The Master recalls the terrible crisis from last year, when the market went down and nobody cared for books anymore. The publishers forced him to significantly cut down on the words in his stories.

He shows me a *"before and after"* sample.

While the *before* sample is beautiful – *"Everything around Marie was dark, deep green. The forest embraced her tightly, with long, greedy branches, caressing her face with an aggressive, overwhelming desire of keeping her there forever"*– I personally find the *after* one interesting and compelling as well. *"Dark, deep green. The forest wanted her."*

I let the Master know right away that I like both. He agrees.

However, there was a problem. The shortest version couldn't pay the bills. He needed to come up with something.

Inspiration struck as he was talking to his landlord. The landlord informed him that if he didn't pay the rent, he would get kicked out the following week. That night the Master couldn't sleep. He walked in circles a lot, until he stopped and asked himself this simple question: "How can one add more words – money – when they are not allowed to add more words?" Then, the miracle happened. The neighbor next door coughed. The neighbor's horrible, deep cough filled all the apartments with fear. However, the Master's apartment filled with joy.

It was the joy of discovery. He suddenly knew how to pull this off. He would have to simply add more descriptive words.

In other words, he would make all his characters choke, hiccup, cough and vomit, until the readers can't take it anymore. This way, the shortest, most powerfully edited dialog, will still have to contain "hiccup," "cough," or "scratch."

I immediately express my deepest respect for the Master, and demand to learn more.

The Master explains. "For example," he says, "a simple scene, where a young man declares his love, can be skillfully transformed into an intense money maker." He shows me a sample. I read with my eyes glued to the paper.

"I know, love can be scary," Larry says (cough)

"Scary?" Miriam says (choke)

"Oh ..." (Powerful, deep cough)

"You should stop smoking," Miriam notices (in between two hiccups)

"I don't smoke," Larry defends himself (cough and hiccup)

"Don't lie to me," Miriam says (cry, hiccups)

I am indeed impressed. May I kiss the Master's hands? He says yes.

Then he shares another gem of knowledge, his masterpiece, *The King of the Hiccups*. It is the amazing story of a man, who couldn't control his hiccups. The Master figured that with one hundred thirty-eight hiccups paid at 75 cents each, he could resume his trips to the neighborhood coffee shop, indulging every morning in his favorite latte.

An unexpected help came from a trip to the cleaner's, where the Master entertained in a short, hazy conversation with the owner's three-year-old triplets. His pages, filled with two and three-year-old kids and their meaningless sounds, paid at 45 cents apiece.

I am stunned. Speechless. Overwhelmed. Can I be on my knees while listening to the words of wisdom? The Master allows.

But even the Master of the Words is not perfect, nor can he always achieve perfection. I raise my eyebrows. He explains, "Publishers are not the only ones I have to keep happy and satisfied. Sometimes my words might upset the reader. Therefore, I have to write with the reader in my mind. Naturally, this has a significant impact on the plot and the characters." Does the Master care? Not anymore. He has to pay his rent. Sometimes you just have to give up. He tells me how he had to give up a short story named *Desire*. It was a story about a young man who has a crush on this hot, extremely sensual woman who lives next door.

He would watch her every day, carrying out the trash bag, bending over to pick it up, followed by the graceful momentum of the actual discard in the big trash container, the Mother of all trash bags. He pictures himself as a trash bag, fantasizing for hours about her picking him up, touching him with disgust and just out of necessity – disposal. Then he fantasizes about her knocking at his door late at night, with hungry eyes, asking simple questions, like "Do you have any trash?"

He knows the answer. "No, except for myself. Take me!"

Then he learns that she is actually married to this ugly guy who moves in unexpectedly. Aside from being mad at Fate for allowing ugly misfits to own gorgeous women, did the fact that she was married prevent him from aching with desire? Heck, no!

I admit I am intrigued by the ending. I clean my face with the improvised toilet paper napkin.

The Master of the Words confesses he never did get to finish the story the way he wanted.

His work sparked controversy while still pending review. Groups of feminists from all over the country stepped in. A fellow writer hissed at him and showed teeth at one of the writers' meet-ups, disgusted by the "misogynist pig"who sees women as trash collectors. The Master of the Words tried repeatedly to explain that his character is rather submissive, placing himself in a much inferior position than his feminine counterpart.

The leader of the most powerful feminist movement and acclaimed author of the revolutionary logo, "We too can grow a mustache!" immediately took position, publicly calling the Master "a small craftsman" who "has never gone beyond the vocabulary of an angry teenager." She also called upon all the religious leaders to express their disapproval at the outrageous desire for a married woman. "We need good literature," she added, "literary works that will promote healthy erotic habits, offering role models for the masses; literature about good, perfect people, who feel attraction exclusively for their partners."

The Master sighs while sipping some coffee. A little drop of coffee falls from the cup, hitting the grass with extreme noise.

The Master resumes.

Maybe the story would have passed the review, after some major remodeling, if it wasn't for the racial issue.

In the original version submitted for review, the guy is black and the woman is white. This was bad. *Really* bad. The Master tried to bring up Shakespeare, but who reads Shakespeare nowadays? The publishers demanded in a very aggressive tone that things should be either black or white. Anything in between is highly unacceptable.

I learn that the Master had to completely change the story. In the final version, which helped pay not only the rent but covered two car payments as well, the guy is white, attracted exclusively to white women – "*he would sometimes see a beautiful woman of color, but, deep inside, he knew that if God wanted him to feel attracted to black women, He would have created him black as well.*" The white guy likes the mysterious woman next door, but when he learns that she is married, he backs off immediately and seeks penitence.

I express my admiration for the Master's flexibility and literary playfulness. Some artists would rather get beheaded than change a word in their works. Now, how silly that is!

The Master smiles at me with compassion. I feel like a three-year-old who listens to stories told by old wise grandpas. I clap my hands. Please, Grandpa, one more story!

The Master pinches his nose. He'll tell me one more story. It's a recent success story, about another work that didn't pass inspection. The hero is a male genius who feels misunderstood and rejected. The words the character uses to express his struggle with the Others sparked hatred and were scrutinized intensely. He was, once again, accused of arrogance, infatuation, and chutzpah. I want to read those words. The Master pulls a roll of toilet paper from under the chair.

He explains again. When he submitted this work, concerned citizens filed complaints, and the police had raided his house repeatedly, searching for the "seeds of social anarchy." So he had to transfer his manuscripts on low quality material.

He has to unroll almost half of the toilet paper roll, so I offer my help. He finds the fragment. I smile while reading. "He knew he was highly intelligent, unlike most of the people around him; he never expected them to understand; they were merely worms crawling on the ground, unable to cherish the sunrise or sunset." Wow!

I think I have learned something today. I leave the Master of the Words' house not with crumbs, but with two heavy suitcases filled with Knowledge. Thank God, Knowledge is compact and not too heavy, for I plan to take it with me on my annual trip to Venezuela.

This is all I want to take with me: *Knowledge*. This way I will significantly reduce the amount of time spent at the border crossings.

Customs always look for narcotics, weapons and such. But nobody bothers to look for Knowledge. I picture myself like a powerful citizen of the world, smuggling Knowledge from one country to another, taking it everywhere I can.

I get home fulfilled, peaceful, and rested.

The Healing Session at the Retirement Home

It's snack time! I call my cat. She does not respond. No problem, I know how to make her get out of her hiding den. I pull out a piece of salmon and leave it on the table. Guess who lands on the chair with big, charming eyes? As I try to explain to her that raw fish can be bad for our health due to risk of food poisoning, the phone rings. It's Aunt Lyla, who else? With no introduction, she starts telling me that yes, it is happening again. I admit I'm puzzled. I want to ask her what she means, when revelation strikes. I suddenly remember that my beloved aunt has the unusual habit of picking up conversations where she left them off years ago. As a child, I had witnessed her many, many times picking up the phone and telling her sister, "Larry was right." Nobody could ever understand what that was all about, since Larry, Aunt Lyla's cousin, had passed away thirty-four years ago. Yet her sister would reply right away, "I know. They don't make them like they used to."

Knowing my aunt so well, I have no problem understanding what she wants to tell me. She just had a mild stroke again. I look at my cat and she brings me the small First Aid kit in silence. We jump in the car and we are on our way to Aunt Lyla.

Aunt Lyla had more than just a mild stroke – red eyes, hair standing on end, lifeless arms. I rush to call an ambulance. At the hospital we learn that her condition is stable but she'll require permanent medical supervision. My cat and I are overwhelmed. What are we going to do? I get out to smoke forty-eight cigarettes and cool down. When I'm about to light up the forty-seventh, a messenger from Heaven, impersonated by a cousin of a neighbor of a former high school lover of Aunt Lyla, approaches me with sympathy.

He has just placed his grandmother in this beautiful retirement home, not far from where I live. Can I have their phone number? I sure can.

I run back inside to pick up Aunt Lyla and physically remove my cat from a child's backpack, where she's secretly indulging in the little boy's tuna sandwich. I give her a harsh lecture about love, family, unity. In return, she jumps on my lap and burps tuna in my face. I must have a serious conversation with her someday.

We jump in the car once again. No, my cat and I jump in the car, while Aunt Lyla crawls into the car with our help. On our way to the place, a shy, naughty thought starts running through my mind like a spring; unfortunately, other springs join in, and before I know it, a river of thoughts is crossing my mind, only to find its way to the sea and from there to the ocean. By the time we get closer, here I am, a skillful captain, navigating the unchartered waters of my own ocean of thousands of unanswered questions about retirement, the aging process, and death.

I drive like a maniac only to pull into the wrong driveway where a banner reads "When was the last time you had a thorough eye exam? Have your eyes checked today by Dr. Perkins!" Isn't that a little bit insulting to say the least? We all pull into the wrong driveways now and then and this doesn't necessarily mean that we have to undergo a comprehensive eye exam. I ask my cat to remind me to file a complaint with whomever.

I find the retirement home. It looks like a little house from the fairy tales. I encourage Aunt Lyla to go in right now and surprise them; find out what it's all about. She agrees. This way we will know on the spot if this is one of those dreaded places where they suffocate the unwanted elderly with fluffy pillows when the night falls. A nice nurse – pale complexion, narrow nose, red locks – invites us to see the house and meet the residents.

I learn that every resident enjoys their own physical and mental privacy since they have the privilege to pick a room that suits their needs. Yet, the desire to socialize is encouraged as well, by offering the residents multiple activities like chess, tango lessons, storytelling, and last but not least, the monthly darting competition, where the winner – once he or she is proven physically fitter – is moved to the "healthier" section of the house that gets less attention from the medical personnel. I learn that the management is an active promoter of the survival of the fittest.

As we stand there, exchanging views with the Head of the Nurses, an eighty-something gentleman proudly pushes his walker by me. I see the spark of adventure in his eyes. This man has a story to tell! I ask the nurse right away about this charming character who seems to welcome Death with such oblivious grace.

She introduces me to the fascinating old man. I learn that he used to be a pilot, flying planes during World War II. Wow! He also tells me he hasn't had sex since 1982. I feel for the veteran. Suddenly, I realize I myself haven't had sex since 1982! I tell him my story, in order to build his confidence in a better future, seasoned with sexual adventures. He feels for me as well.

Once the mutual compassion is established we move to deeper issues.

I want to hear war stories! Yay! I want to know everything. How did he join the Air Force – Flier? Friend? Word of mouth? – and where he fought. Everything, everything. I want a nice, beautiful fairy tale.

I'm about to discover, however, that the human mind does not create spontaneously well-formed, defined stories, with plot, beginning and end. The human mind is images, raw and uncensored. Therefore his story is more like, "Boom, boom, phew, poof, poof." I try to tune that avalanche of sounds out and retain the essence. I catch a few words. Among them, the name of the village where my grandmother was born. I'm curious to know why someone would remember with such accuracy a small village in a small country on a small continent. He explains that he might forget a detail or two, but he always remembers the places where he dropped bombs. What? This lizard dropped bombs on my grandma?

I picture my grandma, young and innocent, trying to hide and save her life while this glorious bastard is up in the air, almighty and untouchable, chasing her with a small plane packed with big bombs.

Let me tell him a few thoughts of mine right now, before I forget them and they lose their freshness.

Our conversation is brutally interrupted by a scream coming from one of the resident's rooms. A feminine voice begs to be put to sleep. I ask a nurse, who passes me while pushing the medication cart, what's going on. She explains that the lady in question doesn't have enough money in her retirement fund to afford the care she needs. Therefore, she's on government help; the government pays a small amount, just to keep her alive and miserable as long as possible. I try to help both the old lady and the government by suggesting my crimson red and white rope. The nurse looks at me in awe. Do I have a heart? I want to say something but Aunt Lyla's sharp, deep gaze tells me that I should move on.

We move on. Aunt Lyla likes the place. However, she cannot move in, just like that. Given her condition, she agrees to spend a few days there; if she likes it, we can proceed with the paperwork.

I leave my aunt having tea with one of the nurses in the enchanting garden. On my way back home I realize I don't want to grow old. No, let me rephrase. I *refuse* to grow old. I will do whatever it takes to avoid this state of advanced helplessness. So will my cat. Actually, she does a much better job than me. I can tell that just by looking at the cat spa and pedicure bills.

We go home and turn on the TV. Luckily we get to watch our favorite program, *Minds in Search of Knowledge*. Today's episode is about the life after life. I like that a lot. While watching the commercial I fall asleep. My cat jumps on the remote control turning on the volume and shaking me, fearing that I might become vengeful – no tuna snack – if I miss my favorite show. I wake up pissed, anxious, and distressed. Am I alive? Again? Do I have to survive another day? But wait, these are not my thoughts. I think the show has just started. Today's guest is Brahmaputra Patel, a well-known Buddhist researcher who has fathered numerous studies about life and essence of the afterlife.

Listening to the words of wisdom, I decide to give up suicide. This means I will still have to face "the Golden Age" along with partial or total decomposition of mind and body. A horrible truth conquers that half of the brain that is not yet rotten. What if this guy is right? Here I am, killing myself to escape this hell, and then, "Surprise!" there's even more suffering to come! What if he's right and it's not that easy to escape the pain of the soul? The thought of my self being tortured even more in Death fills me with anxiety.

The only thing I don't understand is why is Buddha so fat and joyous? He looks like he just swallowed five huge pizzas – deep dish.

I fell asleep smiling, with the image of the fat, joyous Buddha in front of my eyes. In the morning, guess what? A phone call from the retirement home. My beloved aunt has had an asthma attack and can barely breathe. I rush to see her. I demand to know what happened overnight. The personnel on duty inform me that the nurse who was working last night is in love. As we all know, love needs reassurance, validation, repetition; therefore, "the love of her life" kept sending her short erotic messages on her cell phone. She was just about to review my aunt's chart and administer the medications, when the misfortune struck. The phone beeped. She knew right away it was not the emergency beep. It was *the beep of love*. She rushed to read the message. *Your breasts are so firm; I cannot sleep thinking of them.* Caught in the flames of love, the nurse forgot to administer Aunt Lyla the medications and moved to the next resident, in spite of Aunt Lyla's purple face and desperate movements of the head and limbs.

The medical personnel apologize for this minor incident and ask us to have understanding for the young people's feelings. Of course, we do. I assure them that this insignificant situation will not diminish the respect and the consideration we have for this noble profession.

I'm a little embarrassed, but I have to break the news to them, though, that we decided to take Aunt Lyla back home and have my cat watch her. In an emergency my cat can call me or meow at the neighbor's door should the situation require rapid intervention.

Just a humble request. Can Aunt Lyla get her medications now? We would have never dared to bother them with such requests but she might not survive the trip back home – again, purple complexion, tongue sticking out of the mouth, facial spasms. But, of course!

We get a bag of medications along with a miniature oxygen tank. Isn't that nice? We blow kisses at each other and part ways in an exhilarating state of joy.

I will definitely not allow myself to grow old and helpless even if I have to battle a thousand fat, joyous Buddhas.

The Healing Session at the Balkan Wedding

"You need more social interactions," advised the garbage man, on the occasion of the last trash pickup. "Socializing is good," he added, before vanishing into the dirty city.

The almost-French perfume of the trash – deep, persistent, unique – stayed behind, along with an empty popcorn bag that fell out of his trash truck.

I truly believe in Fate. My personal beliefs are once again reinforced. I open the mailbox and I find an invitation to a Balkan wedding. The mother of a nephew of a cousin of the ex-mother-in-law of Aunt Lyla was born in that interesting part of the world. She introduced me to these people some time ago. They are a little bit different from us, who have been born here or transplanted at early age. They are usually happy people, but they can also turn aggressive very fast. Guessing their emotional state – Happy? Angry? – is always a lottery since they're noisy, gesticulate a lot, and carry knives with them at all times. When they pull out their knives I never know what to expect. In most cases the ham is cut too thick and their aesthetic senses are bruised.

They passionately slice the ham into thinner pieces and then put the knives back into their pockets. Once their aesthetic requirements are met, everything turns back to normal and all the people around them exhale in peace and stability. Stability is one word that seems not to exist in their vocabulary. They fight over everything: land, women, and piglets. I have heard about a war that broke from a dispute over how to cook beef stew.

They also treat depression with alcohol, music and sex, not with therapy and pills like we do. My cat encourages me to attend this rare event.

Overall, I think it would be a nice experience. I have previously interacted with these people, yet have never seen them at large. Time to do that.

On my way to the wedding I accidentally look in the mirror. There's a nest on top of my head. No, it's not. It's just me following the advice of a friend, an engineer with a sharp mind and a great sense of Time.

One night, he decided to share more than the usual drinks with me. He shared his theory about personal grooming. I learned that just grooming the hair takes up a lot of daily time. This adds up if you think about it, weeks, years. A total of one thousand five hundred thirty-two hours and thirty-nine seconds per year, he claims. Hooked on his technical approach, I braided my hair in three main horsetails then I masterfully brought them together with the help of an elastic band removed from a floral arrangement.

Since then I've been showering happily *without* combing my hair, saving ten minutes and one second per day. I've been spending those precious minutes wisely, either staring at the walls and thinking of my depression, or staring at people and thinking of their depression.

I look again at my "nest." No, not even the Balkan wedding can force me into combing that.

On my way.

The wedding is supposed to take place at the community hall, where people meet occasionally to listen to news from the region – new wars, murders and rapes – while drinking wine and being carried away by the rhythms of traditional drums and flutes.

At the entrance, two huge males with mean faces screen all the guests. They check everyone and everything. I'm told they're looking for weapons. Why weapons? I step back and verify one more time the information I've written on the invitation. Yes, this is the place.

A grandma in front of me is crying and trying to convince the guys that the Kalashnikov she is carrying in her purse – do-it-yourself-kit – is actually her wedding present for the groom. This is outrageous! How can one attempt to confiscate a present, offered in good faith, by an old, gray-haired grandma?

I make my point right away. I wake up five minutes later with a bag of ice on my left eye.

It hurts a little bit, but it's okay, apparently I got the punch but I *skipped* the check point.

I don't want to be biased, though. You know me, always multi-cultural and open-minded.

***

The ballroom is beautifully decorated with balloons, glass from the broken bottles, and cigarette butts. Intoxicating rhythms fill the air and I almost start dancing involuntarily along with a bunch of extremely hot women – long legs, firm breasts, short skirts. I have to give up because of the armed guys who shadow them at all times. Those women must not only be hot. They must have some amazing wisdom encrypted in their genes since everyone feels the impulse to shadow them.

I learn that all of them are "taken." One is the bride's sister-in-law, married. Another one is the Master Fiddler's girlfriend, and the red-haired hottie on my left is the groom's mistress. Oh, these guys move faster than the agents selling retirement plans, always thinking of the future! He's not even married yet, and has managed to secure himself such a cutie on the side. My respect for the people from this land!

With no available women around I decide to stop fantasizing and head straight to the bar. I order a generous round of plum brandy. Mmmmmm…strong and healthy. Someone taps me on the shoulder. I turn around and I freeze.

It's one of my classmates from the Celtic meditation sessions. She is truly gorgeous and she messed up my meditations many times. What is she doing here? I learn that she was actually born in the Balkans and she immigrated here when she was a little girl. Lucky me! Maybe, just maybe, I will get laid tonight.

I make my move aggressively. I buy her five plum brandys – can't they use bigger glasses? – and wait. Although delicate, this woman drinks like an elephant. To make it worse, she starts telling me stories from her childhood. I'm not interested in listening to stories that took place *before* she reached sexual reproductive age. I sit there listening to her confessions about the little Yorkie – her pet – that waits for her to come home from work, every day, happily wagging his tail.

I want to tell her that I am, too, a joyous Yorkie who yearns to wait for her every day, happily wagging his tail. Apparently I lost the battle with the plum brandy and verbalized my thoughts, for she turns around and leaves without saying a word.

I've learned that women are the same everywhere, regardless of their place of birth.

As no one seems to care for my presence, I decide to blend in with the elderly. It is well known that the elders from this part of the world can share powerful wisdoms even when severely intoxicated. Or, especially when severely intoxicated.

An old toothless man – pink fluffy shirt, half-closed eyes, small scar on the forehead – invites me over to his table.

I meet his wife, his wife's lover and their three children. One of his children is actually a stunning eighteen-year-old blond beauty and I express my intention of dancing with her.

The old man shares his theory about moral values. He wants to know if I'm married. I tell him that I am not. Hmmm. Do I have a girlfriend then? No, I do not. Do I go to the church? I admit I haven't been there in a while. While I sit there going over all possible aspects of my intimate life – religion, background check – a heavy dark guy pulls her on the dance floor and they start dancing. Wow, that was easy…

I demand an explanation. I learn he's one of *them*, a man with strong moral values, while mine haven't been checked yet. I manage to reserve the next dance in return for participating the following day in a six-hour Mass at the Orthodox Church. I will kneel in front of Him, begging for salvation. I will also help the old women's fund, raising money for new and better weapons.

The old man invites me to have a drink and asks me about my political views. I tell him I'm not into politics. A few guests who accidentally overheard my statements drop their glasses on the floor, in a mass effort to help decorate the ballroom even more. What? I'm not into politics? The news travels fast around the small ballroom community.

The old toothless man tells everybody to fuck off and takes me aside.

He *knows*. He has been there. But one day, he felt the deep connection with the people, the world, and the universe.

This world is not where it should be. Where should it be? "Nobody knows," he says, stuffing a chicken drumstick in my mouth. A few young men start fighting each other not far from our table. I point at them with my mouth full of chicken. Why? "They're fighting over *Principles*," the old man smiles.

I learn that while we are rather resource oriented, fighting over oil, gold, and grains, people in other parts of the world fight over Principles. They demand *respect* and when their requirements are not met, the fight is on. Everything is about history, symbols, the deeper meaning of Life. Sure, they also fight occasionally over minor issues – "Your mother is fat" – or for pleasure – "I really, really want to break your nose" – like everybody else.

But nothing pisses them off more than messing with the Principles, the Tradition, and the Wisdom.

I'm curious and I demand, as usual, explanations.

The old man sighs. He empties the small bottle of plum brandy he carries in the pocket of his fluffy pink shirt. He thinks that the civilized world has lost the connection with the Principles. For example, why are we getting married? I don't know, I am not married. I think of my sister. She got married because her girlfriends did. The pressure was on. She had to have an expensive ring, cool dress, the most impressive wedding. Otherwise the girls would have looked down on her.

My parents had to play along, otherwise she would scream – "Nobody loves me, nobody gives me money" – and pull hair. Who cared that she divorced "the man of her life" two days later? Yet everyone remembered the wedding. Especially my parents, who had to sell the house to pay for it. Luckily my godmother allowed them to pitch a tent on her property and they could enjoy a decent existence until they died of coordinated, simultaneous strokes, two months later.

The old man lights up two cigarettes. Why two? He explains that the cigarettes he smokes are very cheap and sometimes they don't burn properly. So he has to have a backup. I agree. I immediately secure myself two glasses filled with alcohol.

He shares his views about marriage. "Marriage," he says, "is made in heaven and the man cannot undo it." So regardless of the outcome of the union, they have to live together until death sets them apart. He gives me his own example. His wife has a lover, so what? Why would he leave a woman just for this reason? Is she mean to him? No. Is the soup cold when he gets home from work? No. Is she a bad mother? No. Does she have good, healthy teeth? Yes, she does.

Then, why would he do such a stupid thing? Who is he to break the Tradition? Besides, they both enjoy their children and want them to grow up enjoying the harmony of a true family. That's one of the Principles that the civilized world forgot about. The Family, the Marriage.

I want to say something but the old man sticks another chicken drumstick in my mouth. In my desperate attempt to breathe and communicate at the same time I accidentally bite my tongue. The freezing pain goes straight to my brain. I try to speak but no sound comes out. The pain is so overwhelming I have to give up.

An idea knocks at the door of my restless mind. *Come in, please.* What if I sit quiet and try to communicate using my body language? I like that a lot. I wink at the old man. He winks back at me. I drink some plum brandy. He drinks some plum brandy. I turn around and wink at one of the handsome guys who sit at the adjacent table. He doesn't wink. I wink again. He raises his eyebrows and calls another handsome guy. They both approach the table with the knives in their hands. Am I gay? I deliver weird facial expressions. I hope they understand I have a facial spasm. They smile and they leave us alone, not before cutting the cheese on the table in smaller pieces and kissing me on my cheeks repeatedly. Now wouldn't that be considered a little bit gay?

I leave around 10:00 a.m., carrying with me one more crumb of Knowledge in my pocket. Yes, social interactions are truly a blessing.

On my way back home I suddenly crave to be hot and handsome, like the guys I saw at the wedding. I sign up for body building at the local "Pete's Gym." I'm told I will meet my personal trainer in ten minutes. Yet I am so anxious to be handsome I cannot help it. I go inside and start randomly playing with the weights.

Someone is gently tapping me on the shoulder and I turn around only to see this gorgeous feminine entity trapped in the body of a goddess. I let go of a hefty twenty-five-pound weight; it lands right on my left foot. So what? I keep smiling like an idiot at the goddess. I don't feel pain at all. The goddess smiles back and informs me that my foot is purple. Never mind, it will heal. People around me don't agree and call an ambulance. On my way to the hospital I have this amazing dream. I'm putting together a Kalashnikov – do-it-yourself-kit – and one piece is missing. I keep asking other people if they can help me find the missing part, and no one seems to know how or where I could get it.

Someone is calling my name. It is the garbage man, anxious to hear how my socializing went. It's all good, but I cannot find the missing part. He smiles, "One man's trash is another man's treasure." He holds something in his right hand. Oh, it's my missing part. He found it in one of his trash expeditions. Enlightenment strikes and suddenly some of my questions are being answered. It is true, one needs trash to start a war.

The Healing Session with Herman, the Pool Boy

I need a tool from my shed so naturally I start walking toward the little structure situated adjacent to my house. On my way to the shed I stop for a second to enjoy, once again, my backyard. It is indeed dirty and neglected! Two weeks ago my cat started pulling out the weeds again, in a modest attempt to save face – visiting cats. I told her to stop and focus on what is of essence for us now. That is, healing our depression and Kung-Fu lessons.

As I stand there enjoying the ugliness of my personal universe – like owner, like house – I feel something wet on my left foot. I look down and see a hefty frog. My cat just hunted down a frog and dropped it at my feet. I highly appreciate her desire to show respect and bring me prey. However, the question begs, where did the frog come from? I'm stunned. I look around and suddenly realize that my pool has become a pond, a true haven for frogs as well as for other life forms. It is green, swampy and uninviting. Time to address that! On my way to the Homeowners' Association meeting I call the Pool Service. They assure me they will send someone right away.

Herman, the pool boy – blue, crystal-clear eyes, muscular build, assertive smile – gives me a short course on the history of the pool. I learn that our ancestors have always yearned to have water around the house; their desire to enjoy the precious element has culminated with the invention of the modern pool, a treat and a retreat from noisy society. I enjoy the short introductory course – it is included in the price of the cleaning – yet I have to curb Herman's enthusiasm. I bring the frog. He picks it up and after a careful examination he tells me that, judging by the size, color and developmental stage of the frogs, he will estimate precisely the type and quantity of chemicals which will be necessary to fix my pool.

Herman's knowledge demands respect. I want to learn more about his craft and the man-water connection. Yet this interesting encounter will have to wait. I have to thoroughly clean my front yard as I just proposed generous fines for those who do not contribute to the beauty of our small and odd community. Naturally, before I moved to proposing life-changing laws, I sent my cat out to perform a few discreet inspections. She confirmed my theory that all our neighbors take great pride in keeping the front yards spotless, while their backyards enjoy a natural state of disorder similar to ours. I clean my front yard and get back to Herman, who is ready to dive in my pool wearing state-of-the-art diving gear. Apparently, while analyzing micro organisms under the microscope, he came across a very unusual life form. He wants to take a closer look, get some samples, and take them to the lab.

I like his scientific approach. Any other pool boy would've dumped a bucket of chemicals in the pool, and have me sign the bill. Not Herman. Herman is a true professional. The phone rings. It's Aunt Lyla, who wants to invite us over for lunch. Now? When Herman is looking for unusual life forms on the bottom of my pool? We deeply regret, but we will have to pass on this one. Back to the pool. My cat and I sit on the side, biting our nails and anxiously waiting for Herman to surface. He surfaces a few times, stares at us from behind the ugly mask only to deliver short messages like, "Life has begun in water," or "There are hidden messages in water." This forces me and my cat to change plans. We cancel the Kung-Fu lesson. I head straight to the restroom anxious for some bladder relief, but my cat turns on the TV, right on time for the documentary on the origin of life. I watch the documentary standing – bladder pain – and I learn new things like the theory of the Russian scientist Oparin and Darwin's opinions on evolution of life.

We're eager to share our freshly acquired knowledge with Herman, who is on his fifth dive. I want to ask him when can I get my sparkling blue pool back, yet I totally understand his scientific approach. We have to take it slowly.

We choose to eat something instead. I fix a low calorie lunch – steamed vegetables, one fish tail, two peanuts – in order to maintain the nutritional balance prescribed by our dietitian and role model, Dr. Pumpernickel, whom my cat and I respect and hate at the same time. I keep thinking of water, this precious element.

Water...everything is water...our bodies are made of water. There's water in the oceans, seas and rivers, and in the air – rain. Water is basically everything and everywhere. My cat doesn't seem convinced that even our favorite sausages contain plenty of water, so I have to squeeze a few in front of her, just to emphasize the importance of this vital element to her.

Aunt Lyla calls again. She understands we cannot attend lunch, but she has an idea. One of the women she met at the Pastry Enhancement Group told her about a Feng Shui specialist who can share priceless words of wisdom and help me to improve my habitat.

Aunt Lyla keeps talking to me, but I can no longer pay attention to her. Through the kitchen's window I see Herman pulling out his mask, taking out his left flipper and gesticulating like a gorilla in full mating season. I look at my cat. She shrugs. I drop the phone and run outside.

Herman is convinced he has "something." A rare microscopic life form, which hasn't been seen in fresh waters up until now. However, he will need help to assess the importance of the discovery. A team of seasoned marine biologists, lead by Alfonso Figueroa, Ph.D., will join forces with him in a few days. A few days? I try to negotiate a closer arrival date for the team of scientists. Unfortunately, Professor Figueroa has to deliver a revolutionary lecture at an International Symposium in Berlin. But Herman assures me that we are next on his itinerary. I go back in the house and pick up the phone.

I catch the last words from a longer story. Aunt Lyla wants to know if I am available tonight to meet the Feng Shui gentleman. Of course I am. I have to. Since Herman started his research I raise my voice quite often and my cat threatens to sue me under the Animal Welfare Act. Really? This is not fair, but I will not comment on that. There is no Human Welfare Act I could sue her under when she screams in the middle of the night, possessed by feline demons.

Time flies by and "tonight" is here, along with the Feng Shui specialist. As Herman fell asleep by the pool, holding his gear tight, we cannot have the conversation outside as I initially desired.

We will have to sit down in the house. The Feng Shui specialist – watery eyes, flamey hair, earthy complexion – doesn't waste time with useless social graces. He points at the window. Then, he points at the sofa. Then, he points at the fireplace. He thinks that my house is a typical example of poor Feng Shui. Do I have water around the house?

I do. I also have Herman snoring by the water, so I have to politely excuse myself in front of my guest.

The Feng Shui specialist doesn't like the pool to begin with. I ask why. He explains, "'Feng' means 'wind' and 'Shui' means 'water'. Gentle wind and clear water have always been associated with good harvest and good health. This is 'good Fengshui'." What is happening right now in my backyard is "bad Fengshui." I see. Did he say "clear" water?

Herman is eavesdropping on our conversation. He stands up abruptly and tells me that he doesn't like the fact that I betrayed our cause. "Our cause?" He starts lecturing me about the significance of water. So does the Feng Shui guy. They both like water. There is only one thing they don't agree upon. One says the water should be crystal-clear and pure. The other one is a devout supporter of the "natural state of being as the primordial state." In other words, what is good

Feng Shui for one is bad for another and vice versa. My cat helps with bringing the state of chaos to an end. She brings not one, but two hefty frogs and drops them in front of my guest. The Feng Shui guy leaves the house full of disgust while Herman picks them up and looks at them mesmerized.

I knew it! I knew I would get more exciting answers from him than from anyone else!

Two days pass fast and here I am, greeting the team of marine biologists led by Alfonso Figueroa. He gives a strong, emotional hug to Herman. I learn that Herman, the pool boy, was actually one of his best students. He was working on his doctoral thesis when he left the scientific community due to a dispute with another researcher. Since then he has been cleaning pools, enjoying an insipid, blue existence. Yet the sight of my dirty pool awoke "the Researcher" in him. I like this story. I like it a lot. It reminds me of Sleeping Beauty.

Since time is of the essence, the glorious team starts working right away. My cat and I watch them in true and profound – not socially acquired – respect. They scan every inch of the bottom of the pool. They examine samples, showing them to each other and making those lovely concerned faces. It's like watching a documentary! We bring popcorn and encourage the researchers to completely ignore us, except when they need us to attend to their immediate needs, like hunger or thirst.

Three days into the hunt for the mysterious microscopic critter and nothing. The researchers are nervous. Herman is nervous as well. Finally, Figueroa decides to give up. They have to leave anyways; they are due in Galapagos in two days. Herman begs them to stay one more day. They refuse. Herman pulls his hair. They ignore him and start packing their gear.

Herman is pissed. He brings a big bucket with chemicals. He dumps the bucket in the pool.

I try to talk to them and see what is going on, yet nobody wants to talk to me. As I stand there watching them leave, my cat meows and points at the pool. The pool is clean again!

My pool is sparkling clean and boring like everybody else's. I do not enjoy it at all. My days are long and lonely. I miss Herman and I feel guilty. I let him down. Herman was right. Each of us has his own Feng Shui and his own habitat of balance, the primordial state of nature that should not be disturbed.

The Healing Session with Zen Master Catfish

I am summoned, yes! Summoned by Aunt Lyla to go and seek advice from Zen Master Catfish. The advantages are obvious. It's free, does not involve traveling. Master Catfish will hold a short conference tomorrow at the local pet supply store, and it cannot be harmful, even if it doesn't help, says Aunt Lyla. I wouldn't go that far with the "harmful" part. I have had my share of "Masters"; I know what they're capable of. But can I pass on the opportunity? Definitely not! I embark on my short trip *emotionless*. I hear that those monks are balanced, stern, and awake. They rarely talk, if at all. Instead they communicate via mind messages and they can read people's thoughts as well. Really? What if I put on my famous expressionless face, so they cannot use their power against me?

At the pet supply store, I stop to admire the elegant, colorful fish – light green, yellow, orange – playing in the store's main aquarium.

Suddenly, someone is pushing me from behind. I feel a pointy, unidentifiable object in my lower back. The anonymous handler of the sharp object tells me to get out of the store.

I do as I am told. I don't want my cat in one of those "Adopt-a-cat" shelters. I keep following the instructions given by the mysterious man. We both end up in the narrow street behind the store. I try to turn around, but I'm not allowed to do so. Apparently, the man wants to see my ID – wallet – first. While I find this method of establishing one's identity a little bit invasive, I do, once again, as I am told. I pull out my wallet. The man panics, thinking I want to catch him by surprise and attack. A short, intense fight follows. I win. He runs away. He has my wallet though. I go to the police to ask for a new ID. At the police station I learn that, actually, the guy was a robber. They caught him already, since he had two more unsuccessful attempts right after he and I parted ways. I file a complaint and express my gratitude for the new ID – much better photo. They will keep me posted on the investigation. I have to run; I am due to meet Master Catfish.

I finally join the crowd gathered around Master Catfish right in the middle of the conference. It is too late to look for a spot in the "front row" and I catch only a few words, mixed with responses from the great audience. I cannot understand anything, yet I wait patiently until Master Catfish finishes his discourse. When he steps down, I approach him with confidence and straightforwardness.

I tell Master Catfish who I am. He tells me who he is. This is Zen already! I ask for a coffee. I get a coffee. This is even more Zen!

Master Catfish starts explaining to me the importance of knowing who you are, along with meditating on the nature of Things.

I ask him up front if he can recommend a higher authority, like God, angels, monks who have attained enlightenment. He asks why. I want to be able to pray to them and ask for *things*, and let them do the meditations for me. He tells me that while there are certain enlightened entities, one cannot ask them for anything. Every individual has to find peace within themselves. I hate that! This reminds me of the conversation I had last year with a priest. I asked him, "Can I pray to God for anything?" He said, "Yes." Then I told him I would pray for more sex. Then he told me to get out. I can ask for *anything,* but this *anything* thing is very limited.

Zen Master Catfish – long, curly whiskers, round eyes, smooth skin – smiles. His approach is different. He will help. He will introduce me to the art of assessing the importance of Things.

He points at the coffee mug. He tells me that the coffee is the object of my desires. Coffee is of essence. The sugar, the milk, and other enhancers are all *optional.*

I think of my long-lost lover. She was the object of my desires. Her mean parents, who kicked me out of the house, were *optional.* That did not prevent them from kicking me out of the house, though. I make my point right away. What is *optional* might be of essence and what is of essence might be optional. The monk looks at me with compassion sprinkled with disgust. He takes my coffee away. Then, he gives me a bag of sugar instead and he invites me to enjoy my coffee.

Those monks are competitive like devils. They don't like to lose.

Well, guess what? Neither do I! I shred a small piece of paper I found in my pocket while looking him in the eyes. Master Catfish wants to know why I am so agitated. Who, me? I'm calmer than ever!

Master Catfish is more than willing to teach me the essence of Zen. He will do so using simple words. "The essence," he says, "is to be able to stop and sit down." So, it's true what I heard, these Zen people sit down a lot. Really? How about this? *I stand.* Alone and happy, here I am, *standing.* As a matter of fact, why don't I establish my own philosophy of standing? I let Master Catfish know right away about my glorious plans of having my own system. Master Catfish seems envious. He tries to convince me of the disadvantages of my meditation techniques.

For example, relaxation. How can one relax *standing*? Then there's a swollen leg, spider veins, as well as a certain nervousness, to name just a few. I'm not buying this. I know a few bad things that could happen to someone who sits down too much. Significant weight gain, which attracts an array of diseases, including high cholesterol, diabetes, high blood pressure. Master Catfish changes the subject. Sneaky, sneaky ... will I surrender? Heck, no! Let's see what he can come up with. Master Catfish understands that Zen is not for everybody. He tells me he is aware of the cultural barriers as well. Westerners seem to think that Zen is some sort of entertainment.

How about a short Zen story? Master Catfish starts telling me a story. It's about a philosopher who dreamt he was a butterfly. When he woke up, he didn't know who he was anymore. Was he the human being who dreamt he was a butterfly, or was he a butterfly who dreamt he was a human being?

His story is naive and lacks depth, but it inspires me. I, too, have a short Zen story.

I tell him how sometimes I dream I am very smart, and I enjoy it a lot. Yet when I wake up, I am again, an idiot. Which raises the *Zen by Me* question, am I an idiot who dreamt he was smart, or a smart guy who dreamt he was an idiot?

I see fear in Master Catfish's eyes. He will tell me another story. Okay, let's hear this one. I'm here already, what the fuck. I wasted half of my day on these Zen *sit-downs* already!

He begins."The Warrior of the Seas and His Meditation on the Herring.

"Once upon a time, there was a wise seal named The Warrior of the Seas. One day, he was lying on the shore, basking in the sun and meditating on the essence of the Herring. And as he was lying there, soaking his silky flippers in the ocean, abandoning himself to the majestic pursuit of the essence of the Herring, the Warrior's meditation was brutally interrupted by someone else's powerful thoughts on the mysteries of Beauty ... hmmm. The Warrior of the Seas spotted the intruder right away; it was another seal, which was perceived by his herring-eating fellows as being extremely noisy in his meditations. The Warrior asked him, 'Will you please stop being so noisy? Your thoughts on Beauty can be heard on the entire coastline and they are more disturbing to us than the presence of a killer whale. You are not meditating, you are screaming.' But the 'noisy' seal did not respond.

"The Warrior appeared to be visibly affected by this unexpected incident. Trapped in the thoughts of the other seal, he started meditating on the Beauty right away. His meditation had been hijacked and taken into a completely different direction. 'Is Beauty beyond physicality?' the Warrior asked himself, sucking on his flipper. He looked at the ocean. 'If we can understand the essence of things we cannot survive without, such as the Herring, then we might be able to get closer to much more sophisticated concepts. And just because someone's meditation is noisy does not necessarily mean that we all have to embrace his thoughts and follow the same path into enlightenment.

"'The paths leading to enlightenment are various and each has his own individual journey,' thought the Warrior of the Seas, while warming up in the autumn sun.''

Master Catfish raises his hand. Gracefully, he stands up and bows before me. I get the message. The healing session is over. I want to say something but I realize in awe that I have nothing to say. I have to fill the void around me, though. So I start generating random sounds. Suddenly I got this idea for my morning mantra. C-c-c-c-c-c-offee ... C-c-c-c-c-c offee.

Pit stop at the Police station. Bad news and good news. They could not build a case against the robber. His lawyer argued that what happened was actually an extremely passionate gay courtship. I agree with the lawyer. I know I'm handsome. And it's springtime, for God's sake! So, legally speaking, there's nothing the police can do. This is the bad news. The good news is that one of the board directors of the Save the Red-Nosed Caterpillar Foundation walked his dog in that area minutes after the robbery took place. While watching his dog sniff some dirt, he noticed a *wounded* Red-Nosed Caterpillar on the ground. Red-Nosed Caterpillars are listed as endangered species; there are five left in the entire country and one happens to live in our neighborhood. A detailed investigation followed. United teams of both human and animal detectives worked hard to determine what could have caused the *near death* of the precious creature. An extremely professional re-enactment showed that the caterpillar's last four hind legs could have been smashed *only* by the foot of a five-foot-tall and one-hundred-seventy-pounds-heavy individual. And that was my gay robber. The Police are happy. They can't bust him for the robberies. But he will get at least ten years for the Red-Nosed Caterpillar.

The police officers smile.

They explain how important a small, apparently *optional*, detail can be. I agree. Master Catfish would not. I think Police are great Zen thinkers.

I get home, my head filled with stories about herrings, meditations, butterflies, caterpillars, monks, and coffee. I'm eager to share my experience with my one and only friend. But first, coffee! I walk with caution, it's almost noon, and this is her nap time. I do not want to wake her up.

As I pour myself a generous cup of coffee I hear movement behind me.

It is she, staring at me with big, expressionless eyes. Did I wake her up? I cannot believe this! I got into the house using the doggy door! I took off my shoes! I used a plastic cup for the coffee to reduce the noise in case I accidentally dropped it on the floor! I put on my camouflage costume so I could blend into the house environment should she wake up unexpectedly and panic at the sight of me dressed as a Zen monk!

She meows at me in a very serious tone, "Your meditations have become so loud that I could hear them from the bedroom."

The Healing Session in Epistolography

Sundays are days meant to be quietly enjoyed with family and close friends. On Sunday mornings I love to sit in the kitchen, sip my coffee and stare at the walls. Today is no exception to the rule.

My cat brings in the mail from yesterday and we both start opening letters. She mentions a funny incident that took place a few minutes ago. The postman, who was just about to leave, greeted her with "How are you?" My cat stopped in the middle of the driveway, not knowing what to say. She finally told him "I don't know," when she realized she couldn't describe her general mood. Her insight into daily social interactions makes me wonder if we could ever give honest answers to this question. I picture instantly a world where the answer to this greeting is, "I have no clue," "Moderately pissed," "Oblivious," or "Out of order." Would that be possible? Probably not.

I pick up my favorite magazine, the monthly *Angry Testosterone*. It's written for men by men and read by men only. I hear that even the cleaning lady at their main office is a man. I like their unbiased approach and I trust their views a lot. Here it is, an interesting article. I read it aloud while my cat does the dishes, turning the water off now and then just to make sure she doesn't miss the important lines. Apparently, an international team of researchers which conducted revolutionary experiments for over a decade has finally come to the conclusion that the cat is the manliest pet. They base their findings on the fact that cats are the most independent, relaxed domestic animals. Who could be the man's best companion if not an animal that has some of his thirst for freedom encrypted in their genetic code? I agree.

We look at each other with love and respect. I pick her up and go straight to the big mirror in the master bedroom. I look in the mirror. I see two glossy abstract paintings. I bring a paper towel and some window cleaner. I clean the mirror. I look in the mirror again. Here I am, masculine, unfettered by minor emotions, hard to bend. That's me. And guess who's next to me. My true friend, my one and only partner, my right hand. A gorgeous, proud-of-her-feline-heritage, solid, stand-alone meowing structure. My cat, the manly pet.

We go back to the kitchen. I open an invitation to a titanium wedding anniversary. Titanium wedding anniversary? I learn that Aunt Lyla's grandfather and grandmother will soon celebrate seventy-five years of togetherness. How come they are still alive? I call Aunt Lyla right away and flood her with questions. She tells me that they got married when they were twelve years old. That makes sense. Also, according to the laws governing the old world, seventy-five years together does not mean seventy-five years of mutually agreed and desired partnership; they are mostly a proof of endurance, since the old world refuses to recognize separation. Basically, we're talking seventy-five years of beatings, fights, jealousy, alcohol and cheating. The old world is ruthless, especially to women. I endorse that. I personally believe women should be locked in the house and their only occupation should be pleasing the man in every possible way. Aunt Lyla is happy to hear that our ancient manly views are still embedded in me, in spite of our family being exposed for four generations to the empty concepts of emancipation promoted by so-called civilized societies.

I have no desire to watch those veterans celebrating their bitter seventy-fifth anniversary or my cousins engaging in their favorite after-dinner pastime – trying to kill each other after a few drinks.

I let Aunt Lyla know that I will probably go, but just for the mouth-watering crêpes.

We finish reading the mail. Time to read the virtual mail. We move our headquarters to the computer. I go over twenty insipid emails when suddenly one of them manages to pique my interest.

It is from a friend of mine, who has recently added me to his mailing list. He travels a lot in his job and feels an urge to keep us posted with his whereabouts.

His emails haven't bothered me so far, since they were mainly descriptive narrations of business meetings or short outings with his co-workers, when their busy schedule allowed. This one is different. It seems like the little angel has now less work and more fun than the average business traveler. I read it and I can feel the anger gradually taking over my system.

Where is Mike lately? In New York (Manhattan) for two days, now in Belize. Plans were to trek into the jungle, blend into nature. Yet Mother Nature herself has put that on hold. Heavy rain and massive flooding forced Mike to change plans. Normally gentle rivers are overflowing and raging. Friendly locals tell Mike that the flooding is the worst they have ever seen. Thank God that food is fresh and interesting. Plenty to do around here, but if boredom sets in, there are planes to all sorts of interesting places. Perhaps sailing on catamarans tomorrow, chess or fancy dinner at the Local Gentlemen's Club, if the weather is still hostile.

I finish reading, overpowered by a mélange of negative emotions that overlap with the initial state of anger. What is this flowery style? Is he some sort of smart writer? Does he know more words than us, the humble addressees? And why is he writing in the third person? Does Mike think he's cool? I don't.

I need a neutral opinion, so I let my cat read it as well. By the time she finishes it she already has the not-so-clean-litter-box grin. This is all I need to know. But, what should I do? Should I reply or should I just ignore it? I bite my nails for an hour. I scrub the kitchen sink for another hour. I excessively water the flowers for another hour, which in turn gives me the amazing opportunity to clean the floors for another hour – flooding. Finally I end my repetitive activities, sit down in front of the computer and write the following answer:

Where is Me lately? At work, enjoying plenty of activity…and interacting with all sorts of freaks…then plans are to fly home to the neglected backyard – lazy workers who never showed up to finish – maybe get something to eat…Not-so-friendly locals tell me that our grocery store has become sooo expensive…I might have to finance the grilled chicken and the veggies I threw in my shopping cart…normal gentle educated people living in our white and clean community are overflowing and raging…why? Because they have to lower their living standards…this is highly unacceptable!

Perhaps taking out the trash tomorrow, bathe my cat or even ice cream if our unstable financial situation allows it. When boredom sets in, there is a small psychiatric clinic close to my house and they do accept my medical insurance. Yay!

I hit the "Send" button with the confidence of someone who has just delivered a humbling lesson of life.

The following morning I run to the computer *before* I even get to make the coffee, an unprecedented behavior which does not go unnoticed by my cat. She brings me the coffee and sneaks quietly behind me, occupying a strategic spot on my left shoulder. I see no response from Mike. I have a few new emails however. I read the first one:

Heavy snow here in Vladivostok. The traffic was a nightmare; I spent four hours in stop-and-go and slow motion. Misha got the flu, so my husband had to pick up Grandma Irina to look after the kid while we are at work. I called the doctor but he would not do a house visit; he has no gas left in his car. Other than that, greetings from Vladivostok. Where is Belize, anyways?
Ekaterina Stepanova

I move to the next email.
First of all, thanks to whoever decided to stop Mike's ink flow.

Sunny day here in Bombay. – Bombay?! I hear a thick noise. My cat just fell off my back – *Not for everybody though. Unlike Mike, we do not wander the streets looking for souvenirs. My mother was diagnosed with schizophrenia. We were not aware of her condition until we noticed that the soup she had cooked for us had bubbles in it. Apparently we have been eating soup seasoned with laundry soap for over a year!*

No worries, we have seen worse than a few bubbles, we will survive.

Gotta go now, a war broke out in the neighboring village.

Amitava.

My mind is wrapped in happiness. I stand up and dance, carried away by my virtual victory. I started a revolution! My cat knows it, too.

By noon though, we have a problem: forty-nine new emails. All over-full and raging, resembling the rivers from Mike's email. I scan them quickly, getting updates on people from all over the world. I learn that Marie – Lima – is squeezing her pimples, Paul – Melbourne – is trying to get custody of his children and Baris Onal, a well-respected Turkish businessman, has a gambling problem. And all this is happening right now, as we speak! Real time human experiences!

How we will respond to this? We need professional advice. And where to look for it? My cat reminds me of our long-lost friend, Atanas Hysterios, an eccentric philosopher and a man of extreme words. His thoughts on existence are extremely optimistic or extremely bleak, so bleak that a few of his readers actually committed suicide after reading them. This wouldn't have bothered him – after all, they killed themselves *after* buying his works – if one of the casualties hadn't been his so-close-to-his-heart nephew.

He knew he had to do something about it. Just before the funeral, he rushed to put some happy, mobilizing words on paper. Then he grabbed the paper, he jumped in the first available cab and summoned the driver to take him to the cemetery as fast as he could. He made it on time. Few of the attending guests were actually contemplating the brutal farewell to life, after expressing their curiosity to read the words that killed their relative. Yet Atanas swiftly replaced the word of death with the one of life. The funeral turned out to be one of the most joyous parties ever, and Atanas went home happy that his depressed philosophy didn't take another victim.

My cat is right. My friend is the only person who can give us the so much sought-after advice. I no longer have his phone number, so I call Aunt Lyla and ask her respectfully to launch an investigation. Ten minutes later she calls me back. She has the number. I call Atanas right away. He's glad I still remember him. Does he want to meet me? Of course, he cannot wait. However, it will have to be *before* 5:00 p.m. or *after* 8:00 p.m. I tell him that we can also meet tomorrow or whenever he is available. He explains that it is not about availability; it is about the *cycles*. What cycles? My cat stops purring and sticks her left ear to the phone. We both learn that Atanas' daily activities are scheduled taking into consideration the cycles of his depression. In the morning Atanas happily welcomes the new day. He washes his face, feeds the birds, and fixes himself a nice breakfast. Then, he goes to work. While driving to work he doesn't listen to the news, as he's not curious to learn who shot whom at the local gas station. He wants to be positive.

At work, he sees people and looking at them he suddenly becomes aware of the miserable fate of the human race. By noon, he is severely depressed. Yet, right after lunch, he takes a walk to his favorite park and listens again to the birds while meditating on nature's beauty. Depression is gone. However, for some unknown reason, when the clock strikes 5:00 p.m., so does the depression. It is not until 8:00 p.m. that this cycle ends, politely giving the right-of-way to the good mood. I express my gratitude to Atanas for sharing his daily cycles with me. I cannot help thinking how deep his respect for us is. He does not want to show us an arrogant, depressed self. What a shocking contrast with Mike.

We meet Atanas in his favorite park, a peaceful, and inspiring setting upon which we both agreed. He has not changed a bit. After listening to my story, Atanas – same big eyes, same square head, same acne – gets straight to the point. In his view, we are all discovering the lost art or practice of writing letters, also called epistolography. The only problem we have is that we all share various shallow thoughts instead of taking advantage of the fast communication system available and share who we really are. What is really behind our virtual confessions? My cat and I look at each other puzzled. We don't know.

We want to ask Atanas to share more of his knowledge. I open my mouth but the clock in the park's tower strikes 5:00 p.m. Atanas pulls out a gun and directs it to his nose. We get the message. The healing session is over. We want to give Atanas a hug, yet the idea of a gun in between our noses makes us somewhat uncomfortable. I fetch the cat and start running without looking back. I don't stop until I am in the living room. The computer screen is flashing.

We get closer, fearful, yet curious. We have another fifty-eight emails to read. I read a few, and oddly, I seem to discover a hidden meaning in each of them. There is a story about loneliness and insecurity in each of them, a desire to share and a hope that maybe their silent virtual scream will be heard.

I no longer have any willingness to delve deeper into this art of communication. I sit down and boldly compose my last email.

Where am I lately? Where I am is irrelevant. What is relevant? The fact that wherever I go, I cannot find what I am looking for.

The Healing Session in Fortune

Aunt Lyla told me once that each of us has a grain of beauty and grace in them. Really? I question her theory as I watch the odd family of five who just moved into the house across the street. When I saw them for the first time, I thought they were clones of the same stupid, insipid individual. Yeah, they were that much alike. However, serious research showed that Mom and Dad were actually distinct entities with totally different genetic codes. Tormented by the scary impact their presence has on our daily lives, I broaden my research. I ask the neighbors about the odd couple's children. Have the nine months of gestation been completed? The answer is yes. I would love to hear my cat's opinion, but I decide not to allow her to see them – I, myself, can barely cope with the shock – and I cover her eyes whenever the odd family passes us by.

Today is Wednesday and my cat reminds me about the lottery ticket. Every Wednesday at 3:00 p.m. sharp we walk to the lottery kiosk situated in front of the grocery store and purchase one ticket. I consider my cat to be my personal "charm," so I encourage her to do the drawing, secretly hoping that one day we will both become rich and famous.

As we get closer to the kiosk I suddenly notice the odd family behind us. In order to limit or prevent my cat from being unnecessarily exposed to traumatizing events, I follow Dr. Applebaum's – my cat's behaviorist – advice and I carry two sets of blindfolds with me at all times. I blindfold her quickly and then try to walk slower and let them pass us. Unfortunately, the ugly social group tends to gravitate around us. We start running to the lottery kiosk. I pay for the ticket. We have a problem though. How will my cat draw the lucky ticket if she cannot see? The omen family is there, trying to catch up with our brisk walk. I finally give up and throw the cat in the big bin with the tickets. I give her a little bit of time to shuffle them and I pick her up a few seconds later, dizzy and shaky. In her mouth, a lottery ticket. We leave immediately as our Wednesday event has been compromised. We will have to wait until next week to fully enjoy our lottery routine.

Upset by the incident I totally forget about the ticket until Aunt Lyla brings it up in a short two-hour conversation about late payments.

I ask my cat to get the ticket. She goes to the laundry room and starts searching all my pants. An hour later an exhausted cat delivers the ticket and crashes at my feet, with the grace and dignity of a marathon runner. I put Aunt Lyla on hold. I open the ticket. Then I tell Aunt Lyla we have a winning ticket. Then I crash myself at my cat's feet. Aunt Lyla's scream of joy brings us both back. What are we going to do now? We won, but we're not prepared to handle it. I tell Aunt Lyla to call our rich relatives and ask them for guidance. Naturally, her relative of choice is the distant uncle of my late cousin's third wife. He is filthy rich. Hearing the great news – more money in our family – Uncle Emanueli starts bouncing like a teenager. Unfortunately, this causes his heart to stop, and he dies while talking to Aunt Lyla. Aunt Lyla rushes to his place, only to meet Uncle Emanueli's lawyers who inform her that we are the only relatives entitled to inherit his fortune.

I'm happy to hear that we are even richer than we initially thought, yet we did not get the guidance we needed from Uncle Emanueli. What are we going to do?

My cat pitches in, walking around the house with packs of ice on her neck and back and thinking. She brings me a brochure she bought two years ago during our short stay in Madrid. It is *The rich man's guide through the poor, hostile world.*

We both read it, shaking our heads in disbelief. We didn't know that being rich is so difficult and time consuming.

Before we know it, we live in a castle and we have dozens of people at our service. My new schedule – yes, I am on a schedule – is very busy.

Golf from 7 a.m. to 11:42 a.m., fencing from 12:00 p.m. to 13:47 p.m., Mongolian meditation from 14:01 p.m. to 14:22 p.m., lunches with important people, meetings with various charities and line dancing courses at the end of the day. I discover that by the time night falls I'm so tired that the only dance I can execute is a modest zigzag dance towards my bed. Being rich has its advantages so I propose the zigzag dance instead of the boring line up. People embrace my idea, and I don't have to try to coordinate my movements anymore. We crawl, bend, stumble and fall as we wish, as we are our own instructors – nobody teaches the rich how to dance, okay?

Besides, I want to be fresh and rested in order to enjoy my new sex life. No, I rephrase, my sex life. My sex life that has just begun! The time of restitution has come! I order exotic prostitutes from all over the world. My agent informs me that he managed to find a woman with three-not-one-pussies – radiation exposure – and he is currently working on relocating her from the poorest village in the poorest country in the poorest region of the world. I greet the good news with a smile and I give him the freedom to buy the entire village if he has to. I want the three-in-one deal!

I'm flooded with requests for donations. I take my responsibility as a filthy rich person very seriously. I want to save everything on this planet, from battered spouses and four-eyed kids to abused bats and politically persecuted Yogis. However, during one of those charity events I make the mistake of asking about their government's involvement. My cat scratches my hand discreetly. Am I crazy? We play Sunday golf in most of those countries. She's right. I immediately take that back and make a few hefty donations for the governments in question. Problem solved.

Still insecure about how to solve the sex issue, I decide to get, among others, a woman just for myself; mine, all mine. I need to be sure she does not cheat on me. There is only one way to make sure a woman does not become interested in other men. Confinement. I find her. Beautiful, educated, rich. That's my girl! After a short ceremony attended by close family – her parents, Aunt Lyla, my cat – I lock her in my two-hundred-ninety-eight-bedroom wing of the mansion. She's all mine and at my service. I leave the wedding ceremony happy and relaxed. On my way to the three-hundred-twenty-bedroom wing I get a phone call from my agent. The three-pussied woman is here, along with the villagers, and with thirty-seven other dancers. He got the village as a "combo" and the dancers for a discounted price. This is indeed good news. I tell him that the villagers can share one big bedroom – they're poor people, used to share – while the dancers can have one room each. Of course, the lucky owner of three reproductive organs will get three.

While giving the agent instructions, I mentally check the outgoing mail on my desk, something I'm usually not used to doing. I hired an army of writers who deal with this on a daily basis. But now, I'm curious.

I spot a thank you card, written in response to a half hour snack I had yesterday with the Mayor. It is signed by me, so why don't I get naughty and read what I wrote to him?

Dear Mayor,

Last night we were sitting at the enchanting Lili's restaurant. The stars sent their light upon us. Enlightened by celestial forces, we made a major decision: to enroll more orphans in 'My City, My Home.'

In joy and fraternity I want to follow up by putting a check on the words. Yes, it is true what they say. We, the ones blessed with fortune, never forget our humble beginnings. Yours ....

The letter ends with my signature – I don't remember signing it though; my cat must have done it.

What? I had a quick snack with this guy, during which I spent most of the time at the restroom – hung over from previous parties.

I want to know who wrote this! I call all the writers. Here they are, creative little monsters. I announce to them I do not need their services any more, and I let them go after offering them a generous severance pay. From now on, my cat will handle the correspondence.

I'm tired. Since I have become rich I get less sleep than ever and a terrible pain in my neck prevents me from participating in the regular rich guy's activities.

This reminds me to gather immediately my team of three-hundred-twenty-nine doctors and researchers and inform them about my condition.

After a five-hour session, during which they share medical and scientific wisdom, their representative delivers a blue pill.

Three days into treatment, my neck pain is gone. However, my happiness is incomplete. A new condition has made its way into my system. I have chronic insomnia. Basically, I can enjoy my healthy neck 24/7.

I call them again. Three hours later a green pill is delivered, along with a five-page long "Get well" card – signatures of three hundred twenty-nine people take up a lot of space. I fall asleep and sleep for three days. I wake up refreshed but when I try to enjoy my breakfast, a violent nausea shatters my body. I'm pissed. Can money buy health? If so, I should be extremely healthy. I learn that an international team of doctors – including one hundred fifty from my crew – are currently working on a non side-effect drug. They assure me that whatever I take might have a mild side effect, but I shouldn't be worried. I wouldn't call healing a migraine at the cost of loss of sensation in all four limbs "mild." Never mind.

Being rich starts to be boring. Same repetitive actions, no fun. At night, when the guards snooze, my cat and I sneak out of the mansion and go have tripe soup at a modest ethnic tavern. I play poor and so does my feline companion, who plays a stray, hungry animal, and gets yummy leftovers from the cooks. People are friendly here. As I sit there listening to the music played by a Gypsy fiddler, I realize I'm free. I can eat whatever I want, whenever I want, with whomever I want. I'm no longer on a schedule and I don't have to meet people I do not wish to see.

The only thing this place has in common with the fancy restaurants is the food. Olives, cheeses, real bread and real butter. I like it a lot, although the cooks become confrontational when I tell them that this is the diet designed for rich people by Dr. Pumpernickel. They don't recognize Dr. Pumpernickel's contribution to science. They insist this has been the poor sheepherder's diet for centuries. One of those people is lying to me, but I don't know if it's them, or Dr. Pumpernickel.

I ask the fiddler if he's not tired of moving around the world. He gives me a toothless smile. He tells me he has never found the perfect place for himself. I'm struck by the fact that, just like him, I'm a traveler, always looking for something. Will I ever stop? I don't know.

I tell the fiddler to play my favorite song. I will write him a generous check. He refuses politely. He only accepts cash and this song is on him. He sings for pleasure as well. I tell him I can buy whatever I please. He smiles. He asks me if I can get him a woman with three pussies. My pleasure, it's a phone call away! He smiles again. It was a joke. What idiot would want a woman with three pussies? We can barely keep up with one!

We sit there listening to the Gypsy song and suddenly become very sad and lonely. We can feel the song is old and it carries an excruciating human experience along with an inexplicable anxiety. We hate the setting, the song, ourselves.

From there we run to a casino. I feel more depressed than ever. My cat suggests that we play all our fortune. She's right. I don't care about money that cannot buy what I really want.

I pick up the dice, blindfold my cat, and let her do her thing. In a second of misfortune she loses everything. We take a deep breath.

It's time to go home. Behind the doorman, five distorted shadows watch us as we head to our limo. It's the omen family.

We get in the car in silence thinking that maybe, after all, they're not real and they're not humans.

The Healing Session at the Job Interview

I get a phone call from the pawn shop where I applied for a job yesterday. They want to know if I'm available for a short interview.

I ask my cat if she has any plans for tomorrow afternoon, then I politely confirm the meeting with the prospective employer.

On our way to the job interview, I meet Aunt Lyla's cousin's granddaughter, Lily. I remember Lily! Lily is twenty-something years old now and one of those sexy women-to-be, whom we watch in kindergarten and secretly wish they grew up faster and that they were not our relatives; this way we cannot be accused of incestuous fantasies. We resume our journey toward employment after a quick, conversation with her. She wishes us Happy New Year. I'm surprised to hear that we are greeting a New Year again. I totally lost track of time. We wish her moderate happiness, as extreme joy is always evened out by extreme suffering. Better enjoy the happiness responsibly. I am glad that we met. I cannot help thinking we are such a lucky family! We have Lily!

The position I'm applying for is that of a cashier at the local pawn shop. I do not want to be one of those desperate people who rush to interact with Society unprepared, so my cat made an appointment with the highly skilled, highly trained resumé expert Jean Pierre Trique, Ph.D.

We meet Jean Pierre – a "professional winner's" face, cold grin, tired writer's fingers – just before the job interview. He does not waste time and gives us the enlightenment we seek right away.

He asks us why I need a job. I tell him we need to pay off the new car and save some money for our annual trip abroad. We do not want to bake in the Tahitian sun and drink plain water just because we have been handling our funds irresponsibly and cannot afford the martinis.

Jean Pierre jumps out of his chair with an expression of genuine horror on his face. His sophisticated facial movements can be easily translated into one word: No! We learn that this is the most common mistake job seekers make at their job interviews. Revealing their true intentions, that is.

Jean Pierre falls back into his chair, shaking. My cat brings him a glass of water. I try to give him a short neck and back massage.

We apologize to the great resumé writer and express, once again, admiration for his craft. We are stupid and unsuccessful. That's why we're here, to learn and become stupid and successful.

Jean Pierre teaches us that, when applying for a job, we have to display a positive attitude along with a happy, continuous smile. A successful candidate is the one who can prove that he can identify himself with the goals of the employer. A powerful job seeker tries to learn as much as he can about the employer.

A true job seeker tries to show he knows a lot about their products or services. Do they make preserves? He tells them that their preserves taste like his grandmother's. Do they sell mushrooms? He surprises them with at least five ways to prepare delicious mushroom dishes. Is this a condom manufacturer? He lets them know he is grateful for the safety their product offers. Actually, he is so into safety that he uses them even when he is making love to himself in the morning. This cute joke will make the future employer smile, and at the same time it will deliver a strong message about the job seeker's morals.

My cat and I agree. I do not want to create the impression of a man who would sleep with just anyone, even in a safe context. Our logo: Play a gentleman, no matter what!

Jean Pierre stands up. The healing session is over. He reminds us to keep our heads straight and to walk tall. We thank Jean Pierre for his precious instructions and we continue our journey.

On the way to the pawn shop, we practice the questions that the manager might ask us. My cat plays the manager and shoots one question after another. And why do I want to work in a pawn shop? I smile. Isn't it obvious that I am a people person? I crave seeing people give up items that they hold dear. Why? Because this is who I am, a deep connoisseur of human nature. I want to help them, to guide them, to introduce them to the world of "owning nothing." My cat approves of the answer.

Next! What are my methods of keeping the old customers coming back while attracting new customers? I tell the imaginary manager, played by my cat, that while Internet and aggressive advertising are to be considered, word-of-mouth is key in this business. People in need do not have access to the Internet and even if they had a computer, by now it must be resting on one of the shelves of a pawn shop. It's good for the business to be remembered as someone who did not try to take advantage of them. The feline manager claps her paws.

Excellent! Now we can move on to the personal set of questions given to us by Jean Pierre. For example, how do I spend my free time?

Shall I tell the prospective employer that one of my favorite pastimes is staring intensely at hot chicks, hoping that one day they will acknowledge my presence? Of course not. Instead I'll tell them that I volunteer for a local charity, as I'm actively involved in sponsoring hungry children from Zimbabwe.

Jean Pierre told us that the employers not only have the questions but the answers to them as well. You got to tell them exactly what they want to hear. Otherwise, you lose.

Then, there are those nasty personality type questions. I hate them, especially since my cat likes to repeat them over and over again. What are my strengths? No kidding, want to hear my strengths? Here they are! I am a fast-learner, a fast-thinking and fast-acting being. And what are my weaknesses? Here I have to proceed with caution and remember Jean Pierre's precious teachings.

Jean Pierre taught us that even weaknesses have to be cute, appealing and interesting. The future employer must see potential even in your weaknesses. Otherwise, you lose. Is that so?

I look my cat in the eyes – body language by Jean Pierre – and I recite my line. One of my weaknesses is being too dedicated and wanting to give one-hundred-fifty percent at the workplace. Another one is being way too humble, giving a lot yet never expecting anything in return. My cat hugs me. She thinks we should be fine.

The moment is here! We walk in, shake hands, share smiles, armed with Jean Pierre's magnificent tools. The man in front of me wants to introduce me to his crew. Cool. I didn't know this was a group interview. Not only do I have to convince him that I could make more and more people to bring their stuff to his pawn shop, now I have to conquer the team. I agree.

Let me take a closer look at "le crew." One is an anorexic, miserable fifty-something woman with big eyeglasses. Do I really want to see her face every morning? Right next to her, a huge imposing young male with mean dark eyes prompts my cat to deliver a few hisses. A Granny opens the door and asks us if we want coffee. I learn that she's their bookkeeper and coffeemaker. Do I really want to be here? I'm suddenly scared by the characters in front of me. I give them the "good" answers. They seem happy. I am not. I pass the personality test as well. I convince them that I'm positive and charming, even if my charm borders on insanity.

I think in awe how scared I would be if people knew who I really was. Should I tell them that I'm a sensitive and loving being? Heck, no! Whenever I let "the sensitive me" get out and manifest himself, I get hurt, so we've learned to hide that side of me. I've always had this problem. My cat convinced me that there is nothing wrong with that.

We hide our true selves just like people with fair complexions use tons of sunscreen to avoid getting sunburns or even worse, skin cancer.

Otherwise, we lose. She might be right, but I still feel awkward hiding who I am. No, I take that back. I feel awkward *being* who I am.

The odd prospective employer starts telling me that they're like a family, always together, working and being there for each other. At this moment, I tune them out. I'm not looking to start a family or to join a family. I have Aunt Lyla and the cat. And let's not forget the beautiful Lily.

In a mysterious, inexplicable and unexpected turn of events, the roles are reversed and I become the interviewer. I ask them questions that are not in their – nor Jean Pierre's – literature. My cat helps too. Mind you, we are very creative!

We must say, we do not approve of their answers. I want to meet and hire interesting people, aware people who have something to teach me. Where is their awareness? Where is my awareness? And last but not least, where is my cat's awareness? We do not know.

I ask my cat, "How can we identify awesome, intriguing people?" She shrugs. Maybe they should wear a tag that reads "I'm interesting."

I agree. That would be helpful for all the people who are unable to see their true potential.

In this world of successful, insane people who look for a job just because they "want to make a difference," or they "want to thrive in a friendly environment," or they "want to expand their professional horizons," here we are, once again, two freaks who need to pay their water bills.

We end up working night shifts at a small bakery, where we pass a short, informal, one-line interview with the Senior Dough Analyst, consisting of "Hey, can you lift those fucking heavy trays?"

The Healing Session in the Gay Community

There is nothing more rewarding than watching your favorite football game. *This* is the essence of masculinity. I open myself a beer, burp vigorously, and get ready for some passive action. My cat jumps into my lap and looks me in the eyes while hitting the remote control with her right paw. She wants tuna crackers. I assure my furry significant other that we will get them first thing in the morning. This is not a good answer. She rephrases. She wants tuna crackers *now*. I get up and grab some money in hatred and resentment. She's like a wife, and we enjoy the dynamics of a heterosexual couple. I'm single, yet married to a cat.

I enter the store like a hurricane, anxious to catch at least a few images of the game I've been waiting to watch for so long. I stand in line glued to the small screen behind the salesperson. During the commercial break I spot a hot woman right in front of me. She is truly hot – curly hair, green eyes, shapely body – yet I cannot display weakness. I put my tongue back in my mouth where it belongs and pretend to be interested in the baby food commercial.

Suddenly, I'm taken back in time. I am four-years old. It's Sunday morning. My mother, my father and I are having breakfast. My mother tells me that all women are dirty whores. "You too, Mom?" My father administers a short, painful sample of paternal punishment. I spend the entire day asking all the kids in the neighborhood if their moms are dirty whores as well.

I'm back at the store. I hate women. Why does the attraction I feel for them make me so vulnerable? On top of that, my team is losing the game. The future looks grim.

I get the tuna crackers and I'm ready to leave when I hear someone calling my name. It's my gay friend Toto. He too wanted to watch the game, but his dog demanded bacon strips. I'm not alone. Toto has an idea. Why don't we go across the street to the gay sports bar and watch the rest of the game together? We can tell our feline and canine partners that we are late because we couldn't find their favorite snacks and we had to drive to another store. I love Toto. We both feel we are cheating on our partners, yet the togetherness helps us achieve powerful guilt management skills.

At the gay bar we enjoy a relaxed time watching the game and drinking beer. A handsome guy stops by our table. He gives Toto a hug and me a venomous gaze. I ask Toto about this young man's odd behavior. Toto explains. The gentleman in question is his ex-lover's best friend. He thought Toto and I were a couple. Naturally, he could not hide his resentment for Toto leaving his partner for me. What? This is indeed funny. We share a few more drinks and part ways blissful and content.

By the time I get back home, everybody in the neighborhood knows I'm gay. My cat is waiting for me with her hair standing on end and a few skillfully crafted lines. How could I lie to her? How could I be gay and not share this with her? She is indeed hurt. My explanations are not well received. She doesn't even want to sleep on my pillow as she used to. From now on she will sleep in the closet, as an act of protest.

I'm stunned, incapable of understanding this stupid situation. Maybe this is a sign. I think of the ordeal a man has to go through to get laid. Boring dates, "bonding," rings, and expensive lobster dinner, along with the uncertainty…we never know if we are on the right path and if our efforts will be rewarded. One mistake, one word can make our secret dream of mating disappear in seconds. Maybe it's true what they say, that, when it comes to sex, gay people get straight to the point.

A shy, devilish thought moves into my mind, settles in and makes itself comfortable. I need to learn more about gay people right now! I open the closet and apologize to my cat. Is she willing to join me in a new adventure? Yes, she is.

I call Toto and I ask him about any upcoming gay events. He tells me that my cat and I can join them for the gay Halloween party. Deal. All we need are costumes. We start browsing the stores in search of the cutest costumes.

As days pass by I discover the benefits of being gay. At the store I am no longer doomed to try my outfits in the men's fitting rooms. I walk into the ladies' booths with confidence and curiosity. I'm gay. I open doors, I admire naked bodies, I even give advice. Women welcome my presence and I indulge in touching, squeezing and pinching their breasts. Nobody slaps me in the face anymore; all I get is sexy giggling. I love being gay! Now and then I bump into one who resists, yet the resistance melts when I look at her with an indifferent smile and inform her about my freshly acquired sexual orientation.

My cat doesn't want a costume since her coat is charcoal black. She fits in as she is. I do not insist. I know she's stubborn. Instead, why don't I pick a witch's costume so we are a fun couple?

I find the one I like. The only thing I will have to change is my hair color. I want to be a blond, sexy mama. I get a hot short black dress, black veil, black stockings and a beautiful blond wig. My cat suggests shaving the hair on my chest, but I want to leave that sign of masculinity untouched. She agrees. Balancing Yin and Yang has always been our top priority.

We walk back home in peace and joy, stopping now and then just to check out the hottest females.

At the gay Halloween party we are warmly welcomed by Toto and his friends. Music is good, atmosphere is good, and people are having fun. I'm anxious to touch some female ass, yet, I have to be cautious because it is hard to tell who is who – good costumes. I spot a couple of women. Mmmmm ... one of them is black and has a gorgeous firm ass. I walk up to her, give her a hug and ask her if she's a waitress. She's surprised. I quench her thirst for explanations by telling her she can literally carry trays on that gorgeous ass. Yeah, it's that firm. My compliment is well received. She kisses me on my lips. Her partner kisses me on my lips as well. I need a drink to control the convulsive arousal that took over my body. It's good to be gay!

My cat is much more detached than myself. She sits in a corner sipping tuna cocktail and observing the people. When I take a short break from massaging strangers, she delivers the essence of the feline observation. She thinks that right now, we're watching a society within a society. I think I shouldn't let her go to the feline philosophy meet-ups anymore.

It's getting late and we have to go. Our gay friends are sad, but they express the desire to see more of us in the future. My costume was a hit, and on my way out I get a lovely pink and red corsage from Mimi the drag queen. Mimi calls me a sweetie. I deliver a graceful "thank you" to her. I also kiss her girlfriends, Fifi and Wiwi and head to the parking lot. My cat is hungry. Can she wait until we get home? No. Pit stop at a snack bar. Unfortunately, in the parking lot I meet my boss along with his happy, unanimously-accepted-by-society, heterosexual family. They're going to church. What? Is it morning already? My boss looks at me in awe and disgust. Can he talk to me for a minute? He sure can. He takes me on the side and tells me in a dry tone I am fired. I demand an explanation. Silly me! A heterosexual, confident boss never gives explanations.

He just does not want to see me again. It's that simple. I get in the car thunder-stricken. As I pull back I accidentally look in the mirror. I am wearing a black dress, blond wig and lots of makeup. I think that might have helped him in making his quick decision. However, we live in a democratic society and we enjoy, among other fancy rights, the equal opportunity employment one. He cannot fire me just because I am gay! My cat agrees and suggests we should contact the Gay Rights Association and file a complaint.

I always listen to my cat, and minutes later we pull up in front of the Gay Rights Association building, full of hope.

As we expected, gay people are ready to offer full help and support. However, they don't believe the fact that I am straight. They think I am in denial. They will help. A counselor is called in. Surprise, surprise, the counselor is Mimi, the drag queen! I tell her the truth. Her face expresses sadness and compassion. She will guide me in this long, painful journey to self-discovery. What? I keep telling them I'm not gay but all I get is a collection of books – *Discovering your Gay Self, The Gay Me, The Person who Lived Inside*. A few days later Mimi calls me. How am I doing? Am I reading the books? Yes, and I'm almost gay. Good. It's a good start.

It's obvious that they do not believe me. But they like my defensive mode. They want me to be the Head of the Equal Opportunity Employment Commission. I ask my cat what to do. She wants to learn more. I do too. My cat has already made friends with a couple of gay cats she met behind the club yesterday while looking for the cats' restroom.

Fast forward. Time is compressed by unseen forces. Before I know it, I am a strong activist for gay rights. Phone calls, letters of support, invitations, people who want to talk to me and learn more about the discrimination I have been subjected to as a gay person.

Here I am, straight and disoriented, sitting in my gay office and fighting passionately for a cause that is not mine. The only person who would be happy to see that I'm finally away from whores would be my late mom.

I take my responsibilities as a gay activist very seriously and I cherish every accomplishment as if it were mine. The only success I have achieved so far though is our community's recognition of the gay parking spots. They do not have to carpool anonymously anymore. The mayor agreed to pass the local law, but there are rumors that he calls me an "infatuated blond faggot" and his cats are no longer allowed to play with mine. I'm pissed. I will not tolerate this!

Can one be a MAN, wear a blond wig, and not get fired in this country?

I feel an urge to delve deeper into this gay issue and the social aspect of the gay movements. What does Society have against them?

Do they pay taxes? Yes, they do. Do they actively participate in the citizens' "Clean the Highways!" programs? Yes, they do. I personally saw Mimi in her colorful outfit, picking up straight cigarette butts on Highway 33. Do gay people donate canned beans and tuna for the poor on Christmas? They do that, as well.

Then where is the problem? I think of the hostility in my neighborhood when I was officially declared gay. I keep thinking and thinking of the mysteries of the gay social movements. Thinking is an exhausting pastime. My cat and I take turns; when I'm too tired to think she takes over, allowing me to catch some sleep. Then, when I get up with a fresh mind, she passes the thinking back to me. We need to keep the thinking relay going no matter what!

A few days into non-stop thinking, we both realize that this adventure has depleted us mentally and physically. I've lost weight. She, too, has lost weight. I've lost some hair. She has lost some as well and her coat resembles Aunt Lyla's old, dusty mink hat. Yet our thirst for knowledge is still there.

My secretary brings me a study about the dynamics of gay couples versus one about heterosexual couples. I have no intention of reading it. There is only one dynamic I recognize, the one governed by a deeper understanding of human nature. And there is only one question I don't have the answer for: Is it true what they say, that when it comes to sex, gay people get straight to the point?

The Healing Session on Foreign Land

I get my medical insurance bill and I shake. Why? Why do I have to pay so much money just to say "Hi" to the doctor? My cat agrees.

I think of the neighbors up North who have free medical insurance.

I'm pissed, frustrated, depressed. I feel like a child who's rejected by his mother. To make it worse I get a phone call from a neighbor of a cousin of an uncle, who's on a work contract in one of those medical insurance-friendly places. How is he? Fine. Just got back from the doctor's office. Why was he at the *doctor's*, is he, God forbid, sick? Oh, no. Far from it. But since medical care is free, why not stop by now and then, and socialize with the doctors, nurses and billing specialists, who are all bored to death? They kill time drinking coffee, eating chocolate croissants and exchanging views on existence.

I admit that I have zero tolerance for someone else's happiness. I hate this guy and I let him know right away. I think enjoying free health care must be extremely fulfilling because he gives me a joyous "See you later, my friend!" before he hangs up.

My hatred is now the size of a huge, greedy hurricane, threatening to devastate everything on its way if I do not take immediate measures. Naturally, I take immediate measures. I look at my cat and apparently we think the same thought. She meows at me conspiratorially. I pull out the big suitcase from under the bed. She brings her tiny feline travel kit I got for her two years ago in Brazil. We both start packing, fighting powerful emotions. But where are we going? Well, this is a tiny detail I might have overlooked, but I address it right away by calling the nephew of my late mother's aunt, who is well connected in my favorite country's Department of Labor. He gives me great news.

As a fisherman I qualify for a work visa, since there is a huge demand right now for fishermen. He will arrange everything for me.

All I have to do is grab my paperwork, go to the Embassy, and pass the interview.

He was so right! We have a little problem with my cat, though. The visa officer wants to know my cat's main occupation. I totally understand. I smile and tell him that, basically, she eats all the smaller fish I catch. Big fish go to the market, small fish are hers. The guy seems to be totally satisfied with my answer and issues the cat a dependent visa as a "small fish eater."

We go back home, full of enthusiasm. A few high speed travel arrangements later, we land in the neighboring country wearing herring amulets and big smiles.

I want to learn everything about this wonderful, welcoming country.

But first, I want to get my medical insurance card. I have never thought I could get one that fast! Yet, I cannot be easily fooled. What if this is only propaganda? Why don't I check this out right away? I end up spending my first three days in this country seeing one doctor after another – my favorite specialties are Neurology and Dermatology. Although it's obvious I suffer from imaginary ailments – I enjoy an admirable state of health – the medical personnel examine me carefully; they take their time, ask thorough questions about my childhood and even send me home with pink chewing gum and fruit balls – traditional dish.

The little settlement where I work is close to the border, so I indulge in late evening walks with my cat, to and from the crossing point. Once I get close to the border, I take great pleasure in clenching my fists at my motherland. "This is for the expensive medical bills, Stepmother!" Then I go to bed, relieved. I love my country, but some things need to be spelled out. Love is a two-way street.

I enjoy my days at sea. I enjoy the time spent with the other fishermen. My only concern is their food. The food is very different from that back home. For example, they eat fruit balls and they're very proud of their national dish. I have to eat them, too, because otherwise they will be offended. They just cannot understand that my system is not used to them and I always get severe diarrhea. The only thing that fills me with joy – and occasionally, fruit balls – is the free medical care available, in case I end up severely dehydrated.

When I'm not at sea, I watch talk shows and I exchange views with people I've met here – new friends, or my cat – old friend.

So far, so good.

I go to the bank to cash my first check. As I stand in line to the teller, I accidentally look at the paycheck. My paycheck reads one-thousand dollars, but I only get two. I'm sure this must be a mistake! I ask the teller. No, it is not a mistake. The nine-hundred-ninety- eight dollars I am inquiring about are taxes I owe to the government; money which is used mainly for health care and education.

I go straight to work and expose my views about the taxation system right away. My colleague fishermen do not seem to understand why I'm so disturbed. They want to know why I am so convinced their taxation system is high. To them it seems just right. You have to pay *something* in order to indulge in free social protection. Really?

To make it worse, a young fisherman tells me that he could never live in a country like mine where health care is a luxury and a privilege. I don't like this. I don't like this at all. *Nobody talks like that about my country!*

I show teeth. I respond in a venomous tone that we have a higher authority to turn to. We have God. We can pray to God that we do not get sick and if He is merciful, we can keep our money. Whereas here, in this Godless country, they rip you off upfront, whether you're healthy or sick. Nobody seems to agree with me. I feel like I have never really left home. Why am I here, if I get the same treatment? I think I like this place, maybe *because* it reminds me of my homeland. Same problem. No one seems to have healthy reasoning skills. Will I surrender? Never!

In between two arguments fueled by everything and anything, I purchase a second cat. "One cat is a joy, two cats are a blessing," or so the saying goes. The felines seem to get along just fine and I don't have to entertain the old one with discussions about global warming anymore.

I look in the mirror and I cannot believe my eyes. Since when is my beard gray? Time must have flown by indeed. I realize that it's been over five years since I landed in this place.

The phone is ringing. I learn in shock and awe that I just got laid off. They don't need fishermen anymore, since the pollution in their waters is so high, they are basically lifeless. So am I. Lifeless. Speechless.

You cannot do this to me now, when I just financed my second cat!

I need an income to pay off the cat. I call my distant relative in the Department of Labor. He's not sure if I qualify for unemployment benefits as a non-citizen. Why don't I try and let him know how it went? I rush to the unemployment center. I stand in line ten hours only to learn that I do not qualify for any help from the government.

But I have been paying taxes for so many years! The clerk does not agree with me. She says paying taxes is a privilege and guess what? I am still allowed to enjoy it! I turn around ready to go. She calls me back. I find out that while non-citizens only have the right to pay taxes, my second cat qualifies for a substantial help, since she is a citizen. I feel relief. This will help me to pay off the cat, cover the rent, all the other expenses and maybe even get a new car. It's good to be a cat and have full rights.

On my way out I see a group of young people smoking pot. They celebrate the generosity of their government, for they have been awarded – again!– hefty unemployment benefits. Why? Because they all suffer from a condition called ALS – which stands for "Acute Laziness Syndrome." Poor kids! I would have never guessed they're sick. They look healthy and strong to me. But you know what they say, "Never judge a book by its cover." True, very true. As I pick up my shirts at the cleaner's I notice an ad on the wall. I suddenly remember that the deadline for the poetry contest my cats signed me up for is close. I panic. A few weeks ago, all three of us allowed creativity to blossom and wrote an existential, philosophical poem. I wrote it on the back of a receipt I got from the same cleaner's. The poem is short – small receipt – but full of essence.

I, the Gosling. I, the Gander
A naive gosling. Eyes wide open
A leap in time. Same eyes wide open
A strong, wise gander. Eyes half open
A detached look at the universe
I, the gosling. I, the gander.

I look for our masterpiece in my pockets and I cannot find it. I panic. After desperate attempts I manage to find it. I run to the post office. They're about to close. More panic. I beg them to send my humble letter. A few bows and they agree. Panic is gone.

Since I cannot accept to be supported by the citizen cat – although she has expressed her willingness to help – I try to find a job, a job that will allow me to maintain my legal status here. I look in the occupational classifieds. The only positions that need to be filled in this country are Clown III and Caregiver in retirement homes. They had some openings for Toilet Cleaner Specialists but those are filled now. I remember I have a Master's degree but the woman at the job bank strongly advises me to delete that from my resumé. Nobody needs educated people. As a matter of fact, any country on this planet will kick out a seasoned top-notch professional and retain a clown instead. Why? Because governments are tired of dealing with their own gangs of "open minded," "intelligent," "creative" monsters. Why import some more?

Taxpayers don't want their money spent on education and such. They want to laugh instead and have fun; life is short. I leave the job bank illuminated and happy. As a matter of fact, I'm almost flying.

As soon as I get home I try out a few clown costumes. One is really cute, and I decide to save it for my job interviews. I'm eager to share the joy with my feline friends, but they both have serious faces. Am I crazy? I execute a couple of graceful tricks but they both watch me in silence. There is no meow. No purr. No hiss.

It's tough not to have support, but I will survive.

Luckily, a neighbor of a cousin of Aunt Lyla's has an entertainment company and will arrange for me to get hired. I will provide fun for children stressed after so many exhausting hours at school.

I go to the immigration office to check on the status of my application. I'm directed to a nice, polite clerk. She wants the number of my application. I give it to her. She types it into a computer. Then she hits a big red key on her right. A panel with multiple lights beeps. The immigration officer smiles and congratulates me. Apparently I hit the jackpot. My application is approved! I express powerful curiosity at this screening system.

She agrees to introduce me to the new, revolutionary immigration system. Until recently, the immigration offices would receive tens of thousands of applications and never had enough trained people to process them. There were backlogs, unhappy taxpayers, demonstrations and political movements.

One glorious day, during lunch break, the immigration staff at one of those insignificant, small field offices was eating and occasionally playing with the applications as usual. They were tired. Why do they have to do this miserable work? Why? Then, the miracle happened. One of them put together all of the three thousand applications received that day and shuffled them. Then he randomly picked out one of them. An amazing, revolutionary idea was born! All the officers present agreed that a reform was imminent. Why not make the immigration process a lottery – playful and entertaining? The advantages were obvious: less paperwork, more green trees, fewer frustrations – people have always complained about the long waiting times and the "unfairness" of the system. There were also other benefits. The joy, yes, the joy that immigration brought into people's lives. It was no longer an ordeal but a game, setting free the inner child in every applicant as well as in every immigration officer. There was also a significant return to God. The society gradually became religious and fearful, since there was no authority left to turn to but Him. Evidence was Faith, and Faith was Evidence.

I leave the office singing and dancing. Life is good, not only for me, but for millions of people in this situation. I get home excited and I show my cats the winning ticket the officer gave me.

I also check the mail. Today is my luckiest day ever! I learn that I was awarded an important literary prize for my poem *I, the Gosling, I, the Gander*.

Both cats give me a bored look. So what? They do not care for being here anymore. They want to move back South. Why? The old one convinced the local cat that here it's cold and down there it's warm.

In order to adapt to the new climate, the old one grew a thick coat and grooming had become very time consuming. And guess what? The local cat wants to have short hair as well. Who wears long hair nowadays? They cannot take it anymore.

I am about to give them a lecture about being grateful for my entire struggle. But I suddenly realize that I grew a thick coat as well. They are right!

Once again, I think of Astrakhan's words of wisdom. He told me that if I took two identical cats and relocated one to the North Pole and the other one to Africa, the Northern one would grow a thick coat while the African one would gradually lose her hair. Why? To improve their chances of survival. Sure it takes time for them to blend in; usually the second and third generations of cats are fully established. And only the first settlers retain the memory of their original coats.

Astrakhan, where are you? I want my coat back!

The cats bring me the suitcase in silence. We all start packing, fighting powerful emotions. The gates of a new adventure open in front of us.

I don't care where I go anymore. People are the same everywhere. They just wear different coats.

The Healing Session in the Military

I am completely immersed in my favorite poem, *Alone Again, Alone with You*, when a dreadful noise brings me back to my gray reality. Apparently my cat needed an energy booster and jumped onto the table; from there she climbed on top of the refrigerator and sneaked into the "dried fish" drawer. Right now, she is on the floor, licking her paws, oblivious to her surroundings. Really? I pick her up and sniff her nose. Her dried fish breath tells me a different story. I check the area around the table, refrigerator, drawer. It's messy. She made a mess again. Yet I have no intention to be her cleaning lady.

I give her a short lecture about respect. She hisses back at me. I hiss at the walls. She scratches the refrigerator. I scratch myself.

Enough! Our Hawaiian cat trainer of international fame is wrong. Just displaying affection, being calm and practicing the ukulele together every night won't work. She needs discipline.

I call him right away. He does not answer. I leave five messages. Nothing. An hour later I call again and leave a message asking him to meet me downtown to get his cat therapy consultation fee, a three-hundred-dollar check. He calls me back before I get to hang up. When he learns that he won't get any money – joke – he suggests I might need discipline as well. What's the purpose of introducing the cat to the principles of discipline, if the owner is anything but a disciplined person?

He's right. Yet discipline does not grow on trees. Where can we get some? As usual, Fate pitches in. A nephew of a girlfriend of a neighbor of an estranged uncle tells me in a short conversation at the bakery that his brother has just joined the military. Did he say *military*? I wave goodbye to him and rush back to my cat and house. While packing I remember Aunt Lyla's stories about my deceased uncle and her brother, *before* and *after* he joined the military. Before he joined the troops, he used to take off his socks and drop them wherever he would see fit: in front of the house, in the kitchen and even on the garage floor. Only a few months later, Aunt Lyla, along with the entire family, fell in love with him again. His closet displayed a rigorous arrangement of socks, based on the following characteristics: date of purchase, place of purchase, method of payment – cash, credit, or debit card; color, length, pattern – number of dots, waves, or lines; category – casual, hiking, diabetic, ski, and thread count. A small category – miscellaneous – grouped the ones too original to be classified.

I close my eyes and picture our fish drawer being beautifully organized and my cat on patrol in and around the house.

Discipline is indeed a key factor in attaining inner balance. The other advantage the military offers is that it relieves you from the burden of thinking. You have to do what you are told to do and that is it. I like that. I like that a lot.

We spend long hours, enjoying our– hopefully – last manifestation of this civilian bad habit which is thinking.

We think of a unit that would suit us best. Aviation? Artillery? Expeditionary unit? Maybe Logistics?

I call my aunt to give her the great news. She is deeply moved by my decision.

On my way to the recruiting office I have to stop by her house and pick up a charm my uncle used to wear when he was active. It is a stuffed chickadee. I express my disappointment. Why not a large, imposing bird of prey, which would inspire fear and make the enemy's knees shake? Aunt Lyla explains. My uncle ended up being a sniper, taking out the enemies, unseen and unheard. Had he been arrogant, had he displayed his skills, the enemy would have detected and overpowered him. But who would fear a chickadee? The enemy was relaxed and so was my uncle when he pulled that evil trigger of his. She's right! She pulls the stuffed bird's legs. The little bird automatically spreads her wings and I can read a small inscription. "Never underestimate your enemy."

I leave Aunt Lyla's in tears. She assures me she will visit us.

In the meantime, while trying on various outfits, my cat reaches the conclusion we were both hoping for. She thinks she looks sexy in camouflage. I do, too. Besides, with her by my side I do not need night vision. Another powerful life-changing decision has been made.

After a long, boring conversation at the recruiting office, about my life, my expectations and my goals, we're directed to another office to fill out a few applications and forms. Mine take ten minutes to fill out. My cat, though, has to undergo detailed screening as she will join the feline unit. Unlike the human units, they don't accept crazy cats. But we made it! Joyous and relaxed, we walk into the building that will be our new home. A few unpleasant surprises. Nobody informed me that I would have to give up my long lasting, refreshing bubble baths as well as sleeping until 2:00 p.m. on weekends. I want to express my outrage, but I have to postpone that since the training begins in a few minutes.

The training consists of very exhausting exercises which neither my cat nor I enjoy. Tired and pissed we crawl to the eatery. The food is bland and horrible. Is this how they treat brave people who, day after day fight the worst enemy ever, the Almighty Laziness?

I will have to inform my superiors about this unbelievable situation!

But now I have to endure. I show great strength and will while secretly indulging in the sausages stolen by my cat in her night missions to and from the kitchen. Our days and nights – mostly nights – become more pleasurable. I have to be careful, though, and not exhale garlic as well as other sausage-specific spices when I'm around other people. What if they sniff my mouth, like I used to do with my cat, and reveal my little secret?

While I enjoy a short two-second nap in between those three thousand nasty pushups, I feel the little stuffed chickadee against my chest and think of Aunt Lyla. Someone taps me on my shoulder. I look up. I see nothing. I look left. Still nothing. On my right, a fellow recruit keeps doing his pushups on one arm, while he hands me over a letter with the available one. My cat opens the letter for me. A fast, rhythmic reading follows. It is from Aunt Lyla! She will come and visit soon! Hearing the great news, my cat loses control and screams in such joy that she's immediately placed in solitary confinement for twenty-four hours. This means I will have to survive the night without any culinary treats. I find it extremely hard to fall asleep without my "goodnight sausage," but I manage to step into the land of dreams while holding my precious feathered charm.

In the morning I go to pick up my cat. We're allowed a thirty-minute meeting with Aunt Lyla. I know what to expect. Fake smiles and true lies. She's not allowed to convey any negative messages or emotions to us. No stories about unpaid bills, illnesses and misfortunes. In order to give his personal best on the battlefield, a soldier must be worry-free. I have never been worry-free, really. *If I were worry-free, I wouldn't be here now.*

We spend a few enchanting moments with my aunt, listening to her nicely designed lies. I offer mine in return. We part ways happy and fulfilled, feeling that we did "the right thing."

On my way back to the main office I learn that tonight we have an opera event. I learn that watching ballet or opera, especially before deployment, has been a tradition in my unit for a very long time.

My superiors think cultural events like opera are meant to build mission-like tension and help the soldiers attain real time alertness and readiness for action. Really? We crawl to the theater, overwhelmed by hunger, thirst and boredom. Tonight's show bears the signature of the Rear Admiral (ret.) Ignatius Mirage, who, after a glorious career in the military, discovered his true vocation: Fine Arts. He is also very original, introducing a new concept, the multi-ended opera, or opera-octopus. His works never have one ending, but at least three or four. Mirage wants the viewer to be involved in the creative process and to pick the best ending.

This one is a story about a warrior who is too old to fight. Although honorably discharged, he still wants to fight. But there is no battle to be fought. After singing alone and with other characters – fiancée, mother, other warriors – he chooses to die in dignity. The opera ends with him administering himself a vigorous seppuku. We all stand up, rhythmically clapping our hands, ready to leave when the second ending of the story strikes. It's a joke! The old warrior never intended to commit seppuku, but just to scare his fiancée. The third ending surprises us with a seasoned twist. The guy is actually dreaming of scaring his fiancée with the seppuku thing.

It is just a dream...yet when he wakes up, he immediately introduces the fourth ending, meant to deeply move the most sophisticated viewer, which is that he is actually schizophrenic and the entire show is a creation of his illness-ridden mind. There is also a fifth ending, for the most demanding military personnel – higher ranks. We watch with bulging eyes. I try to keep the powerful, convulsive emotions under control, while discreetly checking my vitals – pulse 50,000, respiration rate 50,000. The lights wander around only to freeze in the corner, where an old warrior watches TV. The audience learns that he himself is just a viewer, fueled by curiosity to learn more about what he is capable of. Wow!

We walk towards the exit thinking of the opera. We all line up in silence and we're administered a strong muscle relaxant. This opera was tense, like a mission! We all yearn for a real adventure, though. And here it is! We are ordered to report as soon as possible to the main office. Our unit will be deployed to the exotic island of Kuaku.

It is close to midnight when the boarding takes place. There is nothing but silence around us, except for the occasional interferences from the feline warriors, strategically taking their positions in virtually every bush and tree.

While up in the air, a strong vibration shatters the carrier. Yet we are highly trained not to allow panic to take over. We are informed that we should remain calm, since this is just a diplomatic misunderstanding. Apparently, someone forgot to get the clearance allowing us to fly over the neighboring countries. Consequently, they try to take us down. However, our pilots are well known for their skills, so we should fear nothing.

And we do not. After a bumpy landing we learn that the clearance has just been delivered to our headquarters. We are safe!

We land on the beautiful island, yet there is no time for fooling around. We are very excited and eager to learn more about the mysterious mission. We bite nails and claws and count minutes and seconds.

We want to see blood and we make no secret of our intentions.

As we stand there waiting for instructions, my cat hisses in my right ear. I cannot believe my right ear! No! Just like one of Ignatius Mirage's shows this is not a real mission, but just one of their dirty drills.

On our way back home we show our thirst for revenge. We sing, clap, and scratch the windows. They can put us in a cage as far as we are concerned, we do not care anymore.

I want blood! Is this why we have endured hunger and nasty push ups for so long? My cat approves. She, too, wants to see some of that red liquid. I suggest that we try to open some cans of food, as we systematically cut our fingers and paws while we desperately try to get to the precious content. This seems the only way we could see some blood.

On another note, I'm drained, mentally drained. I hate crawling, jumping, hanging in the trees like a monkey, rolling in mud and dirt.

I remember what my father used to tell me, when he was in his eighties. "My son, I might look like eighty on the outside, but I feel like a teenager on the inside." I feel exactly the same, just the opposite. My soul just turned eighty.

I'm summoned to report immediately to the main office. A stern officer – swollen nose, big hands, narrow shoulders – tells me that they decided to discharge me and my cat. Why? Why?

He tells me why. Our superiors think that my cat and I have poor self-esteem, poor morale and low expectations. To make it worse, we are very convincing, and we have a lot of followers. Other fellows started misbehaving as well.

I see. I'm told that we are a failure, yet a very popular one. I look at the officer in silence. As my heart beats faster and faster I feel the tiny stuffed chickadee against my chest. I take it out from under my shirt. I pull her legs while looking the officer in the eyes, smiling.

The little bird spreads her wings, delivering the powerful message, "Never underestimate your enemy."

The Healing Session at the
Small People's Society

I am sitting on the porch, enjoying a bitter coffee and listening to my cat's complaints. What is it this time? Apparently, last night I closed the door to the bedroom and she could not get in, sleep and leave hairballs on my pillow. Okay, I'm sorry. As we sit there arguing over last night's incident I hear a noise. I jump out of my comfy chair and run to the door. It is the newspaper delivery time! This gentleman always drops the newspaper with such noise that my cat and I automatically start the fire-earthquake-flood-evacuation drill.

Today he seems happily intoxicated. I haven't seen him in such a good mood in years. Why is he so joyous? He tells me that our neighbors who own the beautiful house next to mine are going through a painful divorce. While I express my deep compassion, my cat's reaction is shocking, to say the least. She welcomes the news with an evil grin. She wonders if we could buy their house for pennies. I have never seen this side of her personality and I want to understand her approach. Naturally, I invite the delivery guy to have some coffee with us.

I start shooting one question after another. Are they suicidal? Are their kids suffering a lot? Is he cheating on her? Is she cheating on him? Feed us with some information! My cat's new friend in hatred smiles. Happiness can and should be induced by other people's tragedy. While I watch him and the cat, I learn something disgusting about myself: I start liking it, too! I wish I could derive more pleasurable experiences of this kind, but how?

The delivery guy shows me an ad in the newspaper. While reading it, tears start falling down. I count them all. There are four tears of joy and two tears of anger. Joy, for I have finally discovered a possible venue to personal fulfillment. Anger, for I have never suspected myself of such negative emotions. The ad reads "Are you truly a small, mean and selfish person at heart? Is someone else's misfortune your significant source of joy? Does a tragedy make you smile? Join us and we will teach you how to control people's lives and bring true pleasure into yours! Join the Small People's Society today!"

The cat encourages me to pursue this right away. The floodgates have finally opened. How could I live until now in such a deep, self-perpetuating state of stagnation?

I see my unexpected guest out and I start dialing the number from the ad. Luckily, I can still register for the afternoon workshop. But they also warn me that if I'm not a true small person, I'd better stay home. My cat assures them that I am an aspiring devil and a swift predator on human kindness.

We spend the rest of the day practicing various "mean" faces in the mirror. She shows teeth. I do the same. She hisses at me. I respond in the same manner. She looks down on me. I look down on her. She hides in the corner pretending to be asleep, and then she takes me by surprise attacking my legs. I try to do the same, but I fell asleep following her movements instead.

Since I've not been blessed with sharp claws, I employ any available means. Knives, axes, discreet makeup. I try to bring my intellectual input to our enterprise and I purchase a book about famous criminals and their facial expressions. I read a few fragments to my feline partner in between making "mean" faces at the furniture.

Apparently, famous mean people have narrow foreheads and small eyes. Or, broad foreheads and big eyes. But never narrow foreheads and big eyes. Or pointy heads. Unless they're Ku Klux Klan. Wow, I've learned so much already!

I kiss the cat and rush to the meeting. I spend a lot of time trying to find the Society's headquarters. I'm expecting an imposing structure, but I'm surprised to discover that they share the building with the "Quilting Maidens" group. A gentleman – short hair, medium size nose, hefty chin – opens the door. He seems to be very nice. Is this the Small People's Society? Yes, it is. He lets me in and, as I am introduced to the others, I feel disappointment. These mean people look just like good people. No, I take that back. They look like very, very nice people. That's not fair! How am I supposed to tell them apart?

They ask about my qualifications. And what is the worst thing I have ever done to someone? I blush, embarrassed. I admit to some of my mean actions: secretly poisoning my neighbor's Chinese fish – they had big eyes; I didn't like their gaze – puncturing all the tires in my cousin's bride's car on their wedding day – tremendously enjoyed at seeing her cry; encouraging Cousin Vivo to sleep with my best friend's wife – gladly watched their triangle of love. Back then I thought that was bad, but now I see it's good. Jean Pierre Trique was right, you never know what you might use in your next resumé.

They all listen to my humble deeds with patience and agree that I am good material. But I need intensive training.

They are generous teachers. They will teach me how to be really cruel, pushing people to suicide by skillfully maneuvering them as I see fit; or turning people against each other by seeding pure, unrefined hatred and joyously watching it grow.

Will I be limited in my actions? Of course not. Their logo is "Mean by all means." Cool, I cannot wait. When can I start being mean? Right now. Do I have to wear any distinctive clothes? Not at all. On the contrary, a really small and low person tries his hardest to resemble a noble human being. My cat never hides her true nature. Maybe that is why she is an animal while we are superior human beings.

As I start training, a new territory reveals its beauty to me. Before I met these wise, experienced devils, I was dormant like a larva. Just being around them makes *being mean* effortless. I feel like I swallowed a rattlesnake which fuels me with venom on a constant basis. I knew *mean*, but these people are so treacherous I didn't even know such people existed!

I still have mixed feelings about this adventure. The cat says that I think too much and I should just have fun.

A week or so into training with the cat I hiss and spit most of the time. I also have a tendency to catch and kill anything around me, from flies to rats and other small mammals. I play with the flies before I smash them, although the feline trainer insists that actually *they* play with me.

Where is this destructive aggression coming from? I do not know. I realize in awe that my thoughts have become so evil that I'm afraid someone might actually hear them. That is why I protect my thoughts from being read by occasional mind readers by coating them with other thoughts. For example, I think about measles, but I coat this thought with dots. I do not talk to anyone. Make sense? And I never draw anything. A naive, apparently insignificant drawing might give me away. I know I have a tendency to play with my pencil on the paper and sketch herrings. For the experienced eye, this is a lot of information. It tells a story about sea, fishermen and drowning.

At the Society, I'm slowly introduced to the fundamentals of how to lie, be deceptive and treacherous. I'm a dedicated student. I make notes, both mental and written. I write down every punctuation, cough, and gesture. I want that saved, for I see a hidden meaning in every posture, every whim.

Finally, I'm informed that we are getting closer to the testing day. Testing? I cannot sleep anymore. I'm scared and excited at the same time. The D-Day is close. I will be shown a "target," that is a miserable human being, and instructed what I have to achieve. *How* I will do it –

that's up to me. But I'd better be good at it; otherwise I will never become a member of this selected Society.

My "target" is a guy who teaches Fine Arts at the local college. My mission is to make him lose everything that truly matters in his life.

What makes him a target? I hear that he is a strong, balanced, self-sufficient being. The Society does not like such specimens and for a good reason. Does the tiger like a healthy strong deer? No, he prefers a limping one.

The guy is also good looking, which fuels my desire to destroy him. Oh, I wish I could tell him "Congratulations! You have been selected to participate in a very classy and cruel experiment! All you have to do is *be yourself*, I will take care of the rest, ha ha ha!" But I have to control my pleasures. Discretion is what makes those people so powerful. Yes, true predators are discreet.

I must find out the weaknesses of this man. Observation is a key factor. I sleep well, drink plenty of fluids and exercise a lot, in order to keep my mind free of unwanted thoughts and focus mainly on the mission.

My mission is not easy. If I were a woman, it would be easy to control him. All I would have to do is become his girlfriend and deny him sex. But being a guy makes it tougher. Sadly, he is not gay. Will I give up? Fuck, no! I feel proud of myself.

I start gathering information about this teacher. Does he have a family? A girlfriend? A beloved pet? None of the above, really. Sometimes he talks on the phone with his mother. I have to find something, give me something! Perhaps he has a hobby of some sort I could work on. Yes he does! He likes to watch the news. That's an easy one. All I have to do is basically cut his cable off. Which I did. Next!

After enjoying watching him nervous and puzzled at the cable "accident," I follow up when the night falls. I destroy a little bench he built for his garden, poison his roses, misplace his gardening tools.

However, I do not see him desperately pulling his hair yet. For example, yesterday he talked with his mother and he didn't even *mention* the events.

Since my actions are not taken seriously, I decide it's time to move to more meaningful acts. This guy must lose his job! I arrange to send a fake filthy email to his boss. My cat attaches dirty photos of "him" surrounded by some cheap underage prostitutes. The header reads "Should we trust these people with teaching our children the difference between *right* and *wrong*?"

The strategy works. I watch him the following day being literally kicked out of the school. I sit down on the bench in front of the school and eat ice cream – vanilla, strawberries, whipped cream. As he passes me with a sad expression on his face a powerful orgasm shatters my being like an electric shock. I smile at him while picking a hefty strawberry. "Good morning, teacher! How's it going?"

I spend the rest of the day monitoring his house in silence and making plans. As I watch him mowing the lawn it strikes me that it would be nice if he lost the house, too.

Kicking someone out of their home could and should be my signature mission. But how should I proceed? After losing his job, the bastard took a modest job at the local library and he never misses his payments. But what if the community expelled him? I am all about action, so I get a small printer and I print out hundreds of ads reading "A child molester lives among us. Are we truly a clean community?" and depicting "him," again with the underage prostitutes. All I have to do is sit and wait. Not too long, though. I remember what they taught me at the Society. There is one good thing about people, they never question anything. Just feed them and they will do the rest. The hatred I spark in the neighborhood makes my days enjoyable. I stand across his house and I watch him packing his stuff. Where will he go? I am dying to learn more about his plans.

At night I dream sweet dreams in which I'm playing with his life just like my cat plays with the half-dead mice around the house for hours.

But when I wake up, I'm forced to face harsh reality. I do not see him manifesting his anger or sadness. He seems pretty calm for someone in such a situation. What the fuck! I need to find out *why*.

I spend my meaningless life hoping to become a star and monitoring him. Opening his mail. Listening to his conversations. Following him step by step. At night I crawl in the bushes behind his house to observe, make notes, monitor – my cat joins the fight perched on my back. I sometimes pop out of the bushes, allowing the feline periscope to get an accurate visual. Yes, we are that resourceful! What does Sun Tzu in his *Art of War* say? *Be extremely subtle, even to the point of formlessness.*

The target's house is sunken in darkness. Yet Aunt Lyla's words of wisdom – *All the darkness in this world cannot put out a single candle* – give me strength and faith. I picture my being as a tiny stubborn candle, hard to put out, boldly crawling in the darkness…

Bold or not, I am desperate! I have tried everything with no success, except for some minor perennial suffering.

The cheerleader cat is tired of missing her favorite nighttime TV shows. She suggests a nasty letter, *accidentally* dropped in his backyard. We pour out venom, pure, crystal clear venom. "You lost everything. You have to learn your lesson, miserable creature. When you lose, you lose, that's it. Ha!"

I drop the letter off and then indulge in an almost endless, deep and rewarding sleep. Early in the morning I sneak behind the house. I see him happily greeting the new day with a smile while watering the roses. My heart sinks.

I want to go home, lock myself in the house and scream like a beast. Yet I lay down there in the bushes, motionless, soundless, and hoping for a miracle.

I suddenly feel something underneath my right thigh. It's a small envelope. I open it and I cannot believe my eyes. The bastard actually replied to my letter. I read through my tears. "I have lost nothing, for I have never owned anything. You cannot take away from me what I do not possess. All we can really have is merely an image of the material things we once loved. I will save mine. No one can take that away from me. I appreciate your efforts, but you are just another *small* being. Have a great day!"

Have a great day? Have a great day? Miserable caterpillar! I tear the letter into small pieces then I burn it down to ashes and bury them in my backyard, in a ritual of peaceful, calm and controlled hatred.

But his words keep bouncing off the walls of my brain, giving me terrible, insurmountable pain. I close my eyes and try to bring back the images of the things I once loved. All I see is a void.

I enjoy a depressed walk to the Society. I get a cold handshake. A voice informs me that I failed. I cannot be a part of the Small People's Society. In a desperate attempt I show them the letter from the "target." They cannot do this to me *now*, when my target called me *small* and I myself started feeling *small*.

They don't see it that way. My target is a winner. Had he committed suicide, had he hurt other people, had he changed his true nature, then yes, that would have been a victory.

I feel smashed. I feel the heaviness of the entire world on my shoulders. On my way back home it occurs to me that I haven't tried to hang myself in a very long time. As soon as I get home I pick my favorite rope – off-white and crimson red. I also pick the favorite spot, right where the chandelier is. My cat tells me that she loves to make pit stops on the chandelier, just like that, for the view.

That's the spot where I want to fly and dance in the air; just like that, for the view.

All I need is a strong hook. A frantic search for the right hook begins. I have to give up. I don't have one strong enough, but I can improvise. My cat is instructed to go and deliver deep meows at the neighbor's door, should my attempts become ridiculous. I start putting everything together, while whistling a happy song I used to sing with Agatha back in high school.

Oh, no! There is someone at the door. My cat and I crawl on all fours and peek under the door. We see Aunt Lyla's slippers. I definitely cannot hang myself *now* and greet beloved Aunt Lyla with my tongue sticking out of my mouth. That would be very, very disrespectful!

Aunt Lyla greets me and asks me what I am up to. *What I am up to? Dancing. Same old dance.*

Aunt Lyla needs an aspirin. She has a terrible headache and it's been like this for days now. I offer my beloved aunt two glossy, beautiful aspirins.

She also asks me who are the people? What people? The people hiding in the bushes behind my house.

I send the cat out on recon while I start putting the rope back in the black velvet box. It will stay there for a while.

We are not winners, but we are not losers either.

The Healing Session with the Tribe of Cannibals

A friend calls me, disrupting the harmony of my early morning snooze.

He wants to get together and merge our individual depressions into a greater one. While I would love to do that, my cat reminds me about the appointment with the Persian herbalist. I ask my friend if we can unite our depressions tomorrow afternoon instead. My friend says yes.

I brush my cat's coat, put on some clothes and here we are, curious and excited to meet the well-known Persian healer. The Persian herbalist – big belly, long toes, basil-like scent – looks at us with amazement and amusement. Of course he has the cure meant to slow down the aging process and keep us in great shape! All we have to do is stick with the vegetarian diet prescribed by our doctor, and sprinkle the food with the secret herb called "Everlasting Life." He brings a small jar. My cat protests, since she's afraid she will lose her feline skills if she keeps eating vegetables. I have no skills to lose. What do I care? She sniffs the lid and passes out in the sweet, unusual scent of the mysterious Persian herb. I pick her up and apologize for the incident. The Persian herbalist smiles. He brings some pine tree extract, which is meant to have exactly the opposite effect. Indeed, my cat is back to life in no time, with her tail standing up like a pine tree. The herbalist wishes us everlasting life and hopes that we will return to him for more advice and herbs.

We get home and I try to explain to my cat the advantages of the magic "Everlasting Life" herb. My cat suggests that we should also take into consideration the quality, not only the duration. Who would want to live a *boring*, vegetable-like life? I've noticed that whenever she says "vegetable" she frowns and her whiskers point at me in a very vengeful demeanor.

I change the subject. Let us watch the news while eating dinner instead. I fix some steamed veggies and sprinkle them with the Persian herb. Tonight the news is truly exciting! We learn that somewhere, on a remote island, a team of researchers has just bumped into an ancient Tribe of Cannibals. We watch the short, intense documentary motionless, carrots glued to our teeth and tongues. Apparently, this Tribe is thriving. The researchers are stunned at the overall health these Cannibals enjoy. The lifespan is stunning as well. My cat and I agree that we haven't seen such handsome, proportional people in a very long time. What is their secret?

We look at each other. Then we look at the veggies. A quick assessment of our big bellies follows. We pick up the plates and toss them away. I know what has happened. She knows it, too. Watching this short documentary about the most primitive people on the planet forced us to review our opinions about society, rules and individuals. And while we know we enjoy one of the most advanced states of civilization, we feel we might get some answers from these flesh-eating folks.

We both endure a sleepless night thinking of a new adventure. I call my travel agent first thing in the morning. By noon we have the tickets. We are going to meet the Cannibals!

We are already boarded and very happy. As usual, my cat finds something to complain about. How come that we didn't get first class tickets? I know, I know, it was short notice; what can I say? Yet the perspective of traveling with poor, average people fills us with fear and concern. I explain to my feline friend that sometimes we have to sacrifice the comfort for a greater, noble cause. She survives the long, horrible trip during which all the children on the plane want to play with her.

As I expected, as soon as we land, the cat reminds me to call Professor Funfbackstumpfl, a well-known psychiatrist who specializes in treating the so common "Traveling with Poor People Syndrome."

We look for a cab. The cab driver tells us that the Cannibals do not live close to the airport, but far away, hiding in the deep forests covering the wild, unpopulated area of this oasis of civilization.

The driver agrees to take us close to the edge of the forest, but not farther. No problem. My cat and I agree to walk a few miles. Who would be picky under such circumstances? We are close to experiencing an amazing encounter! We keep walking, oblivious to our surroundings. We are haunted by unanswered questions like, "Do they wear a bone in their noses?" "Do they eat their meat raw or do they cook it?" and "Is a pregnant woman a more desirable meal?" We decide to stop reminding each other what we *do not know*. We shall learn soon; that is why we are here in the first place.

I do not realize my cat is no longer walking in front of me until I see a familiar face popping out of the bushes. It takes me a few seconds to realize that this might be one of the Cannibals. His eyes express extreme aggression and he waves a cat at me. I do not like to see my friend treated like this. I approach him with caution and I would like to say something when it dawns on me that he might not understand me.

Surprise! He does understand English. A short, nice conversation and I learn he actually took his Master's in Social Sciences at Harvard a few years ago, as an exchange student. World has become a small village indeed. How come he chose to return to his people? Wasn't he attracted to our perfect society, based on respect and other moral values?

He explains. While we see him and his people as being primitive, the Cannibals are convinced that we are the most ruthless vegetarians on the planet. He ended up being torn apart between two worlds, both equally wild and fascinating. He tried to stick with the so called "civilization." He almost got married and settled down, in spite of his parents' concerns.

Yet, his fiancée soon started displaying hysterical behavior when missing important sales at the most popular designers' stores; he *knew* that civilized women were not for him. He seasoned her with sauce remoulade and vegetables and had her for dinner. Then he packed his stuff and boarded the first flight to freedom. Since I made friends with him, I have to ask him *the question:* Am I in danger of becoming their meal? He smiles, showing impeccable white teeth – Oh, my God! White teeth without the latest tooth whitening technologies? He assures me that I am in no danger. Cannibals do not eat civilized people since the food we eat is so packed with chemicals that our flesh has a bad taste. Besides, they are at high risk to develop our diseases. As a matter of fact, when he returned from Harvard, he had to undergo a strict detoxification program – his fiancée was a big fan of fat foods.

The young, charming man agrees to take me to his father, the Chief of the Cannibals.

As any other enlightened individual, the Chief – small bone in the nose, crappy hair, imposing machete – doesn't waste time with pointless observations. He espouses in a few sentences the fundamentals of their society. The old, the sick and the helpless need to go. This is the law of nature. I'm extremely enchanted to discover that our society follows basically the same rules. We have not lost our deep connection with nature, as those silly environmentalists pretend. I have a question, though. Aren't they afraid that by eating human flesh they will pass the diseases on? The Chief looks at me with contempt. He pulls out an advanced medical book about viruses, bacterial infections and cross-contamination. It is a precious gift from a English doctor who had studied them years ago, hoping to bring them back to civilization. Can I talk to the doctor? The Chief points at the jars on shelves behind us. Not unless I can communicate with the preserves his great grandmother prepared from the Doctor's flesh, in case the tribe were to face harsh times, like last year's, when everyone enjoyed extreme health. I'm disgusted and outraged.

I make my civilized point right away. How can one eat his own people? The Chief gives me a bitter, distorted smile. He explains that in his view, we are ruthless, soulless and heartless creatures. We do not eat bodies, we devour minds and souls.

We do not let our peers die according to the laws of nature; yet we derive a lot of pleasure from not allowing them to enjoy their lives.

Being ostracized in our civilized society is worse than being eaten alive. He sounds convincing. May I pierce my nose and wear a little bone out of respect? Of course. As a matter of fact, their fascinating culture has always been a source of inspiration for the civilized fashion designers. Every body is pierced at least a couple of times nowadays; one can see pierced noses, tongues, and piercings in those places we are not allowed to show in public! How come fashion is *the only thing* we learned from them?

The Chief wants to know if we would like to join them for dinner. While my mind is busy trying to find a decent excuse my cat delivers a double meow – a sign of approval. I always forget she's a carnivore. I crawl to the dinner table with the excitement of someone on death row, waiting to be given the lethal injection. I do not want to eat human flesh! My eyes scan the dinner table. I'm looking for familiar anatomical parts like eyes, ears and such. I suddenly spot something resembling fingers. I feel sick already. They're fingers and they're green! I ask the Chief how they prepare the fingers and why they're green. He smiles. These are not fingers. They're tiny pickled cucumbers, a well-appreciated Bulgarian import.

The Cannibals respect their guests, so they decided not to serve the delicious teenager thigh stew tonight.

My relief must be obvious for the Chief looks at me with understanding. He sees me out in silence. Before we part ways he shakes my hand and delivers one more piece of cannibalistic wisdom, "Things are not what they appear to be."

The Healing Session in Boredom

I pick up the fairy tale book. The cat jumps into my lap. It's fairy tale time! Our reading sessions have roots in ancient times, when she was a kitten and I started reading her bedtime fairy tales to help her cope with baby cat colic. In time, this became a routine and we both saw it was a good one. Today's fairy tale is *The Happy Prince* by Oscar Wilde. By the time I finish my reading, we're both in tears, contemplating various activities meant to help us improve ourselves and become better beings. However, our desire to change our inner selves vanishes instantly as I open the refrigerator. Here we are, standing in front of the magic, big food box, like two ruthless predators, ready to make their move. After a few moments of indecision, I make mine. I snatch the chicken. My cat snatches the tuna salad. I also need bread. She wants some ham. I, too, consider a couple of slices of ham. I'm faster than her and I get my hands on the ham. I hide in the master bedroom, holding the ham tight, with passion, as if the piece of meat was my mistress. But where is my cat? I look for her everywhere. Nothing. Finally, I realize that the ham is somewhat heavier than it should be. I look *under* the ham. She's right there, glued to the ham, holding her breath, with all her claws penetrating deeply into the piece of meat. Shaking the ham brings no improvement. A few selected lines from *The Happy Prince* and she finally lets go of the ham. We eat in silence, avoiding eye contact. We're *small* and we know it.

I have to run; I'm late for my Collective Breathing Classes. I cannot wait to become a part of this simultaneously inhaling and exhaling group of twenty people. I manage to catch most of the green lights on the way there, yet one tricky red forces me to come both to a sudden stop and a conclusion. I'm in such a hurry lately and no matter what I do, I'm always late. My life is fast and impossible to keep up with.

I think of my childhood friend, Phineas Schwartz, who was never late. On the contrary, he was so obsessed with being late for work, that he started getting there ten minutes early. Soon, he would go there twenty-nine minutes early and before he knew it, he was parking his car in front of the office an hour before they opened. In time, the "safety" time buffer grew to two hours, and before he retired he was known for getting there the night before, sleeping in the car, just to be on the safe side. Why can't I be like him? Okay, maybe I'm not willing to sacrifice my family life – my cat likes the comfort of our king size bed – and get to the meetings the night before. But just not being late anymore would be a step forward.

I get to the Collective Breathing place and exhale, relaxed. The instructor gives me a nasty look. I learn that my timing is bad. I ostentatiously exhaled just when everybody else was *inhaling*. I apologize, but it is obvious that I do not fit in this marvelous group of high standards. It's not the first time that I find myself on a collision course with members of our society. Never mind. I look at my planner and there's still a few interesting meetings in the area. I decide to go home and have a quick conversation with my cat. On my door knob, there's a flier. I read it with interest, since every little message of this kind helps me take the pulse of the greater family I belong to. This one is an announcement for an upcoming meeting of the extremist religious group "White ... *powder*." I immediately call my cat. She admits to have scratched a "d" in the group's name, on her way to the bushy restroom. She just couldn't help it. She points at her coat. She's black. Now, how offensive that is, to hang such announcements on a door behind which lives a black cat? I assure her that I totally understand her approach. I know she's black, but does she realize that a single letter can change the meaning in the social, political and religious message? Where is her social awareness? How can I trust her when she's the one who actually distorts the oh-already-so-distorted messages? She promises not to do that anymore, in return for five albacore tuna snacks.

We sit down and go over the most appealing social gatherings in our area. We both agree that there are at least two that sparked our interest. One is a meeting about the upcoming citizen's vote regarding the type of grass our city should predominantly cultivate. The other one is a strong lecture about social empowerment. We would love to taste a little bit of both!

I pick up my cat and walk boldly to the first meeting – a small hall packed with people of all colors and social statuses who generate a lot of noise. The noise grows stronger and stronger as nobody really understands the purpose of the meeting. Finally, a bald representative from the City Hall brings two big boards. One of them reads "Vote YES for rye grass," listing under all the pro's – low maintenance, beauty, softness that demands immediate contact with bare feet. The other one reads "Vote NO for Bermuda grass" – speedy growth, highly durable. I admit I don't understand why one of the boards promotes a YES while another one is about NO. My cat says it's not fair. She thinks saying "Yes" for one thing implies somehow rejecting the other options. Maybe she's right, what do I know? We watch the people around us screaming at each other. We do not approve of such manifestations. Yet, we feel compassion for the human frailty. They will have to vote soon and they do not understand the messages they get from the organizers of this meeting. We watch the situation getting tense with interest.

Three hours into the meeting and nobody knows what they're here for. We smile. Unlike them, we do know why we are here. We are here to watch. I look at the people around us. It's like a country that can barely fit into the room. What if I declare this bunch of people *my* country? I could be a dictator and what a cool little country that would be! I smile at my stupid thoughts. Maybe I should get some sleep?

Back to the grass thing. Someone taps me on the shoulder. It's Rafaello Mariani, an eccentric sculptor and relatively good friend of mine. I consider him a "relatively good" friend, because of his unusual behavior. He seems to be the master of odd announcements. This time he announces to me that he just got into a car accident. One might say, so what, you're still breathing. Not Rafaello, though. He assures me it's just a minor bumper to bumper incident, yet his car will have to be fixed, and he won't drive it for a while. Instead, he might be spotted in a green car – his father's, or a blue car – his girlfriend's. Why is he giving me all those details? He seems surprised. Why? He thinks it's obvious. He does not want me to panic at the sight of him driving an unexpected model and make. I respectfully thank him for his social awareness and I assure him that I will not panic at the sight of him driving a car other than his own.

He wants to show us his latest masterpieces and he invites us to his creative studio. I'm afraid to go there! His works always compel me to ask about the completion date. "But, they're finished," smiles my relatively good friend. Then he starts telling me the history of each stone he's ever carved, always bringing up the piece carved ten years ago when he was in New York, trying to buy a house. Just seconds before buying the house a deep anxiety overwhelmed his being. He rented a small apartment instead and carved the piece we all know as *Fear of Commitment*. I let him know I cannot visit him today, since my cat and I are very involved in the community and we want to see the outcome of this fruitful gathering. But we will visit him soon.

We shake hands happy and content. Sadly, I cannot promote him to the "good friends" category, although my cat insists that most people we interact with also consider us to be real freaks, except perhaps for Aunt Lyla.

We step off the grass and move on to the next exciting experience: the debate on social empowerment. We are definitely into such unplanned, life-changing events. After all, one goes to the grocery store to get cabbage and ends up falling deeply in love with someone, or at least answering powerful questions on the meaning of life. Or both. We walk to the conference place scanning people's faces. The faces are not interesting today.

We join an impressive mass of a hundred-something people, who are listening to the words of wisdom of some elevated researcher. We sit down and immerse our minds in sophisticated concepts we will never understand. I soon learn that such things as the mind-body connection truly exist. The audience is drowning in boredom and yes, there are inherent visible physical manifestations of the inner pain. The researcher's voice is monotonous; the topic is boring.

I look at the guy sitting next to me. He is experiencing ruthless abdominal cramps induced by the boredom. We admire the physical pain that embraced the half-asleep audience. People are almost screaming a mute scream; eyes are crossed, and faces are distorted by inexplicable, never-ending suffering. We do not want to become small prey, so we look discreetly for the exit signs.

The doors are locked! The organizers had locked us in. That's why all these people are so desperate. I look at my cat. Be strong, sister! We have to last until this symphony of boredom ends. One more hour. We are so pissed that we almost fail to notice when it's over. Shame on us!

I jump out of the chair, holding the cat over my head to prevent her from getting injured in this impressive Exodus of bored entities. The masses are moving faster and faster, roaring. One or two unhappy creatures who fell asleep during the ordeal, wake up screaming, thinking that their nightmare is still on. On our way out, I hear someone saying that the conference room is equipped with automatic doors and the organizers have been known for trapping innocent people in by just pushing a button.

We get out of there, shaking. We cannot believe we are free. I tuck my cat under my arm and minutes later we both crash in the comfy chairs of the cafe "Le Mimose." I am about to feel relief when suddenly, I notice the Boredom sitting at our table. She must have followed us! She is there, ugly, bitchy, staring at me with mean eyes. Luckily, the coffee shop fills with colorful people.

I call the waiter and learn that they're members of the selected creative group named "Thunder." Just like the thunder strikes, announcing powerful weather changes, so they strike with astonishing creative ideas. Wow! Can we pull our chairs a little bit closer? They allow us. We want to know where their "thunders" come from.

They explain. Each of their sessions has a theme around which they work. At the beginning of the meeting, the organizer – I am shown a guy chewing gum nervously – announces the theme. Then, the creative process begins. Next thing they know, they all go home thunder-stricken. Today's theme is "birthday." Each participant has to compose a short one-hundred-word essay about birthdays and – do I have to say it again? – bringing in the thunder. May we participate?

We're not invasive; we're just trying to kill the Boredom. They tend to be selective and turn us down, but when I show them my Boredom's repulsive face, they all display their profound empathy by delivering a mass "Whew!" The waiters step back and we all start thinking. I think thinking makes me burn extra calories but I'm somewhat embarrassed to disrupt the creative process by ordering food.

Unusual thoughts start flowing in, like, for example, when I invited the hairstylist and the postman to my birthday party in spite of everyone else's protests. Even Aunt Lyla was visibly worried by my decision. Don't I have friends? Why would one celebrate his birthday with someone he barely knew? I'll tell you why, to get to know them better. Why do we have to invite the same old faces we've known for years, over and over again, instead of expanding the horizons of friendship? Besides, I consider the hairstylist to be one of the closest friends ever. How many of our good friends get to touch our hair, really?

I stand up thunder-stricken. I know the answer. I will show my social awareness by organizing a party. I will invite all the people I never get to know, like the butcher, the gardener, the real estate agent, the clown I hired last year for my cat's birthday and many others. On this occasion I will find out what their thoughts on the rye grass are.

I look for Boredom. She moved to another table.

The Healing Session in Time

I pull out a piece of paper from my cat's mouth. Is she depressed and eating paper again? Not at all. She was trying to show me a flier advertising glorious retirement plans. The paper consists of two sections. Section one depicts a sad, poor and sick eighty-something gentleman, still in the work field. Section two shows us a wealthy, cheerful old entity, which did not miss the amazing opportunity of choosing the right retirement plan.

I want to sign up right away but my cat looks at me amazed. We do not believe in *Future*. Our perception of Time includes only *Past* and *Present*. We have to have some awareness of Time, so we recognize the *Past*. But *Present* is the most dynamic and intense dimension we enjoy. We both agree on that one, yet none of us can understand our innate ability to feel the *Present* and totally exclude the *Future* from our plans. I need an answer.

I call Aunt Lyla. Does this Time perception have anything to do with our heritage and the way our ancestors viewed the flow of Time? Aunt Lyla says yes. She confirms what my cat and I know already: for us there is no *Future*. Just a very tormented *Past* and *Present*. *Present* must be exploited at maximum, for tomorrow might bring another war, dictatorship, some sort of crap we cannot escape. Once again, we might lose all we've worked so hard for. We always lose. Everything we build vanishes right under our eyes; it's almost like a curse. I look at my cat. Aunt Lyla is right.

Maybe that's why our emotions are so strong. It's obvious that we both take *Present* very seriously. This might also explain why most people seem lifeless to me. I sometimes feel an urge to take their pulse to see if they're still alive. It took me many years to understand *why*. Because those people have nerve and they actually believe in *Future*. They plan every little thing in detail, like retirement plans, various activities. They look for ways to enjoy the golden age. Hahahahahaha…we never think of such things because none of us expects to hit the retirement really.

That's why we hate people who waste our Time and lie to us. Those worms take away from us the only thing we have left: the *Present*. They can afford it, because they believe in *Future*. Boring and miserable, but it's there. For us, everything happens NOW. However, one cannot build a solid *Future* without having the awareness of the *Past* and the *Present*. It appears to me that we have the elements but we are unable to understand them and use them in our favor.

I politely thank my aunt for the steep insight into our collective being. We might have something! My cat stops sucking her right paw and asks a simple feline question, "What if, God forbid, the *Present* becomes unbearable? Where do we find escape?"

I tell her that when this happens, we will go to bed and dream endless dreams, like three years ago when we both went to sleep because we could not handle our failures anymore. My cat is annoyed at the shallowness of my answer. Don't I see the people around us? Thinking and hoping for a better, prosperous *Future* helps them to handle the hideous *Present*. What do *we* have? What are our tools? We are hopeless! On my way to the kitchen, I drop the paper towel, unable to listen to the feline verdict and coordinate my movements at the same time. I stand in the living room, staring at the cat's fluffy tail with empty eyes.

How could I miss this one? I had the opportunity to learn more about this during my healing session at the detention center, when I met Panda Bear, the specialist in Time Management. Yet I failed.

We need to do something about it right now! I don't hesitate to call my friend Anatol Broom, a specialist in Time. His family is originally from the same part of the world as mine, so he must have some answers for me.

We meet Anatol at his place, a little charming house with no windows. Why no windows? Anatol is tired of seeing the world, so he decided to prevent himself from watching the misery of other people. His house might be dark, but it is filled with music, played by the traditional wedding and funeral orchestras. I ask Anatol why those orchestras are so big and have so many instruments. I find paying attention to each instrument extremely distractive. Anatol smiles. In the old world everybody has something to say. A song is basically a conversation. How can we refuse someone the right of expressing themselves? The violin has a story to tell and so does the drum. But can we say no to the joyous trumpets? We are a welcoming society, so we listen to everybody and give each entity their share of Time.

Speaking of which…I tell him upfront why I'm there. I ask him how does he feel the Time? Is he passionate, does he suffer at the sight and touch of *Past, Present, Future*? Anatol sighs. He knows what I'm looking for. He hates to speak about himself but this time he will make an exception and give me his own example.

He tries to use simple words, as we have known each other for some time now and he is familiar with our inability to process sophisticated concepts. When he married his current wife he was devoured by passion for her. I understand. We both seem to have a problem with handling passions. Passions and Time. So, he is deeply in love with this woman. He feels insecure, fearing some catastrophic event will end their love story. What does he do about it? Nothing. Year after year he lives in fear, unable to cherish their life together. One night, while he was searching the house, desperately trying to find her – she went to the restroom – he has this revelation. He understands that finding Peace is just a matter of Time. He will have to wait until they grow old and only then fully enjoy her and stop fearing that he will be abandoned. And here he is, tens of years later, happy and content. Is he afraid that she might get tempted by other males and cheat on him? Heck, no! Is he afraid that one day she will pack her things and move back to her mom? Not at all. As a matter of fact they just bought themselves very nice burial plots at the local cemetery. This way they will be close to each other even in death. After that, the flow of Time ceases.

He knows that no matter who leaves this world first, the other one will have to unconditionally follow.

Our session is interrupted by the wife herself, bringing in coffee and homemade preserves. I look at the tiny, wrinkled creature. Anatol is right! How can one feel insecure around her? I envy him for his wisdom, patience and true happiness.

Now, how powerful is that! My cat sobs quietly while I impulsively swallow huge amounts of cherry preserves.

We leave Anatol's house making small, well-measured steps. We want to show deep gratitude to the Fate, for whenever we needed advice we have been blessed with the wisdom of our friends.

Once in the street we allow ourselves to be carried away on a brisk, joyous walk. "Listen, the cuckoos are singing!" says my cat. We buy flowers and we knock at Aunt Lyla's door with big smiles on our faces. Aunt Lyla doesn't smile. "Are we insane?" We shrug. "Since when is a genuine smile a sign of insanity?" Aunt Lyla explains.

Normally, a smile is nice, but right now the country is in recession. How can one genuinely smile in Time of desperation? I stare at her in disbelief. When did this happen? Aunt Lyla says that all started two months ago. Two months ago? How come we've never heard of it? Aunt Lyla is stunned. But we haven't seen each other in two months. Last time she spoke to me, I was getting ready to visit my friend, Anatol, but she hadn't heard from me until now. I cannot believe we spent two months with Anatol, although coming from him, that wouldn't be surprising – he is highly trained in distorting the Time. But, back to the recession.

Aunt Lyla gives me a short orientation tour along with a loaf of bread. I politely refuse the bread; my cat and I are on a new diet. My aunt is surprised, the bread is rationed and every citizen gets a loaf every other day. How can I refuse such an amazing gift? Hearing Aunt Lyla's introduction to poverty my cat snatches the bread and starts eating it right away. Really? I, too, swallow huge pieces while Aunt Lyla explains how and where we can find food. If we find money, of course. If we can find money? What happened to our investment funds that promised hefty returns? What funds? Everybody lost everything, there are no funds. How come? Where are the retirement fliers, showing us happy old people who chose the right fund?

Aunt Lyla mentions Cousin Mendi, who lost his lifetime savings and retirement funds overnight. But Cousin Mendi is not a rookie. He got a second job, and immediately starting contributing to a new retirement fund. His reasons might appear strange for the average citizen, yet make perfect sense to me. Mendi knew he was going to lose again. Yet in good old tradition he wanted to lose even more, to feel complete in his losses. He craved to be an accomplished loser. I agree. Even in failure, completeness is more important than anything else. The truth is, we all might end up working like slaves until we die. I tell my aunt that we still have our properties. She sighs. Their value is so low now that we can probably get twenty loaves of bread for them. Creative and resourceful as we are, we think of other ways out. My cat suggests selling some of our designer clothes and jewelry. I learn that nobody is interested in buying anything but food. And when they need clothes they just break into the stores and steal them. People are really poor. Actually, Aunt Lyla spotted a few gentlemen wearing designer's clothes, waiting in the queue to collect their unemployment benefits.

We thank my aunt for the update on the new and exciting life experience and we rush back home. We need some bread so we'd better go and get it. I put on my favorite mouton jacket and the fancy hat with the pheasant feathers. My cat wears five red ribbons on her tail. We might be poor, but we have class!

We stand in a long queue, consisting of at least two-hundred hungry and pissed people. This gives us the opportunity to analyze the grim situation. Maybe we should get a job? Why would we? We do not believe in *Future*. We shouldn't be afraid of something we do not believe in.

My cat suggests going back to Anatol's place and spending there those few days of recession. Loaves in hands and paws, we go back home again. I try to reach my friend, but he doesn't answer his phone. We run to his place but the house is no longer there. I ask a neighbor and he tells me that they moved. Does he have the new address? Of course. We spend the whole day looking for Anatol's new place only to end up at the cemetery. Here he is little scoundrel, hiding from the earthly, painful survival drill. We sit in silence by his grave.

We envy him for quitting just in Time. He didn't lower his standards. He and his wife live in the same small house with no windows, far from humans and their misery. We cannot hear any music, yet I bet they indulge in some fine sophisticated tunes down there. How happy he must be! We are not. We wave goodbye to Anatol and his wife and we swim back to our recession.

In the street we cannot help noticing people eating hot dogs. Hot dogs? Are they rationed, like bread? They must be; they smell so nice. My cat plans to steal one – recession habits – but I stop her. Let's learn more first. She picks up the scent and takes me to the hot dog source. It's a small stand and the man behind the counter seems friendly. I ask him how come he can sell hot dogs in time of recession and poverty. What recession? This was years ago. Now we are all wealthy and happy again! He is right! I look around and I see the same irresponsible happy people from the *Past*. Oh, we are indeed back to our normal life. I knew there was no *Future*, just *Past* and *Present*. What a relief to be aware of such deep knowledge while millions of people still believe in a better or at least different *Future*.

I know there will be no retirement fund. I have no intention of putting money aside. The only thing I save and put aside is madness.

Anatol and I have one thing in common: we like the anxiety that builds up before pleasure, we like the anticipation. Time is irrelevant. I never get mad on the spot, but instead save the madness for later and indulge in delaying the catharsis. There is no doubt about it, I will explode soon. And I would love to take my Time. Basically, I plan to regularly deposit madness into my retirement fund. And when the Time comes, I will gloriously become mad at myself, my cat and all of mankind.

The Healing Session with French Film Critic Setupp

I get out in my backyard to enjoy my weeds. Some people take great pride in homeownership. I do not. That's why I rarely pull out the weeds and clean my yard. Why would I waste time doing that instead of searching for healing? An ad, accidentally brought by the warm autumn wind, lands at my feet. I pick it up. It is a glittering advertisement, promoting the movies now playing at the neighborhood theater. I remember my grandpa's stories about people picking up fliers in the streets and joining the Communist resistance. That's how he ended up fighting "The Enemy." He thought it was a good cause. Then, they nationalized his house. They even confiscated his toothpaste! Then, he changed his mind. After reading another flier, he joined the Anticommunist resistance. While spending ten years in Siberia and building those cute little cabins – resorts for the working masses – he changed his mind again. He passed away at the tender age of sixty-two, hoping that one day his children would pick up another flier and keep the fight for some good cause going. I think picking up fliers and getting extremely excited runs in my family.

Although this flier announces just a movie, I rush into the house and give the cat the good news. We're going to the movies! We are giddy and frisky yet we do not manifest our feelings openly. First, we're very private beings. Second, we don't want our temporary happiness to be detected by other people. We do not need to be envied and make new enemies.

I look again at the flier. I scan it fast, trying to find one movie that would truly entertain us. Here it is, a catchy title, *Wild Hearts, Tamed Souls*. The presentation also includes a short dissertation with the well-known French film critic Setupp, following the premiere.

I literally pick up my cat, throw her in the travel bag, and run to the theater. Can we get front seats? Yes, thank God. We can. And we get them.

We sit down in silence, waiting. The movie begins. No wonder it has such good reviews! The actors are hot, the scenery beautiful – green lawns, lavish houses, nice cars – and the plot is simple, yet unique.

Maria loves Miguel. Miguel loves Maria. Yet Miguel's feelings are tested when his new secretary Amanda, expresses her admiration for him. Will he give up the love of his life for an office adventure? I look at my cat. She is completely immersed in action, with her eyes glued to the screen, occasionally biting her dew claws.

There are a couple of things I don't get, though. The heroes seemed confined in a big living room or in Miguel's office.

They rarely leave the house, the safe place where everybody sobs, cries and suffers. Suffering takes place mostly on the couch. On rare occasions they stop to suffer in the door, by the door, and in front of the window.

Then, there's this lovely woman, Maria. She has a dark, mysterious secret.

For many, many years she's been suffering from depression, anxiety, tremors. Her ordeal comes to an end when she meets a great therapist who specializes in hypnosis. After many sessions, he finds out what has been haunting her for so long. The cause of her depression is actually her mother. Twenty-nine years ago, Maria's mother refused to buy her an expensive Russian doll. Since then, Maria has panic attacks whenever she's refused something. Simply put, her fragile mental and emotional structure cannot handle the average, no.

In spite of his love for Maria, Miguel cannot understand her. Why is she so upset when he tells her he does not want to close the window, or to take the dog out for a walk? Unlike Maria and like any other man, Miguel is very much used to no. No sex, no beer with the boys, no fun. That's when Amanda steps in. No matter what he wants, her answer is yes. Sex? Yes. Golf? Yes. How about a tap dance offered by a hot shapely dancer? Yes! Yes! Yes! Hmmm.

Before knowing it, Miguel is devoured by passion for Amanda. He is sucked in a whirlpool of desires, love and unbelievable emotions.

Miguel is lost, confused, torn apart.

He's trapped between yes and no. But one day, while shaving his mustache, Miguel has this revelation: the seed of the conflict of the misunderstanding lies in the no's he has been delivering to Maria. They both hate the no's. And if they both hate the no's, how come all they have for each other is no's? Miguel rushes to Maria's bedroom with his face covered in shaving foam.

The timing is perfect, for she is actually shaving her legs. A strong, passionate, foamy hug follows. They look at each other with love and their eyes seem to say yes. The movie ends with a close-up of Amanda reading the farewell letter from Miguel. She screams, "No … no … no." The echo of her voice fills the theater. People stand up in fear and leave the theater in slow motion, looking over their shoulders at the almighty, shiny screen.

I learn that the dissertation offered by the famous film critic has been rescheduled. It will start an hour from now. I have to kill some time.

Wow, that was a good movie! As I hold my cat tightly I feel her entire body shaking. Her left eye pupil is dramatically dilated. I know what this means. She wants to pee on the carpet. I open my mouth to say no, but I realize how traumatizing that would be for my one and only friend. I let her be and pay the $50 fee for littering with a smile, while people around us mumble something about us being "dirty." Oh, really? My cat and I might be a little bit dirty on the outside, but on a deeper level, we are very clean.

For example, I do not allow my thoughts to get dirty. I wash them carefully and I sanitize a lot. If for some reason they cannot be washed and disinfected, then I quarantine them. This way I make sure they will not interact with the good, clean thoughts and taint them – I have a few quarantined areas packed with porn, so what?

I stop at a fruit stand to get some fresh plums. The banner on one of the fruit boxes reads "Yes to legal prostitution!" I point at the banner with supreme disgust. I ask the fruit salesman where his moral values are. The fruit salesman – green face, mean mouth, pointy nose – explains. He thinks that if we, as a society, fully accept a woman who marries a man for his $500,000 estate, then we shouldn't be outraged by those modest feminine beings who choose to accept a thousand smaller installments instead of a lump sum. I totally disagree. I pick up a plum and I carve it with my front teeth in disapproval and defiance.

The fruit salesman insists. He wants to share the intricacies of his reasoning with me. He tells me that one day, while he was arranging strawberries for a home delivery, he had this epiphany. He had *what*?

What is an epiphany? I am struck by the fact that I haven't learned a new word in a very long time. My cat and I used to open the dictionary every day, just like that, to learn a new word and expand our horizons. It was a good habit. We didn't care if people around us wouldn't understand why we chose to obsessively use a certain word, even if it didn't make sense. It made sense for us.

But, we stopped doing it, and now I see it was a bad decision. I think the last word we learned was *laparoscopy*.

I admit my ignorance to the fruit salesman. He smiles. He pulls out a Merriam-Webster's from under one of the fruit cases. I learn that *epiphany* is a word he just added to his vocabulary yesterday. We decide to learn a new word together. We randomly open the dictionary.

Today's word is *paraphernalia*. I spend an enchanting hour at the fruit stand using the new word as often as I can.

Then I enter the bakery and praise the interesting collection of bakery *paraphernalia* owned by Norm the baker. Norm the baker does not seem to react to my knowledge. He throws a challah bread at me. I used to play basketball in high school, so skillfully catching flying challas is a piece of cake for me.

I'm back at the theater along with my paraphernalia – cat, plums, challah. I learn more about the distinguished gentleman who will lecture about *Wild Hearts, Tamed Souls*. He authored the highly debated book *Contemporary Entertainment and its Characters as Role Models*.

I look at my cat in awe. We both have an *epiphany*. We do not have a role model! Geez…I mean, we do so many things to better ourselves. We learn new words, we interact with carefully selected people, we think of ways of overcoming our own intellectual limitations. How come we overlooked the importance of having a role model? I cannot forgive myself for this one. How am I going to explain this to my feline friend? She trusted me with important decisions. She looked up to me. Shhhhh … the lecture begins.

The film critic Setupp – bulldog eyes, chic pink sunglasses, preoccupied face – deserves the fame that surrounds him. His words are deep, consistent, penetrating the minds and souls of his audience. I yearn to write a few of them down. I struggle to find a pen and paper in my *para* – short term for *paraphernalia,* much easier to memorize and pronounce. I have the paper but I cannot find a pen. My cat pitches in, scratching the words on the paper with her claws. One of them is "affection." The other one is "denial."

Master Setupp analyzes the characters briefly. Take Miguel. The Man, the masculine entity looking for completeness. The critic uses concepts unknown to me. And I consider myself a masculine entity. "What is a man looking for in a woman?" the French thinker asks himself. Yeah, right. What does Miguel want? I know what I want. When I was dating this girl, who was moody, bitchy, territorial invasive and didn't like sex, I yearned for the opposite. Then I met Agatha. She liked sex. She didn't control me. Yet, for some reason, I kept seeing the one who refused me everything. She was a challenge. One day, Agatha had enough and stopped the sex flow. Suddenly, I realized what I really wanted. Too late. I ended up alone.

The French critic analyzes Miguel's feminine counterparts as well. While he explains the mysteries of the feminine universe to the audience, I think of Aunt Lyla's confession about coping with the physical and emotional trauma of breaking a freshly polished nail.

In deepest secrecy, Aunt Lyla shared her journey into womanhood with me. She told me how much she used to suffer over nail breaking when she was a young girl. One day, though, she had an ... *epiphany*. She realized that she didn't have to trim and adjust all the nails to match the length of the broken one. Instead, she could get the beautiful, everlasting fake ones. It was a long, tough transition from being a girl to becoming a strong, independent woman, a true decision-maker.

Setupp is right. I remember the scene in the movie when Maria breaks a nail. One would think she lost someone from her immediate family. Everybody held their breath at the sight of the desperate woman. Not me, though. Just a nail, just a nail.

Setupp wants to finish his outstanding presentation. Few words on the "Happy ending" part. I learn that a carefully designed happy ending is crucial in keeping the morale of the viewers in place.

What if we all know that, in real life, the happy ending is rarely an option?

The viewers will not take a no. Who wants to watch tragedies and go home from the movies depressed? The audience raises their hands in unanimous approval.

I do not. I want to know why everybody in the movie chooses to "suffer" on the couch. I think the movie lacks action.

I need to ask the film critic about this right now! The audience is numbed by my chutzpah. Although equally startled and unpleasantly surprised by my ignorance, Master Setupp chooses to smile. He explains that the movie I just watched is a masterpiece, fathered by one of the most appreciated and acclaimed contemporary movie directors. Unlike the average action-packed box office successes, his movies are a landmark of "non-action" along with the introspection and in-depth self-evaluation of the characters.

Setupp adds in an amused tone, "If Miguel didn't have an office job and a couch to suffer on, and he were a fireman, always breathing heavy smoke, jumping like Spiderman from one fire to another, would he find time to stop and analyze his feelings?" People start applauding. Everybody agrees with the film critic. I do, too. Now I know why the divorce rate is so high among firemen. Those people are way too busy to stop and take a closer look at their own lives. They just live it.

My intense reasoning is interrupted by an anxious meow. The cat wants to know if we are getting that role model or not.

I assure her I didn't forget about our role model. I humbly pay my respect to the French film critic by offering him a plum and buying three tickets for the upcoming show. I do not intend to watch the movie again, nor do I have the intention of inviting someone else to watch it. I just want to help this amazing work to become a blockbuster.

Then I take the cat and walk straight to the fruit salesman. He's happy to see me. He's learning a new word: *Resocialization*. I like this word. I think I might have heard it a few times in my childhood. I just cannot remember who used it.

A decision has just been made. I pick the fruit salesman to be our role model.

It is almost noon. It's time to go home. I carefully put all my *para* in the backpack and walk a brisk walk towards the house. As I open the door I have this *epiphany*.

Resocialization was my late grandfather's favorite word.

The Healing Session in Censorship

I have to put the phone down and turn on the TV. Aunt Lyla is literally screaming at me. Don't I read the news? Don't I listen to the radio? Don't I watch TV anymore? What news? What radio? What TV?

Back to the phone. I tell her that my cat and I had decided to take a break from all this strenuous life. We needed some rest so we lowered the blinds and enjoyed a long, refreshing sleep. Aunt Lyla is shocked. Now? When the world is about to teach its citizens the ultimate lesson of respect? I'm puzzled. Back to the TV.

We watch the speech of a well-known politician in silence. Apparently, after centuries of social and political turmoil, the International Law of Censorship has finally been passed. Unanimously. I catch his last words: "The world welcomes a new era. An era of respect for each other, an era of understanding and everlasting social unity."

A couple of commercials promoting rye bread and mustard follow.

I look at my cat. Maybe she can explain to me what this is all about.

Of course she can. She's a female. She has intuition on her side. According to the new law, we're not allowed to express ourselves just like that, tell whatever comes to mind and offend other citizens. Every word has to be weighed, measured, polished, and only when we are absolutely sure it will generate unanimous, spontaneous approval, shipped to its addressees. What are the consequences of breaking this new law? Oh well, fines, imprisonment or both. Not counting the lawsuit the offended party can follow up with. Wow! We are indeed witnesses to a new world.

We're happy. This means no one will dare to call me crazy anymore. Unless they're ready to sponsor our vacation in Tahiti, he he.

My cat brings the champagne. We toast for an insult and offense-free future. Just in the middle of my sophisticated mental toast a raw revelation cracks my skull open. I realize that, while I can enjoy my days without being called crazy, mental and retard, I, too, cannot return any compliments anymore. We are bound to silence. We can no longer let our inspiration flow. I have to be very careful with my cat who has a very nasty habit of expressing her dislikes. She's also very opinionated. Whenever asked about something, she delivers the most outrageous, social and political feline perspectives. Right now, we need to cool down and watch the other people's behavior. We also need bread.

We go to the bakery in fear, avoiding looking people in the eyes. I see they started implementing the new law already. At the store a clerk makes some unorthodox remarks about the height/weight proportion of one of the customers. He tells the woman she's skinny enough to eat every day five muffins without gaining weight. The woman is offended. She doesn't think she is skinny. She thinks she's just fine. Police are called in and they bust the rude citizen right away. I ask respectfully about his immediate fate. Three years in prison and a substantial fine. As we pass the woman, we hear her crying on the phone and making a pledge to sue the clerk for at least a million. She is so offended. Will she ever be able to recuperate from this traumatic experience?

My cat looks at me. I know what that look means. I stuff her mouth with pretzels and stick her face in the bag. In the car I take her out and allow her to repeatedly call the woman "bitch." She also calls me various names. I agree with her, but she has to get it. If Daddy goes to prison, who will be here to look after her?

We have to understand how this new law works. *We were sleeping when they passed it, for God's sake!* Now, we have to wake up.

We go straight to Aunt Lyla. She is watching a short documentary that teaches citizens how to express themselves politely while preserving the initial meaning of their thoughts. It's not easy but she can see some progress already. I tell her about the bitch at the store. She tells me about a fuck up she met at the butcher's shop. I learn that we cannot use the term "fuck up" anymore. Instead, we can safely use "disoriented citizen."

There are a few things she likes about this new law though. I snap. Like what? How can one like this? I call her crazy. She calls me an idiot. We decide to call the police and sue each other. My cat hisses at us. Who's going to take care of her if we start this sick game? The cat calls us both "severely disoriented citizens." Aunt Lyla and I turn around and look at her. Can we sue a cat? We have to read the new law, word by word.

We part ways filled with anger. I feel like the blood in my veins has been replaced with boiling lava. I need to understand this. I am happy we got some sleep already, because I do not see too much sleep for us in the near future.

A gallon of coffee and eighty-nine cigarettes later, the sun shines upon me again. Aunt Lyla calls. She agrees to drop the charges for the "idiot" if I take back my "crazy." We make peace. Resourceful as she is, she managed to get two invitations to a very select, unique meeting with Ishmael Popcorn, the father of the concept of the censorship coming from inside out, as a citizen initiative. For more than a decade, he has actively promoted the idea of a society where the censorship – read: good citizen's manners – is no longer imposed from outside by the government but, by repeated educational measures, it becomes a citizen's initiative. The current law is actually based on his theory.

My heart starts beating faster. We better get ready; the meeting starts in less than an hour. I give my cat a bath. She hates baths, especially when she gets shampoo in her eyes. I show her The Law. I try my new daring prêt-a-porter. I ask her if I'm hot. She doesn't say a word. I ask her again. Nothing. Now I get it! She wants to tell me that I look like crap. Really? Why don't we sit down for a minute and quickly review the main aspects of…The Law? She starts purring and she tells me I'm hot.

We leave the house. On our way to the meeting I sue two neighbors. One called my cat "food aggressive" – *it's "resource protective" idiot, read The Law* – another one called my fancy prêt-a-porter "outdated" – *Really? Who are you, moron, the fashion police? If you want to enforce the Law, read it first! Ha ha!*

Caught in my fresh unexpected lawsuits we get there later than we planned. We know we are "disoriented citizens." We apologize to Aunt Lyla who, in order to save the seat for me, put on three sweaters and pretended she was pregnant. Nobody dared to question her extreme desire to give birth at the tender age of sixty-seven – The Law, Art.23, Par.4. We sit down in silence and position our antennae in the direction of the great speaker.

Prof. Ishmael – ageless face, mummified body, shaky voice – appears to be at least one hundred years old. Aunt Lyla corrects me. He is actually ninety-eight. I politely apologize – The Law, Art.9, Par.2.

His discourse is simple and meaningful. He gives the example of so many societies that failed to gain absolute control over their citizens.

So much useless pressure, dictatorships, anarchy. With such poor results. The idea of the ultimate censorship came many years ago while having coffee with a couple of select dictators. He just couldn't watch them struggling to eliminate the free-thinking using such brutal inefficient methods. Why use so much pressure coming from the outside? Why not place the pressure inside the citizen and then watch it grow? He knew he was on to something big. Seventy-nine years later he authored his glorious study, *Censorship Like a Seed*. According to his theory, the censorship lives inside the human brain.

It's like a seed, planted and watered by a loving parent – government. Once the plant is mature and vigorous, and most important, can sustain and reproduce itself, it doesn't need help from the parent anymore. The parent rests while watching his children grow, living their own lives, producing offspring.

Another advantage of this theory is the low cost of the law enforcement. The law is based on eternal human features: poor self-assessment skills, lack of competitiveness, and, of course, the almighty smallness. The great thinker estimates that after the initial phase, the police will gradually step down and let the citizens themselves enforce the law. Human smallness is eternal.

We express our gratitude to Aunt Lyla for bringing us here. We start walking towards home, muted and respectful. We pass a gray, tall building. The street is narrow, and so are my thoughts. My cat points at a tiny cross hanging on the door. The gray building is actually a monastery and according to the wall plate, it hosts the Carthusian Order. I knock at the door and a reluctant monk gives me, in a few words, all the information I need. What makes the Order so special? The monks are taught to cultivate the spirit of the exterior silence – speaking only when truly necessary. Solitude and silence are the keywords. I look at my cat. She approves. We step into great silence. We both feel we will be here for a while. There is nothing for us out there.

The Healing Session in Self-Evaluation

I've never been aware of the fact that a small incident, like being late for dinner, can be a life-changing event.

Naturally, I try to avoid the consequences and I sneak into the bedroom quietly, but when I try to get to the bathroom I step on her toy and a horrifying squeaky sound fills the air. Here she is, frying pan in paw, glossy eyes penetrating the darkness. After a stormy argument, we decide that the dinner incident is not an isolated case.

Something is not right in our relationship!

We need to get counseling! I promise her to call the well-known counselor for couples, Prof. Wilhelm Blueberry, first thing in the morning. Prof. Blueberry – bags under his eyes, coarse hair, huge listener's ears – is more than happy to listen to our problems and to facilitate the exchange of ideas between us.

We sit down in front of him waiting for a sign. He points at my cat, curious to hear her complaints. My feline partner pulls out a small diary. I didn't know she was so organized. She starts reading. I'm shocked to discover that she kept track of all my missed dinners, unanswered phone calls, as well as my inability to provide her with fresh fish upon request. I almost start snoozing listening to the never-ending list of complaints.

However, one of them catches my attention. She complains about the fact that, when I went to pick her up at the pet resort, I was unable to tell her apart from other black cats. This is ridiculous!

This unjustified complaint reminds me of a black friend who grew up in an all black community and never saw white people until he started college. He met this white girl, and they decided to get together the following day in the same place. A small problem, though. Once there, he could not identify her. All the white women around him seemed pretty much alike. He started walking around and shyly approaching all the young blonds – "Mary?" – until he finally addressed the right one. Although funny, my old friend's story has nothing to do with my cat problem. I went to the pet resort and I called *her*. It is not my fault that ten other cats rushed to get the salmon crackers. I wish women were like cats!

I look her in the eyes. I need not put my unhappiness on paper. I recall every detail of her mean actions, designed to curb the significant other's pleasure. Little things like peeing on my freshly built snowman two years ago in Colorado. Or scratching my hand when I wanted to play with her – mood swings. Or telling people what we think about them, without obtaining consent from me – social embarrassment.

My cat pulls out a second, smaller diary. Prof. Blueberry and I have to listen to another long, boring list of complaints, including, among others, constantly refusing to take her out to cool, exotic places; abusing her verbally and emotionally; refusing to cover her grooming expenses. And last, but not least, giving her a $10 Christmas gift card in exchange for her $20 gift card. Now, how cheap is that!

Prof. Blueberry listens to both sides with compassion and understanding. He gives us his famous *You have to change* brochure and invites us to read it thoroughly and work on ourselves. He suggests that we should emphasize the activities we both enjoy and create a daily ritual around them, gradually adding other exciting activities. This will help us rediscover each other, rekindle the romance, and eventually step into new territories of togetherness.

Prof. Blueberry informs us that we will resume our counseling session in a week and shows us out with a graceful smile.

I do not smile. Neither does my cat. Actually, we are pretty concerned. Why do we have to *change*? We don't like the idea. We were the same when we met, why do we have to change *now*?

However, we both have a deep respect for Knowledge and we decide to follow Prof. Blueberry's advice. After all, if we didn't trust him, we wouldn't be here.

At home we spend time in separate rooms, reading the precious guide to a perfect partnership, making notes, and then getting together in the living room to analyze them carefully.

We start having short sessions, during which we politely emphasize certain events in our relationship that triggered negative emotions along with resentment. I recall one such painful memory.

It takes me back in time two years, when I had packed twenty pounds on my belly and I was fat and miserable. I finally decided to cut down on fats and sweets and start a diet the following day consisting of seafood, rice, potatoes, matzos, and such. No chocolate. Unfortunately, before I made the decision, I got a huge, nine-inch-wide fruit tart. Because I couldn't function properly, knowing that "the enemy"was hiding in the refrigerator, I decided to eat "the enemy" that very day, so there would be no temptations in the future, as my fridge would gladly host only fat-belly-friendly foods. Then, I felt remorse. And guilt. What did she do? Was she supportive of me? Was she *there* for me? No. She laughed at me. She took pictures of me in my bathing suit and emailed them to our friends. How can I possibly forget this? My cat apologizes, although she admits she hardly remembers the fruit tart incident.

She, too, has a major complaint to make. It's not an isolated incident, but an ongoing, unpleasant experience. I learn that I seem to have a major communication problem lately. She doesn't recognize me anymore. In the shortest conversation or announcement I feel the urge to describe a series of facts or situations that are absolutely irrelevant to the message itself. The partner cat is pissed. Where is the straight-to-the-point man she once knew? Why do I have to give so many details when there is no end to it? Why do I put her and others through this ordeal? I admit I have no answer. I just use more words lately, so what? Do I have to undergo separate counseling in order to socialize the way I want to? Are there any guidelines for free expression that I have to follow? My cat says yes.

I call Prof. Blueberry right away and I ask for an additional session. He would love to help, but his expertise in communication and socializing is very limited. He kindly offers to call his friend, Prof. Strawberry, who is a leading expert in verbal communication. Five minutes later we have an answer from Prof. Strawberry, via Prof. Blueberry. He tells me that every message that needs to be conveyed to our counterparts consists of three basic elements: introduction, the message itself, and conclusion. For example, "Hey" – introduction, designed to catch the attention of my counterpart; "yesterday I went to the movies" – content; and "the movie I saw was bad" – conclusion.

Okay, I can tell you right now, I hate this! I politely thank my counselor and hang up. Then, I turn to partner cat. I want to tell more. I want to say a few words about the construction workers who snored through the entire movie. I also want to bring up the dirty restroom. And the fact that my pants were too tight and I felt discomfort during the show. However, I want to nurture my relationship. I will work on my ways of expressionless expression and take it to new levels! My cat smiles. In return she will practice along with me, ready to intervene whenever I'm in danger of giving too much off-base information. We spend a lovely day practicing and correcting each other respectfully, as a part of our "You have to change" strategy.

We also practice the small, innocent lies Prof. Blueberry taught us. Before we sought counseling, we thought lies would only damage a relationship. However, Prof. Blueberry suggests that a tiny lie now and then would only reinforce our desire to be safe and looked after. I agree. Our favorite lies are "I love you" and "Who, me?"

Since we decided to change, we both have plenty of time on our hands. I had to give up beer at the small neighborhood tavern, for my cat never approved socializing with the boys at the cost of the activities meant to make us a better couple. She had to give up playing with other cats early Sunday mornings when I indulge in my weekend sleep.

She protests as I try to limit her outings. She does not want to lose her freedom. Really? Who leaves the house whenever she wants and shows up at midnight with dust and spider webs in her coat? Not me! I am *here*, glued to the house, waiting with food and water. And by the way, whose food is more expensive? Some sessions are fruitful, some are scary. We end up sleeping in separate beds.

A week later we meet in Prof. Blueberry's office, both deeply disturbed, carrying bags of diaries.

Prof. Blueberry looks a little bit scared. He asks us to bring out the most relevant moments and disagreements of the past week. I look at her. She licks her paws gracefully for about five minutes, and then delivers yet another outstanding sample of femininity.

I learn that I'm cheap with her but a very irresponsible spender when it comes to my pleasures. Prof. Blueberry sanctions me with a parental gaze. What did I do this time? The counselor advises me to remember humble beginnings or to look in my past for an event that would trigger respect and appreciation for modesty. This will make me a humble, modest human being, and a wise spender. Is there any moment in my life when I was forced to cut down on costs and just live on a budget?

I'm pissed. Why do I have to re-live those moments instead of those when I was rich and money was plentiful? What kind of sadistic counseling is this? I'm taken back in time, against my will. When I was a kid, my cousin and I used to play different roles and make up silly games. One of them was that of a very poor widow – played by my older cousin, Eliza, who had a young kid – played by me. We were sitting in an improvised tent, made of branches and we were eating nothing. We were too poor to afford food. This was the game. I used to hate it and I protested a lot. I didn't want to be poor and eat nothing even if it was only a game! Why would I embrace a humble, modest lifestyle now, just to please my partner cat?

It strikes me that I do not want to change. At all. After all, when we met I was the same person. She was the same cat. She had her bad habits but I loved her anyways. I had mine and she didn't seem too bothered by them. I realize that neither of us has changed; maybe we were just immature and unable to see ourselves and each other for who we were. I write a generous check for Prof. Blueberry.

Do we wish to delve deeper into the misshapes of our relationship? We decline politely. We are who we are. On our way out I show my cat a painting on the wall. It's a girl with a fresh smile holding a big bunch of wildflowers. I want to tell her that I like the painting, but instead, I spontaneously create a story about flowers, femininity and freshness.

My cat smiles. We go home happy, aware of the flaws of our relationship.

The Healing Session in Abnormality

I take a deep breath and I recite our original poem again. The message contained in our thorough poetic fury seems to make my cat melancholy and resigned. Is our poem bad? Not at all. We have been humble scholars of the Master of the Words Whiteout himself. But who will broadcast our creativity? And then, who will read it? And last but not least, who will understand it?

My cat examines her freshly polished claws in the warm afternoon light. Then she turns to me with a glittering grin. It is hard to sell yourself in this market and we are no whores, except when it comes to Knowledge. We are *such* whores for Knowledge! We need someone to promote our original works. We need a literary pimp!

I tell her that I'm not sure I could use the services of such gentlemen. She laughs. She thinks I'm funny. No, I am not funny, I am honest. But maybe she is right and honesty is indeed a funny thing. What bothers me is that there is only one tiny step from being honest to being stupid and she should know better; we have proudly taken that step many, many times.

Caught in the conversation about promoting arts, we forget about the Annual Literary Mental Awards, *Stigma*, a show we have been watching religiously for the past several years. We start like athletes, at the same time and place, but in opposite directions. She rushes to get the remote while I quickly improvise dinner. How could we forget about this important event? That, I don't know. This is the Nobel Prize of the literary mental illnesses, and every time the great prizes are awarded we shed artistic tears, trying to imagine that we are *there* in the audience, sharing the stigma and the joy of the true artists. We have also watched the healthy people's awards, but for some reason, we found them tasteless and overdone. Same bland stories about happy, flawless people, who attain physical and emotional perfection only to give it up later and go mental.

Of course, we are saddened by the fact that we have not been blessed with some heavy illness. We are envious, and deep inside our hearts we hope that one day, the average depression will get the so-deserved international recognition, and all of us will be able to enjoy a universal state of abnormality. Or, maybe one day we'll discover that we are carriers of an exotic craziness, just like our neighbor Romy. Reunited with his long-lost Asian relatives, he learned from them that his depression was yellow. Sure, the color of his skin always made him wonder, but it wasn't until he turned fifty that he finally took a closer look at himself in the mirror.

While I watch the introduction, memories from the past start flowing in. I have always asked myself, when should I break the news about my condition to my lovers? Should I do it right after we meet? After the first night spent together? Or better wait until we are deep into a relationship and only then take off the clown costume? Surprise! I'm severely depressed and I love you. Boo!

My cat shushes me so I stop thinking. Here are this year's prizes. The Gold Stigma goes to a relatively unknown Swedish artist for his demented, conflict-less work *My dog's umbilical hernia repair*. The Silver is claimed by a paranoid poet for his lyric journal *Hooves* and the Bronze is shared by twin sisters who happen to be identical in every respect but their condition – one is schizophrenic, the other one anorexic. Their autobiographical work *Identical and Different* did not impress me, although the moment when the schizophrenic one received her sister's award was a little bit emotional. Would her sister have still committed suicide knowing that they would be awarded a "Stigma?" We don't know.

An honorary mention goes to a South African artist for his work *Taming the Characters*. I might want to read this one. It's about a writer whose characters become so smart that they start talking back at him, protesting when he wants to place them in one situation or another.

I need some chocolate. I stand up and walk to our secret place, where we keep huge amounts of dark chocolate for even darker times of uncertainty.

I put one piece on the table for myself; right next to it, my cat's treat. I also save a tiny piece for Agatha, hoping that she will stop by and watch the "Stigma" awards with us. This way I can secretly watch her while she watches the show.

I know I shouldn't be doing this. Is this abnormal behavior to share chocolate with the imaginary love of your life? But…have I ever been normal? I even saved the paper from the chocolates she brought me for my birthday. When was this? It seems like an eternity and a second ago at the same time. When is my birthday, anyways? I feel that while I do have a birthday, I have never been born really.

I'm basically waiting to be born, get named and start my life.

I choose to be born, unlike my dearest delusional friend, Cesario Parsley. Cesario was a genial shoemaker who suddenly realized that he was very unsatisfied with his life. He felt that, at a deeper level, he could not evolve anymore, so his Being took him on the great journey back home. Slowly and steadily, he went back to better times, when he was a happy young man; then a happy teenager; and finally a happy toddler. He loved it so much that he decided to go even farther and become again an embryo in his mother's womb.

Once he rediscovered how amazing it was to be an embryo in his mother's warm womb, he simply refused to come back and make shoes anymore. Why would someone want to be helpless and exposed to the cruelty of his peers when he could enjoy the endless maternal protection instead?

Sure, the people around Cesario had tried to stop this regression. They couldn't do much, not even the best medications available helped him. True, they managed to keep him at the adolescent stage for a while, but overall they failed.

My cat recalls an interesting conversation we once had with Cesario. We were about to go to the lake for a swim, and we invited him along. He then confessed that he couldn't swim. We didn't believe him but he insisted that he grew up in the woods and nobody ever took him to the ocean to teach him how to swim. My cat and I laughed at him. Of course, we did not expect everybody to be exquisite swimmers like ourselves – we took expensive swimming lessons with a Tahitian dwarf nicknamed "the Titan of the Pacific." Cesario told us that he was not capable of signature swimming. The only thing that he could do was to stay afloat and this made him feel miserable.

We rushed to assure him that *staying afloat* is actually the most important survival skill. True, my cat and I were masters of enchanting ourselves and the audience with signature tricks, yet we had been close to drowning way too many times in our lives.

Cesario Parsley is to this day a happy embryo, sending his inexplicable thoughts to us via occasional, chaotic swimmer's movements. Is he truly happy? We don't know.

I send my cat out to get some more booze. An hour later, she's standing in front of me with a bottle of liquor in one paw and some unsettling news in the other. The neighborhood cats told her that the healthy people also awarded prizes to the "Stigma" winners. What? These healthy people are so greedy and invasive. They even want to claim the geniality of our conditions!

We do know that normalcy is extremely boring and cliché, however sharing our craziness is highly unacceptable!

I don't get to hear the end of my cat's story. The phone rings.

Aunt Lyla's voice is indefinite. Yes, she did watch the show. She tells us that we have to be strong and then excuses herself as she has to get back to her apple pie.

Some dude calls as well – who gave you my phone number? – willing to share his outrage with us. I want to be alone so I tell him that I'm busy. He cannot understand why I am so busy. I explain to him that I am busy because I have nothing else to do. My explanation ends the conversation naturally and gracefully. This creature and I used to drink together until one night when he told me he is smarter than me. My cat rushed to bite him, but I did not approve of her instinctual reaction.

Instead, I told him that I would be honored to share a glass of wine with such a smart person. I love when people think that I'm stupid or crazy. I like to boost their arrogance and make them think that they are special and unique. I watch them taking off and getting higher and higher, propelled by the almighty ego. I know that the higher they get, the more abrupt their landings will be. And I like to watch them crashing. Watching them free falling is one of my simple pleasures. Simple pleasures of a madman.

I'm not quite satisfied with this year's "Stigmas." I want to share the deep dissatisfaction with my cat, but she scratches my right arm gently. I raise my eyes and I see a stunning, long-haired Fairy standing right there in front of us. She is indeed beautiful, but for some reason I remember my father's words of wisdom. He told me once when I was young not to go at night with a woman I wouldn't want to be seen with in the daylight. My father is right. Who would want to be spotted with a Fairy?

What is she saying? Oh, she asks if we have a wish. Yes, Ma'am! We do! Can she make us stupid, but you know, really stupid, immune to knowledge and wisdom-proof, so we do not suffer anymore? She smiles with sadness. Unfortunately, she cannot help us. She can only make us smarter. Are we interested?

We decline politely. Telling us that you can make us smarter is like telling someone who's got a mole that you could turn that into an invincible melanoma. And we plan to stay healthy. Abnormal, but healthy.

I look at my cat. She pushes the whiskey bottle aside.

The Fairy is gone.

The Healing Session in the Unknown

We're walking back home from our early morning archery session.

It's still dark and some might argue that shooting arrows in the dark is not the best way to test your abilities. *We* think it is.

When we send our arrows into the unknown, my cat and I feel like ageless warriors. What an awesome pastime! Here we are, taking our beautiful poses, proud and undeterred, hoping we will not kill anybody accidentally. Then we gracefully release the arrows and let them find their own way. Fly arrows, fly! Our message to all of those irresponsible, cowardly people out there is simple: if you haven't tried it yet, do it!

My cat takes a pee-pee break and I'm forced to stop as well and wait for her. What a good opportunity to quickly review the most insignificant moments of the last week! I think about the garage door I failed to fix and about my cat's odd request to quit my job at the postal office. She demanded that I quit my part time job just because she couldn't stand to see the face of my co-worker Nataniel.

She would only see him once a day when she brought me lunch, but apparently even the shortest encounters with Nataniel drove her crazy. Personally, I found Nataniel awkward yet harmless.

Nataniel was notorious for his slow motion, slow thinking and overall, slow being. Nobody really knew if he was absent-minded, crazy, or just incapable of following instructions. He would stick stamps for Europe on packages that were meant to reach Australia and charge international rates for the local mail. He would also sell decorative items that were not for sale, like the post office's mascot, the used mop, and one two-turkey corsage he was wearing. But the most intriguing aspect of his slow being was revealed in his stories and aspirations. He would tell us about the books he was working on and about the thrilling screenplays he sat down and wrote after the postal office would close its doors at 8:00 p.m. sharp.

One day he took me aside and told me that he was working on this book about a woman who was haunted by visions; aliens would have children with her; she was chosen from nearly two-thousand people;

but then she had their children; but they were like dogs with huge ears; and she was also playing the trumpet.

I was mesmerized. I kept thinking of his madness and his last words, that he would not forget us when he would become famous. It was obvious for me that Nataniel was a true, born, not raised, idiot.

I tried to convince my cat that we do not meet a purebred idiot every day. An encounter with a gracious, natural idiot should be cherished just as much as one with one of the wisest fathers of Mankind. Both have a lesson to teach, and extreme wisdom is as interesting as extreme stupidity.

Most people are either smart who feel like idiots, or idiots who think they're smart. But a purebred – someone who is truthful to their nature – oh, what an amazing case study!

For some reason, I didn't have to leave my job at the post office. The manager fired us all and kept Nataniel. I don't know why he fired the others; I might know why he fired me. Nataniel's story sounded inspiring so I went to my co-workers and I told them I too was writing a book about a flower that falls in love with a brick, and then there are vampires involved as well. The brick starts bleeding but only occasionally. My manager didn't laugh at that, but I did not suspect that my joke would constitute grounds for immediate dismissal.

The pee-pee break is over and we start walking towards home again. I want to sit down on a tiny bench, but an older woman reminds me politely that this is a bench for the disabled and the elderly. I apologize right away but I cannot help thinking that I'm fully qualified not only to sit down here but to spend the rest of my life on this bench. While my infirmities are not visible, I was born old and brainless. I've always felt that I lack brains or that life puts me in some crazy situations, especially designed for me, that I cannot handle.

I think I should probably get another job since I am no longer a proud employee of the local post office. My cat suggests a food place or at least a bakery – one of those places where employees get fed now and then. I cannot believe how small she is! I only think of spiritual food, while all she can see is free sausages.

We try the recently opened sandwich place, owned by our odd friend Miss Bubblebaum. Miss Bubblebaum recently split with her husband of twenty years.

This is an interesting story. The husband knew little about his kennel mate until they divorced. He was never interested in her or her aspirations. Actually, nobody was ever curious to know her, just like nobody ever cared to take a closer look at Nataniel.

Yet, once the divorce was finalized, he became intrigued by this person, whom he had ignored consistently for so long. His substantial indifference was instantly replaced by a vigorous interest one glorious afternoon, when they were arguing over who should get custody of Yossi, the stuffed puppy. While he hated anything that could remind him of the years of lonely togetherness, Yossi had a funny face and he wanted to put him in his office and watch him in between meetings with important people. Getting Yossi was a matter of manly pride.

However, Miss Bubblebaum saw Yossi as her closest companion, the one and only presence that would fill the empty, cold bed in those endless, shapeless and soundless nights when her husband was away from home. While for most people toys become live presences to whom they talk and with whom they share impressions, to Miss Bubblebaum, Yossi was not alive. *She* was the one who felt stuffed, lifeless and unable to move around and make her own decisions. She felt that throughout her entire life she had been moved around just like she used to move Yossi from the bed to the couch when she needed to dust the house. She had never complained or opposed resistance. She just kept asking herself a simple question: Who kept moving her around? Was it her husband? But then, who moved *him* around? There was only one way to find out, so one day she just announced to him she wanted to be alone. She was no longer willing to wait until someone else made things happen. She decided to try to be the one who makes things happen. After a long legal battle over Yossi, she moved out and started her own sandwich place. At first people were reluctant to go there, but they were all curious to taste the sandwiches fixed by a stupid woman, so they all ended up swallowing huge pieces of bread seasoned with various toppings, under the pacifying, non-judgmental gaze of Yossi.

I eat the bread in silence while my cat gets the ham, mushrooms and olives. I look at Miss Bubblebaum. Yes, she is definitely a natural, successful idiot. Maybe we should ask her if she needs a helper and we hang around here for a while, just to delve deeper into this matter.

We offer our services to Miss Bubblebaum. Then we leave, hoping that she'll take advantage of them.

It is almost midnight and it is not the first time that Aunt Lyla called us at odd hours. She's yelling at me.

She just watched an interview with Nataniel. He published the book about the woman giving birth to dogs fathered by mysterious aliens. People loved it so much that he had to follow up with a screenplay that a famous director brought to the big screen. My cat shakes her head in disbelief.

I warned her that any encounter with a purebred idiot should be cherished accordingly, for unlike him, we are merely mutts. This explains Nataniel's huge success. Unlike us, or the smart idiots who bought his book, he had a Certificate of Pedigree.

She hisses at me with vengeance. She, too, will write a book. It's a book about a cow that was a cow by day and an airline pilot by night. She would enjoy awesome green pastures during the daytime, making mental notes as to their exact location, only to land there at night enjoying safe, smooth landings.

I sigh and crawl to bed, crushed under the heaviness of the recent revelations. Yes, this is a good question. Who moves Miss Bubblebaum and Nataniel around?

I dream a simple, challenging dream about Nataniel and Miss Bubblebaum, waving at us graciously from a train that passes us quietly while my cat and I stand motionless on the platform.

# The Healing Session in Charity

Some people think it's relaxing to take a walk in the neighborhood park in the early morning. We do not. We hate to grope in the semi-darkness, but we are pursuing our lovely new neighbor – small fig-like breasts, curly eyelashes, mole on her left cheek. We pray to see her again and our prayers are heard. We say "Hi" and she says "Hi" as well. Then we continue the bonding we started five days ago, hoping that soon we will get our greedy hands on her body.

My cat advises me to get it on. I tell the beauty about my lonely nights and the empty cold bed. About the breakfast I share – sadly – with an animal. About the Christmas cards I send to myself. This is a new strategy, and we are curious if it works. Women need to be impressed. We decided to give up our old strategy when my cat used to play sick – one of the best tear-generating shows ever. We also decided to try something different than borrowing my estranged sister's toddlers and displaying strong paternal instincts – another unbeatable chick magnet.

I recite my lonely male poem and wait. The hot neighbor looks at me with compassion. Then she tells me that she's not a charity. Then she excuses herself; she just signed up for the trial of a new medication for migraines organized by the Homeowners Association. We would love to follow her but my cat stops me. In order to qualify you have to have at least three strong migraines a month. Unfortunately, the never-ending one and only migraine we have doesn't qualify us for this trial.

But…what is her answer supposed to mean? Do I look like a poor desperate man who needs help? My cat says yes. I hate her and I hate myself. We decide to go back home and skip the morning coffee shop pies.

We're close to the house when a big red truck passes us. The banner on the back reads "Help the Hungry Children of the World." In less than an hour we knock at their main office door. We need to find out how this charity principle works.

An old muscular lady with a mustache explains. The essence of charity is to help the ones in need and donate things that you don't need anyways. How many times we clean our houses and we find items we haven't seen or used in years? Too many times. Isn't that terrible that we might have twenty towels in the house while a poor child doesn't have any, and stands there, in the bathroom, dripping wet? We agree. We sure have a few items we can dispose of. Our donations will not only help the hungry children in need, but will also help *us* defeat our selfishness. At least this is what the muscular lady says. She also tells us that the ultimate donor will gladly give up not only items he does not use anymore, but items that he actually holds dear.

Wow, amazing words of wisdom. At home, we start looking feverishly for things that we don't need. Surprisingly, we need them all. Even a sock with a big hole in it seems now dear and useful. My cat and I end up putting the donations on the big kitchen table and then taking them back in a precise, continuous come-and-go. We take trips to the table without talking to each other like vehicles on a busy two-way street. Trying to make donations can be a very healthy way to self-discovery, though. We learn that we have five beds and four coffee-makers. Four coffee makers? My cat smiles, bored. They were "Buy one, get three free" and how could I forget? Besides, what if three of them break down? We still have one that's running!

At the end of the day we count the few items that we *think* we can live without: a can of beans, an old dish rack, and some expired baby rat formula. Are we really selfish? Do we have an inability to be generous and caring at least once?

The cat frowns. Her eyes wander the living room only to stop on the painting that has been in our family for generations. I'm surprised and, need I say, unpleasantly surprised. Whenever we tried to sell that painting and be able to buy useful items – refrigerator, couch, shoes – we received many death threats from otherwise very distant relatives. Even Aunt Lyla threatened to leave town, assume a new identity and never speak to us again, should we behave selfishly and allow the family treasure to get into wrong hands.

I look at the painting. True, it's a masterpiece signed by the well-known Auguste Ilya Toilette. But for us, the humpbacked skinny, bowlegged "Resting Ballerina" has no value, unless perhaps we can trade her in for a new refrigerator along with a new, bigger house.

We recall in awe the first days after we inherited the precious painting from our beloved Uncle Yusuf. We were so overwhelmed by the value of the ugly woman that we couldn't sleep at night fearing that someone might break into the house and steal it. We even worked shifts guarding our Toilette and my cat was on constant patrol. We rarely left the house and only when Aunt Lyla was available for house sitting. Before we became the proud owners of the famous painting we had no clue how hard it was to live with Toilette hanging on your walls. Even a trip to the bathroom was a risk we proudly assumed, until one day when we decided to hang it right there, in the bathroom where it stayed for at least ten years. Once again my cat was right. What burglar, no matter how sophisticated of an art connoisseur he is, would look for an authentic Toilette in the bathroom?

Owning such valuables had a negative impact on my intimate life as well. On the very rare occasions when I had a woman over, I had to cover the painting days before the event, since her ugliness bothered me immensely and led to poor sexual performances. Just thinking of such skinny legs in my bed made me shiver.

Since we were forced to spend so much time around the house, in time we grew closer to the ugly expensive image. Oddly enough, we could no longer imagine our life without Toilette. Over the years we had many offers, but the pressure from the family was too high. Now that pressure is gone. Most of the family members who used to send us death threats are gone as well. What prevents us from getting rid of the painting? True, we will have to convince Aunt Lyla, but only after we convince ourselves.

I look at my cat. She looks at the sandwich I'm eating. I put the sandwich in the refrigerator so we can focus on the topic and not allow the instincts to take over.

The question is will we be able to donate the Toilette? Will we have that strength? My cat says no. We can hardly give up the baby rat formula – who knows when we might need it. I do not agree. What if our Toilette helped with finding a cure for sleeplessness or cat colic? She shows teeth. And what if our Toilette helped with finding a worry-free life for us? I call her selfish. She calls me stupid and honestly, at this point I don't know what is more desirable.

We argue a lot, and we even stop talking to each other for a few hours.

The dawn catches us in front of the painting, sleep-deprived and clueless. I stand up. Enough! I will not listen to a cat. The only one I am worried about is Aunt Lyla, so I call her right away. Will she still leave town, move to an undisclosed location and assume a new identity should we give the Toilette away? Of course not. She is old and sick and let's not forget that she is the only beneficiary on our life insurance policy. She won't be able to cash in if she changes names. We are moved to hear that she is so supportive of us.

In the morning I take the Toilette to the Hungry Children. I offer it to them with respect and joy. I'm aware that the hungry children will need food and hopefully the value of the painting will help with feeding a small country for a year or so. The people at the charity office express their admiration. They think I am the ultimate donor, a person with strong values, a pillar of our community.

They are wrong. Had they asked me to donate the baby rat formula I couldn't have done it. Who knows when we might need it to save a baby rat? Deep inside I feel small, but somewhat happy. At home I hang a $5 poster on the wall where I once had the famous Toilette. It is a half-naked Hawaiian woman with a big ass. Yeah, baby!

There's something odd about our place since I brought in the cheap Hawaiian beauty. She doesn't fit in our elegant living room. My cat suggests that maybe we should get rid of the leather sofa and replace it with something more casual. We do that but it's not enough. We decide to give up our entire universe. One after another, the beds, the coffee makers and all the items we have clung to so desperately disappear in the hands of the Hungry Children of the World.

We should be sad but we're not. Instead, we feel great relief. There's more air in the house. We couldn't sleep on five beds anyways. Did we really need forty-four exquisite hardwood chairs? Have we ever used the thirty-nine silver forks? How about the ugly plastic egg holder that we had dumped many times only to run later to the dumpster and retrieve it?

My cat totally approves of our new simple life. Sure, we've been poor before, but we have never given up anything willingly. The truth is that we don't need more that one bed, two chairs and a table to be miserable.

However, as I hide the baby rat formula and the sock with a hole in it in the drawer, I still think of the words the hot neighbor told me and I still wonder what she really meant by telling me that she was not a charity.

The Healing Session with Music Teacher Theodore Quartet XI, Esq.

I sit in my car and wait for the green light. My cat's monotonous purr helps me to fight the fatigue triggered by the heavy silence. Some time ago we decided to stop listening to the radio. There's nothing wrong with listening to music. Yet the thought of listening to those verbalized feelings and emotions attached to the tunes drives us mad. We are not unlicensed therapists. We refuse to participate in this insane social pastime that is mumbling lyrics and identifying us with some dude who misses his father. Instead of doing that, my cat and I started a challenging adventure: listening to word-free music and creating the lyrics ourselves, making the music *ours*. The joyous Chopin proved himself to be our favorite, and we authored numerous glowing lyrics to match his music. We kept creating soul-touching lyrics to Chopin – *Long, long days/ one thousand-mile-long days/ I never get to see their end/polar nights are shorter than my days/ I envy you, polar bear for your endless dreams/ I need to rest/ But how?* And then we moved to Beethoven – *I do not miss anybody really/ Occasionally I miss the train/ or perhaps a meaning/ but I do not crave anyone's presence/ and if you think I am deceiving/ you are the one who missed something/ you missed my point.*

We have spent countless hours in the car, listening to the Titans of music, simultaneously following the lovely rhythms and shaking our heads. What can be more beautiful than enjoying a relaxed ride in your little-wheeled, air-conditioned-box, amazed, and at the same time indifferent to the world's daily happenings? The word-free music gives us the strength to pass the shootings, robberies, neighborhood rapes and even the rising gas prices, with grace and wisdom.

Our connection with the world of harmonious sounds has become so obvious that I decide to share our little secret with Aunt Lyla.

Aunt Lyla is not surprised at all. She hates those stupid lyrics our brains are forced to accommodate along with the nice tunes. But she has no idea as to how to fight this cultural plague. Luckily, her maid also does some Sunday cleaning for Theodore Quartet XI, Esq., a distinguished music teacher and composer, who lives not far from my house. Born and educated in Vienna – where else? – Professor Quartet has enchanted his audience with glittering musical journeys like *The Word-free Symphony, Silence,* and *Empty Acoustics.*

I beg my aunt to get me in. It's not easy; the famous music teacher has not been seen in public since 1987. However, Aunt Lyla's maid has a connection. A friend of the mother-in-law of the waiter, who caters for occasional family gatherings held at the composer's house, is the butler's brother.

Needless to say, I can hardly control my excitement, so on my way out I break an antique vase that has been in our family for over two-hundred years. Once at home, my cat and I start getting ready for the event – afternoon tea at the Teacher's house – that will take place three days from now. We both choose activities that will bring out the vigor in our systems while maintaining the balance and dispersing the negative energies. Only this way will we be able to grasp the essence of the glorious music teachings.

She goes to the hairdresser. I go to the hockey game. She gets a paw massage. I go to the strip club. We meet at the end of those endless three days, happy, relaxed and ready for yet another attempt to find *the healing.*

We do not want the great musician to think we are some invasive, desperate fans, so we use the servants' door to get into the property. A nice butler sees us in and takes us to the patio, where the Magician of the sounds is ready to share his tea and musical wisdom with us. At the sight of the genius, the lines I have been religiously practicing for the past three days vanish. I skip the introduction and I ask the music teacher directly why Theodore Quartet XI? I have heard of I, II, III and IV, but ... XI?

Theodore Quartet XI – red hair, deep wrinkles, pitted-plum complexion – explains. Music has been in his family since ancient times. His great-great-great-great-great-great grandmother, Theresa von Marzipan was an official provider of home-baked cookies for Mozart himself! I push my chair closer to him, once again overwhelmed by the desire to submit unconditionally to Knowledge.

I confess. I tell him about my hatred for the lyrics we automatically have to buy along with the tunes. I tell him how one day, while I was driving to the cleaner's I asked myself if we could do a little cleaning in music and get rid of those nasty lyrics, those true stains on the canvas of sounds. He agrees. He gives me his definition of a real musical event. He thinks that the musical work should resemble a whirlpool or a tornado that sweeps the listener in, growing bigger and bigger, tumultuous and restless on the outside yet quiet and peaceful on the inside. Once inside that breathtaking fast moving column of sounds, the listener can experience everlasting emotions. When the work ends, the giant tornado gently drops the listener off, and moves on to the next listener. The mission is accomplished. The listener goes back into the bland daily world of nothing, yet the emotions triggered by the work will live as long as he is alive. The music that cannot trigger such powerful life-changing intensity is not music. It is merely noise.

So are the poorly crafted lyrics. Noise. Useless noise.

I feel blessed. Master Quartet is a true genius who makes me feel at home. I close my eyes and picture the history of art and literature manuals from elementary school. Their pages were filled with photos of wise, concerned artists. As kids, we always think that people who have in common so much concern must be friends or belong to a universal, big family. How disappointed we were when teachers would tell us that the artists were born three-hundred years apart? I used to think they lived among us. I used to imagine them having coffee together, sharing their views on culture, society and even daily problems – conflicts with their mothers-in-law, lovers, unpaid water bills. Master Quartet seems to be one of those wise fathers of Mankind who can have dinner anytime with Mozart, Liszt, Thomas Mann. But he prefers my company instead.

Will the Teacher allow me and my cat to mentally create the lyrics for one of his masterpieces and immerse ourselves in his music? He allows. The bell on the table rings, and here comes the butler, pushing a piano. Today we will create the lyrics for *The Wrinkled Mistress*, one of the Teacher's earlier Viennese impromptus.

I pick up my cat, stand up and let the inspiration flow. I hold her firmly while the lyrics come to life naturally, effortlessly, embodying the experiences of a great musical journey – *I can enter minds/and visit them/I feel like a tourist without a guide/ I discover the awkwardness of the mind sitting next to mine/but then I have to go/ before I start deeply understanding/ someone else's oddity*. It is indeed a life-changing event. Unfortunately, the butler feels the urge to bring his humble contribution – *Sir! perhaps you wish me to relieve you / from holding your feline alter-ego*. I promptly sanction him – *You have to go/ before you start understanding/my oddity* – ready to move on to my next reflection. He insists – *The law of deep respect requires/ the utmost comfort/ for your feline friend*. I, too, insist – *Respect? who shall decide/ upon the comfort of a dear odd friend/ if not a dear odd friend?*

Finally, my cat decides to end our poetical confrontation. She jumps on the piano. She meows. She scratches Theodore Quartet's hands. The Teacher and Musician hits the last note with his hair standing on end and with the gaze of a madman. At his sign, we all bow in front of each other and step outside the musical tornado.

In silence we watch Theodore Quartet XI, Esq., who stuffs his face with bagels and miniature croissants and drinks the tea straight from the pot. May I disturb the Teacher's oneness with the snack with one more humble question? He looks at me as if he sees me for the first time. Then, he smiles. He introduces himself. I learn that his name is Theodore Quartet XI, Esq. and he is a musician. I play along with the adorable game and introduce myself again to the famous artist. He wants to show me his music box, a gift from his late father. He points at a beautiful red box resting on the table by the sugar jar. He pushes the lid. The box opens and a mature chimpanzee pops out and starts dancing, but there is no audible music. Maybe the box is broken? I ask Theodore Quartet XI, Esq., "Where is the music, why can't we hear a sound?" He seems oblivious to me, cat, and tea, staring at the chimp. It's time to go. I leave him smiling, immersed in the inaudible song.

The servant sees me out. Before he closes the doors behind me, he apologizes for his Master's behavior, but he hopes I will not take the Master's musical confessions too seriously. I'm very intrigued and I want to know why he undermines the great Theodore Quartet XI, Esq. while being in his service. He looks at me surprised. He opens his mouth, trying to say something, but a small, yet strong musical tornado shows up unexpectedly and before we know it, the butler is swept in another unforgettable experience.

We leave Master Quartet's house tired, puzzled, impressed.

The Healing Session in Success

We are headed to a pottery display bearing the signature of Wilhelm Ladybug, my cousin of my late mother's uncle. We wouldn't be going, we have totally lost interest in creative pottery – cups with five handles, plates with holes in them – since high school, but Aunt Lyla insists. She thinks that our cousin Ladybug is a successful, accomplished pottery maker. Besides, this is a wonderful opportunity to meet other successful people like nephew Corgi, a successful plastic surgeon and his wife Picky, a successful plastic surgery; their neighbor Vivianne, a successful lawyer with her two successful daughters; and the list can go on and on.

I ask my cat if we really want to be there. After all, we are not successful. We have never achieved anything. All we have is a bunch of questions that no one can answer.

My cat has a different opinion. She thinks that this is the reason why we should go, to see real, flesh-and-bone Success and understand what it gives to people. Also, the Ladybugs always serve good food.

We pick up Aunt Lyla in front of the bakery for debriefing. I cannot believe she doesn't trust us with being able to behave around successful people, especially since they are family. Aunt Lyla agrees with us. They are indeed part of our family but unlike us, they belong to the successful side of the family. We belong to the other, less successful side, with prominent members like Uncle Didi the thief, or Uncle Sasha, the renegade who spent the family's money drinking and pinching the dancers' breasts in the taverns.

After being instructed by my lovely aunt how to temporarily fit in our own family we get into the car with our hearts beating faster. Will we be able to hold high-quality conversations and prove that in an emergency even our blood can be used for transfusions?

We hope to get some answers. First and foremost, what is success, really? Recognition from your peers, or enemies, or both? Is success everlasting?

Once we get there we sigh relieved. There's nothing to be afraid of, they're people like us, just successful. As I expected, the conversations revolve around their successes. Everything they do is a great success. Naturally, success attracts success, so they tend to flock together.

As we try to put as much food as we can on our plates we catch the words flying around us. One of the younger daughters of Aunt Lyla's successful older sister is dating again, and need I say, she's dating a successful engineer, who authored three books about the gooseneck lamps. The wife of Eduard Pishkot VII, Esq. passes me in a hurry screaming, "He went! He went!" I turn around and I see her holding her three-year-old son's potty. The audience learns in great content that little Pishkot VIII just went potty for the first time. It is true, success starts at an early stage in life.

My cat tries to say something but I shovel caviar down her throat. This is definitely not the time and the place for sarcastic remarks.

I have to quickly remind her of Aunt Lyla's teaching that successful people don't like jokes. They cannot laugh at themselves, only at the unsuccessful people. They like positive things and reject the slightest reference to unaccomplishment as if it was plague or worse. They hate to hear that other people have problems – what problems? Life is so beautiful – and they consider them inferior, initiative-less and whining creatures.

I am surprised I have to explain this to the cat, over and over again. Doesn't she remember the times when we were rich and worry-free? It's the same mechanism.

My cat scratches the table. She points at nephew Corgi, who is thirty-nine but looks like eighty-nine. Why? Because he's the owner of a success he didn't ask for. When he was young and playing in the garage with dead old mice, trying to make them look younger, he just dreamt of being a good plastic surgeon. But then he graduated and he met his wife-to-be, a sneaky bitch with a taste for gold. Ten years, two kids and two greedy in-laws later, Corgi felt that his ideals had been hijacked. He felt that he had given in to the pressure of the society. He ended up working day and night just to maintain an image, the image of success. Corgi wanted out, but it was too late. When he finally realized what he really craved, there was no room in his life for…his life. He was a slave, a slave of his own success.

My cat thinks that even with no life, Corgi is still in a better place than Uncle Didi, the thief.

I strongly disagree. Uncle Didi was successful in his line of work. He was a successful thief. He got caught by Interpol eventually, but only after he had skillfully robbed all the major art museums in all the major capitals of the world – our famous Toilette painting was one of his successes.

He would have become even more successful, if it wasn't for the police who caught him. Basically the law enforcement officers took Didi's success and made it their own. Uncle Didi lost everything while the until-then average cops turned instantly into successful cops overnight.

My cat wants to know if success is portable. I'm not sure about its portability, but I am sure it is pretty volatile.

Success can also be elusive and mischievous. Let's take Auntie Mirabelle. Her life was miserable. She gave up everything as she was trying to become a famous hairstylist. She never married. She spent most of her time practicing, trimming wigs and occasionally the neighborhood retirees. She even introduced her signature "Three pointy bangs" and was close to achieve stardom when she died unexpectedly from a hair allergy. Right after she died, the Academy of Beauty recognized her contribution to the industry and named the three bangs "Mirabelle bangs." But she never knew of her success and all she got from life was misery and struggle.

My cat arranges her three Mirabelle bangs and sighs softly. Oh well, life is strange.

Then, there's Uncle Sasha, a misfit, drunk and outcast, one whose name inspired embarrassment and disgust altogether. Why? Who has the right to name someone else unsuccessful and based on what? I stand up and discreetly approach Aunt Lyla who is having a mind-freezing conversation with Corgi about his older son's academic successes.

I remove a bunch of hair off my aunt's café-au-lait outfit. Ah, the shedding power of a cocker! I deeply apologize for interrupting their precious word exchange, but I need to know where Uncle Sasha is. Aunt Lyla frowns in deep disgust. Where? In the same old tavern where he's been spotted for the past fifty years.

We cannot take the car and leave Aunt Lyla at the mercy of successful people in order to get back home. We call a cab and are on our way to the tavern! We've seen enough Success. We feel that we need to experience firsthand failure as well.

While the cab driver tries to find his way on the narrow filthy streets of our uncle's select neighborhood, we review the information we have on him.

People expressed outrage when Sasha left his wife and three kids fifty years ago. He was wealthy, well respected in the community; in other words, successful. But Sasha had other plans. He started spending more and more quality time in the tavern, enjoying the dancers and the good wine. He loved it so much that one day he decided to leave his house and sleep on the bench in front of the tavern. He thought that would be more comfortable than trying to walk home drunk and falling asleep in various unfriendly ditches. And he was right. Of course, the community condemned his devilish deeds and he became a part of the unsuccessful side of the family. But he didn't care at all.

We find old Uncle Sasha easily as he is a very popular presence. He sits in a poorly lit booth with two dancers in his lap and he seems pretty happy. It might sound strange but he looks very young for his age. And what is his secret? I ask him what success is.

Will I do him a favor? I say, "Yes." He needs to relieve himself but he feels lazy. He asks me to go to the restroom and pee for him. I look at him stunned. This is impossible. I cannot pee for him just like he cannot pee for me.

"The secret" he says, lighting up the candle on the table, "is knowing what you need to do and no one else can do for you. This is the real success."

Sleepy cat in my lap, I empty one glass after another. We're not successful yet and we know it. She is not a successful cat. She has never caught a mouse without considerable help from me. But I've never caught a mouse without considerable help from her either.

We watch the candle burning out slowly. The door is closing behind someone and when we turn around we see Corgi. He's drunk already but he hopes to achieve a more advanced state of successful impairment. We wish him good luck.

In the semi-darkness of the old tavern success is invisible.

The Healing Session in Death

Aunt Lyla stops by to bring me the invitation to Cousin Jello's funeral. She knows that I have a tendency to avoid such events so she insists that I participate. She also knows that I met Cousin Jello twenty-four years ago at someone else's funeral and since then I've barely spoken to him. However, not showing up at the event would be a very, very big mistake. Really? What if I refuse to go? What is he going to do, get mad at me and never have me over again?

I assure Aunt Lyla that my cat and I will be there. She leaves happy reminding me that for this special occasion Jello's brother hired a group of mourners from overseas. Being on time would not only show respect for Jello and everyone else, but would give us the opportunity to listen to all those beautiful traditional songs.

We get there right on time, a fact that does not go unnoticed by Aunt Lyla and "the rest" of the family. I didn't know I had such a big family. They just keep coming. Honestly, if I were to see them on the street I would have never guessed they're my relatives. Every day I meet a new relative!

They talk a lot and ask a lot of questions. And how have I been in the last twenty-nine years? And why am I not married? Have I ever been married? Do I want to get married? I don't get it. Why should I answer to people that I'll not see again until thirty years from now? Let's hope next time when we meet it will be on the occasion of their funeral party. Or mine. This way I will skip the unwanted questions. Luckily, the mourners start their performance so my cat and I excuse ourselves from the ordeal. We make sure the mourners get hefty tips so they'll keep singing for a while. Perhaps this wasn't the best idea, since their songs induced severe depression and fear. My cat jumps into my lap with eyes filled with tears. "I don't want to die!" We won't. But in order to stay alive we need alcohol.

Thank God, it is plentiful. I have always said that the only cool thing about our funerals is that they serve alcohol and they encourage vigorous drinking. After all, if I cannot drink as much as I want at a funeral, where should I drink? Weddings are a good occasion as well, yet if you miss a wedding there will be more to come, whereas people don't die that often these days. It will take a while until someone else in our family dies and we'll be able to enjoy again this type of gathering.

But where is Jello? Everybody is anxiously waiting for him. They worked so hard to cook his favorite dishes, arrange the house, and bring in the mourners. It is almost like a surprise party, just without balloons, or excessive joy. Although I can read on many faces the hidden, unspoken joy of being alive, overcast by isolated outbursts of fear. Finally the door opens and here comes Jello, straight from the funeral beauty parlor.

We get close to the carefully decorated coffin. I haven't seen Jello in years, yet I don't remember him having blond hair. I pinch Aunt Lyla's right arm and point at his hair. She confirms that he was a dark-haired, dark-skinned man, like most of us. I ask one of the mourners if that is him or they accidentally switched coffins at the beauty parlor. It is him. Dyeing his hair was his brother's idea. As Jello was very sick and basically awaiting Death, his brother thought that if he altered Jello's physical appearance, he could trick her into picking someone else. They dyed his hair and changed his name, according to the ancient beliefs, but who can fool Death? They were extremely careful not to accidentally call him by his real name since they knew that Death was there, waiting for the right opportunity to serve Jello. Unfortunately, one morning, Jello called his mother and asked her for a glass of water. Unsure if the voice coming from the living room was her son's, the woman asked, "Jello, is that you?" and thus blew his cover. She rushed into the room only to see a lifeless, thirsty Jello. The story is indeed moving and speaks of the endless imagination and the sense of humor our forefathers had, although trying to escape Death sounds like pathological chutzpah to me. The fathers might have passed on to us some elements from this amazing tradition. We, too, use fake names when we log on to the dating sites and wear wigs when we go on blind dates. My cat agrees. A bad date can be worse than death.

As the party progresses, more and more people stop by Jello's coffin, making various remarks as to his appearance. Even Aunt Lyla says he is very handsome, compared to late Uncle Lionel, who at his farewell party greeted the guests looking pale and with bags under his eyes. Another woman says she couldn't sleep after her aunt's funeral. The deceased woman was stubborn even in death, and she decided to keep an eye on the guests, staring at them and making them uncomfortable.

A severely intoxicated man tells them that his father continued to grow his beard even after he died. Yes, they had to shave him every day, for three days in a row.

I'm surprised at their insight. This cruel society will not steer away from sanctioning one's appearance even at your own funeral party.

Speaking of appearance, a group of relatively sober women shushes the audience as the leading vocal mourner delivers an excruciating cry. It's time to listen to the traditional, "Why do you have to leave us, Jello? Jello, come back!" I hope it's a metaphor and we will not see the blond Jello getting out of his coffin and joining the group.

We need more alcohol. I'm going to fix myself a cocktail! In the kitchen I meet ninety-nine-year-old Uncle Milo, who takes a break from his snoozing only to assist me in my work. Unfortunately, the only cocktails he can fix are the Molotov's. He's been fixing them through the entire evening, picking up the bottles emptied by the guests unnoticed, like a ghostly presence of the past. Since I saw him last time, Uncle Milo's memory has severely declined. For him, Time stopped seventy-two years ago, when he was a proud member of the Resistance Movement. He looks me in the eyes and offers me two Molotov's. He knows I will not disappoint my people.

I tap him gently on his shoulder and I assure him that tonight we will fight and defy Death like never before.

My cat checks her watch discreetly. She wants to go home. I take her aside and explain diplomatically that if we leave before the traditional gift exchange Aunt Lyla will never forgive us. And I mean *never*. The cat tends to take my parental advice easily, but I remind her that Aunt Lyla can and will eliminate her Sunday bacon treat. She ends up agreeing to behave until the end of the party. It's obvious that we're going to witness a painful gift exchange as people become more and more intoxicated. A group of old women bring the few things Jello left for his immediate family. The only problem is that the immediate family counts fifty-nine people. A set of scissors, a pair of slippers, one toothless comb, the cage that housed Jello's childhood parrot, five watches, two pillows, the sunglasses he used to wear on his annual trip to the sea resort, as well as other priceless artifacts, which are brought in and placed in the middle of the room. While his sisters agree to share the ownership of the scissors, his daughter claims that she should get all the items since she was the one who cared for Jello in his last days. The sisters are pissed and all the women start hissing at each other. Their husbands join the fight, proudly standing by their significant others.

Jello's son-in-law helped him fix his car two years ago. The sisters' husbands helped him replace the oven last summer. Other relatives join in, taking sides and pouring more wine in the glasses. We watch the public argument that lasts over two hours. I find interesting the fact that everyone wants the toothless comb, while nobody really seems to care about other items. We get a tiny watch, Jello's first Christmas gift from his father. We feel embarrassed and do not want to accept the gift, but Aunt Lyla's desperate hand signals along with continuous eye blinking makes us reconsider. We *cannot* refuse Jello's last gift. We politely accept his gift and we place it by Jello's shapely wooden outfit. We, too, have a gift for him. We would have brought him intimate apparel like everybody else, but since we haven't been too close to each other, we chose to get him one of those adorable lavender sachets. Lavender is well known for decreasing stress and covering up bad smells, two high-priority issues down there.

The exchange ends on yet another excruciating mourning song, followed by Jello's sisters thanking everyone for coming and planning on how to get to the cemetery. They cannot decide who should give Jello a ride. We decide not to wait until the end. For some reason I don't want to give him a ride nor witness his fabulous descent into the ground.

Well-mannered as I am, I go to say goodbye to Jello. I hope he enjoyed his party. People were nice to him. They knew he wouldn't be able to dance so they abstained from dancing this time. They wanted to make him feel good at his last party. They drank and ate and listened and so did he. He exchanged gifts with his friends. I hope he likes his gifts because, as my father used to tell us at Christmas time, there won't be any other gifts. I don't care for gifts anymore. I have learned not to be attached to material things.

Before I leave, I place the tiny watch back in the coffin, right on Jello's chest. He might want to check the time now and then. I do not.

The Healing Session in Hobbies

I'm bored to death. Yes, it is happening again! I deliver the bad news to my cat. The news makes her hair stand on end. She hisses at me in frustration. Why am I unable to find a hobby to entertain myself and spare her my existential issues?

I pick up the phone and start dialing the number of the famous astronomer and celestial professional reader Lucretius Lichtenstein, but my cat displays visible scratch-and-hiss resistance. She thinks that I should stop paying hefty consultation fees for some useless advice and try to find my own way out. Why don't I set up a savings account and deposit all the fees I manage NOT to pay to these people? This will not only contribute to our welfare, but it will also boost my self-esteem.

The idea of a do-it-yourself kit seems appealing. I decide to try this out so I make my first three-hundred-dollar deposit – astronomer – along with the fifty dollars I was about to pay to an old woman who promised to read the coffee grounds for me.

Now I have to find a hobby and keep myself busy. I have never had a hobby, really. My cat suggests fencing, bowling, even modeling. I could also try photography although as a kid I had always feared that people captured in photos can get out and talk to me.

Listening to them wouldn't be a problem, but what if they ask questions? What should I tell them? I decide to do some grocery shopping while thinking of the perfect hobby.

At the Farmer's Market I ask an old woman why the potatoes are so expensive. The woman explains. The market has experienced some fluctuations lately but given favorable conditions, the prices should go lower and the economy should improve by the end of the third quarter.

I smile. Who said formal education is everything? Most likely an idiot, who had no respect for the innate intelligence and the vigor of our people, these simple holders of complex answers. I want to express my gratitude for her input when I realize that I have my iPod on and the answer was actually delivered by Prof. Maurice Schweitzer, a lead expert in global economy, whose conferences I have been listening to while performing daily routine activities – taking out the trash, mopping the bathroom, shopping.

Back at home, my cat is biting her claws, worried that I will not be able to find a hobby. Anything else? She's also worried about the housing market and about global warming. Enough! We decide to share our worries, just to make it easier for both and to minimize the stress. As of today she is only allowed to worry about the housing market, while my official worries will be "hobby" and "global warming." She agrees, but who's going to worry about *us*? We will respectfully ask Aunt Lyla to pitch in and worry about us. Problem solved.

Back to the quest for a decent hobby. I think I need to be a little bit more organized. Let's see, what are the most popular hobbies? Hiking, biking, hunting, playing an instrument, bird watching. Hmmm.

I leave the bird watching to my cat. I like to watch, but mostly women, not birds. And do I really want to play an instrument? Okay, I agreed not to seek formal, in person, advice. But I will continue to follow the news in the scientific community. What do the teams of scientists and researchers say? I love those guys. We owe them so much; we just don't know it. Without them and their guidance we would be lost. I think of them as our teachers and chaperons, for whenever one of us strays from the righteous society and heads in the wrong direction, they bring us back on the right course, with love, patience and understanding. The united, international teams of wise people say that the right hobby improves general well-being, lowers cholesterol, and makes you look up to nine years and a half younger. The right hobby makes one truly blossom.

Blossom. The word sticks to my brains and I cannot take it off. How can I dare to dream about blossoming when I cannot find a stupid hobby? Aunt Lyla calms me down. She says that I shouldn't panic. I do not have a hobby now, so what, so what. What if I'm a late bloomer – one of those people who discover themselves and their hobbies later in life? She gives me the example of her cousin Iovan, a shy, powerful introvert, who had been struggling for over fifty years to understand the differences between sexes.

He finally discovered his sexuality in his late seventies. Sure, he could no longer perform, but he was happier than ever knowing that a masochist like himself would not have enjoyed it anyways.

Was his revelation less valuable? Not at all. Was the lesson of life less significant? Far from it. Was his personal journey a little bit longer? It depends on how one looks at his struggle. For those irresponsible beings like us, who delve into sexuality in their teenage years, Cousin Iovan might have appeared to be terminally mentally ill. But for the true connoisseurs and thinkers, forty or fifty years of observation means nothing.

I am humbled by Cousin Iovan's personal journey. I tell Aunt Lyla that I don't mind waiting a thousand years if I have the guarantee of a nice hobby waiting for me at the end of my struggle. Once again, she is right. Each of us has to patiently wait until they reach their best moment, the moment of blossoming. I know so. Aunt Lyla is herself a role model, waiting for twenty-seven years to find the perfect Cocker Spaniel, whose coat would match the colors in her living room. I could not be oblivious to her mental pain, and I felt compelled to donate to her the long-haired cat I brought home with me from my last trip abroad. The cat was a success, perfectly matching the drawers in her kitchen and my dearest aunt could find the so much sought-after inner peace.

The profound exchange between me and Aunt Lyla is butchered ruthlessly by one of those unpleasant household incidents.

My cat wants to drink bleach water out of the mop bucket. I rush to physically remove her and place her in the proximity of the clean water bowls. Then I explain to her that this is not the best way to have your teeth bleached.

I say goodbye to my relative and go back to my strenuous thinking. The cat is visibly disturbed by my failure, yet she doesn't say a word, fearing that I will remind her to limit her worries to the housing market as previously agreed.

I know what I need to do to de-stress. I need to go jogging! It's dark already and a heavy rain starts just as I am about to leave the house. Will this prevent me from enjoying quality time with myself? Never! I put five more waterproof coats on top of the light, chic jogging costume my cat bought me five years ago in Paris.

I run two hundred feet and then I start walking a brisk walk, confronting my body with the rain and my mind with the deep darkness.

I walk ignoring the world until I get to a small hill. From atop, the view is different. I notice another human shape sitting not far from me. A few watery words and I learn that the man whom I might have unwillingly disturbed is Samuel Frunza, a famous writer whose writing started as a hobby and took him to celebrity status. How was this possible? My instant friend in hobbies explains. Years ago Samuel Frunza looked for a hobby yet all the activities that appeared entertaining were way to expensive and he could not afford them. One after another, his favorite potential hobbies vanished, leaving him hobby-less and unaccomplished. Facing the grim perspective of joining the crowd of poor, hobby-less people and even dying without having enjoyed any decent hobby Samuel came up with this amazing idea.

What if he started writing about all the things he will never have? His first novel, *The Hobby Man*, was an instant success and bestseller. Samuel went to bed poor and hobby-less and woke up rich and indulging in one of the most affordable hobbies ever: writing. Locked in his bedroom, he would close his eyes and dream about breathtaking hobbies like raising chickens, playing tennis with rich people and winning, and last but not least, having his own collection of those colorful, eclectic socks quilted by peasants from Southwestern Ukrainian villages. I give Samuel Frunza a vigorous hug and I express my admiration for his success. This gives me the strength to keep looking for a hobby.

However, I have a question.

Even in the deepest darkness I cannot help noticing that Samuel Frunza is anything but a happy man. What is a man of such glorious hobbies doing here, in the company of a hobby-less, miserable creature like myself? Samuel explains again. Along with fame came money. For the first time in his life, Samuel could finally fulfill his fantasies and get all the hobbies that up until recently, he could only write about. He could not resist the temptation. Before he knew it his life resembled one of his books, intense, adventurous, colorful yet lifeless, empty of realm.

As if this was not enough, a second horror struck. He stopped dreaming as there was no purpose in dreaming. He also stopped writing. Basically he stopped *being*.

And here he is, sitting in the dark and the rain, hoping to *be*, once again, *alive*. The truth is that Samuel, proud owner of a few expensive hobbies, is devastated. I am very concerned for the well-being of my new friend so I assist him in stepping down the hill and safely getting home. In front of his house, a meow in the dark awaits me. It is my cat, who broke the ban on worrying about me and left the house armed with two, not one, flashlights. The joy of seeing my dear partner dissipates as she aggressively asks *the question* while pointing at me with one of the flashlights. Do I have a hobby? No. She is not mad at me as I expected. Actually, she is rather happy; at least this time I saved a lot of money by searching on my own and not turning to those expensive advisers.

At home she fixes me a hot tea, covers me with her favorite blanket, and brings the newspaper. I'm tired. Before I fall asleep, I hear the Depression knocking at my door, and my universe becomes instantly bright. Here she is, my very affordable hobby. She has been with me for a very long time and she will probably never leave me.

I have never been aware of her presence and significance. Yet I know that if I am ever in danger of settling down, my hobby will kick in, taking me into yet a new, unplanned and unpredictable, blossoming adventure.

The Healing Session in Euphoria

I am at one of those gatherings where you go just because you have nothing else better to do. However, my cat did find something better to do. She chose to stay at home and purr. She is smarter than me and she knows it. Why would someone be here instead of being elsewhere?

At the end of the meeting about the most desirable things in life, I expose my humble thoughts briefly. Most people approve of my thinking, except for one small creature in the back who appears to be in the challenge mode. Other average people rush to join him in what is becoming a greater work of rejection.

Annoyed, I look over the masses, broadcasting my declaration of war. Who are you, tiny beings? No, let me rephrase. Who *invented* you? I might seem aggressive. Not at all. The truth is, I despise those intellectual terrorists, shooting at people's ideas without bringing in any creativity and freshness.

Can you teach me something? No? Then move on please and leave room for someone who has something interesting to share. I stand up, ready to leave. I'm pissed because I am going back home in a much worse mental state than I was in when the meeting started. What do I want in life? A nice pen, fluffy pillows and comforters so I don't feel the cold ever again. I want to feel warmth around me. Warmth and Beauty. A man approaches me. Naturally, I put on the "Go away" smile, but he doesn't seem impressed. As I finally decide to look at him, I recognize my "almost-friend," Maki.

Why "almost-friend"? Maki and I have been seeing each other at these meetings, but never got a chance to get closer to each other even though it was pretty visible that we shared the same views. Every time we planned to get together, inexplicable life events made it impossible. One time it was me becoming rich and banning the people from my poor past. Another time, we were ready to meet in private when someone set his house on fire. Three months later when he finally rebuilt the house, we attempted to meet for the third time, but he got a flat tire on his way to the coffee shop.

This way, Maki remained just an "almost-friend," someone you would like to get together with, but you never do.

Tonight it might actually happen. I ask him if he is okay. He smiles at me. Why wouldn't he be okay? I cannot help noticing how harshly life has treated him. Maki starts laughing at me. His life is very interesting. Why would he be upset by a few unpleasant incidents, like a flat tire? We're talking about different things. I'm shocked that he seems to focus on the flat tire and overlook other incidents from his past like the house burning down, his wife cheating on him with the bakery boy, and his car having transmission issues. Maki seems oblivious to the things I find to be really devastating. And I know he can help me with some answers.

I want to know how he can handle life with such grace. Why is he always relaxed, sending the world a message of peace and inner tranquility? I want to seize the opportunity, so I grab him by his arm and literally push him into my car. We are going to have dinner and talk. This time I will get what I want! Maki admits that he, too, was very interested in getting closer to me. To him, I am the personification of ongoing human dissatisfaction. He has always wondered why I am so tormented and unable to enjoy life as it is. He thinks I am his exact opposite. And he is very happy we can finally sit down and talk before he goes on his annual trip home. I ask him where is home. He proudly shows me a few pictures of Euphoria Island, the place where he grew up. Really? Is this where you grew up, little angel? In this heaven of beautiful tall palm trees caressing the shores together with the cerulean blue waters of the ocean? No wonder you seem to be happy all the time.

I ask him if he and his people live in an ongoing state of fearless optimism. Not at all. But they do not seem to carry any dramatic experience in their collective memory. If something bad strikes, they suffer only *after* it happens, never *before* it happens. I am extremely curious to learn more about those laid-back, almost surreal entities. Maki explains. Suffering is part of life and no one is spared. Yet some seem to be inclined to pass the suffering from one generation to another while his people do not. People should live their lives in a continuous state of euphoria and never think of negative events. Nature is friendly, people are friendly, why suffer? Nature, huh? I finish my dinner with a smile, while my brain is processing the freshly acquired data at lightning speed. I would very much like to learn more, so I offer to give Maki a ride. Sadly, he declines my invitation. He would rather walk home.

I get in the car and I dial Professor Gustav Turtle's number before I start my engine. Professor Gustav Turtle is one of today's leading scientific authorities in anthropology, as well as other "ologies." As usual, Professor Turtle's insight is useful, powerful, and deep.

In his view, the landscape and climate play a very important role in our development as individuals and, on a larger scale, as societies. He gives me the example of the people living in northern parts of the world.

Professor Turtle thinks that cold weather makes people reserved, introverted, quiet, whereas warmer climates encourage noise, passions, joy.

I put Professor Turtle on hold and call Aunt Lyla. Can she describe the weather in that part of the world where our forefathers grew up? Stormy. And what does she mean by that? Ugly? Not at all. Just sun today and rain tomorrow. Unstable, volatile weather, extreme temperatures, extreme tempers. Back to Prof. Turtle. One more question for him. Does he think that being transplanted at birth and raised in a different climate could change who one really is? Prof. Turtle says yes. I thank him respectfully and I fly back home.

I'm anxious to introduce my cat to the latest Euphoria experience. She is intrigued as well. She wonders if creating a Euphoria-like environment could help us defeat our depression and emotional insecurities. There is only one way to find out, as a massive remodeling project is on its way.

We work long hours to make our home a place of endless joy, by hanging blue ocean wallpaper, bringing in exotic flowers, and even resetting the Jacuzzi tub in the ground in order to create the impression of an ocean shore. Various stuffed marine mammals, ordered by my cat at a discounted price, add authenticity. We think that it was a successful project, and we cannot wait to enjoy it and improve our general well-being.

A few days into our program and we do not see improvement. Severely depressed, we bring in songbirds, hoping that their joyous singing will help us smile. We end up smiling, but only after we caught and ate them all.

Just when we are about to give up and leave the understanding of the euphoric lifestyle to the much more gifted citizens, we get an invitation to a divorce party. Not only was I not aware that divorce parties existed – I called Aunt Lyla and sought advice from her; as soon as my relative heard today's theme, a deep silence fell; I suspect she might have passed out – but I myself am close to passing out when I see who the happy divorcee is. It is Maki! Oh, this time he will have to answer some questions! Especially since the invitation card has a beautiful picture of himself passionately embracing a voluptuous, long-haired woman. Who is this woman? His new lover? What is this all about? I call him right away and demand explanations. I can almost picture Maki smiling. Of course it's a metaphor. The woman symbolizes Freedom, his one and only wedded wife. All his life Maki yearned to be free. Marrying his now ex-wife did not bother him, since he loved her dearly, but in time she started poisoning his life to such an extent that he found himself at high risk of losing his Euphoria citizenship and becoming one of those average depressed and suffering people from elsewhere. His entire being was in danger. He lost weight, avoided people, became an animal. His existence was purely minimalistic, formed on basic instincts. He did not want to go home anymore. He felt rejected and unwanted like a stray dog.

Year after year, Maki tried to find the best way out. He even became suicidal!

His relationship with his wife worsened to the point where one morning he craved separation so badly that he could not hide it anymore. Oddly enough, the thought of the divorce filled him with joy and happiness, as if he was falling in love for the first time and wanted to be with that person forever. He knew that his marriage was over. Healed and emerging from a long, life-threatening convalescence, he also felt the urge to share the joy of being alive again with his closest friends. He thought that throwing a divorce bash would be a pretty cool idea.

I do too, and one week later my cat and I knock on his door. We knew that by accepting his unusual invitation we would place ourselves in a very unusual situation. And that's why we decided to postpone suicide to begin with, to be in more and more unusual situations. Of course, we also took into consideration the fact that our insurance policy does not cover suicide in the first years, so my cat carefully reviewed the policy and told me that in order to leave Aunt Lyla financially secure we would have to stay alive for another two-hundred-sixty-seven days. Today is day number thirty-four and hey, we are anxious to get closer to euphoric people.

We are not greeted by Maki, as we expected, but by the genderless Amelie-Johannes. I look at my cat but she, too, is unsure if the smiling face in front of us belongs to a man or a woman. We shake hands and paws in great fear and we try to blend in with the mass of celebrating people. After a short informal conversation with Maki, I ask him who the androgynous person who let us in is. Oh, it is his friend. We rephrase our question. "*What* is this friend, a man or a woman?" Maki explains. Amelie-Johannes, a chosen individual with a deeper understanding of human nature, is the honored guest at all the divorce parties. As we all know, the deep understanding goes beyond gender and those who can attain that state of true knowledge need not refer to the masculine or feminine principles. They can identify themselves with both worlds and enter any emotional and physical realm they wish to explore. Really? Well, then who am I?

I'm thinking that since I am not able to understand neither my masculine nor my feminine side, I might not even be human. Maybe I am a goat. Here we are, a goat and a cat, screening the guests. I totally understand that Maki is euphoric. After all, he is, again, a free man. But what makes the other people happy? This I want to learn. I send my cat on reconnaissance. I, too, pick my targets. We meet an hour later, drunk, annoyed and far from euphoric.

My cat is worried that by trying to understand euphoria we might become even more depressed. She worries too much; she has become a true worrier. And every time she gets drunk she starts worrying that we will become poor again. She cannot forget the fact that three years ago I had to sell her French doll to buy food. I assure her that we will never become that poor again. I have learned, throughout the years, that there is poverty, and then there is poverty!

I wouldn't have made this discovery if it wasn't for the amazing encounter with Leopold Hedgehog, an exquisite Swiss pharmacist. He was ten years younger than me, yet forty-two years senior in Knowledge. We had barely stepped into our friendship when Leopold announced to me in a sad tone that we could no longer be friends.

Why? According to him, we were both facing poverty, yet mine looked glamorous when compared with his. We were not a match. To me, poverty meant giving up the Sunday lattes at Mireille's Bistro. To him, it meant skipping one meal; a homemade meal, that is. To me, poverty meant no more sex toys for my cat. To him, it meant forfeiting the deeply discounted prescriptions for his heart disease, and walking around with severe palpitations. Back then I could not understand him and frustration fueled my thinking. It took me a long time to realize that Leopold was a "never-friend," in spite of our great mental connection.

Years later, I attempted to make friends with Tito Sponge, a great mind with whom I was hoping to survive another stage of poverty. But unlike the previous poverties, this one was gruesome and my cat still brings up the French doll. We were selling things to buy food and reading "Introduction to Poverty" guides, while Tito's worst experience was letting go of his vacation home in Tahiti. It struck me that his poverty was chic and desirable, while ours was scary.

Hedgehog was right to defend himself and steer away from incompatible friendships. I tell my cat that I decided to follow Hedgehog's approach and give up the young friendship with Maki.

I thank Maki for having us over. We envy him for turning such a painful experience such a divorce, into a euphoric event. We are humbled by his teachings but...birds of a feather flock together.

We cannot be friends with him as his constant euphoria fuels our endless, life-threatening depression.

We are, once again, back to square one. What should we do to switch from ongoing genetic depression to ongoing genetic euphoria?

I crash on the couch helpless, staring at the inviting ocean and luxuriant vegetation that I personally glued to my walls. I wish I could glue them to my mind and spirit as well, but I just don't know how.

From where I sit on the couch I see a stern yet euphoric, omniscient Amelie-Johannes staring at us from behind a greener than green palm tree.

The Healing Session in Homelessness

We lie in bed motionless. I know we're supposed to join the amateur ping-pong group but we choose not to go. We will close our eyes and imagine that we are playing a very dynamic Tuesday morning game. Actually, the imaginary ping-pong is much, much better than the real one. I never lose and my cat does not have to retrieve the balls. And last but not least, we don't have to go through those after-ping-pong-arguments sparked by the awkward places she has to look for the balls – cleavages, pockets, mop buckets. This is truly a win-win situation. We do not go there to learn something, we just need to see the others playing miserably and to boost our self-esteem. We finish our imaginary ping-pong game and we congratulate each other. We agree to repeat this memorable experience next Tuesday, same time, same place.

We are hungry. Time to grab a bite! My cat turns on the TV. We drop the coffee mugs as a tired woman with big eye rings points her long, red fingernails at us, screaming, "You have to think positive! Join us for the glorious teachings in Light!" We are afraid of pushy people, so we turn off the TV right away. As the screen is black, silent and safe again, we look at each other bewildered. What *is* Positive Thinking?

My cat thinks that this must be one of those new trendy things. People just repeat to themselves everything is wonderful, just to avoid facing their miserable lives. After all, what can you do when your own life turns against you and becomes your greatest enemy? Talking to friends, therapists and such might help a little bit, but in the end you are the only one who has the power to make a change.

I analyze the feline friend's words while baking muffins. I wonder what my family's history would've looked like, had my ancestors applied the rules of positive thinking. Aunt Lyla told me a few stories about her grandparents' villages being occupied and entirely destroyed. What if her grandfather, instead of grabbing the axe to fight back, along with other men, would have sat down, looked at his weeping wife and the six underfed, overstressed children, and told them that they just have to think positive?

I think my cat is right and this must be some new trend. One cannot think positive unless they are secure in one way or another. Yet, *who are we* to draw such quick conclusions? We both feel that we need to learn more about this.

My cat finishes her snack. God, she eats so much! I think of Miss Bubblebaum, the idiot with a stuffed pet. She must be so happy with her low maintenance companion. I like to learn from idiots so I immediately consider a stuffed pet for myself. It's cheap, does not eat, and it's washable. My cat is pissed. She wants all the attention. She feels threatened. So did my last girlfriend and guess what? She's no longer with us – hint, hint. In between hisses and scratches I manage to convince her that a new, fresh voice in our house would be beneficial for both of us. She agrees to try to give a warm welcome to our new friend.

We choose a beautiful Bichon Frise to be the third presence in our house. This way we have a social group, a well-defined social structure. Comte de Champagne, as his name might suggest, is bubbly, flamboyant, and excessively sociable. My cat gives the "hate at first sight" look to the creature with black, sparkling eyes.

I offer Comte de Champagne a nice comfortable spot on our loveseat.

Before the evening sets in my cat eats half of the Comte's tail, and she starts working on the right ear already. I do not pay attention to the manifestations of her insecurities, yet when she asks for dinner I pretend not to hear her pathetic meows.

I indulge in memorable positive moments in the company of the French socialite. I feel compelled to get a nice leash for the Comte for the morning walks to the park. I enjoy the walks immensely and it appears that my neighbors are envious. Unlike them, I do not have to pick up after my beautiful new pet. He is a little bit shy with the other dogs. So what, so what? The only drawback is that he is not a fast learner. I only managed to teach him two or three tricks.

The morning walks are extremely inspiring. I think a lot as usual, but it seems that this time my thinking actually might take me somewhere.

For some reason I think of my old friend Armadillo, the one and only to offer me the deepest insight into human loneliness. Armadillo is indeed very unique. It appeared that no other human being could last too long in his company, no matter how hard he tried to get closer to those he cared about or at least those he wanted to keep around for a while. Why don't I pay him a visit? One like him would be very pleased to learn that someone actually seeks his company.

Armadillo is in "confession-mode" and agrees to share his misery with me. His days are lonely and boring, following the same precise routine. For example, if I ask him if he recalls what he did five years ago on September 4th, he can give me the exact details. How is this possible? He explains that September 4th from five years ago is identical with any other day of any other year. In the morning he wakes up, takes a shower, and pampers himself with lotions and candles. Then his grandmother stops by to bring him fresh homemade doughnuts and to express her fear at the sight of the burning candles, since candles are lit in her old village only when someone close has just passed away. Armadillo sees her out and then he looks in the mirror, wishing that a hot woman and not his grandma stopped by, delivered doughnuts, and made wild love to him right away. Unfortunately, this never happens. Then he calls his friend, Maurice. Maurice, too, would love to get laid, but knowing that chances are slim, he will pay Armadillo a short visit instead. Armadillo tries to make Maurice stay longer, to spend some time with him. But Maurice stands up and is ready to leave right after he finishes the adorable espresso fixed by Armadillo. Then Armadillo goes to the coffee shop where he has his third strong coffee. His hands are shaking already and it is not the caffeine overdose. None of the people in the coffee shop want to take him beyond the usual social graces. Even the lonesome regulars prefer their solitude to a conversation with my friend.

At noon his girlfriend calls. They will meet for lunch. Armadillo is happy, but his happiness is short-lived. As soon as the lunch is over, the girlfriend stands up and leaves. Alone and rejected, Armadillo feels that the only person he can turn to is his mother. His mother weeps listening to her son's misery. She just cannot understand why her special little boy is systematically turned down. However, after she expresses her compassion she too tries to escape his company, choosing to go shopping. Solo.

I look at Armadillo. I dare not ask about the positive thinking but he seems to read my thoughts. Has he ever tried it? Yes, he has. He tried to work on himself, to meet different people; and he even changed jobs, cities, countries. The truth is he never felt at home in anyone's company. He is *spiritually* homeless.

I leave his house puzzled. I talk to my cat but she too is flummoxed and has no answers for me.

If true positive thinking exists, then it should manifest itself in people who are indeed hopeless. Armadillo is spiritually lonely, but he still has a house. How about talking to the homeless guy who lives downtown, under the main bridge?

We drag the Comte on his new Cerulean blue leash to the bridge. We have to stop a few times to dust his coat and paws. Catching all the dust and filth on his coat is one of the dirty tricks I managed to teach him.

The homeless man – frozen luciferic gaze, caveman hair, built-in intuition – is leery of us. Aunt Lyla remarked once that for the average person our original duo might appear slightly freaky. With that in mind we leave candy under the bridge and we wait patiently until he approaches us. We introduce ourselves and express our curiosity to learn more about his lifestyle and views on life.

We hear that homelessness is relative. Most of the people who think that they have a house are truly lonely and homeless since there are voids in their lives that cannot be filled. Before the events that sent him into homelessness, he, too, was living an empty life, void of warmth. He had a house, true. But it was merely a structure, just a bunch of wood, metal and glass. Besides, losing everything helped him focus better on the real issues. As a member of our society he had to deal with a lot of problems: house, kids, wife, jobs. All this vanished and it was replaced by one major problem which was homelessness. And who doesn't know that having only one problem is much better than having a myriad of problems? My cat and I agree. Comte de Champagne is silent.

Life is tough indeed, but our homeless friend is not desperate. It took him many years to realize that, on a deeper level, he had much more than many other people. He pulls out a bunch of drawings. The drawings are truly stunning. What does a man of such extraordinary talent do here, sleeping under bridges? He smiles. Drawing, of course. He hasn't drawn anything significant lately, though. This paper is so expensive! Time to ask the question I am here for. I tell him that he looks like a positive thinker. He bursts out laughing and he shows me some drawings that make my hair stand on end. Abandoning oneself entirely to the Great Positive might not be the best choice. The world's fundamental principle is neither positive nor negative. We have to embrace them both and learn from both. The homeless guy thinks we should never be afraid of the negative principle.

I do not like this guy. Here he is, basically having nothing, and at the same time having so much. Now I understand the hatred my cat felt towards the Comte. There are some guys you just have to hate, and that's it.

Is there anything for which he yearns? Of course. I expect him to tell me he wants a home, but he assures me that art is truly the coziest place ever. There's no place like art!

However, he would like to have a close companion with whom he could share artistic impressions.

I offer the positive Comte de Champagne to the homeless artist, along with a modest allocation for future drawing expenses. He bows in front of us, holding the Comte to his chest.

We go back home without looking back. I do not feel positive at all.

I look at the house. Yes, it is a bland structure, empty of warmth. Will I ever be able to fill the void inside me? We don't know.

The only one who is happy that Comte de Champagne is homeless as well is my cat.

The Healing Session in Beauty

I need to go to the bathroom. On my way to the magic place, I notice accidentally that it is 6:00 a.m. 6:00 a.m.? A few minutes later, I am relieved and happy, yearning to find my way back to the warm bed.

Sadly, my cat is up and seizes the opportunity. She wants us to practice for tomorrow's Inuktun language course. The Inuktun language course is our recent and very fulfilling hobby. Mastering the communication tool used by barely a thousand people from Greenland has become a priority for us.

I cannot say no to my cat, and we start practicing the original lesson our teacher created especially for us in the dark. I take a deep breath. "Excuse me, sir, are you an idiot?"

"Yes, I am," my cat says, pouting her lips for a perfect pronunciation. I smile while I recite my answer, "Me, too! It's good to see that, no matter how far you travel, you can still meet people like yourself!"

It's good to learn languages. Who knows, one day we might travel to Greenland and actually meet those people.

The sunrise catches us by surprise. Tired and grumpy, we try to go back to sleep, with no results.

Since I'm up already I browse the channels, resigned and hopeless. I notice that there is nothing interesting to watch. My cat suddenly remembers the International Beauty Contest. It should be broadcasted live and, given the time difference, we could catch at least a few images. I like the idea, and I am grateful to my cat for reminding me about this event. The thought of hot women in swimsuits keeps my eyes wide open and my brains in a state of deep shock. Here they are, beauties of all races, statures and backgrounds. I argue with my cat as to which one is the hottest. A few glasses of wine clear my mind, and I realize that women see in women details always invisible to the manly eye and vice versa. Why is that? I do not have an answer to this question and neither does my cat. Does she ever have an answer? To make it worse, now she thinks she is some beauty and she walks around the house like a model, staring intensely at herself in all the mirrors and even in the water bowl.

In order to make her happy I have to crawl on my knees, holding an imaginary camera and pretending to take pictures of her.

Half an hour into the show, the verdict comes like thunder, catching me off guard. Yes, my cat is pretty. The only problem is her black coat.

A lighter coat would make her beautiful. Pretty...beautiful...do I see the difference? I admit I do not. I like all colors and sizes.

Another half hour and I see the difference. It is in the price of the coat implant. Coat implant? I slip and fall in between the couch and the coffee table. We have to talk about this. She gives me the "Have you been drinking lately?" look. I learn that the coat implant is a standard feline beautifying procedure, during which the original coat is removed through a series of revolutionary, advanced and sophisticated medical surgeries, and then replaced with the more desirable one.

While we argue over the purpose of what appears to be a true feline ordeal, a red cat distracts us by repeatedly scratching the window. Who is this red cat? It is Emma! Emma? Emma used to be white! My cat explains while she lets her friend in. Emma was indeed white and she hated her life. She always wanted *that sexy tan*. So Emma underwent the same coat implant my cat brought up, just the other way around.

I think of those millions of dark-skinned women who bleach their skin wanting to have a lighter complexion. I also think of most of the white women who visit the tanning salons regularly and have their skin burned in a professional manner. Why? Just to get that sexy, darker look – along with a few thousand wrinkles.

I have to stop this insane enterprise. Aunt Lyla is not surprised at all. Her best friend's dog wants smaller ears. Yes, they have tried to explain to him that he is a Papillon.

We need to ask someone who is really beautiful. Aunt Lyla is skeptical. What do I have in mind? Strictly physical beauty? I tell her that for now, we will limit our search to physicality. She does not agree with me. She gives me the example of niece Melanie. Niece Melanie was a perfect beauty. However, she was very stupid and unwilling to work on herself. Everybody warned her to get smart, just in case and be prepared for the times when her sex appeal would diminish. She ignored everybody and grew old, stupid. And who doesn't know that there is hardly something worse than an old, ugly, and stupid person?

This takes me into another unpredicted journey. Things become complicated, something that I have always hated.

I am suddenly turned off by the beauty contest and I want to take off. Literally. I pick up the phone and call the well-known flight instructor Nono Cloud. Can he reserve a couple of hours from his oh-so-busy schedule for us? Yes, he can. I throw on a jacket, annoyed by my cat's insistent questions about her appearance. Yes, she is sexy. Yes, if I saw her on the street right now, I would definitely turn my head and look at her. Yes, there is something about her. And that something is the fact that she is always late. I remove two hefty tears from her big blue eyes and I push her through the door. We do not want our first flight lesson to consist of us on the ground, watching the plane taking off, do we? We agree to make a short pit stop at the premiere of the movie *Settling for Dust* directed by our dear friend Francisco Watermelon. We are glad that we stopped by, even if for just a few minutes. His short "Thank you" speech might give us a new perspective on Beauty and Life in general. Or not.

Unlike most artists, who thank their mothers, fathers, siblings and even distant relatives, Francisco rushes to thank all the people who made his life miserable and forced him to put himself together and become famous. From what he mentions briefly, the worst and most inspiring beings were his wife – who left him working three jobs and raising three already spoiled kids, and then married a tattooed thief, and his mother – who categorically refused to pitch in, being way too busy with her new twenty-two-year-old gigolo. Since then Francisco experienced a powerful mega shift of his Being. Simply and gracefully, he shifted from outer Beauty to inner Beauty.

We do not understand what he is saying, so we ask for a generous five-minutes of his time. We go behind the scenes to get a cup of coffee and some details. Francisco explains. Up until the life-changing events, he wasn't too picky about the people around him. Now he is. No, he is not a psycho. If he needs a gardener to rake his lawn, he cannot care less for his quality as a human being. But if that person has to be his partner and friend, then they'd better live up to his new standards.

We say "Okay" and continue our journey, partially illuminated by the seeds of Knowledge delivered by Francisco. He is right, and my cat and I hope that one day we too will shift from physical to inner Beauty.

However, as we get close to the airport we are struck by the fact that Watermelon's seeds of Knowledge landed on barren land. We barely remember his words. As a matter of fact, we went there hoping to see the hot actress playing the main character.

We are indeed two worms crawling on the ground and lacking awareness and perspective. Oh, well, at least we know it.

We are anxiously awaiting our first flying lesson. My cat looks funny with her headset on, however I'd better keep my mouth shut, otherwise she will start questioning her sex appeal over and over again. She appears to be saying something to me. It is noisy and I cannot hear anything. But...do I really need to hear her in order to understand? She and I are one!

The flying instructions, per se, are a little bit boring. Thank God for the colorful buttons that seem to invite us to push them. My cat responds promptly to the invitation and pushes them all, curious to see if we are still able to take off. We are not. Instructor Cloud gives her a nasty look.

But where are we flying? We are shown maps yet we have no idea how to use them. We are completely directionless. What if we decide to land wherever handy, just like that, to test our fate and see what it might offer to us? Instructor Cloud does not approve of our impulsive creativity, in spite of our repeated attempts to land on a barn, tennis courtyard and even on a radio tower.

We give up. He is way too uptight for our taste, but he can fly and we cannot. Not yet, that is.

We like the take-offs and we like the loops. But most of all, we *love* stalling. It is the physical state closest to our mental attitude. Being up there, looking down and not knowing.

I try a shy loop. My cat wants to do that too. I explain to her that we cannot do *everything* together.

This reminds me of one of my ex-girlfriends who complained one night that her bed was cold and empty. Mine was cold and empty as well, yet the only thing we could do was to pull our beds closer to each other.

This made both of us feel warmer.

As the flying lesson comes to its end, instructor Cloud shows us some seasoned aviation tricks. We clap hands and paws in great joy. We want to be able to do that too! Instructor Cloud thinks that we should be able to master that pretty fast, but only if we quit drinking.

We thank him politely yet we have no intention to quit drinking.

Back at home, I try to relax. My cat suggests that we shouldn't be concerned about our limitations. Another day passed by and we have learned *nothing*. So what?

As for the beauty topic, I am empty of ideas. I do what Aunt Lyla taught us to do when we are empty of inspiration: I prepare a delicious herbal tea.

A question wearing camouflage pops out like a skilled enemy, catching by surprise the warrior's mind, tired after so many lost intellectual battles. My protests – "I thought this was a question about weather!", "Go away! I don't want to think of you now" – do not help.

The question is, am I beautiful? Good question. Why don't I assess myself like my cat does? And how could I overlook such an essential, yes! essential, fundamental thing?

My cat suggests that in order to be able to generate a healthy self-assessment, we should detach ourselves from ourselves. Her idea is good if not brilliant.

Here we are, living in the third person.

Detached and relaxed, we watch this guy who lives with his cat and walks around asking bold, odd questions. We start well and practice detachment with dedication for almost a day.

Yet right when we are about to let the *assessment* speak, the *self* kicks in brutally. Our view about ourselves becomes distorted and biased. We think that the human-animal couple in front of us is attractive, smart and sexy. My cat does not like this self-assessment. She thinks that we are awesome. Awesome. Awesome. This time I am the one who is completely dissatisfied with the outcome of our assessment. The couple I see cannot be described using simple words. We will have to re-invent the English language. My cat suggests creating a longer word like *marve-miracu-aweso-extraordi-amazi-wonderful*. I decide to end this dangerous game, fearing that we might fall in love with ourselves. You cannot blame us, we are so beautiful.

The herbal tea is ready. We say goodbye to the adorable human-animal couple and we retreat to our cozy bedroom.

On the side of the bed, the childhood plush toys approve of our latest discovery and deliver in a soft voice one more Inuktun sentence: Beauty is a state of mind.

The Healing Session in Politics

We make the mistake of watching the News again. Cat resting on my feet and curious eyes, I try to understand the way this world is ruled.

We hear in great satisfaction that the economy is good. The PBIWW is higher this year and the DLOYY is lower, which means that overall, our life has significantly improved. We do not comment. We keep drinking and try to memorize the odd economic indicators. These names are so complicated that we need to be drunk in order to remember them.

A politician with strong jaws assures us that the interest rates for the first time homebuyers will drop soon. We don't care. If we ever buy a house again – which I doubt – we will be last time buyers. The interest rates are a hot topic for us, though; we just financed a chicken for our birthday.

We look around trying to understand the wealth these politicians talk about all day long. Where is Wealth? "It is not here," my cat suggests pointing at our cheap furniture. As I question everything, even her assessments, I look under the furniture, behind the curtains and even in the closets. She is right. The promised wealth is not there.

Tired of playing hide-and-seek, I decide to get advice in this matter. The best person to get unbiased advice from is our dear Aunt Lyla.

Aunt Lyla is, as always, to the point. Most power people are greedy and ruthless, what do we expect? What do we expect? We put them up there to solve our problems!

Not only do they not seem to be interested in solving them, but we get more and more problems every day. We don't understand quite well how this works, but we feel something is wrong.

I'm no longer willing to put up with this and settle for the low interest sausages. I want a decent life.

We don't know where to start, so we keep watching the news with indifference. We see the president opening schools, closing banks – or the other way around, I am not sure – and mediating conflicts between the first generation of homeless people and the second and the third ones. We also listen to declarations and announcements made by important politicians with bodyguards. The bodyguards are very big, while the important people are very small. We do not understand why it takes so many big people to protect the small ones. But Aunt Lyla tells us that apparently, the third generation of homeless citizens has guns and is very well organized.

The international news is equally unsettling. Our politicians, along with politicians from other countries, decided to print out more money and give it to the people. That's nice though. I mean, the money has no value, except for the comfort value. Money is to us what pacifiers are to the restless infants. Here's another one. Some official from a tiny country is caught in a hotel room with three, not one, prostitutes. Male prostitutes. In the few broadcasted interviews, impoverished toothless citizens express outrage. However, when asked if they would still vote for him they say, unanimously, "Yes."

A week later I realize that I have totally lost my appetite for life and, even worse, for sex. My cat looks at me in awe. I know, I know, coming from me this is a huge, scary statement.

We pay an expensive visit to Dr. Leon Iceberg, RN, Ph.D, DDS, DVM, CD – what is CD? – a recognized authority in low sex drive. He assures me that the lack of desire is not unusual at all, and most distinguished members of our society have it. It is caused by stress along with the financial instability. People are desperate. How can they not be? It's tough when you have to hold three jobs. They put all their time exclusively into survival; there is little or no room left for pleasure, be it sex or playing Frisbee with their pooch.

Dr. Iceberg gives us precious medical advice. He tells me to talk to my partners about what arouses me sexually. I don't think so. I've done that in the past. I've tried to share my fantasies with women just to watch them walking away with their hair standing on end. It's better to save some mystery for the intimate encounters.

He suggests reading erotic materials, watching erotic videos, or indulging in sexual fantasy, if these appeal to us. My cat looks at me with compassion and points at the shelves packed with porn. I have done that in the past as well. As a result, I became a selfish jerk-off. No woman could offer me what I could offer myself with the help of the porn stars. Besides, real women are not predictable like the porn stars. Those are awesome. You pinch their ass, they moan; you squeeze their breasts, they spread their legs, and so forth. Real women come with manuals and instructions, and you better be ready to do your homework. Otherwise, they won't work properly.

Is there anything else Dr. Iceberg can recommend? Of course. The magic pill that will increase our sex drive up to 358%. Can we have one, just in case?

We get the pill and leave the doctor's office happy. At home we put the pill in a safe place and we go outside to feed the squirrels.

It started with one squirrel. She had big wet eyes and we felt for her. She was alone and her coat was ugly. We started feeding her and she turned into a sexy red-coated mama. In order to offer her a quiet, welcoming environment, we gave up practicing the African drums in the backyard. She must have liked it here. Before we knew it, a boyfriend showed up. After he moved in, little young squirrels kept popping out of nowhere. But when we went up North and there was no one to feed them, she kicked out the young, the boyfriend and tried to survive on her own. Three months after we came back and resumed the steady nut-and-seed supply, the squirrels multiplied again.

I think of Astrakhan and his simple observations. The lesson is obvious. No nuts, no little squirrels. Too much African-drum-induced stress? No little squirrels.

My cat speaks words of wisdom. Dr. Iceberg is right; it has to do with the poor economy and the financial instability. Aha, so the government does not give us nuts, therefore we lose interest in having sex. There we go, so we owe these scoundrels more than just the daily poverty, we also owe them the lack of desire for intimacy.

We want our nuts back along with an even lower DLOY or whatever they call it. And we want it now!

I go to pick up my shirts at the cleaner's and I hear heated conversations about taxes and the gas price. I have a coffee at the place across the street, and I watch a few customers becoming confrontational over the reforms in Transportation. I am interested.

At home, the cat is fixing a green tea for Aunt Lyla. Without saying a word, my aunt hands me a pamphlet. They're hiring at the Prime Minister's offices. They are mainly looking for maintenance guys and housekeepers, but they also mention terrific advancement opportunities. We kiss Aunt Lyla's hands repeatedly while calling the four numbers listed on the pamphlet simultaneously. She is a fast thinker, so she has the recommendation letters, signed by select members of our family all ready.

Needless to say, we got the job. We start as a Garbage Collector Aide for the right wing offices. Yet our ability to profile the workers based on the trash collected from their offices does not go unnoticed and we are promoted to Security Advisor III. We will work in one of the offices that we used to clean until recently. We send Aunt Lyla flowers.

Our job is very interesting but it is not the job that keeps us here. It's the people. We interact with them with extreme curiosity but also extreme caution. We do not want to be sent back to the Garbage Section.

The most important occupation here is to "look" busy, as if you really cared. Then it's five o'clock and you go home. Sometimes we have to use the back exit as the building is assaulted by angry strikers fighting for some perennial cause, but we don't mind. I like that, and my cat likes it, too. I am happy because we rarely agree on anything.

Now and then, the office doors open and a very important man calls one of my colleagues, "Hey, Tim will you give me a break?" And next thing we know, voila! A new tax break, especially tailored for Tim's friend, is passed. *This* is true friendship.

Although our duty is to screen potential enemies of the government, sometimes they ask us to perform other tasks as well. We don't mind, we are skilled in more than just one field. For example, today we are requested to translate the messages of our Prime Minister and his counterpart on the occasion of a short visit. They do not trust an outsider as a translator, and rightfully so. They do not want distorted messages to reach the masses.

As our guy delivers his speech, my cat and I freeze. The officials turn around and stare at us intensely, waiting for the translation. But how can we translate "the joy of bringing together the people, whose efforts have been intensified by the international action, along with the fight against everything, and the recent events, especially now when we are inhabitants of a global village..."?

The cat asks me discreetly where the subject, predicate and object are. I don't know. I don't see them. All I can see is the world as a global village. I instantly picture my grandma's village, the horses, the cows...and us, the happy villagers. Moo! Moo!

My cat has enough. She picks up the microphone and tries to save face by delivering random phrases like, "Let the peace triumph! Let us fight against everything!" and even, "I want tuna!" Oddly enough, the audience applauds. No one seems to notice anything unusual, as they rush to the banquet.

We are startled by this experience and we promise each other to avoid translations from English to English in the future.

In the meantime, a new international scandal erupts. Can we get a peaceful day at our new and exciting job? This international scandal prevents us from enjoying our coffee. We need to sit in our office and listen to the President's message.

We get the message. For the average citizen the message is about economic turmoil, misfortunes and pensions that the government won't pay. But seasoned advisors like us can translate this from

English to English. Simply put, someone at the very top stole again and now we have to pitch in and cover the losses.

While I do not encourage stealing, I listen to my cat's theory. She thinks that maybe they do not want to steal *that* much but they get sucked into a whirlpool of greed. Maybe they are good people and they start clean, like we do when we start a new diet.

What does Dr. Pumpernickel say? No food after 6:00 p.m., just water and meditation. We cannot do that. We cheat, but just a little bit. We won't have food, as in real food, just a few carrots. We start with two carrots and by the third we are looking for the dip. After all, how many calories can hide in a very light dip? What are they, secret agents? We dip a few carrots in the mayonnaise-based culinary treat and…we could use some bread. And who doesn't know that bread, olive oil and spices are best friends forever? From here to sausages, chunks of ham with garlic, salamis and burgers it's just a tiny step. And once this symphony of greed, this tsunami of unstoppable cravings, this waterfall of hunger has started, nothing can be done.

Once again, Knowledge is power. We are no longer moved by the fact that someone up there walks away with a country or two in his pocket.

What annoys us is the fact that we were hoping for an inside view, a view that would be different from what we can see from the outside. Yet there is no epiphany and this saddens us immensely.

We pack our things slowly. We are going to miss the coffee. Their coffee is awesome and the packages display cute tanned kids from third world countries counting coffee beans; behind them three guerilla fighters smiling. There is also a message to it. It reads "No children have been exploited while picking this outstanding coffee."

Right in front of my office, I meet a few colleagues. We talk about stress and I expose my thoughts about sex, nuts, squirrels and governments that suck the life out of us.

They all look at me as if I was an idiot. They give me a bland expressionless look while they swallow Dr. Iceberg's pills.

The Healing Session in Friendship

I was hoping to take a shower and watch the early Sunday morning food show, when one of those unplanned events crept again into my existence. Wasili invited himself over for breakfast. My cat hates Wasili and for a good reason. Severely depressed, Wasili is constantly searching for friends to listen to his confessions. This would not be a problem if he allowed us to share our thoughts as well. But Wasili wants *us* to listen to *him*, skillfully avoiding the situations that would place him in the listener's seat. He never seemed to understand that friendship is a two-way street, and whenever we tried to escape the hell of his confessions we have been reduced to silence with the almighty "I thought you were my friend." Throughout the years we have all learned to "Wasili-proof" our lives – by offering him creative excuses, prepaid therapy sessions, et cetera. However, he has improved his techniques as well – climbing walls and entering our houses through the bathroom windows is one of them – so now and then, we are forced to tolerate him for a while, listen to his confessions and give him advice he will never follow.

I can hear Wasili's voice from upstairs, so when I descend, I am fully prepared to handle his latest sufferings. My cat pretends to be busy fixing breakfast, besides she is totally safe, wearing the state-of-art feline earplugs. Polite as she is, she stops from her errands now and then, making compassionate faces at Wasili as if she was closely following the plot. I join the duo with a before-coffee distorted smile. Wasili neither stops the flow of confession nor does he update me as to the main events. I pick up not necessarily related to each other fragments, like his dislike for small cupcakes, and the emotional pain he had to cope with when he broke up with his last girlfriend and the mother-to-be of his not yet conceived, unborn son.

I offer him coffee. He offers me another confession on how he discovered that huge amounts of coffee helped him stay slim.

I offer him a pancake. A short confession about olive oil and low cholesterol blends in the conversation. I'm afraid to show my hospitality so I eat my pancakes and drink my coffee shyly, while Wasili opens the heavy floodgates of true confessions. We are flooded in less than an hour. I learn about his turmoil, emotions, break-ups and financial issues. All this crochet on the same old canvas, that we are his best friends. Finally, my cat intervenes and reminds me – wink, wink – that we have to go to the Sunday Mass. Wasili understands, yet, while seeing him out I have to listen again to the oldest and most famous of his confessions, the one about the religion and mystical life.

The door is closed yet we do not feel safe enough. We lock it and then use chairs and a heavy loveseat to barricade the main entry. We also call Aunt Lyla and advise her to lock the doggy door as we fear she might be Wasili's next target.

My cat takes out her earplugs and the question is delivered to me telepathically as no words are spoken. Yes, she is right. I, too, cannot understand the freeing power of friendship and confessions. We have learned, the hard way, that the best way to cope with dissatisfaction is to bury it inside you and only when it burns your entire being inside out, seek professional advice. This will help you realize that those professionals not only have no clue about what you're talking about, but they are able to give you advice. How is this possible? We don't know. But it is way better to do so than talking to the average citizen friend. I only made one confession in my life, when I was in high school. I told Agatha, whom I considered to be my friend, that I hated low-rise panties. Naturally, she used that against me, bringing it up whenever she could, making people wonder what was wrong with me. She also wore them when we were having arguments or we were just disagreeing over different things. Since then, I do not feel comfortable giving out information that can and will be used against me. It appears to me that every friend wants to make a citizen's arrest now and then, for personal validation purposes.

My cat opens her mouth and I see her struggling with the right choice of words. I encourage her to skip editing and use simple kitty words instead. She reminds me of our sources of knowledge like for example Atanas, as well as other friends who listened to us and offered guidance. I correct her right away. First, we did not make confessions, we asked questions. Second, we did not repeat ourselves. We are cute and creative, not a burden. Who wouldn't want to be around us? She does not seem convinced. In my cat's view, we should go to the Sunday Mass and maybe try to talk to the priest and see what he thinks about this. I agree. After all, maybe the lie she told Wasili about us going to the Mass was not a coincidence. Maybe it is a part of the Big Plan. I want to know how a man of God would handle Wasili. We dress up in great joy and walk to the church proudly, looking people in the eyes. They do not know that we are close to yet another powerful life lesson. We feel pity for them. Most of them will never sign up for life lessons. Some will, but will not graduate. And only a chosen few will eventually graduate, but they will never be able to use or share their knowledge, due to the final and most compelling life lesson, which is Death.

At the church I ask my cat to introduce ourselves, as she enjoys superior social prestige. As I expected, she is warmly welcomed by the elderly awaiting the most compelling life lesson, while my flamboyant masculine presence goes unnoticed.

The Priest – moderate smile, arched back, swollen legs – is more than happy to listen to the human-feline grief. But first we will have to participate in the Mass. Obviously, the church we picked is one of those old rite Orthodox ones, so we will have to stand and hold the candles throughout the entire Mass which lasts less than six hours. No wonder those priests have swollen legs. Six hours later we crawl in front of the magic black booth, the Mother of all one-way friendships. While waiting for the man of God, we eavesdrop on the word exchange taking place inside. As the sound enters my ear, brain and is finally processed, I drop the cat. Normally, such act of animal neglect would have severe consequences. Not this time. It is Wassili's voice! We both freeze with our ears struggling to pick up more and more sounds. We are curious to hear his confession like never before! Our curiosity is satisfied. Wasili's main problem is the fact that...he does not have friends, real friends who would be there for him, day and night. His voice is shaky as he confesses he cannot find warm hearts to offer him comfort and support. The Priest suggests lots of prayers and meditation. Warm Christian words end Wasili's one-way friendship session.

Wasili's voice is probably well known here, for we watch the priest discreetly removing his earplugs on his way out. I send a triumphant "Aha!" to my true and only friend. We are on the same page. I would be surprised if anyone except perhaps God could handle Wassili's selfishness and human selfishness in general. We both agree not to wait and talk to the priest, as our questions have been answered already.

As far as I am concerned the only confessions – and friendships that might develop from them – that drive me crazy are Wasili's and the after-sex ones. I do not like to connect, bond, and hold hands after sex. While I am fully aware that this is the price a man has to pay for the short-lived pleasure, I most definitely do not encourage such behavior. I see women like predators who skillfully trap their small prey and force them to listen. If they have to tie them down for this purpose they will do it. Yeah, it's that bad.

Again, a phone call from Wasili. I put the phone on the speaker and immediately summon my cat for the impromptu phone conference. She crawls to the phone holding the newspaper. What is it this time? Wasili just broke up with the girl he met yesterday, another mother of his unborn son. How come? Oh, well, she wanted him to listen to her endless insipid … confessions. She wanted him to be her friend. Outraged, Wasili tells me how he has tried everything: sex, changing subjects, distractions and even threats. He admits that he, too, likes to share his feelings with people, but he is always careful not to cross certain boundaries. Hearing his last statement my cat's face turns yellow and she clenches her fists at the phone. I try to end the conversation by telling Wasili I have some important things to do right away. Not before I answer one more question though. Wasili wants us to tell him how he can keep happy both his body and mind, how he can satisfy both his instincts and soul. I look at my cat. She is the one who can give advice as to the simplest basic animal instincts and cravings, while I handle mostly the other, most hideous part. My cat sets aside *Feline News* and allows the animal voice to speak. Her advice? When your instincts call, follow them, do not try to analyze and think. Where should we place the soul in this picture? She does not know. Her wisdom ends here. A cat cannot give what she hasn't got. She sends a muted growl to an imaginary Wasili on her way to the bathroom. I get to finish the one-way conversation with Wasili on the background of her peeing and whistling.

I finally realize that today we are blessed with such beautiful weather! As usual, we decide to enjoy the beautiful weather in our own way, which is sitting in the kitchen and watching it through the window, wishing we were out there. We are grateful for this simultaneously useful and useless life lesson about friendship.

We soon get tired of enjoying the nice weather. We are thirsty. We decide to leave the house and have a beer/tuna shake at the sports bar. We enter with caution, observing the surroundings and looking for the waitress. I hear my cat introducing herself as Felicia. Felicia? Her name is not Felicia! I want to ask her what is this all about but she sanctions my unfinished intention with a hiss. I bet this has to do with her secret activity on the dating sites.

Yet I do not want to listen to her confessions. Selfish and undisturbed, I sip my beer laying one more brick in the wall of friendship that divides me and my best feline friend.

# The Healing Session in Pain

I pick up my cat at the vet clinic. She's still drowsy after having her wisdom tooth removed. I try to make jokes and to cheer her up, telling her that now her wisdom is significantly reduced. She hisses at me. I do not like whining. I politely remind her that I, too, underwent a few surgical procedures in my life, yet I handled the pain in silence, like a true man. Her numbed face does not prevent her from laughing at me hysterically. She does not consider laser hair removal to be a surgical procedure. And she remembers how I walked around for days with ice packs under my arms.

I decide to change the subject.

Her quiet, unassuming demeanor seasoned with mischievous hisses makes me think that maybe I shouldn't change the subject. The subjects my cat and I tackle are usually the type that cannot be easily changed. I think of the Pain, the physical pain I had to go through in my life. Like when I broke my arm. So what, so what … it hurt a little bit. Okay. It hurt a little bit more. But I recovered fast and never complained. However, when Agatha broke my heart, I suffered like a dog for years, never recovered, and complained a lot. My cat sighs.

To this day, when I mention the hotel incident, the cat reaches for her earplugs. I find that to be a manifestation of her feline selfishness. The question is on. Why can we handle physical pain gloriously while the pain of the soul is unbearable? Why? Why? We do not know. We wish we knew.

Just sitting and contemplating future sterile years of suffering is not a solution. Time to find out more about our pain of the heart.

We need to be careful as to whom we choose to turn for advice.

Yes, we are lonely and unloved and we have questions. But we do not want to be desperate, like we were a few years ago when we joined the Single Parents' Network, just to belong somewhere. True, we had no kids, yet we learned so much about parenting. That's the scary part. We learned so much and we identified ourselves with "the parent character" to such an extent that we almost felt the presence of the children in our house. Even Aunt Lyla started bringing candy to Amos, my imaginary son. That was truly an unhealthy experience.

We need someone to teach us pain management. There are so many remedies for physical pain, yet can we find a soothing one for our bleeding hearts? My cat smiles. Do I want to try the muscle and mind relaxant that her vet prescribed? No, I do not. My intention is to be able to face the Pain and stop living in a continuous state of denial. She wishes me good luck. This means that I am on my own. No problem, cat buddy, I will prevail!

I go to see Amadeus Steel, the Pain Management Specialist, secretly hoping for a ray of Knowledge. The Pain Management gentleman – expressionless face, expressionless body, detached demeanor – listens to my grief with the utmost attention. I ask him why, after so many years, I still go on dates driven by the silent, burning hope that when I get there I will see my Agatha and not some woman I do not even want to know?

He says that this happens because I have not been able to *release* her yet. In my heart, she is still *the one and only*. I admit I am a little bit confused. He explains, "While it is pretty easy to *release* the Past, along with the Pains of the Past, people just don't know how to do it. All you have to do is embrace the Pain, fully accept it and only then *release* it for good."

Sounds easy. But how am I going to achieve this state of ultimate wisdom? I learn that if I split up with someone, all I have to do is make what he calls a "healing" list. The healing list is a list of good and bad traits of the person who hurt my feelings. Reading the list, over and over again, should convince me that I could not have been happy with such a person.

But what if the good traits outnumber the bad ones? Wouldn't that only deepen my Pain? Not if I "cheat" and add a few imaginary bad traits. Talking yourself into the fact that the person in question was not a desirable choice for you, is of the essence. When this method fails, repeat to yourself that men and women are not created to love and complete one another, but just for the sake of practical, reproductive purposes. This method can be tailored to a specific type of Pain. If the one who hurt your feelings is your mother, no problem. Take a look at the animal kingdom, after all, at core, we are just a bunch of talking animals.

Any creature on this planet will kick their young out of their nests or dens after bringing them to a certain degree of independence. Why would your mother be different? Grow up, will you? With fathers it is even easier!

While I sense the strength encrypted in Mr. Steel's words, I still think it's pretty hard to cope with the Pain of the heart. I cannot help wondering how such a great specialist would handle the pain induced not by other people, but by the simplest facts of life.

Maybe that is why I have never thrived in relationships. I am afraid to be in a relationship. I *refuse* to be in a relationship. Being alone carries a significantly lower risk of being hurt and *abandoned* again. My Pain Manager does not agree with me. He says that by isolating myself, I only increase the Pain. Really? I don't remember isolating myself from the very beginning. My cat and I joined various pain therapy groups, including the famous informal chit-chat therapy led by Dr. Enrique Blasé. Although useless, his therapy sessions were fun and my cat still remembers how people who did not know each other would sit around the table, tell stories about pain no one else could relate to, and then walk away. They served good cookies so we kept going. I think that this was the main reason why other people kept going there as well. Nobody could let go of their pain, but everybody enjoyed the cookies. I learned something interesting there, though. It became obvious to me that the first onset of Pain is the excruciating one. Then, you just learn to live with the Pain. It's like living with arthritis. You know it will never heal really; on the contrary, it will only get worse. But you do whatever you can to make your life easier.

Or...not.

As for the rest of the humanity, and its ways of coping with the Pain, it seems to me that they navigate carelessly in an ocean of suffering. A pill or two, a night-out, a few cheering words, and the pain is gone. How do they do it? We don't know.

My cat sanctions my hasty statements and brings up the painful story of Aunt Madeline, who for most of her life, managed to hide her pain from everybody else including herself. Every day Aunt Madeline would put on a happy mask and would head out to face the world.

Who would have guessed that under that mask of calm, impersonal happiness, a deep, profound pain was growing unhampered? Slowly, almost imperceptibly, the internal pain was taking over the happiness that Aunt Madeline's mask was displaying so effortlessly.

Day by day, people watched in awe as Aunt Madeline's mask deteriorated. One sad gaze here, one sigh there, until the volcano of suffering erupted, burning everything in its path. The positive mask melted, unveiling a face unknown even to the closest members of her family. Seeing the true Madeline for the first time was a very traumatizing experience for everybody. Parents would cover their children's eyes, fearing that the unhealthy early exposure to pain could have a negative impact on their development.

The older members of the family, who were secretly hoping to end their lives without having ever to face their own pain, expressed unanimous disapproval. How could she dare? Wasn't she aware of the fact that, by publicly expressing her Pain, she was endangering an entire clan's well-being and self-esteem? Have a heart, Madeline!

A very tense period followed. Everyone avoided Madeline, except for Aunt Lyla and the ice cream truck driver, each of them for different reasons. Aunt Lyla was sensitive and supportive, while the ice cream truck driver had a big fetish for sad women. Pain on a woman's face was a healthy turn on for him, so he ended up driving the ice cream truck in circles until he ran out of gas and the ice cream melted just like Aunt Madeline's positive mask.

I look at my cat. And where is the wisdom I am supposed to get from her story? She shrugs scornfully. It goes without saying. Even a cat gets it!

I am lost in thought and so is she. We are not convinced that we have an answer. And maybe we are not interested in a particular destination but in the journey itself.

The journey is what keeps us going.

My feline friend offers to fix dinner for the two of us. I sit at the table, defeated. It is late night already, and she lights the candles. I try to slice some bread, but I slice my fingers instead. The cat freaks out at the sight of blood. Never mind, it will heal.

I look over her shoulder. Outside in the dark, an individually blue and haunted-by-memories Agatha sends me an enigmatic smile. The omniscient Pain Management Specialist failed to teach me where to put *that* smile in my "good traits/bad traits" healing list.

The Healing Session in
Bad Relationships

I wake up shaking, covered in cold sweat. I see my cat's big, round eyes moving over my face. Am I OKAY? She rushes to check my pulse. I assure her I am fine. Another nightmare, what else? And who is afraid of nightmares, after graduating from Dust Devil's Academy of Nightmares? However, a few elements of this dream give me the goose bumps.

I have to call Aunt Lyla, the woman who hasn't lost the deep connection with her ancestors. I'm sure she will have an explanation for the unusual assembly of creatures and events from my dream.

I call my aunt and give her all the details. In my dream, my cat and I are asleep. We seem to enjoy an endless state of dreaming, to be more precise. At some point we wake up, yet our movements are slow, clumsy, as if we were still asleep. Oddly enough, when we are up, everybody around us seems to be awake and asleep at the same time. What could this be? My cat and I are anxious to hear the ancient wisdom brought to us by Aunt Lyla. At the other end of the phone, Aunt Lyla is silent. I summon her to say something. Finally, she breaks the silence. She does not know. What? I respectfully remind her that she is our closest relative alive and our spiritual guide. She must have an answer for us! She promises to call Cousin Natasha who is very knowledgeable in this field. We should have an answer by tomorrow afternoon.

I feel better already. I tell Aunt Lyla that I want to do something with my life and I don't know where to start. She suggests a fresh Turkish coffee as one of the best places to start. My cat approves. We need an energizer, so we move to the kitchen. The Swiss cuckoo pops out of his little cuckoo house and announces to us it is 5:00 p.m. 5:00 p.m? I thought it was early morning! I thank the cuckoo and allow him to return to his wooden solitude. Once again, my cat fails to get him and her abrupt landing on the wet tiles reminds me that I forgot to put out the "Wet floor" sign. I apologize to my best friend. Courteous as she is, she agrees to get over the incident.

Half-asleep, we review the most recent events. I know where this is going. She cannot help it and brings up my last relationship with the

Croatian widow. How could I get involved with that woman? Yeah, how? I admit that every single day I ask myself the same question. I stare in the mirror for hours repeating, "Why? Why? Who are you?"

I have been in many bad relationships, but this one drained me totally. Why do people end up in relationships anyways? To feel protected? To feel loved? To get laid more often? Why can't we be like animals, mating now and then, and occasionally raising an offspring or two?

My cat cannot understand me. Why do I have to be with someone just to be with someone? True love is different. *That* she can understand. She supported me when I was deeply in love. She spent countless nights in the cold outside the house to give me the privacy I needed. She stepped down from her position of best friend, and allowed the women of my life to get closer. She even skipped a few meals and agreed to move the Zen meditations from Sunday to Monday. She does not regret showing support, but she wants to know if I learned something from my adventures.

Have I learned something from the past experiences? I might have. I also learned a lot from other people. I think of my cousin Aram, who married a woman with two children. In vain, we tried to stop this insane move. He kept telling us he wanted a family and such. And he got one. He ended up with a bitch, her children, and since they were both in their forties, an awesome set of old relatives to care for. Ten years later, he looked as if he was in his early seventies while the sick and old relatives blossomed and looked like teenagers. Aram did not realize where *love* had taken him, until one glorious summer morning. He was sitting in the garden in his wheelchair. His adopted fifteen-year-old boys were playing football with his adopted set of grandfathers. The grandfathers won. Aram was only fifty-three and he suddenly felt very old and lonely. He missed his life, the times when he was free to chase the chicks around without having to take their fathers to the doctors. What went wrong? Perhaps life went wrong.

I decided to learn from Aram's scary journey through life. So after I liberated myself from the Croatian oppression, I met another sexy, freshly divorced thirty-something woman. This time I had the questions ready. Does she have any parents? Are they healthy? To be more precise, how many sets of sick, old people do I have to care for when love fades away? Aunt Lyla taught me that love fades away quickly, while the old, sick grandparents suffering from urinary incontinence tend to stick around for a while.

The sexy creature called me blunt and insensitive. Really? My cat and I laughed at her vigorously. We did not even bother to hide our feelings. You won't trap us, hot mama! Yes, knowledge is indeed power! We decided to test her, just to have some fun. We tell her that we have to take Aunt Lyla to the dentist. Will she join us on our short forty-nine-mile commute? The caring, sweet feminine angel sitting in front of us suddenly remembers that she has a very important doctor's appointment. We smile triumphantly at each other and shake hands and paws under the coffee table. We tell the young woman how wonderful she is. Yes, we cannot wait to get together again. It looks like we clicked and we might have a wonderful future together. Of course, we could tell her that she is a bitch, and uncover her smallness. Yet if we do that, she will improve her skills and become a better bitch. More and more men will suffer as a result of her actions. By not telling her that we *know,* we are actually encouraging her to stay an average bitch, thus saving many innocent lives. *This is wisdom*, my friends.

My cat approves. We have been blessed. We are safe. After hearing so many "success stories," I admit that whenever I meet a chick, I picture instantly a family of old sick relatives in the background. The images are so intense and so colorful, I sometimes feel an urge to introduce myself to the army of ghosts. While the ability to detect the clear and present danger is very empowering, we cannot find a woman's company enchanting any more. I wonder why. When I was young I used to have much more patience with new relationships and even with bad relationships. Whereas now, we recite our questions, get the answers and move on. In some cases, we move on even before we hear the answers to our questions. But how long are we going to keep moving on? Is this because I'm a male? My cat starts laughing. Of course, not. She gives me the example of Carmen, the niece of Aunt Lyla's grandfather.

Carmen was this beautiful, highly educated and polished young woman. Everyone was hoping to see her marry a successful man and settle down, in good old family tradition. But Carmen had different plans. Unlike other women, Carmen was looking for much more than a successful man. She wanted a man to complete her. She wanted *integrity*. While men usually go to extreme lengths to shower women with rings, flowers and other artifacts, Carmen was oblivious to their efforts. She couldn't care less for a man who was trying to cover up his mental, emotional, and sexual insecurity. She just wanted a man who could give her a *home* and not simply a house. Although it appeared to everyone, including herself, that she wasn't asking for that much, a gruesome revelation was waiting. It was the other women who settled for little or nothing. Carmen wanted *a lot*.

Aunt Lyla teamed up with the powerful informal group of old wise women and they decided to bring in a famous matchmaker. Yet he, too, had to admit helplessness. There was no *integrity* in the masculine world that he knew so well.

Carmen ended up dating one idiot after another. Then she stopped. As she grew older, she eliminated the dinners and the whole dating ordeal and went straight to sex, focusing only on the physical dimension, and totally tuning the rest of them out. In time, she narrowed down her search so well that she could tell even before getting close to them if they were worth those two hours of her precious time. She started visualizing her colorless and insipid men as handsome golems, waiting for her to put the right words in their minds and mouths. What was her problem? Her problem was that she had no problem. She realized that whenever she allowed a man to get closer, she also got a bunch of problems. She got tired of living just to solve other people's problems.

Carmen's story is indeed frightening. One might think that a person with such an awesome insight and knowledge of humans should be happy or at least empowered. Carmen was anything but. Twenty years in her quest for integrity and there she was, back to square one. What went wrong? Perhaps life went wrong. But what if this runs in our family – this unusual thirst for things that nobody cares about, this bad timing in everything we do?

Finally Aunt Lyla has an answer for us from Natasha. Apparently, we make the most important decisions in life while half-asleep. I am speechless. Do we ever wake up? But, of course. We wake up only when we have to face the consequences of the decisions we made in the dream-like state. My cat frowns. We decide to avoid making any important decisions for a while and we go back to sleep.

The Healing Session in History

I do not have time to go home, pick up my cat and be on time at the National History Museum for the interesting lecture about the Old World and the New World, given by the community college drop-out turned into neighborhood historian Prof. Gyrba Elf.

My cat agrees to hop on a bus and meet me in front of the museum. I wait twenty minutes, fearlessly defying the icy winds. A hot woman passes me by, hiding her delicate features in a classy chinchilla coat. Who created such sexy beings? I hope they come with a manual and instructions. I would not know where to start with one like her.

Frozen and annoyed, I give up and go inside only to see my cat and Aunt Lyla getting hot dogs at a small kiosk. I've told Aunt Lyla many times not to buy her food anymore. But she can be charming when she wants to, and she definitely wants to be charming when she smells hot dogs.

I clean the icicles off my face. All three of us are ready to take a look at the most significant events in the lives of our ancestors. Since the lecture starts in less than an hour, we agree to quickly review the gallery, hosting impressive images of rulers and empires. Here we are, walking slowly, breathlessly, overwhelmed by the ancient times of glory. But were those indeed times of glory or rather terrible times of despair for mankind? The eyes of a fifteenth-century ruler with hedgehog hair and his right arm wrapped around a medium size sword seem to say yes. I move on, humbled by the message. As I pass the images depicting those warriors trapped in a glowing reality, I become impatient. So does my cat, who starts scratching the glass box hosting an eighteenth-century Declaration-of-something. I've always wondered if history does really teach us something or if it's merely a dusty chain of events.

Prof. Elf – raisin-like eyes, irregular mustache, old coat – seems to have just gotten off one of the battle scenes we just viewed. He delivers a short yet ambiguous lecture about major events in the Old World; events that caused mass migration along with the foundation of the new worlds.

"How did our ancestors feel the History?" Prof. Elf asks rhetorically.

"Were they aware of the significance of the events they witnessed?" An older woman holding the hand of her three-year-old grandson sobs quietly. A few high school students play poker under the loving guidance of the History and Science teachers.

I close my eyes and think of my grandfather Meno who, on Sundays, used to ride his coach to what he thought to be a bigger village than his own. I doubt he was aware of what Prof. Elf calls "historical moments." Civilization moved into the big village unnoticed and one day when Grandpa took his beloved horses to the bigger village he was in for an even bigger surprise. He awoke in the middle of a metropolis, a humongous, evolved animal that was eager to devour his inhabitants. To him, this was History. Obviously, he could not find his Old World anymore. He turned to his horses and told them, "Boys, we do not belong here anymore, take me home." But things got worse. Grandpa Meno felt History pushing him out of his house, his village, bigger village, and even his country. He finally decided to cross the ocean. He packed his humble belongings, the horses and the wife and he ended up in a virgin land, where he could finally build his own History and establish a new village, along with a New World.

An extremely simple man, Grandpa Meno never ate in a tavern or a restaurant. He just could not touch food prepared by people he did not know. He would stay away from taverns yet the demanding work would not allow him to go home and have lunch. This major problem forced him to make another radical change in his life. He established his own restaurant and this way he could take lunch breaks and enjoy food prepared by friendly hands.

His brother saw things differently. He refused to move to the so-called New World. No, no, no. He will greet the New World here in the Old World. Finally able to escape poverty and decently feed his twelve children, he built the house of his dreams. It even had a golf course. However, he could not break up with the Old tradition, so he made sure the sophisticated mansion was equipped with a beautiful outhouse overlooking the golf course. People laughed at him, mocked him, and even raised their voices, trying to make him realize the absurdity of his enterprise. Why would someone want to have a mansion with an outhouse? They could not understand Grandpa Meno's brother, whose thinking was actually pretty simple. He did not believe in the New World. To him, it was just another experiment. That's why he did not feel compelled to follow his brother across the ocean. Years and years later when the war struck again in the Old World, bigger and smaller villages, people and houses vanished, and along with them the memory of an entire universe. However, the outhouse that everybody laughed at became overnight a standard of a new civilization, since no one had a decent bathroom anymore. Except for Grandpa's brother, whose strong, stand-alone structure and legacy stood tall, overlooking both centuries and the golf course. Once again, the new was old and the old was new.

It appears to me that History welcomed the practicality of both Grandpa and his brother. New and Old were relative.

I hear the voice of Prof. Elf going on and on about glorious wars, statues and historical moments. What is a historical moment? We humans are never aware of the historical moments, be them at a personal or larger scale. We just seem to prefer faithfulness to the old bad choices than to something new. We like to cuddle up to the same old mistakes. I share my thoughts with Aunt Lyla. She agrees. She can prove that with her own mistake. I know what she is talking about.

The day when she told me, full of excitement, that she was going on a date is still fresh in my memory. Hearing the news my cat fell off the chair and landed on her head so I had to rush her to the hospital with head trauma. I don't know about mankind, but for us, that was indeed a historical day. But who was the lucky man going on a date with my precious aunt? A few years ago, Aunt Lyla had decided to take belly dancing lessons, just to refresh her memory and keep the ancient tradition alive. As expected, she had made friends at the belly dancing club and one day they organized an informal party. While Aunt Lyla, along with other old ladies, was practicing her seductive moves, two predatory eyes were following her from across the room. It was the newly single, freshly-emerged-from-his-ninth-divorce and consistently-looking-for-the-next-prey, Augustus Ordeal. When Aunt Lyla took a short lemonade break, the handsome eighty-seven-year-old approached her and praised her sensuality. It was love at first sight; naturally, she agreed to meet him in front of the Monday a.m. ice cream truck for a short date. Some women would prefer to arrange their dates in a restaurant or a coffee shop. Not Aunt Lyla. She hadn't been seen with a man in fifty-three years. What would her girlfriends and the entire neighborhood say about her? She took great pride in never compromising herself in those fifty-three years since she'd been a widow. Of course, the ice cream truck driver would sense that something was not right, but he would not be able to prove anything, either. After all, who doesn't love his famous vanilla ice cream? To make it even safer, I agree to lend her my cat. The plan was the cat would meet her at the ice cream spot, and, in case a nosy neighbor saw them, Aunt Lyla could pretend she was not on a date, but just wanted to show the handsome gentleman her kitty.

Aunt Lyla was totally infatuated with her date. Augustus Ordeal was not only handsome, but also severely educated and well traveled. All the men she had met in those years lacked the level of knowledge and savoir-vivre that only he displayed. Even my cat tried to suggest delicately that those nine ex-wives must have tasted something more than just his charming personality. But Aunt Lyla was deaf to our advice. She kept praising him with passion. We ignored her. But when she mentioned that Augustus reminded her of her late husband, a deep fear entered our minds. Aunt Lyla's late husband was definitely charming. Until they got married. Then the charm had been gradually replaced with alcohol, beatings and intense gambling. God must have watched over her, and one night he had too many drinks and he died in front of the house while trying to take an imaginary shower under the old walnut tree. Yet Aunt Lyla firmly believed that he was a great man and it was the alcohol that caused all the problems.

And here she was, fifty-three years later, back to square one, ready to make the same mistake. It was hard to believe that this was just a coincidence. We cannot watch this happening again, so my cat and I take the matter into our hands and a few cat attacks convince Augustus Ordeal to stay away from my aunt forever.

While I think of my aunt's unusual attraction for the same disaster, the voice of Prof. Elf overlaps with my thoughts. He points at the fact that in spite of the worst experiences and tragedies, people seem to repeat the same poor choices when they elect their leaders.

They love to be represented by charismatic individuals with savoir-vivre. They choose to be led by "Who they would like to be" and not by "Who they are." And while life is too short, they masterfully pass on the mistakes from one generation to another. I am tired.

A bored Genghis Khan trapped in a painting behind Prof. Elf's desk tells me to go home. I decide to stay and snooze happily with the blessing of the great Mongol leader.

By the time the interesting lecture ends, my cat is nowhere to be found. An hour later we find her sleeping in the lap of the statue of Vladimir Ilici Lenin. I try to pick her up without disturbing the leader. I hate to wake her up, but I also hate arguments in cold weather, so when she starts complaining I pretend not to hear her. I do not want to get icicles running off my mustache again, so I kiss Aunt Lyla and try to get to my car. She insists that we stop at her place and have tea with her and her sister-in-law. We have a deep respect for Aunt Lyla's sister-in-law, a feeling we have nurtured intensively for the past thirty years. However, every time we meet she brings me candy. Besides the fact that I am no longer the little boy she knew, the candy she brings has been rotated as a gift among the family members for many years now, in good Old World tradition of saving and preserving everything. In time, we came to know in detail every bag, the occasions it had been used, every ribbon and every candy in the bag. According to our constantly updated database, there should be five candies left, two glossy red and white, one dark chocolate, and two sugarcoated peanuts. Now we're really curious if our guess is accurate. We hug our old relative and wait for her to offer us the same old bag of candies. Surprise! A new green bag replaces the traditional red one my father used to like so much. Aunt Lyla smiles at us triumphantly and encourages us to taste them. A New World invites us in! We crush the candy cautiously as a familiar old taste invades our taste buds. It is the taste of the Old World in a new bag.

The Healing Session in Love

Every Thursday afternoon I sit with my cat in the living room and watch the exciting soap opera *Love Without Love*. There is one thing I love about these enchanting shows and that is their surrealism. We all know love does not exist. Yet we cannot help smiling with understanding as we move on to the next episode. Today I am dying to learn if Amy will finally split with Joseph, but once again, my high-maintenance partner finds a way to distract me from my Thursday pleasure. She is cold. I have to go out and check the heater, an activity I do not enjoy at all. Can we wait until tomorrow morning when highly trained professionals will look into it? No.

I move slowly, making small and elaborate steps. Here I am, in full winter wind, trying to see if the heater functions properly. As I stand there scratching my head with fingers of fury, a shy bark catches my attention. I turn around and see a tiny poodle on a leash wagging its tail. At the other end of the leash, a feminine hand which continues harmoniously with an even more feminine body. The woman walking her dog in front of my house is gorgeous. I forget about the heater and I rush to connect with her, asking silly questions about poodles, like how many times a day they eat and if they are prone to ear infections. The woman smiles. An extensive weakness takes over my body and mind. I want to see her again, so I ask her to join me for dinner tomorrow evening. She says yes.

I go back in the house singing and I lie to my cat that the heater is within the manufacturer's parameters. We watch *Love Without Love* in cold and silence, yet for some reason I don't care if Amy leaves Joseph anymore. What I do care about is my date tomorrow. While I stare at the screen with an expressionless face, rubbing my cat's back, I think of the times when we were rich. Money could not buy me the woman I wanted, but only pleasure; okay, PG-35 pleasure, yet just pleasure. I suddenly feel overwhelmed by passion for the mysterious poodle owner. Will she show up or not?

I spend the night with my eyes closed and my mind open and awake. The following day is long, wide, deep and unbearable. I do not know what to wear so I rush to the designer store. I give up after trying all the outfits in the store, including the XXX sizes and the funeral, wedding and baby shower ones. I leave before the sales associates kick me out, still uncertain about what would make my personality more appealing.

I call Aunt Lyla and tell her about my date. Aunt Lyla is worried. She suggests wearing my grandfather's manly amulet and discreetly carrying garlic in my left pocket, to help keep the vampiresque spirit of love away. I laugh at her. Who believes in such silly things as love? It's just a date, for God's sake!

Aunt Lyla does not agree with me. She insists that I should be a man and keep love and sex in separate containers. Love can be very harmful to a man. Obviously, I do not listen to her advice, although I know she is right. It took me years and years to heal after Agatha left.

The time has come! When I see my beautiful date entering the restaurant, the weakness is back. I feel helpless and scared. I feel an urge to be on my knees kissing those gorgeous legs. To touch her pretty face. To be her humble slave, begging for her attention.

Next thing I know we are in my bed, passionately loving each other. It happened so fast I forgot to bite my nails and worry about my sexual performance. The only connection with the real world is my cat repeatedly screaming, scratching the windows and trying to get into the house. This woman is so intense and passionate I just cannot let go of her! I step outside the bedroom and immediately lock all the doors and windows, hoping to keep her here forever. Unfortunately "forever" ends as the weekend is over and she has to go to work.

We part ways in love and extreme adoration for each other. When she is away I feel yearning beyond yearning and desire beyond desire. I cannot find my place in this world anymore. I remember I owe this amazing encounter to my cat so I finally let her back into the house. She has lost weight, has a dirty coat and resembles a stray cat.

However, she *knows*. She has a deep understanding of the animal nature. Yet she demands excuses for my freaky behavior. I explain. I need some time off. The truth is I am torn apart. Yesterday and today are situated in different dimensions. My cat is, as usual, wiser. She tells me that, basically I have no reason to complain. I asked for it. I could have settled for some good sex and moved on. Instead I opened the gates to my body and mind. I chose to let this woman into my life. The cat is right but she hasn't seen anything yet.

Things get worse than I expected. I have separation anxiety. A pain, physical pain shatters my body whenever my love is away. I tell my cat about the unusual symptoms I experience. She panics and insists that I seek immediate professional advice.

I call Dr. Lowenstein, the guru of male-female relationships.

I tell him I need special counseling for a special relationship. Are we having the common issues couples have? Far from it. Perhaps we are experiencing major conflicts? Not at all. Basically, we are in an amazing relationship. We are *one*. A *problem* is what we need. We are way too attached to each other. We need to hate and feel insecure, part ways in relief, convinced that it wasn't meant to be and escape this burning suffering. Can Dr. Lowenstein be of any help?

After listening to my confessions and cashing in two-hundred dollars, Dr. Lowenstein calls me a freak. So does my cat, which makes me wonder if my cat has the knowledge of a doctor or my doctor has the knowledge of a cat.

I spend my days thinking of my beautiful angel. I have tried to run away without looking back, but whenever I open the door, Love is there, standing like a ruthless guardian with a deadly gaze. I stand behind the window, watching people passing my house and asking myself repeatedly, where are they going? Aren't they afraid to leave their safe houses? Where can we hide? No, I rephrase that. Can we ever hide?

To cope with the anxiety I try to find exciting activities and keep busy. I try to go back into painting, but the ugliness and the repulsiveness of my art is so obvious I myself cannot look at it. I take on line bakery classes but I only manage to bake distorted muffins, so imperfect, that even the blueberries try to escape their dough prisons, running out and hiding under the baking pan.

I finally let it out. I tell my angel how profound the impact she had on my life is. She looks at me in awe. Then she pulls out a bunch of drawings even uglier than mine. She also shows me a family of blueberries that fled *my* muffins and tried to hide in hers but had been deterred by the perspective of exchanging poor housing for an even more imperfect one.

We are doomed. A series of powerful, existential conversations follows and as we speak, our connection is deeper and stronger than ever.

I wish I never met her. She agrees. There is nothing we can do about it and we know it. Around her I no longer feel defensive. She, too, is driven by thirst for knowledge. So is her poodle, with whom she exchanges powerful opinions on daily basis. She is truly the feminine "Me," my one and only mate.

Time is, once again, compressed by unseen forces. The anxiety makes our lives unbearable. We both fear that the other one will walk away.

When we are together, we lock ourselves in the house. The cat and the poodle are our designated key keepers, trained to prevent us from taking the key and opening the doors, unless extraordinary circumstances require it.

I have never been so close spiritually to any human being. I even remember her name! This is scary!

Oddly enough, I tremendously enjoy sharing my thoughts with her. I can't believe it! I have always been reluctant to give information that later can and will be used against me. I haven't talked at such levels to a woman in a very long time, if at all. I have limited my "expressions" to sex only. I've always wanted to skip the traditional dynamics of the traditional relationship, so boring and predictable. But with her, everything flows naturally and gracefully.

I think of my old theories and approaches to man-woman relationships; none of them perfect, each of them taught me something. After so many life lessons it strikes me that only absolute completeness will do it for me. I am so simple…Why would I want to waste time and be with someone if I have to be defensive? I have always wondered if a perfect state of completeness exists – if there is a dimension where a man and woman could meet, mind and body; where I could sleep and rest; evolve and thrive; and never fear.

I am about to feel relief. After all, I have found the absolute love and truth. However, my feline friend remarks that the thirst for knowledge is not *love-friendly*. On the contrary, it is harmful and somehow prevents us from getting the minimal comfort everybody else does. Basically, it condemns me to be *alone* and feel *alone* forever. Pretty simple thoughts huh, if one does not count the endless years of continuous, strenuous thinking my cat and I had to put into it, just to get to this terrifying conclusion.

As the door closes behind the love of my life, the pain makes way into my system like the poison of a venomous snake. I look at my cat. She approves. We cringe together on the couch, man and cat, in a last attempt to free the terrible pain of soul and mind that existence forces us to bear.

The Healing Session in Fog

I have decided to take yet another short break from my odd encounters. I need solitude. And where can I find more solitude than in the mysterious Northern Forests? Why the Northern Forests? I don't know. I talked to a friend the other day and he reminded me that I should be more down to earth. Then he told me that he had bad sex the other night.

I thought of his words. Yes, bad sex is worse than no sex, although many people would disagree. That's why I want to take a break from seeing people; they always disagree with me. Also, I do not wish to be *down* to earth but close to earth. I want to feel the earth and become *one*. We will pitch a tent or rent a small cabin in a remote spot and just *be* for a while.

After a few hours of packing, my cat and I are on our way to the endless fresh green. As usual, she insists to be in the front seat. I do not like this, and for a good reason. She always distracts me from driving, by pointing at various things that she finds interesting. Blablabla…I have tried repeatedly to explain to her, that what is interesting for her might not be interesting for me. As usual, this brings up the male-female issue. She exposes – again! – her theory about the limitations of the male mind. According to my cat, males learn to speak later in life, around the age of twenty. By the time they reach thirty they are capable of delivering very short, sometimes pointless, grammatical structures such as "Look, chicks, I horny." At the age of forty they should be able of building a basic sentence with subject, predicate and object, such as "I like milk." But only when they reach fifty are the intricacies of the male mind fully revealed; this is the moment when sophisticated metaphors emerge: "I think she smells really good."

My cat thinks that just being thirty-five prevents me from having a decent conversation. Does she have to wait five more years until I am able of building basic sentences?

I tune her out and ask her politely to check the map and see if we are heading in the right direction. She meows annoyed and shows me her impeccable teeth.

I show her mine. She pulls out an appointment reminder from my dental hygienist. Mouth closed and teeth clenched I try to catch her. I slam on the brakes. Once. Twice.

I'm not vengeful yet I decide to stress out my cat by singing songs that she hates. I have heard that certain sounds can and will induce a high level of stress in both humans and animals. It works on rats. Are cats, so different from rats? My friend Astrakhan says no.

We hop on the first available ferry and an hour later we reach our destination, a tiny Northern island, a place of peace and tranquility.

We plan our stay here quickly, yet in detail. We will spend amazing moments in a small cottage by the ocean; behind the cottage, the deep mysterious woods. The orientation of the rooms is very important as my cat enjoys watching the sunrises and I will focus mostly on the sunsets, as usual. We like to share our responsibilities responsibly. I help my cat to set up the room facing the East while sipping a Martini happily. Okay. All we need is booze and maybe some food.

We pull over at a gas station. She goes to the restroom while I get gas and the booze. I notice a small ad on the door, "What does your face reveal about you?" and an invitation to a Chinese face reading course. I learn that Chinese face reading provides insightful and accurate personal information regarding life events, health issues and relationships. I fetch the add in spite of the Chinese cashier's screams. She does not understand my thirst for knowledge. Why would she? She is probably an expert in face reading, like all these sneaky Asians. I announce the glorious change of plans to my half-asleep cat. She freaks out, thinking I gave up on the connection with nature. No, we are still going to experience green and solitude. But first, we will stop to read a few faces, that's all.

A small crowd composed mainly of women and older people is gathered in front of a grayish building. The crowd is surprised to see a man of my age joining them, but as they learn that I am a stranger they leave me alone. Their men are at work and this explains the group structure. Nice. It is obvious that the poor males are small prey, since they go back home from work only to have their faces skillfully read by their loved ones. Now, how horrible that must be! We picture instantly the home-coming Male, having to answer the universal question "Where have you been?" and his unpolished vodka-flavored lie, "At the library." I try to sit quietly but my cat decides to deliver a bored meow. This makes the audience even more curious about us and we are invited to introduce ourselves. I tell them my name. Everybody agrees that I have a cool name. And what is my specialty? Asian faces, European or perhaps African? None. I tell them that I have never read a face in my life. I cannot even read my own face when I look at myself in the mirror. I always ask my cat how I am.

As I talk to them I suddenly become aware of the fact that I am among highly trained professionals who can read my true feelings. I try to cover my face. A pretty lady sitting next to me smiles while passing some cookies. I melt down, totally ignoring the fact that she is a pro. She is very sexy but I am not falling for this again. I look at her bravely and I start practicing my morning mental mantra: "Sex only, sex only. I do not wish to develop feelings for you, go away, go away!" She offers me a candy and tells me that being truly sensitive is a gift and I shouldn't be afraid of my own intensity. Really? Who told you I am sensitive, bitch? I do not like this. I stand up, looking for a seat far away from her. I will sit down next to an older guy with big monkey eyes. Monkey Eyes asks me upfront if I always dissociate mental and physical pain from pleasure. Who invented you, Monkey Eyes? What is this? What is this? It appears that everybody here seems to know exactly how I feel about things. This is a life-threatening situation. I scruff the cat and out we are! I am so scared at the perspective of having my face read by strangers that I almost slip and fall on the doorsteps, where the cleaning lady is masterfully mopping the slates.

I apologize and so does my cat. The woman gives me a stern gaze. She tells me that no matter where or how fast I go, I cannot run away from myself. I am stunned, pissed, numbed. We need to cover our faces and prevent those monsters from reading them. We get into the first boutique and buy colorful silky scarves.

We walk back to the car fearful, covering our faces, passing the ice cream mobile unit drooling and helpless. We *know* that we cannot handle ice cream through the silk. I back up while the cat is holding the scarf in front of my face, like a true friend.

It's time to get lost in the woods!

We race to the cottage, lock the doors and feel safe.

In the morning a squeaky meow makes me regret bringing the feline friend with me. What is it again? I open my eyes in disgust ready for my favorite short lecture about the importance of getting enough sleep.

The air around me is milky. I panic. On the rare occasions when I lecture I like to make aggressive eye contact with the audience. I try to locate my cat. She's by my side meowing incessantly, and rightfully so. Everything appears to be covered in… fog. This means we cannot go kayaking. We are very frustrated.

We walk inside and outside the house, holding paws and assessing the situation. We cannot see anything but white fog. We decide to enjoy our coffee on the small deck and spend half of the day trying to guess what birds are landing and taking off at the shore. We end up trying to be positive, something that is definitely not in our nature. My cat comforts me. We will not allow this minor incident to ruin our vacation. She is right.

The alarm clock shakes me vigorously at an early 4:00 a.m. My cat set it up in order to catch the sunrise. She must have lost her mind. What sunrise? The fog is thicker than ever. I try to fix breakfast but it is tough to find the right ingredients. We end up drinking a sugar-free coffee and chewing on some rotten wafers. In the meantime my cat makes an astonishing discovery while she tries to set the alarm clock for the sunset: the clock is equipped with a radio as well. We are rich!

We appreciate the entertainment provided by the local radio station. The voices from the radio seem friendly although the news they deliver is not. They say that the fog will be around for a while and the islanders organized a Committee, so they can fight the fog better. They think that being blinded by fog will bring us closer to each other. We smile in contempt. I cannot see my cat's face but I can feel her smile. Humans are indeed ridiculous. We never display the slightest interest to know each other unless something bad happens. Then we organize committees and fight invisible enemies. We rarely win; perhaps the enemy has had enough of us and leaves. Then we feel strength and unity.

We think someone might be at the door. I open the doors to the walk-in closet only to greet my cat who was rushing to open the bathroom door. It's just the wind. Never mind. Thank God we do not pee in the pantry anymore. That's us! We adapt fast to any environment.

The Committee broadcasts an encouraging story about a little girl who shows great strength in the battle against the fog and delivers food to the elderly. Yeah, right. I, too, wrote a short story for the Committee for I am a good responsible citizen and I plan to bring my humble contribution to this enterprise. It is a moving short tale about a guy who stands tall and defiant in the almighty fog and masturbates happily ever after – it is his own way of expressing his freedom, hidden from the judgmental citizens' eyes. He hopes that the fog will stay forever and he will continue to focus on himself and his urges, selfish and undisturbed.

Although we do not need food – we have coffee and booze to last us forever – the good neighbors insist that we participate in one of their meetings. After a few hours of sniffing and bumping into bushes we are sitting around the citizens' round table. We listen to the latest news hiding our indifference in the fog. We don't care. We will soon go back to our blue skies. I hear a woman's voice asking us how can we be so selfish? I position my whiskers in her direction so I can smell her better. So does my cat. Wait a minute! It's the pretty one from the face reading group! We move a few inches away from her scanning the fog; we can barely see, yet we *know* Monkey Eyes is there as well. Who are these monsters? Where can we hide from them? No, I rephrase. Will we ever be able to prevent other people from reading us? Are we small prey?

We leave the island sooner than we planned. We are depressed, helpless and we bring up this issue non-stop. My cat has a revelation: our fears are ridiculous. I follow in her footsteps and I have the same revelation. Yes, they are. After all, are our secrets that special? We are not even gay like our friend Toto, who had struggled years before coming out and telling their parents that he liked men. When I came out to my parents and told them that I like women badly, there was no major reaction. My father seemed rather happy.

We do not want to learn how to read faces anymore. We are no longer ashamed of being read either. I think we mostly feared the fact that other people could see our failures. But life itself is nothing but failures and rejection. My cat does not agree. She thinks that only *our life* is nothing but failures and rejection. I correct her respectfully. Failures and rejection constitute the very foundation on which we have built everything. My cat cannot believe her ears! She thinks that I'm a prodigy. I haven't reached fifty yet and I can already build such sophisticated phrases!

We decide to display our inner selves fearlessly as this has become our strongest and most incredible defense.

We have nothing to hide.

The Healing Session in Manhood

We look at the invitation, startled. Every time we get an invitation to an event, be it a christening, wedding or funeral, we feel betrayed. It's like someone just dropped a *problem* at your door. Just minutes before you were happy and worry-free. Now, you have a problem. You have to respond to the invitation. You can participate or not, but you have to respond. Sometimes saying no can be much more difficult than going to the event.

Aunt Lyla thinks that we should probably go. It is the christening of Lejon. Who is Lejon? I learn that he is the newborn son of Aunt Lyla's cousin of a nephew of a grandson. By the rules of the Old World, this is close family.

My cat is intrigued by the little angel's name. We learn that "Lejon" is Swedish for "lion," since the father's mother-in-law is of Swedish descent. I am also reminded that it is an ancient tradition in our family to give males strong significant names in order to preserve our historical manhood.

Manhood…I look at my cat. She looks at me. We both look at the invitation. This is something we might have overlooked.

We step into the chic ballroom with the confidence of a predator looking for its next prey. While other guests are here to have fun we are here to get an answer.

After being introduced to the close family we sit next to Aunt Lyla, asking questions about the strangers around us. I need a drink, and I order it right away. The waiter brings me some sort of iced corn syrup. I am ready to ask my cat to scratch his hands, when a stunning young woman approaches me and apologizes. That was *her* drink, and the waiter must have delivered it to our table by mistake. I smile and I assure her that we are anything but upset by this minor incident. Actually this could be an excellent opportunity to get to know each other. We start talking and I discover that she is not only beautiful; she is smart as well. I do not like this but, oh well, nobody is perfect.

By the end of the conversation I feel weak. The reason is simple. I want this woman. I want her badly. Yet it seems that she has some sort of inner strength – perhaps the Swedish blood – that intimidates males. Not me, though. I get drunk gracefully while I listen to the Godfather's toast on manhood.

I wake up at home in bed desperately trying to find her phone number. My cat replaces the bag of ice on my forehead and gives me great news. She and our beautiful relative exchanged phone numbers while the taxi driver was pushing me into the car. Her name is Amanda.

My cat insists that I ask her out right away. Waiting three days until I fully recover might not be a good idea. She is pretty and we might lose her.

I follow my cat's advice and here I am, having dinner with the gorgeous Amanda. I think about proceeding with my mating propositions. I want her, period. There is a problem though. I haven't been close to a woman in months, and my manhood might not last me longer than five seconds. Should I back off? Should I proceed and – God forbid – embarrass myself offering her short-lasted pleasure? This is a very complicated situation. What should we do?

Right in the middle of dinner, my feline friend meows discreetly pointing at the couple sitting next to us. He is steaming hot, yet his female companion is ugly and repulsive like a prairie dog. I kiss the cat. Yeah, the answer was right in front of me. All I have to do is practice on unattractive women and only when I regain full control over my body, upgrade to breathtaking beauties like Amanda. *I need an ugly woman.*

We part ways with Amanda, not after I tease her with the promise of an everlasting passionate encounter. I show off my biceps, which translates into, "Watch out, pretty lady, I am a sexy beast who will possess you soon!"

At home, my cat signs me up on all the mating sites she could find, while I write a short yet impressive profile. My secret dating name is of course, Lejon. Our ad is simple and the title sends the women straight to the point: "Beauty is beyond physicality." Our profile reads "Young, sensual male seeks extremely unattractive woman with great personality. I am tired of perfection. I am tired of moods. I am tired of being on some beauty's waiting list. Are you available tonight?"

We get over fifty-eight replies in less than an hour. We should be fine, plenty of ugliness and imperfections to sort through. We decide to pick Lillian, a four-foot-one, two hundred eighty-four-pound cross-eyed, single white female. She is thirty-nine and has no money and no education. Can I ask for more?

We send Lillian a glamorous letter, letting her know about our intentions to meet her right away. The response comes back but it is not the response we were hoping for.

Lillian wants to know why we chose *her*. My cat writes a short but concise message: My mother was cross-eyed and what a wonderful woman she was!

We learn Lillian's story immediately. Her parents were poor, simple people, who could not afford the surgery. Being cross-eyed pushed Lillian to eat more, and so she became overweight. This is valuable information. We should be fine.

However, there is a small problem. Lillian is not quite convinced that I am so attracted to her. She thinks this is a game and I am making fun of her. I cannot believe that luring an unattractive woman can be much more difficult than luring a hot one! Yet it is true.

We decide to pursue Lillian aggressively. We start by bombarding her with flowers, letters, and phone calls. She will give in soon, we know it.

In the meantime, we see Amanda almost every day and we melt under the impression of her sexiness. I think she likes me, too, for she seems to get closer and closer. Yesterday she tried to kiss me but I skillfully avoided the contact with her moist sensual lips pretending I needed to tie my shoelaces. I know she will be disappointed by the fact that I cannot see her on Saturdays anymore. I need to practice on Lillian. You will have to wait, my beauty!

We meet Lillian at a cozy coffee shop not far from the house. This way if I feel that she cannot be my practice girl, we can get back home fast and continue our search.

Lillian is actually not as repulsive as I expected. She has a great smile, and I am surprised to enjoy the conversation with her. I am not sure I can sleep with her; I might need that bottle of Jack Daniel's handy. But she is nice company. She tells me more about her and I tell her less about myself.

Amanda calls me every time I am with Lillian. She wants to know what I am doing. *What am I doing?* I am doing everything to make her happy. This is all she needs to know. I think she suspects something. I will have to send her some flowers as well.

Two weeks have passed and my secret double life is in full swing. I managed to convince Lillian to share her body with me and I spend most of the time at the gym and practicing on her. I discovered in awe that her big ass actually turns me on. I also like the scent of her body. My cat is very happy with my progress. She thinks that soon I will be able to kiss and caress Amanda's body without experiencing convulsions and double vision. She is tired of having to resuscitate me so often.

Sadly, I do not have time for Amanda anymore. Actually I stay away from her. Around her I feel weak and when I am with Lillian I feel strong and confident like a true Lejon. I think of Amanda with mixed feelings. I think of her long legs and the provocative signals she sends to me. I feel hatred. What do you care, bitch? All you have to say is yes and then make some fake noises you heard accidentally in some movie. You do not have to work hard to make me happy and even harder to keep me around.

My cat summons me to end the relationship with Lillian and get it on with Amanda. Yet for some unknown reason, I cannot do it. I feel that manhood means much more that we previously thought. I think of how much fun I had with Lillian and how much I have learned from her.

Perhaps true manhood is about giving and not taking; about being generous and compassionate. It is not about ego. I expose the new findings to my cat. Her reaction – hiding the whiskey bottles – predictable as it is, makes me smile.

In the meantime, tired of being continuously rejected, the beautiful Amanda moved on. I cannot say I am surprised or sad. After all, it wasn't about *her*. It was about me and my own performances. I never bothered to know her better. Amanda seems hurt in spite of my deep apologies. We stay friends with Lillian though. She is indeed a cool chick.

My journey into manhood has just begun. We are not resigned; we are just practical. In life we have to let go of things so we have our hands empty, ready to grab, and enjoy the new ones.

The Healing Session with the Traveling Circus

We get a letter from Cousin Emma. We learn that she left her husband and she is now living with her mother. My cat crosses her eyes and sticks her tongue out at the letter. She couldn't care less. She is right.

I have always opened letters in great fear and uncertainty. God knows what surprises they might hide! Why can't we get cool, awesome letters with news we love to hear?

My cat thinks that the answer is obvious. We do not get such joy-generating letters simply because we are not the authors. She thinks that when you address a letter to yourself you know exactly what to expect. There is no better letter than the one addressed to yourself by yourself.

Her idea seems a little bit crazy to say the least. However, I kept thinking of it while chopping onion for dinner. She might have hit a spot.

Two hours later we sit down writing our first letter to ourselves.

We read it a few times just to make sure we haven't missed anything. My cat says everything is covered, from how cool we are in the morning when we sip our coffees to the late nights when she gets the usual cat colic and I fix her natural remedies; from our interesting getaways to our boring silent dinners; from her depression to mine; and finally to our pure, unrefined hatred for the ancient game of chess. We hate chess and the reason is simple. We cannot cheat and win at all. We love to play cards; my cat sneaks behind the other players' backs and then delivers their secrets to me via sophisticated meows and tail movements. But chess…how is she supposed to spy on our enemies and enter their minds?

While I read our lovely letter over and over again, I make a stunning discovery. It is not addressed to "me," but to "us." I don't like this. I don't like this at all. It looks like I have committed myself to being with her. And I am commitment-phobic. So is she, and I think I don't have to explain this. I am a man and she is a cat! Time to review our approach to commitment. What is it that prevents us from being in a relationship? I have gotten close to a few women, I've even loved two or three, yet I have always moved on.

I share my deep thoughts with my cat. She is not quite in the mood for philosophy. She wants hot dogs so she pushes me through the door meowing incessantly.

At the store I overhear a phone conversation between a woman and someone else. She ends it with a graceful high-pitched "I Love You!" A teenager passes me; he is shopping with his grandmother. He, too, delivers a joyous "I Love You" in return for the latest video game. A couple is having a short tense fight in between aisles; he tells her that she is a bitch; she hisses at him. I move on looking for hot dogs, but when I pass them again, they both agree on the brand of the chicken noodle soup, exchanging the same happy "I Love You's."

I realize that I have never told my cat that I loved her. Neither has she. However, there is a lot of affection between us, no matter what. We could never say those empty, cute "I Love You's." Does this make us bad people? Why do we have to declare everlasting love every five minutes? What is wrong with just affection? Not quite love, but just affection, warmth, compassion?

People throw "I Love You's" everywhere and to everybody nowadays. It is like a modern mantra, meant to convince mostly ourselves that yes, we are capable of love and yes, we want to proudly display our commitment even if it's not there.

At home my cat has even more disturbing news for me. She sneaked up on the neighbor's roof and listened to the conversation he was having with the plumber. After fixing the broken pipe and getting paid, the plumber ended with a professional manly… "I Love You." I sit down and take a deep breath. The world is indeed headed to an emotional disaster.

We try to catch a few hours of sleep. We cannot. We finally fell in a deep state of dream but are promptly brought back to reality by an array of exotic noises.

I get up and go to the window. A traveling circus stopped not far from my house. I see people, standing and chatting by colorful wagons. A monkey sitting on top of one wagon waves at me. I wave back at her instinctively. *An important decision has just been made.* I go back to bed and tell my cat we should join them and travel around for some time while trying to clarify the commitment issue. These people are well known for not committing, never stopping, and never settling down. She agrees.

The Director of the Circus – one eyebrow shorter than another, sad puppy gaze, open toe sandals – is actually very happy to hear that I intend to join their team. They need new people, new tricks, and new, fresh air.

I cannot wait to meet and talk to each member of this big family! My cat and I travel light, so we are able to hop in the wagon in less than an hour.

Next to me, surprise! The bearded woman. All my life I have *yearned* to talk to a bearded woman. I have questions, such as how does the beard impact on her femininity? Was she born like this? Surprisingly, she is very sociable and open. She tells me her story right away. She once had a smooth face. But when her fiancée left her for his best male friend, she grew a beard overnight in a desperate attempt to bring him back to her – best male friend had sumptuous beard. I am deeply moved by her love story. Is she unhappy? No. Overall, she is happier now than before. Her job is easy. People stare at her and pay for it. Even the monkeys have to do *something*. She doesn't even have to groom her beard. People will pay anyways.

I envy her for she does not have to work too hard to make a living, unlike us. We move on to the next intriguing character.

The Magician is very sad. He cannot find talented people to share his craft with. All his tricks will die along with him. There will be no one left to entertain the people with high-end tricks. Who will continue his legacy of illusion? Who will make people's wallets and money vanish in his top hat, only to make them re-appear at the end of the show? I think there are a lot of talented people, adept at making money to vanish. They wouldn't make great magicians though because they can only make money disappear but never re-appear. They are more like one-way magicians. My investment agent is one of them.

The dog trainer takes great pride in his Chihuahua show. He claims that his Chichis can do anything he asks of them: roll, jump, sit, have dinner, wipe their muzzles and bark respectfully and politely at the end of the dinner. I am not impressed. I can do the same but only when I want to get laid.

I am so excited to be around these beings. I want to make the most of this encounter. I decide to take some amphetamine in order to increase my alertness and sleep less. I will enjoy long hours of sleep when I get back home; right now I am really interested in being awake as much as I can. The only minor problem I might have is the double vision I get sometimes. But not always. For example, yesterday I saw a monkey with two heads and I decided to reduce the amphetamine. However, a clown who was passing by assured me that I was indeed looking at a two-headed monkey, one of the Circus' main attractions. I felt relieved and I allowed myself to slightly increase the amphetamine.

During the amazing big cat show, one tiger shows signs of frustration and decides to take a closer look at the audience. The masses react promptly, screaming and trying to get out as soon as possible. The rapid intervention teams rush in, trying to capture the beast. I can read the utmost fear on almost everyone's face. Yet, for some odd reason, a small group of simple people, men women and children does not even move. They watch the horror in silence.

I think of Marcus Lavender of my childhood, who terrorized our neighborhood with his threats, child and wife beatings as well as other displays of violence, meant to teach us, the weak, the splendor of the true masculine strength. When they finally managed to contain Lavender in a nice comfy cell and defer him to justice, his lawyer argued that Lavender's delicate being could not cope with the harsh imprisonment, especially since the imaginary conditions he was suffering from demanded that he was under constant medical supervision. The case was dismissed on grounds of medical issues. His lawyer told the judge that Lavender perceived his victims as being enemies of the mankind and he was trying actually to save the world, like Superman. So, Lavender went back to "save" the world. I am thinking that the group who displays no fear at the sight of a furious tiger must be a group from Lavender's good old neighborhood. After all, once you survive twenty years of Lavender, a pissed tiger makes you smile.

I am, once again, tired. My cat tries to cheer me up with one of those bland, pointless cat jokes she inserts whenever she thinks I need an attention booster. I ignore her jokes. She meows at me, disappointed.

As we have nothing else better to do we decide to resume our defiant cry-and-despair sessions. We used to sit down almost every day and enjoy an internal, excruciating cry for an hour or so. It was rewarding and soothing. We held each other tight and we allowed imaginary tears to fall down our tormented selves. We were not able to produce real tears though. Yet no matter how our tears lacked material dimension, they were real and painful.

Right in the middle of our cry-and-despair session a monkey knocks at my wagon's door asking us if we want coffee. I love monkeys! I wish I was a monkey, jumping from one tree to another, oblivious to life itself, never stopping, never thinking and never suffering. My cat wishes she was a monkey too! We start jumping around joyously until she fells in between the small improvised beds and hurts her back. I slip on the wet floors almost breaking my arms. We stop wanting to be monkeys right away.

The truth is that a few months have passed and we do not have the answers we were hoping for. We have seen cool places. We have eaten exotic foods. And all this for free, which is pretty cool.

The Director of the Circus stops me in front of the big tent. He wants to know if I like traveling with them.

I sure do. But we have a problem. My cat and I have never committed to anything. We cannot commit to a person, group, country, language or religion. We wish we could! This way our life would have been simple and we would not question anything.

The Director smiles. He understands. That's why he founded the Circus after living for thirty-five years in the same house, shopping at the same grocery stores, having coffee at the same coffee shop and drinking beer at the very same pub. One day he felt an urge to pack everything and vanish into the world. He has never stopped since then and life is better than ever. Do we care to join them?

We refuse politely. We like to watch. We like to think. We like to have *options*. We fear that if we join the Circus this might limit our options. But we are very grateful for the insight into non-commitment the Circus has offered to us.

They drop us off in front of the house, in the very spot where they picked us up months ago. It is an emotional moment.

We say "I Love You" to the Director and we get inside the house quiet, humble and commitment-free.

The Healing Session in the Tower

I stare at the phone helplessly. At the other end of the line, Aunt Lyla sounds impatient and concerned. Did the water pipes creak again? No. She just performed a Tarot reading on me. One might question the sanity of performing Tarot readings at 5:00 a.m. I do not. The only sanity I occasionally question is my own.

According to Aunt Lyla the Tower is my governing card, foretelling a life-changing event of cataclysmic proportions.

I sigh in great relief. Women! As long as the water pipes are fine, why worry? Every single day of my life is catastrophic.

I thank her for getting me ready for the next cataclysm and I wish her "Happy sunrise." Then, I sneak back under the sheets skillfully warmed by my cat.

Two hours later I stand in line at the grocery store to get yogurt. The old woman in front of me informs me that her son and my former high school classmate Angelo Soychip lives in the neighboring town. Then she tells me that she likes pink bubblegum over the green one. I look at her gray hair. I refrain from telling her that only sissies and idiots like pink bubblegum. We have to respect the elderly. The conversation is over and I rush to my car carried away by mixed feelings.

I keep thinking of Soychip and our long-lost friendship. In high school we used to skip classes and go to the railroad station tavern. Why there? Because Soychip liked to watch the travelers who were desperately trying to get somewhere. Now I know that these journeys take us basically *nowhere.* It's just bodies moving from one place to another. But back then I shared his passion.

Needless to say the following day I call Soychip. He, too, is amazed that we have been so close in space yet so far from each other in time. He would love to have me over for a couple of days. We agree to meet at the railway station tavern like in the good old times and go from there.

I start packing immediately. On my way out the cat realizes in horror that I might have packed two combs. And who doesn't know the old superstition one comb is useful but two bring trouble – they say that one is for hair, while the other one is for combing misfortunes. I didn't. I stare at the cat speechless. Women! I go back and leave the spare comb on the table.

I'm in the deserted, old railway station, waiting for Soychip and sipping on my drink.

It is late night and there are not many people here right now, just a few employees, busy with cleaning or moving things around and a peasant who is sitting on a bench reading the newspaper. I enjoy watching the educated peasants. My great-great grandfather, for example, could not read or write until he reached adulthood. He finally put himself together and learned the alphabet by himself. He could not reap the reward of being literate until one glorious summer morning. He went to the city to pick up supplies. Once he reached the city he forgot about the supplies. Instead he spent hours reading all the street signs, names, billboards. The world was suddenly friendly. He could not believe that he had moved through life solely guided by images and scents he was picking up like an animal. Yet he had.

This sends me back into the pure, surreal times of my adolescence. Soychip and I used to watch the travelers and imagine that they carried in their suitcases not clothing and toothbrushes but secrets. In our twisted fearless minds we were some sort of magicians and we could peek at their secrets and how well they carried them around.

I think that in a way, my dream came true. The childhood happiness is gone, but I am still curious, eager to peek into people's carriers. Life has made me picky and selective, especially since I experienced Uncle Dan's dirty fishing trousers. I learned fast that some secrets should stay with their owners forever as there is no lesson in them for the passionate observers like myself.

Soychip – big, ugly eyes, no lips, Tarot card-like face – is here along with his beloved pet, a small annoying parrot named Lola. I shake his hand several times, happy that I have not brought the cat with me.

We seem to pick up the conversation where we had left it off years and years ago. Angelo Soychip tells me his story in a few carefully selected words. He starts backwards, with his latest revelation. According to him, things are simple. He is all alone, since he has lost all his friends one after another. I express my curiosity. How did this happen? Soychip explains. He quit drinking and he lost a few right there. A couple of months later he stopped smoking and several hard-core smokers avoided him for good. Then he grew old and lost interest in sex as well. His last close friend vanished with no trace. Angelo realized that actually, all this time he had been actively alone and coping with existence. There were no friends, just random acquaintances who were coping with existence as well. As soon as he gave up coping and faced his own misery sober, Soychip experienced loneliness and happiness altogether.

On the way to his house I am tormented by unanswered questions as usual. How old is Soychip? How old am I? How much Time has passed since I started looking for the healing?

Soychip is proud of what he calls "this old house." I get out of the car and stare at the building. It is not a house, it is a tower. I cannot even see the last storey, for God's sake! It is *that* tall!

If there is one thing that sets me apart from other people, it is the fact that I cannot keep my mouth shut. I ask him right away why does he have to live in a fortress instead of a house?

My old friend starts laughing. I learn that coping with poverty led him to overbuilding. In the beginning, there was just a room with a small restroom. But the social prestige demanded that he had a guest room or two. So he added one more room on top of the old one and was very proud of his work. However, his cousin's late mother had visited Soychip, bringing along her six children. Bad news travels very fast and soon the whole town learned about Soychip's questionable hospitality. Five more rooms were added the following year but it wasn't enough. Some people started spreading the word that Soychip treats his guests as one would treat his horses in a stable. In a desperate attempt to make the world happy, my old friend started adding at least three storeys a year, just in case someone wants to pay him a visit. How many rooms does his tower have? He does not know. He stopped counting them a long time ago. I will have to ask Master Architect Pok-Pok, who designed it.

I am invited to pick myself a room and just feel like home which I do immediately. I close the door behind me. This trip is much more interesting than I thought. I want to take a shower and change so I open the suitcase, looking for some clean clothes.

I step back in great horror, as the suitcase is full of...feathers. At least this is my first impression. Annoyed, I invoke my cat's presence, while checking out the surprisingly light feathers. Is this yet another silly joke, like last year's one, when she hid the radio under the bed, turned it on, and tried to convince me that I was hearing voices? Her immaterial presence says, "No." I thank her politely. I am happy I am not hearing voices and my connection with the real world is strong.

I drop everything and leave the room. The hallways are poorly lit but I can distinguish the narrow inviting stairs on my right. I start climbing them with unsure steps. Coming from me, it might sound crazy, but I feel a heavy presence hovering behind me, pushing me to go higher and higher.

The Tower has endless stories and rooms. I, the child, want to see them all! I, the mature one, will probably never get to see half of them, so I try to open a few doors and peek inside, just for fun. I pull the doors with the tenacity of a Pit-bull. They won't open. I realize in great embarrassment that they open inward. Of course they are, they are designed by Pok-Pok! The doors finally open. Nothing interesting, except for some very irrelevant encounters from the past.

As I move to the upper levels, I start seeing more than just lessons that taught me nothing. In some of the rooms, familiar faces and events start revealing their true meanings. How could I not grasp them back then? I don't know. I see myself in early adulthood, wanting to marry the freckled tavern singer. My parents are there, opposing this insane idea. I also see myself yearning to be with Agatha. My parents are opposing again, but this time a good idea.

I see myself hating my parents. They hate me back. I also hate my sister but she does not hate me. She redirects the hatred to her husband whom she will later divorce.

I start laughing like an idiot at their decisions and behavior. I laugh at my own as well, just not that hard.

And when I get to my latest encounters I cannot even smile.

I open one door after another with the grace of a hotel housekeeper, who is entitled to check the rooms and assess the state of cleanliness. Some of them are dirty indeed. In one I have the unpleasant surprise to see myself trying to "fit in" as people convince me that "We cannot say this" or "We cannot do that." I feel anger. Who is "We"? There is no "We," it's just "I" and "I" do and say whatever I want. I see myself instinct-ridden and blurry-minded, looking for answers from Heavy Feather, Dust Devil, Chamomile, Medje and others. I also see my ridiculous, equally unsuccessful attempts to understand how my own soul, body and mind work. It's tragic and funny at the same time.

I turn around. My beautiful Agatha flies into my arms. It happened so fast, I am breathless. I missed her so badly. Finally, I can tell her all the untold thoughts that have been so heavy on my heart since she left me. She smiles. Will she forgive me and come back to me? Yes, she will. But, at a deeper level she's never left me, not even for a second.

I hold Agatha's hand tight. I wish Aunt Lyla and the cat were here! They will never believe me that I reunited with Agatha and my life is finally falling in place.

I am about to move to the next room when I see them both at the end of the hallway. It was about time!

The cat smiles listening to my complaints. Of course, they know I met Agatha, they've talked to her before. What is this? Dr. Schnauzer's clinic? Am I being set up again? Is she going to give me an answer? The feline friend says no. This time, I am the one who holds the answers. I turn to Agatha and Aunt Lyla for help, but they agree with the cat.

It strikes me that I have never thanked these women for their tremendous support, guidance and endless compassion. Men never thank women who care for them, really, but I guess it's just our selfish nature.

Is it too late to say "Thank you"? Not at all.

Will they forgive me from beyond Time? But, of course. It is never too late to thank someone and if I am in doubt, I can ask Anatol Broom, the greatest specialist in Time, of all Time.

Will they join me in my future journeys? They decline politely. They belong to the Past. Taking the Past with me would only make me weaker. But they will always watch over me from the old painting I keep by my bed.

I am grateful for having them around for so long. I have always thought that every second spent with the wrong people translates into years that we never get to spend with the right ones. By the time we realize the ones we're pursuing are the wrong ones, amazing opportunities pass by. Life is indeed ruthless.

Oddly, I am not sad and neither are they. As we embrace each other for the last time, they give me Love and Faith to last me forever. I carefully put them in my pocket.

My cat cannot help it. She checks my pocket to make sure that it is not broken and I am not in danger of losing Love and Faith just like I lost her discounted sauna ticket two years ago.

Outside, the light seems brighter than ever.

I hug Soychip and I thank him for having me over. He is an outstanding host. I do not tell him about the Dream I had while at his house though. It is way too disturbing to be talked about.

As I walk away from Soychip's house I turn around and look at the imposing structure one more time. A deafening sound paralyzes the air around me as the Tower crashes, leaving behind nothing but a glowing memory.

I wake up in the railroad tavern surrounded by people and noise. I need to go to the restroom. While I wash my hands I raise my eyes and see a peaceful reflection of myself in the mirror. The cat is no longer by me, but as I leave the restroom I bump into Shlomo. He is happy to see me alive. I am happy to see him and *be* alive.

Someone is calling my name. I wonder if this is *really* my name or maybe someone else's. I smile and move on. Who cares?

Aren't we all anonymous owners of a greater collective experience?

Nameless, shapeless and light like a feather I fly over the disoriented crowds below, vanishing into the unknown.

I am AWARE.

About the Author

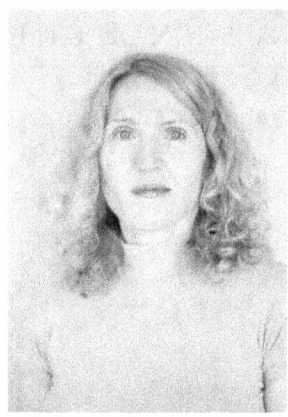

Born in Bucharest, Romania, Oana lived twenty years under the grotesque dictatorial regime of Ceausescu. After the fall of the communism in 1989 she studied languages at the University in Bucharest, then received her Master's at the Jagiellonian University in Krakow, Poland. English is her third language.

She has worn many hats, working as a translator, as a teacher, and eventually caring for animals both domestic and wild. She volunteered and worked for wildlife rescue and rehabilitation centers both in the US and Canada.

She lives in Phoenix, Arizona, where she continues to dedicate most of her time to her animals and to writing. Oana is an active member of Central Phoenix Writing Workshop.

www.ingramcontent.com/pod-product-compliance
Lightning Source LLC
Chambersburg PA
CBHW051633260626
47170CB00004B/1152